OCT 1 2 2016

S0-BOG-510

NAPA COUNTY LIBRARY
580 COOMBS STREET
NAPA, CA 94559

THE TROUBLE WITH TWINS

Henrietta

THE Trouble WITH Twins

KATHRYN SIEBEL

With illustrations by
JÚLIA SARDÀ

ALFRED A. KNOPF
NEW YORK

THIS IS A BORZOI BOOK PUBLISHED BY ALFRED A. KNOPF

This is a work of fiction. Names, characters, places, and incidents either are the product of the author's imagination or are used fictitiously. Any resemblance to actual persons, living or dead, events, or locales is entirely coincidental.

Text copyright © 2016 by Kathryn Siebel
Jacket art and interior illustrations copyright © 2016 by Júlia Sardà

All rights reserved. Published in the United States by Alfred A. Knopf, an imprint of Random House Children's Books, a division of Penguin Random House LLC, New York.

Knopf, Borzoi Books, and the colophon are registered trademarks of Penguin Random House LLC.

Visit us on the Web! randomhousekids.com

Educators and librarians, for a variety of teaching tools, visit us at RHTeachersLibrarians.com

Library of Congress Cataloging-in-Publication Data is available upon request.
ISBN 978-1-101-93273-5 (trade) — ISBN 978-1-101-93274-2 (lib. bdg.) — ISBN 978-1-101-93275-9 (ebook)

The text of this book is set in 12-point Alegreya.

Printed in the United States of America
August 2016
10 9 8 7 6 5 4 3 2 1
First Edition

Random House Children's Books supports the First Amendment and celebrates the right to read.

For my sisters,
Eileen and Mary,
with love

To Any Reader

So you may see, if you will look
Through the windows of this book,
Another child, far, far away,
And in another garden, play.

. . .

He does not hear; he will not look,
Nor yet be lured out of this book.
For, long ago, the truth to say,
He has grown up and gone away,
And it is but a child of air
That lingers in the garden there.

ROBERT LOUIS STEVENSON

THE TROUBLE WITH TWINS

⧽⧼ TWO SISTERS ⧽⧼

Henrietta and Arabella Osgood were born on the second and third days of April. When they were little, they were everything to each other. They slept in the same crib and wore matching baby outfits. They dreamed the same dreams and played together. People said they learned to talk their own secret language that no one else could understand. They were both beautiful girls, but from the start Arabella was somehow more beautiful than Henrietta. And that is where the trouble began.

Since everyone knew they were twins, nobody could understand why they seemed so different. Arabella was always smiling and laughing, her pink cheeks creased by deep dimples, a charming gap between her two front teeth. Her clothes were spotless, and her glossy blond hair was perfectly combed. Every day their nanny, Rose, arranged it in a new and elaborate hairstyle, tying off the ends with bits of colorful ribbon that blew gently in the breeze.

Henrietta, on the other hand, was as quiet and serious as an elderly professor. She seldom spoke, rarely smiled. Crumbs tumbled down the front of her clothes. And her hair! Well, Rose always meant to get to it, but she had such fun fixing Arabella's that she never did.

Their differences had never mattered to the two of them, but they had always influenced how others treated them. When they were babies, Rose always fed Arabella first and held her more. When they grew older, Arabella was the one the girls' parents asked to perform for guests. Arabella would recite a poem or sing a song for the grown-ups before they went off to dinner. The adults would smile at her and clap their hands in delight, and they barely noticed Henrietta as they passed her on the way to the dining room. And even when nobody else was around, Mr. and Mrs. Osgood were always praising Arabella. "Have you ever seen such blue eyes?" they would ask each other, gazing fondly at Arabella. "Doesn't she have the most delicate fingers? Born to play the harp." Of course they were never mean to Henrietta. At least not at first. But it was clear to everyone who ever met them that the Osgoods liked Arabella best. Watching them fawn over Arabella, Henrietta stood back, saying nothing and feeling too much.

At school the girls sat near each other: Arabella at a clean, perfect desk from which she unfailingly gave the right answer, and Henrietta at an older one with gum under the seat. Inside were forgotten peanut butter and jelly sandwiches that Henrietta hadn't wanted to eat and smudgy homework papers that showed, as her teacher Mr. Stilton-Sterne was always saying, that Henrietta couldn't be paying very much attention.

Outside the house, Arabella was always busy with friends. The other girls invited Arabella to their birthday parties, where they ate tiny, delicious chocolate candies from pink paper cups under birthday streamers and balloons. On the playground, they hopscotched together and gathered in tight circles, giggling, whispering, and pulling up their socks. Arabella didn't mean to leave Henrietta out of all the fun; she just seemed to lose track of her sister, and Henrietta had to either find someone else to skip rope with or make peace with standing off in a corner all alone.

But at home they built their own world. They lined up dolls and stuffed bears, poured them invisible tea, and invented their conversation. When the sun shone, they dressed each other in their mother's old dresses; they added paper crowns and wings and ran through the garden, playing fairy princess. When it rained, their heads were bent over drawing paper as they passed crayons to and fro in companionable silence. They were mirror images, touchstones. The sight of the other steadied each of them. They ate the same meals, listened to the same conversations between their parents at dinner, received the same gifts in different colors. Both

THE LAST STRAW

For her part, Arabella was blissfully ignorant of how deeply unhappy her sister was. She knew, of course, that Henrietta was quiet and odd—that she stood apart from things. But it would have surprised and saddened her to know the extent of her sister's suffering. And Henrietta couldn't bring herself to confront Arabella directly—at least not at first. Her resentment was a secret tangle coiled deep inside her, and it went unseen for years until one day an argument and some unkind words finally nudged Henrietta toward action.

The girls had been playing hide-and-seek together. The

sisters knew with a look what the other was thinking, and words were seldom necessary. They ended each day whispering good night across the short space between their matching beds.

Yet as soon as they arrived at school every morning, things changed. There was so much more going on there, and Arabella was always at the center of it all, encircled by her adoring friends. Henrietta, on the other hand, spent her days by the wrought-iron fence on the edges of the playground, staring at Arabella and her friends.

"Mother," asks the girl by the fire, "if Arabella and Henrietta are twins, how could they be born on different days?"

"It does happen sometimes," the mother insists. "Henrietta was born just before midnight at the end of April second. And Arabella was born a bit after, in the wee hours of April third."

"Well, that's very unusual, don't you think?"

"They were very unusual sisters."

"And that bit about dreaming the same dreams. How could anyone know that?" the girl asks.

"I know these two girls quite well," the mother says. "Do you want to hear their story or not?"

game had gone on longer than usual—in part because of a light rain that discouraged going outdoors, but also because of some especially creative hiding places and a bit of assistance from Rose. Henrietta crept across the kitchen on tiptoe.

"Where is she?" Henrietta whispered to the nanny.

"I'll never tell," Rose declared as she arranged some fruit on a plate.

Then Rose glanced at the kitchen clock and said, "Oh dear, it's nearly two. Arabella! You best come out, or you'll be late!"

"I win!" Arabella declared cheerfully as she stepped out of the pantry closet.

"You don't win," Henrietta protested. "And you have flour all over your face."

"We'd better get you cleaned up," said Rose. "You'll be late for the party."

Arabella, it seemed, had been invited to yet another birthday party—this one for a girl named Lacey.

"Here," said Rose, handing the plate of sliced apples to Henrietta like a consolation prize. "Have a snack."

"But we're in the middle of a game," said Henrietta. "You can't just leave."

Arabella sighed. "I told you before. Lacey's birthday party is this afternoon."

Perhaps she *had* said something. Arabella's schedule was full of wonderful things: parties and piano lessons and ballet classes. All Henrietta ever did was bite her fingernails, meet with her tutor, and wait for Arabella to come home.

"Remember?" Arabella asked. "I showed you the present I got for her. The doll?"

Now Henrietta remembered the shiny package topped by a blue bow that waited in the front hall.

"Well, when will you be back?" Henrietta asked. "I thought when we were done with hide-and-seek, we could work on the puzzle."

"I know!" Arabella said. "But, Henrietta, be reasonable! I have better things to do right now than work on a jigsaw puzzle!"

"But it's a thousand pieces," Henrietta said, following her sister to their room and watching as Rose slipped a party dress over Arabella's head. "How am I supposed to do it alone?" Henrietta asked.

The two girls often worked on puzzles in the evening while their mother painted and their father read the newspaper. They had been piecing this one together for days—connecting bits of blue sky and the bright yellow flowers that reminded them of their mother's garden. Now it lay half-finished on a low table in the living room, and Arabella had lost all interest.

"Come on, Bella Bella," Henrietta coaxed. "Please?"

Finally the pressure was too much for Arabella, but instead of giving in (as she often did), Arabella snapped at her twin.

"Henrietta, you're making me late!" Arabella yelled as she buckled her patent leather shoes. "I'll miss the best parts. But I guess you wouldn't understand that, since you never leave the house."

"I go places!" Henrietta shouted back, though she couldn't think of any. "I have friends!" Henrietta insisted, though none came to mind.

"Oh, Henrietta," Arabella sighed. "You'll think of something to keep yourself busy. You always do. I have to go. I have to get this doll to Lacey. It's her birthday."

"Fine!" Henrietta yelled. "Go! Who needs you?"

At this, Arabella's usually smiling face clouded over.

"You're mean," Arabella proclaimed. "That's why you don't have any friends."

And she marched away.

❧ THE PLOT THICKENS ❧

For a few days after Lacey's birthday party, the girls barely spoke.

"Do you want a piece of toast?" Arabella would ask crisply as she passed her sister the plate at breakfast.

The only reply from Henrietta was a dark stare.

"Henrietta!" her mother scolded. "Your sister is asking you a question."

"No," Henrietta said.

"No thank you," her mother prompted.

"Never mind, Mother," Arabella said.

And so it went.

At times they would forget their feud, unaccustomed to fighting as they were. Arabella saved a cupcake that was passed out in class one day, meaning to split it with her sister later. Then she remembered that they were now mortal enemies and licked off the pink icing all by herself, feeling teary. And it was the same for Henrietta, who would store up some story or joke from the school day, meaning to share it later with her sister—until she remembered that they were no longer speaking. These lost opportunities only made them more furious in some strange way, and each was determined not to be the first to give in and apologize. Their quarrel was their newest project, like a puzzle they were solving, and each one added to it—piece by piece.

Arabella no longer helped Henrietta find missing homework or shoes as they got ready for school in the morning. Instead, she yelled to her mother, "Henrietta is making us late again!" And for her part, Henrietta spent a great deal of time dreaming up ways to punish her sister for her disloyalty. Until one day, as she sat in the parlor reading a book, Henrietta overheard her parents saying something that gave her an idea.

"Where have you been off to?" Mrs. Osgood asked her husband.

"Went to the barber," he said as he took off his hat.

"Little short, don't you think?"

"Perhaps it is a bit," he said, turning his head as he studied his reflection in the hall mirror next to the hat stand.

"What do you think, Henrietta?"

Henrietta set the book down and was about to answer when her mother interrupted, "Oh, what does she know! She's just a child. I'd try another barber if I were you."

From across the room, Henrietta considered her father's hair. It did look a little choppy. "I've got it!" she thought triumphantly. And she went off to her mother's sewing room to look for a pair of scissors. Upstairs, their bedroom was empty. Arabella was at a piano lesson. Henrietta pictured her sister's perfect blond head asleep on the pillow and was filled with secret, evil joy. So she stashed the scissors under her mattress.

"Oh my God!" the girl screams, her mouth full of cookie. "She's going to kill her!"

"Of course not," the mother says, dusting cookie crumbs off her lap. "That would be completely inappropriate. What sort of story do you think this is?"

"I don't think I want to hear the rest."

"All right," the mother says. "Whatever you prefer. It's time you were getting some rest yourself."

"Not now, thinking of people stabbed with sewing scissors."

"That isn't how the story goes."

THE DEED IS DONE

Nothing happened at first because Henrietta was such a heavy sleeper. She meant to wake up in the middle of the night and carry out her plan, but every time she would slip into some strange dream of shopping for candy or being chased by dogs, and when she woke, the sun would be coming through the window, and Rose would be shaking her shoulder and saying how if she wasn't careful she was going to be late for school again.

Mrs. Osgood noticed, one afternoon when she sat down to needlepoint, that her sewing scissors were missing. She went around the house muttering and sighing. Then she gave up and decided to work instead on a watercolor picture she was painting of her lapdog, Muffin.

"What a pretty picture!" Henrietta told her, for truly it couldn't hurt to keep her mother in a good mood. "A bunny in your garden."

"A bunny?! That's not a bunny; it's a dog. Muffin, in fact."

"Oh," said Henrietta, staring harder at the muddy swirls in the center of her mother's canvas.

Mr. Osgood, who had just walked by, stopped and gave Henrietta a worried glance.

"Does that look like a bunny to you?" Mrs. Osgood asked, turning to her husband.

"Oh, dearest, you know I can't see a thing without my new spectacles."

"Spectacles?" asks the girl.

"Glasses," says the mother.

"Where are they?" Mrs. Osgood demanded to know.

"Well, dear, that's an excellent question. I'd best find them, hadn't I? Henrietta, would you like to help?"

So Henrietta and her father backed slowly and carefully out of the room, while Mrs. Osgood went on muttering to herself. "Bunny! Preposterous. I think we need to have *your* eyes checked too, young lady!"

Knowing how easily her mother became upset, Henrietta kept a low profile as she waited for the perfect moment to use the stolen scissors. As she was falling asleep each night, she would sneak her hand down beneath the mattress to make sure that the scissors were still there, and she would smile.

At last one night she did wake up before dawn, perhaps because the light of the moon was so strong in the window. She tiptoed across to Arabella's bed. Arabella was sleeping soundly, her hair spread out across the pillow like a waterfall. Henrietta picked up a handful; her fingers shook. The scissors were small and silver in the moonlight. Henrietta dropped the handful of hair and bent over her dreaming sister. She could feel Arabella's moth breath against her cheek as she leaned in. Delicately, she lifted Arabella's bangs away from her forehead and long eyelashes. In the silence, Henrietta could hear the crisp snip of the scissors as she cut her sister's bangs. Bits of golden hair fell onto the pillowcase and slipped beneath the soft blanket. Arabella murmured and rolled over in her sleep, and Henrietta had to tiptoe to the other side of the bed to finish the job.

Henrietta was pleased with her work. Arabella's bangs were short, choppy, uneven—much worse than her father's haircut.

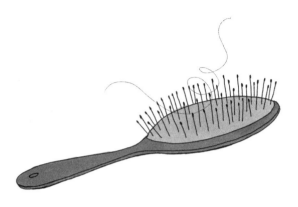

·: IN THE LIGHT OF DAY :·

The next morning, when Rose saw Arabella's crooked bangs, she became hysterical. She dropped the brush *and* the red hair ribbon she was holding.

"What have you done to your hair?" Rose wailed.

The noise sent Mrs. Osgood rushing into the room, still in her blue satin robe, demanding to know what the matter was.

"She's cut her own bangs!" Rose screamed. (You would have thought someone had been murdered.)

"Arabella! What did you do?"

By now Mr. Osgood stood in the doorway, knotting his tie. "What's the fuss?" he asked.

"She's cut her own bangs," Mrs. Osgood said. "Just look at the mess!"

The girl by the fire says, "Geez, it's just hair."

"Well," says her mother, "think of how she must look. And bangs are the worst. You can't fix that with another haircut. And you notice it every time you look at the person."

"So what happened?"

Well, it took some time for things to calm down. Arabella was crying by now and denying that she had done anything to her hair, because of course she hadn't. And then Rose walked toward Henrietta, who was standing at the closet, pretending to pick out a blouse for school.

"Do you know anything about this?" Rose demanded.

Of course, Henrietta denied it, but her face gave her away. On the long list of things that Henrietta was no good at, lying was near the top. Unfortunately, this fact had not made her any more honest.

Finally, with the nanny and her parents forming an accusatory semicircle around her, Henrietta cracked, began to cry, and admitted that she had cut her sister's bangs.

"My scissors!" her mother shouted. "So *that's* where my

scissors got to. Give them to me at once." And Henrietta was forced to march to her bed, head hanging in shame, and remove her secret treasure from beneath the mattress.

"What were you thinking?" her mother asked. "These are not a toy. And just look at your sister! Look at her. She looks ridiculous."

Arabella, who had gone to the mirror to study the damage, broke down. "I do!" she wailed. "I look ridiculous!" Then she threw herself on the bed, sobbing into her pillow.

"Oh dear," said Mr. Osgood, glancing at his watch and slipping out of the room, leaving his wife and the nanny to settle things. Mrs. Osgood and Rose huddled in the corner, deciding what to do while Henrietta began to plead with Arabella.

"It's not that bad," Henrietta insisted, rushing to her sister's side. "Arabella, really, it doesn't look that bad."

But Arabella waved her sister away, too angry to speak through her tears.

"Oh, don't be mad!" Henrietta begged. "I didn't mean it."

Henrietta looked stricken. Her regret was intense and immediate. She knew, of course, that she had gone too far and that Arabella had every right to be furious. Still, she couldn't stand the thought that the rift between them would now deepen. Their hearts, like magnets, once drawn together, would now press apart.

Rose eased Henrietta away from her sister's bed. Grasping her by the shoulders, she locked eyes with her.

"Why?" she asked.

"Why not?" Henrietta burst out. "Everything's always so perfect for her! Let her see how it feels for once."

"Your sister's never done anything to you!" Mrs. Osgood exclaimed.

"She's never done anything *for* me either," Henrietta said. And then the tears overtook her as well.

In the end, Arabella was allowed to stay home from school that morning, and Henrietta was sent off with a note for Mr. Stilton-Sterne.

Dear Mr. Stilton-Sterne,

Please excuse Henrietta for being late this morning. Sometime during the night she attacked her sister with a pair of sewing shears. Naturally, we are all quite shocked. Her poor sister is traumatized. And we won't even speak of the long-term damage to Arabella's appearance.

Mrs. Osgood

P.S. Please be sure Henrietta receives the standard punishments for tardy students.

Mr. Stilton-Sterne raised an eyebrow and said, "Henrietta, this is monstrous. What were you thinking? You are in serious trouble. Go take your seat."

• • •

Mrs. Osgood and Arabella seemed destined to spend the day weeping, until Rose (who was quite fashionable when not forced to wear her uniform) suggested a solution.

"Perhaps a hat," she said as she ruffled Arabella's bangs with her fingers. "Or even an especially nice scarf."

So Arabella and her mother set off for town to find some hats or scarves that would cover the crooked bangs. And as soon as Henrietta arrived home from school, she learned what her punishment would be. She knew that it was serious from the look on her father's face and the fact that he was home early, which had only happened once before (when he ate some bad fish).

The Osgoods had decided that Henrietta was to be sent away.

BANISHED

"She has to leave?" asks the girl by the fire, brushing cookie crumbs off her jumper. "That's a bit harsh, isn't it?"

"They thought it was best," the mother says.

"Where did she go?" asks the girl.

The girls had a great aunt, Priscilla Renfrew, who lived in a small neighboring town. She was a bit odd, but willing. So the arrangements fell into place. And that was that. They packed Henrietta's things, and her father loaded them up, and they left.

"What about school?" the girl asks.

"She wasn't allowed to go after that."

"Isn't that illegal?"

"Parents can do as they please," the mother says. "We have great power."

"Be serious. What about Henrietta?"

"Well, her life was very different for a time."

For now, picture her, her bags packed, tears streaming down her face. Henrietta tried to kiss her mother goodbye, but she just turned her face away.

"What about Arabella?"

As Henrietta was leaving, she looked back at the house, and Arabella was there in the bedroom window, waving good-bye. Henrietta couldn't tell at that distance, but she thought Arabella was crying too.

❧ PRISCILLA RENFREW ❧

Imagine what a wretched ride it was for Mr. Osgood and Henrietta. Her loud sobbing was quite distracting to her father, who had had quite enough of both girls for one day.

"Listen," he said, trying to sound soothing. "This isn't the worst thing. The house is old, but it's roomy. And Aunt Priscilla is very interesting in her own way. You should really try to think of this as an adventure."

Henrietta hiccupped. "An adventure?" she asked.

"Yes. And blow your nose."

Just then they pulled up to the house.

"Go ahead," he urged her, giving her a little nudge. Henrietta walked, knees knocking, to the door.

She rang the bell and was met by silence, so she turned to ask her father what she should do, but he had already left her bags behind and was pulling out of the semicircular drive. Little puffs of dust swirled where he had been, and she heard him calling goodbye as he rounded the corner.

"Now what?" she thought.

She tried to ring the bell twice more, then settled down on the front stoop, head in her hands, for a good cry. Henrietta had been weeping rather loudly for several minutes when she caught sight of something floating down from the upstairs window. It was a fancy sheet of ivory-colored stationery with an elaborate interlocking P and R at the top. It said:

The door is unlocked, you foolish girl.
Stop your silly crying and open it.

P. Renfrew

"That isn't very friendly," says the girl.

"Well," says the mother, taking a sip of tea, "she wasn't a very friendly woman."

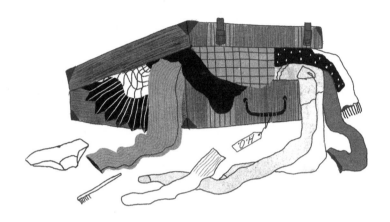

ꜱ SETTLING IN ꜱ

Henrietta opened the door and went inside. The place was pitch-dark, even in the middle of the day, because all the curtains had been drawn. Aunt Priscilla Renfrew was just descending the stairs, dressed completely in black and carrying a large black cat in her arms.

"Don't just stand there," she said to Henrietta. "Come over here and introduce yourself properly."

"My name is Henrietta."

"I know your name. Aren't you going to curtsy or take my hand?" Priscilla asked, tossing the cat to the floor.

The hand in question was wrinkled and covered with

twisty purplish veins and liver spots. Priscilla's fingernails were long and blood-red. On her right hand was an enormous emerald ring, as beautiful as the hand itself was ugly. Henrietta closed her eyes, held her breath, and gave the hand a quick shake.

"Very well," Priscilla said. "Take your things upstairs. First bedroom on the left is yours for now."

Henrietta struggled to get the suitcase upstairs. It was hugely heavy and bumped against every step.

"Quiet, if you please!" Priscilla shouted.

At this Henrietta startled and let go of the suitcase, which toppled down to the bottom stair and sprang open, so she had to stuff her skirts and kneesocks back inside and start the whole exhausting process over again from the beginning. When at last she reached the room, she shoved the suitcase inside, kicking it with her foot. The door squeaked. The room was cold and dark, but it had a large canopy bed in the center with two more black cats at the foot of it. They hissed as Henrietta entered.

"I hope she wasn't allergic to cats," the girl says.

"That was her only piece of luck," the mother tells her.

 DINNER IS SERVED

Henrietta was unsure of what she should do. The room was uninviting, but the idea of going downstairs again was even more awful, so she opened her suitcase and started to unpack her things. It calmed her a bit to touch them, the familiar wool skirts and white cotton blouses with their rounded collars. Henrietta was bent over the suitcase when Priscilla appeared in the doorway.

"I have other ways to occupy you," she said.

Henrietta jumped. Then she screamed.

"What is the matter with you? You're worse than they said."

"I'm sorry," said Henrietta. "You startled me. That's all. What would you like me to do?"

Priscilla took her to the kitchen and told her to make soup. Henrietta protested that she didn't know how to cook, but Priscilla gave her a recipe and handed her a bowl of lumpy-looking vegetables and three packages wrapped in white paper.

"Follow the recipe," she said.

Henrietta looked around the room, examining each detail of her new surroundings. The cutting boards were covered with dark, watery stains, and the room was drafty. Bundles of dried leaves and slightly rusty pots swung from a wooden rack overhead. Henrietta had no idea where to begin. She felt utterly alone and hopeless and was standing stock-still with a blank look on her face when Priscilla stuck her head into the room a second time.

"Well, go ahead!" Priscilla urged from the doorway. "The soup isn't going to make itself!"

So Henrietta gathered her courage, grabbed a large knife, and started to chop up the meat in the first package. It seemed ordinary enough. The recipe called for butter and onions, so she sliced those too. But as they were sizzling in the pan, she realized that the other two white paper packages were still there. When Henrietta opened the next one, a small, wet, red-brown organ fell out into her hand. Henrietta shrieked. It looked like the heart of a small animal.

"And the third package?" asks the girl.

"Fish heads," says the mother. "Quite common in soups, really, but Henrietta didn't know that. She screamed again—just as loudly—when she saw them."

"This is too awful," says the girl.

"It's not that horrible, really. A lot of tasty things have odd ingredients, you know. Steak and kidney pie, for one."

"You know what I mean. She shouldn't even be there. She only made the one mistake. Cutting her sister's bangs."

"Sometimes the smallest missteps have unimagined consequences," the mother says.

❧ NIGHT TERRORS ❧

Believe it or not, Henrietta was not the only one suffering. Mr. and Mrs. Osgood thought that Arabella's life would return to normal as soon as her bangs grew back and her sister went away. Unfortunately, they had underestimated the depth of the attachment between their daughters. For as opposite as they were, Arabella and Henrietta were twins, and twins are connected in strange and mysterious ways that only another twin can really understand.

And so the very night that Henrietta left for Aunt Priscilla's, Arabella woke up screaming. The nanny had to rush to her bedside. It turned out that Arabella had had a terrible nightmare. It was something about a strange house, a woman in black, and an awful bowl of soup with an eye floating in it. She was crying so hard that it was difficult for the Osgoods to understand exactly what she was saying.

"She's cutting up a heart," she sobbed.

"Cutting out your heart? Oh my goodness no! You've had an awful nightmare."

"For the soup," Arabella insisted.

"She's not making any sense," Mrs. Osgood said to Rose. "Get the thermometer. I think she must have a fever."

"Perhaps we should call the doctor."

In the end, Arabella went back to sleep with a cool cloth on her forehead and a small light turned on at her bedside. Her mother slept beside her, in Henrietta's bed, thinking it would calm Arabella. But every hour or so, Arabella woke up with another terrible nightmare about cats sleeping on her bed or long red fingernails. No matter what her parents and Rose did, they couldn't seem to end the bad dreams for the night.

"I have two questions," the girl says.

"All right," the mother sighs.

"First, is that true about the connection between twins?"

"Of course. Why do you think they dress alike?"

"And another thing. Don't you think she acted like a baby by having her mother sleep with her?"

"Well, dear, only Mrs. Osgood and Arabella know the answer to that."

36

 NOTES AND MESSAGES

The next morning, while Arabella was away at school, it suddenly dawned on Mrs. Osgood what had caused the dream in the first place.

"It's Priscilla," she said. "Somehow she's dreaming of Priscilla. Don't you see? The cats and the fingernails and that awful food Priscilla eats."

"That's impossible," Mr. Osgood said, without lowering the morning paper.

"It isn't impossible at all," said Mrs. Osgood. "It's the only thing that makes sense. I'd call her myself if she had a telephone. You have to go and speak to her. She's *your* aunt."

"And yours," said Mr. Osgood, "by marriage."

"Nevertheless," Mrs. Osgood said. "And do it right away. We can't spend another night like last night. Arabella needs her rest."

"But what will I say?" whined Mr. Osgood, who, truth be told, hated any kind of conflict.

"Do you want me to drive over there?" Mrs. Osgood asked, in a tone that suggested it was more of a threat than an offer of assistance.

"That's a lot of bother, dear. Don't trouble yourself. I'll send a telegram on the way to the office," Mr. Osgood said. "Oh! Look at the time! Have you seen my spectacles?"

"They're on top of your head," said Mrs. Osgood.

"So they are," said Mr. Osgood, reaching to locate them and giving his wife a small salute. "I'm off! Bye now."

And so that was settled. Mr. Osgood escaped his wife and avoided a long, painful conversation with his aunt. He sent a telegram to Aunt Priscilla that said:

ARABELLA HAVING BAD DREAMS STOP

"Stop what?" the girl asks her mother.

"That's how they sent a telegram," the mother explains. "The 'stop' is like a period."

"But that doesn't really tell her what to do," the girl says.

"I suppose they weren't exactly sure what Priscilla would do to make the dreams stop."

"What did she do?"

When Priscilla got the telegram, she had the same reaction as her nephew, Mr. Osgood. Priscilla didn't see how *she* was responsible for Arabella's nightmares. So she took out her stationery and a quill pen and wrote Mr. Osgood a letter.

> Osgood,
>   Imagine my surprise at having my lunch interrupted by your odd telegram about Arabella and her nightmares. I cannot imagine what you think I can do to assist. If I am not mistaken, the child has two parents as well as a nanny. And I, you will recall, have already taken in her sister—who, by the way, is prone to fits of screaming and is so untrained that she cannot even follow a simple recipe!
>   Yours,
>   Priscilla

40

· · ·

Priscilla licked the envelope and handed it to Henrietta. "Take this to the post office," she said, depositing some coins for postage in Henrietta's upturned palm.

"Where's that?"

Aunt Priscilla sighed and gave a long and confusing set of directions: up a hill, down a hill, past the bookshop, across from the pharmacy, and so on. Henrietta was sure that she would get lost, but she was afraid of making Aunt Priscilla angry if she asked for further instructions, so she set off.

It was a cloudy day, threatening rain, and Henrietta was cold. She should have worn a sweater, but she never remembered, and her mother and the nanny weren't there to tell her to wear one, so she went without and shivered. Her socks kept falling down and bunching in her shoes, and every few feet she would stop and bend over to pull them up. The wind whipped her hair into her eyes, and the strands stung like salt in a cut. Henrietta was tired and miserable and sure that she was lost. Most melancholy of all was the sight of her parents' names and her own address on the letter she carried. Soon their hands would open this envelope, touch this same paper. Henrietta could picture the letter resting in the wicker basket on the hall table where they kept the mail, and a wave of homesickness hit her as she walked through the unfamiliar village all alone.

HENRIETTA FINDS A FRIEND

As she walked, Henrietta thought of all that had happened since that fateful moment when she cut her sister's bangs. Suddenly she realized that she should have written a letter of her own, apologizing and begging her parents for another chance. Finally she passed the bookstore and decided to stop to see if she could borrow a pencil.

The woman behind the counter had beautiful dark hair and a kind face, so Henrietta decided to test her luck and ask for the pencil, which the woman gladly gave her. The letter was sealed tight, so she wrote on the back of the envelope.

I am very sorry. I would like to come home.
H.

"Would you like me to mail that for you?" the woman asked.

"That's okay," Henrietta said. "I'm on my way to the post office myself, except I don't know exactly where it is."

"Why, it's miles away. Why don't you leave it here? I'll give it to the postman when he comes by."

The woman was so kind and sympathetic that Henrietta felt tears forming in her eyes. It seemed a very long time since anyone had been nice to her.

"Had anyone ever been nice to her?" the girl asks her mother.

"Arabella," the mother answers. "Before their argument. But that must have already seemed a long time ago."

The woman, who was called Inez, took Henrietta to the back of the store and gave her a peppermint from a jar she kept on her desk. Soon Henrietta was telling her the whole story about cutting Arabella's hair and how it had led to her being sent away.

"And this is only the second day," she sobbed. "And already I want to go home, but I know they'll never take me back."

43

"Perhaps they just wanted to teach you a lesson," Inez said. "When they hear how unhappy you are, surely they won't make you stay."

"But I think they will," Henrietta sobbed.

"And she's right, isn't she?" the girl asks her mother.

"Just let the story unfold," the mother advises.

Inez fixed Henrietta a cup of tea and told her to make herself at home in the shop.

"I should go," Henrietta said.

"No need to rush," Inez answered her, smiling. "Have your tea and look around a bit. A book can be a good friend on a cold, blustery day."

Henrietta sipped the tea, which tasted like lemons and honey. Then she tiptoed out into the store and began to look at the books. Inside each one was a whole world. The best had drawings as well as stories: horses and castles and dark, mysterious woods. The bell above the door would ring sometimes, and someone would buy a magazine or pick up a book they had ordered for someone's birthday. Henrietta ignored them, curled up in a soft chair, and read. She stayed so long that soon it was time for the shop to close. It was raining by now, and Inez offered to take Henrietta back to Aunt Priscilla's house. She also gave Henrietta two things.

"Can you guess what they were?" the mother asks.

"A pile of gold," the girl says.

"Not likely," says the mother. "Though Inez was wearing some lovely gold earrings."

"Another peppermint."

"One piece of candy is more than enough," says the mother.

45

Inez gave Henrietta a book of stories and, best of all, a promise that if she did not return home and if Aunt Priscilla allowed it, Henrietta could work in the shop on Thursday afternoons. So Henrietta rode with Inez back to Aunt Priscilla's house in the rain, uphill and downhill, daydreaming the whole way. When they arrived, Henrietta thanked Inez for her kindness. Then she tucked the book beneath her waistband, wrapping her arms around it. Henrietta most definitely did not want to have to explain where she had been, though she needn't have worried, as Priscilla seemed to have disappeared.

That night, Henrietta dreamed she was reading the book of stories in the shop, next to a crackling fire. And far away, in her bed, Arabella dreamed the same dream and smiled.

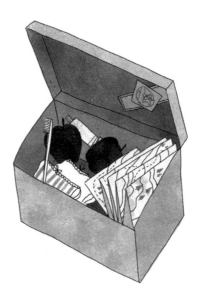

ARABELLA PLANS A RESCUE

Although Mr. and Mrs. Osgood were as happy as could be now that Henrietta was out of the house, Arabella was sad. She missed her sister's company in the evenings, missed their games. This surprised her because before Henrietta left, there were times when Arabella hadn't really paid much attention to her sister, times when Henrietta was, more or less, just a lump underneath the covers in the opposite bed at night. But once Henrietta left, the house was too quiet. Arabella began to miss her sister and worry about her. On the playground at school, her circle of friends speculated about Henrietta and what her life was like.

"Is she a servant girl?" they would ask.

"Does she sleep by the fire like Cinderella?"

"I don't know," Arabella was forced to answer. But the truth was that ever since her own nightmares began, Arabella had suspected that her sister's new life wasn't very nice.

"Maybe she's in danger," Arabella's friend Lacey said.

But this seemed improbable until the afternoon when Arabella noticed a pile of mail on the hall table and flipped through it, which she was not supposed to do. She saw the letter from Aunt Priscilla, and she saw the note of apology that Henrietta had written across the back. Arabella was sure that when her parents saw it, they would regret their decision and bring Henrietta home. Then things would be back to normal, and she could sleep better at night with Henrietta in the next bed to whisper to in the dark.

At dinner that night, Mrs. Osgood asked her husband, "Anything interesting come in the post?"

Mr. Osgood shook his head. "Nothing much. Letter from Priscilla, full of complaints."

"Just like her," said Mrs. Osgood. "What does she want?"

"It's not her so much," said Mr. Osgood. "It's Henrietta herself. Wants to come home."

"Can she?" asked Arabella. "Please?"

"Oh, I don't think so," said Mrs. Osgood.

"Right. Best leave things as they are," agreed Mr. Osgood.

And when the girls at school asked her if her sister was ever coming home, Arabella had to say that she was not. And then, for some reason, perhaps because she felt sad or perhaps just as much because their pity gave her a warm feeling of pleasure, Arabella's eyes welled with tears, just as her sister's had that day in the shop. This got them all excited, and they patted her hair and handed her handkerchiefs and asked her not to cry.

"Why don't you go and visit her?" Lacey suggested.

"My parents would never let me."

They agreed that it was sad, and Lacey gave Arabella a chocolate to make her feel better. Then the bell rang, and they had to go back to class. But Arabella was taken with what they had said. She decided that she should find a way to visit Henrietta whether her parents wanted her to or not. And she started to lay her plan. In a box underneath her bed, she began to store up what she thought she would need: allowance money she had saved and clean underwear and a map she snuck out of her father's study and a couple of apples she could eat if she got hungry along the way. She even snuck Priscilla's letter from the basket on the hall table and copied Priscilla's address on a small slip of paper. Arabella was ready, but she knew that sneaking away might prove difficult. Leaving before school was impossible because Rose kept a close eye on her. And once she got to school, there was no way of doing anything without Mr. Stilton-Sterne noticing.

Arabella confided in her friends, and they discussed the problem endlessly. They loved the drama of it. You couldn't blame them, really—so little happened in their young lives. But soon Arabella's plans to run away were the talk of the playground. The girls even made up a jump-rope rhyme:

She escapes after dark
Takes a walk
Through the park
Mother cries, father frowns
She is miles out of town
One, two, three, four . . .

And the boys were prepared to perform the rescue themselves if the girls proved too timid.

"I can find your sister for you," Brendan Crowhurst bragged. "If you're too scared to go."

"She's not too scared," Lacey said. "She's just waiting for the right time."

As it turned out, the right time presented itself that very afternoon when Mr. Stilton-Sterne announced that he would be away the next day and the class would have a substitute teacher.

"I've got it!" Arabella shouted at recess. "When the other teacher calls my name, you just tell her I got moved to another class."

"That won't work," Lacey said. "She'll check, and we'll get caught."

"Look," said Brendan, butting into the conversation as usual, "when she calls Arabella's name, somebody just says, 'Here.' She won't know any of us. It's easy to fool a substitute."

They had to agree that Brendan had a point. And his tone did not exactly encourage protest. After that, the deal seemed sealed. Everyone was in on it. For once, they were all looking forward to school the next morning.

⁑· A STRANGE DISCOVERY ·⁑

Henrietta, of course, had no idea what Arabella was planning. For her, each day dragged on with no real prospect that her situation would ever change. Without school to occupy her, Henrietta had many empty hours to fill. Even the countless chores Priscilla gave her did not seem to last long enough.

Priscilla was not much of a conversationalist. When she was not devouring one of the hideous soups or stews that sustained her, she could be found in front of the fire reading, napping, or murmuring to one of her cats. In fact, she seemed to have more to say to them than she did to Henrietta.

Left to her own devices, Henrietta began to quietly explore the second story of the house. She examined the books on

Priscilla's shelves, which were mostly accounts of great wars or long biographies of elderly gentlemen Henrietta couldn't quite identify, though their faces all seemed vaguely familiar. Finally she opened the door to a large closet in the wide hallway. Henrietta knew she was snooping, but her curiosity got the better of her. Inside the closet's dim interior were piles of shiny fabric and stacks of small magazines and photographs. One especially intriguing gold-and-lace bundle was stowed on the top shelf. Henrietta stood on her tiptoes and leaned forward as far as she could, stretching toward her prize.

That was when the whole thing came tumbling down: the top shelf (only loosely attached under the best of circumstances) tipped forward, and a gold dress, a pile of fabric, photographs, feather boas, and lace rained down on Henrietta. She took a small step backward, twisted her ankle, and landed with a thud on the hallway floor. The commotion brought Priscilla from her comfortable seat by the fire up into the drafty hallway.

"Oh no!" she said. "My things! What have you done to my things?!"

Henrietta, still in shock, just blinked at her from the floor, a feather boa around her neck and another in her hair. She looked as dazed and helpless as a baby chick.

"I was just—" she started.

"Going through my closet," Priscilla finished for her. "I can see that."

Priscilla rushed to pick up the gold dress, caressing the brilliant material as if it were one of her beloved cats.

"Here," Henrietta said, attempting to stand. "Let me help you."

It was then she realized what she had done to her ankle, which was already beginning to swell. Priscilla sighed, dragged a small wooden chair out of her bedroom, and helped Henrietta onto it; then she went to get ice while Henrietta, humiliated and in pain, surveyed the mess at her feet.

When Priscilla returned, Henrietta asked, "What is all this?"

"My past," Priscilla said wistfully.

"What do you mean?"

"Haven't your parents told you anything about me?" she asked. "Who I am? Who I was?"

"No," Henrietta said softly, as ashamed of her ignorance as of the fallen papers and clothes at her feet.

"See for yourself, then," Priscilla said, handing her a small booklet.

Henrietta studied the drawing on the cover. It was a lovely young woman wearing the gold dress that Priscilla

was now folding. Her hair was in an elaborate bun, jewels hung around her neck, and she had vivid green eyes.

"Is this. . ."—Henrietta slowly realized it as she spoke— ". . . you?"

"Who else would it be?" Priscilla asked.

"But you look so different," Henrietta blurted.

Priscilla was looking at the cover now herself.

"It was a long time ago," she said.

"Tell me about it," Henrietta said. "Please."

And so they stayed there for a time in the upstairs hallway while the ice melted against Henrietta's wounded ankle, and Priscilla described her glory days on the stage: her favorite plays, her favorite roles, the thrill of looking out at the audience's faces, lifted expectantly toward the stage.

"Were you famous?" Henrietta asked.

"For a time," Priscilla said, "I had my admirers."

And she gazed down at her emerald ring.

"No wonder they gave you jewels. You were so beautiful," Henrietta said. "Arabella is too. Not like me."

"What are you talking about?" Priscilla said. "All the women in our family are beauties."

"Not me," said Henrietta.

"Nonsense," Priscilla insisted. "It's a matter of confidence. People will believe what you want them to believe. Every good actor knows that. Here," she said, rearranging the boa around Henrietta's neck and perching a large hat on her head. Then she stepped to her room, and when she returned, she handed Henrietta a mirror.

"It's important," she told Henrietta, "to see yourself as you really are."

Then Priscilla began collecting her treasures and storing them in the dark closet.

"What a disaster," she muttered to herself as Henrietta studied her face in the mirror, turning her head this way and that.

 THE JOURNEY BEGINS

As Henrietta was gaining a bit of confidence for the first time, Arabella was losing hers. The truth was that Arabella was a little afraid of sneaking off. She had heard her mother talking about Aunt Priscilla, and some of the things she said were scary. And despite the map, Arabella wasn't at all sure she would know the way. All through dinner she kept thinking up little excuses for not leaving that she could use at school the next morning. She could say that it looked too much like rain, or that she hadn't had a chance to pack. If nothing else worked, she could fall back on the most time-honored and impossible-to-prove excuse of all: she could tell them she had a terrible stomachache. If Brendan protested, and he probably would, Arabella knew she could whip up some fake tears, and the girls would circle around her until the boys lost interest and backed off.

Arabella was so convinced she could get out of leaving that she began to relax and enjoy dessert. (It was her favorite: chocolate silk pie.) But that night, something happened that convinced her she had to leave after all. Arabella had a dream that she was sleeping in a cold, drafty room in a strange, dark bed. Black cats kept wandering in and out, and she was freezing and hungry. Arabella tossed and turned in her bed until she woke herself up.

"That room is real!" she whispered out loud to herself. "That's the room Henrietta has to sleep in. How awful!"

Arabella looked over at the empty bed beside her, and her eyes filled with real tears as she remembered the day Henrietta was sent away. "She's never done anything *for* me either!" Henrietta had shouted that day. And right then and there, in the deep dark middle of the night, Arabella resolved to take to the road and find her sister.

"Wasn't she frightened?" asks the girl.

"Of course," says the mother. "But sometimes it's the most frightening thing that most needs doing."

"But how did she know where to go?" the girl asks her mother.

"That's the thing. She really didn't."

Arabella located the town on the map and knew that it was north of where she lived. Then she remembered the little signs that her teacher had hung on the walls at school to help them learn about directions.

"Never eat soggy worms," the girl says.

"I beg your pardon?"

"That's how you remember it. The directions. Never eat soggy worms."

"Oh. I get it," the mother says.

So the next morning, Arabella stood in front of the school, watching as her nanny waved goodbye and headed back toward home. Then Arabella imagined herself inside her classroom, facing the side where they kept the class gerbils, Mike and Pat. She took a deep breath, turned north, and started out.

✿ SOME HELP ALONG THE WAY ✿

At first she was walking through her own neighborhood, then another near her school, then out on a country lane, and across a hill covered with small stones and purple heather. She saw goats and small houses and lost track of the road. Finally she saw a crooked little old man who seemed to be taking care of the goats, and she decided she would ask him if she was going in the right direction.

"Let me think," he said. He stroked his stubbly chin. "Seems to me like you *are* going north, but hadn't you better stick to the road? You'll be stepping in cow pies this way."

"Where is the road?" Arabella asked.

The old man told her to walk with him a bit, and he

would get her squared away. She hesitated at first because she had been given all the usual and correct warnings about talking to strangers. But the man seemed nice, and Arabella reasoned that as she was already in the next town over, anyone she met was likely to be a stranger. So Arabella walked beside the old man for a time.

"What brings you this way?" he asked.

Arabella stopped for a minute and thought about how best to describe it. It seemed silly to say that her sister had attacked her bangs and had been sent away and was now trapped in a strange room with a dusty old bed and dozens of dark creepy cats.

"My sister's in trouble," she said instead. "And she needs my help. I'm trying to find my way to her."

"Maybe I can help," the man said.

Arabella took the map out of her book bag and showed him where she was going.

He traced the route she should follow with one long, crooked finger; then he said, "I think we've got you sorted. Healthy walk, but you'll be there in a bit."

"I hope so," Arabella said. "I have to get to her no matter how long it takes. Henrietta doesn't even want to be with Aunt Priscilla—"

"Priscilla?" the old man asked as a strange look came over his face. "Tell me, what's her last name?"

"Renfrew," Arabella said.

"Oh my," the man said slowly.

And then it all came out.

PRISCILLA'S PAST

"He knows her?" the girl asks her mother.

"That's what I'm getting to."

It seems he knew Priscilla from his youth, when they were both aspiring young actors. He was one of the many taken by her beauty and talent on the stage.

"But," he told Arabella, "there was something unnatural about it. The way she seemed to change for every part. It was like she became another person every time, like she cast a spell."

"You see!" the girl shouts. "He's saying she's a witch."

"Well," says the mother, "she certainly had mysterious powers."

The old man described how Priscilla's was always the most amazing performance in any play.

"Nobody ever saw her backstage putting on her makeup. She never seemed to be in the wings waiting to go on. When it was time, she just appeared onstage looking so much like the character that it confused the rest of us. The other actors."

Arabella stood completely still, engrossed in the story.

"You would almost forget your own lines, staring at her face," the old man went on. "The only way you ever knew it was her was by her eyes. Those amazing green eyes."

He said that every actor in the troupe was in love with her. And a funny, glazed look came over his face.

"This must be a different Priscilla," Arabella said. "I've seen pictures of her, and she's as ugly as . . ."

"As a witch!" the girl shouts at her mother.

". . . can be. As ugly as can be. *That's* what Arabella said."

"No," the old man said. "There's no mistake. There's only one Priscilla Renfrew. Of course, she's gotten older, like all of us. She wouldn't look the same now, I expect. But no one knows for sure. Nobody's seen her for years."

"Well, I'm about to," said Arabella. And she thanked him for his help. He gave her a leg up so she could climb a fence and get back on the road. And he pointed the way and wished her good luck. Then he offered her some water from the pouch he had slung over his shoulder, but she politely refused. And then Arabella was on her way again.

❧ THE RUNAWAY ❧

Of course, at home it was quite a scene come three forty-five when Arabella failed to appear. Rose rushed in and said she couldn't find Arabella at school.

"What?!" yelled Mrs. Osgood, putting her art supplies away so quickly that she ruined a perfectly good new paintbrush. Then she called her husband and told him to meet her at the school. And she hurried off to find the principal, who was just leaving for the day. Mrs. Osgood charged into his office, demanding to know if he had seen Arabella.

"Let's see if she's still in class," Principal Rothbottom said, leading Mrs. Osgood toward Arabella's classroom. They arrived just as the substitute teacher, Miss Brittlewhite, was locking the door.

"Have you seen the Osgood girl?" he asked her.

"She has a name!" Mrs. Osgood said.

But Principal Rothbottom was too busy quizzing Miss Brittlewhite to notice how upset Mrs. Osgood was.

"I'm asking you a question. Did Della report for school today?"

"Arabella!" Mrs. Osgood exclaimed. "Her name is Arabella!"

"Which one is she?" Miss Brittlewhite asked.

"This is outrageous!" shouted Mrs. Osgood.

"Well, there are dozens of children; I get them confused," Miss Brittlewhite admitted. "But I had all the children who were on the list. I took attendance. I swear I did."

And, of course, she had. But, just as they had planned yesterday on the playground, another girl answered for Arabella, and Miss Brittlewhite never knew the difference.

Principal Rothbottom turned to Arabella's mother. "Mrs. Osgood," he said, "I assure you we will do all we can to help you find your daughter."

"I should hope you would!" she snapped.

And so on. It was one of those fights that grown-ups have without any shouting. It was full of sighing and nasty looks. In the middle of it all, Mr. Osgood arrived and listened as his wife and the principal explained that Arabella was missing.

"I think the point, my dear, is that it's time to contact the authorities," Mr. Osgood told his wife. "We need to institute a search."

"I'm afraid I agree," said Principal Rothbottom.

Mrs. Osgood turned pale. She began to imagine bloodhounds and policemen slopping through the woods and shallow streams looking for Arabella. Mrs. Osgood started to panic. Mr. Osgood took his wife home and called the doctor to come over and give her a shot.

"A shot?" the girl asks her mother. "What for?"

"Well, to help her calm down. Imagine how upset she must be. Her daughter is missing."

"A shot doesn't help you calm down," the girl says. "Just seeing the needle is scary."

"A certain kind of shot can help you calm down."

"Like the kind they blow out of a dart gun to take down an elephant?"

"Of course not! Where do you get these things?" the mother asks.

Mr. Osgood took his wife home, and their house was full of people: Dr. Waverly tending to Mrs. Osgood; and the police, asking questions; and the neighbors, who said they were worried but who also, as anyone knows, were just being nosy.

Principal Rothbottom, true to his word, stopped by later to see if there was anything the school could do to help.

"What did they do?" the girl asks. "To find her?"

"Well, the first thing they did was to call her friend Lacey to see if she knew anything."

"What did she say?" asks the girl.

"Nothing. Brendan Crowhurst had made them all swear to secrecy."

"You mean she was more afraid of a bully than the police?"

"Well, police and teachers don't rule the playground, I'm afraid," the mother says. "Brendan's word was law there. Besides, Lacey wanted Arabella to reach her sister."

"Good point," says the girl. "And there's never any telling how things will turn out once you let grown-ups interfere."

"Well, quite a few were already involved in the search for Arabella."

Principal Rothbottom promised to have Mr. Northington, the assistant principal, question the children at school the next morning. It would give Northington something useful to do instead of frittering away the day, settling minor playground disputes or mooning over the librarian.

And, as Mrs. Osgood suspected, the police sent out dogs. They asked Mr. Osgood, who asked Rose, for a piece of Arabella's clothing, so the dogs could get her scent. Then they started off. Mr. Osgood and the principal promised to let Mrs. Osgood know as soon as they found out anything about what had happened to Arabella.

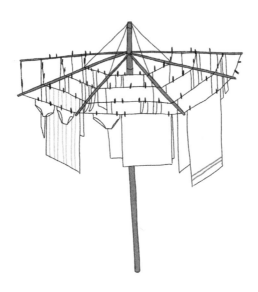

A KIND BUT CURIOUS STRANGER

"What *had* happened to Arabella?" the girl asks.

"Well, actually, it wasn't scary at all," the mother says. "At least not at first."

Arabella, who had stopped to pet a small dog, met a woman who was out in her yard, hanging up laundry.

"Are you lost?" the woman asked.

Although Arabella had done her best to read the map and follow the route the old man had outlined for her, she suspected she probably *was* lost. She was afraid to admit this, however, in case the woman might decide she should call for help.

So she said, "I'm fine. I'm just on my way to my aunt's house."

The bad part was that the woman seemed suspicious and kept asking a lot of questions. The good part was that she asked the questions in a warm kitchen at a table while she fed Arabella a delicious bowl of vegetable soup.

"Vegetable soup is not delicious," the girl says. "Chocolate cake is delicious."

"Chocolate cake is not a meal."

"Why are you so worried about what she's eating?" the girl asks. "Isn't the real point that she just talked to a complete stranger for the **second** time and went inside her house?"

"Good point," says the mother. "It's nice to know you're such a sensible child."

As Arabella ate her soup, the woman studied her.

"That's an interesting hairstyle you have," she said.

"Thanks," said Arabella. "My sister cut my bangs for me."

Arabella, who had pulled off her now-customary

headscarf, was surprised by the compliment. Yet, as the woman began to question her further, pleasure turned to nervousness.

"What did you say your aunt's name was?" asked the woman.

"Worthington," Arabella said. "Sarah Worthington."

That's right. Arabella told a lie. But what's even worse is that the name she selected actually belonged to her Sunday-school teacher. It may be hard to imagine nearly perfect Arabella making up a fib, but the fact was that the journey was already beginning to change her. Her shoes were dusty; her white anklets were smudged with dirt. And now she had told a lie. Arabella knew it was wrong to lie, but she also felt certain somehow that the woman meant to tell on her. She would call the Osgoods and tell them their daughter was here; it was the only thing that could happen next in the sparkling clean kitchen of such a sweet and responsible woman. Arabella sensed it, and she felt forced to lie if she wanted to keep walking long enough to find Henrietta.

"What time is she expecting you?" the woman asked next.

"Could I have some more water?" Arabella asked.

She had only hoped to change the subject, but the truth was that Arabella was beginning to panic. As the woman turned to fill Arabella's water glass, Arabella dashed out the door, leaving the woman to call out after her, "Wait! Don't go!"

 MEANWHILE . . .

Although Arabella was now off on a big adventure, Henrietta's life at Aunt Priscilla's house had settled into a routine. Each night she had to make kidney pie or fish-head stew.

"Each night? They ate horrible things like that every single night?"

"Well," says the mother, "children always complain that they're eating the same things all the time. Perhaps Aunt Priscilla just decided not to bother trying to vary the menu."

Of course, Henrietta never could force herself to take more than a few bites of these dinners, and even then she had to close her eyes and hold her breath to get the food down. Afterward she brushed her tongue with her toothbrush until it hurt. And the rest of the day, Aunt Priscilla kept her busy with odd jobs: catching spiders and teaching them to sing . . .

"What?"

"Well," the mother says, "I said they were odd jobs."

One morning they decided to name Aunt Priscilla's cats.

"They don't have names?" the girl asks.

"Apparently not."

When Henrietta realized that Priscilla was calling them "the gray one" or "the one with the white paws," she asked if they could name them.

"What for?" Priscilla asked.

"That's what people do with pets," Henrietta explained. "We could do it together. I'll start.

"Let's call that one Oatmeal."

"Oatmeal?" asks the girl.

"They were eating breakfast at the time."

Then Henrietta dubbed another cat Lulu, and Aunt Priscilla began to call a third Professor Wiggles. It took them the better part of the morning to name them all. In fact, they only stopped when it was time for Henrietta to go and help Inez. She had gotten Aunt Priscilla to agree that she could work in the bookshop. Of course, she would not be allowed to keep the money she earned, and she had to promise not to say anything about her life with Aunt Priscilla.

"This town is full of gossips," said Aunt Priscilla. "That's why I so seldom go out."

"She never goes out," says the girl to her mother.

"Exactly."

"You'd better get going or you'll be late," said Aunt Priscilla. "Come along, Professor Wiggles," she added, scooping up the cat and wandering toward the bookcase.

. . .

Henrietta rushed off to her appointment with Inez. The bookshop was just as lovely as she remembered, and Henrietta was very happy there. She dusted the shelves and learned to work the cash register.

"There you are," she said as she counted out change into the hand of an older gentleman who had just bought a book of poetry for his wife.

"Well done," said Inez once the man had left. "You're a natural. I should have hired you years ago."

"You didn't know me years ago," said Henrietta.

"Excellent point. And entirely my loss. I plan to make up for it by getting to know all about you right now. What's your favorite color?"

"Purple," said Henrietta without hesitation.

"Lucky number?"

"Ten."

"Favorite pet?"

"I only have the one. Had the one. Muffin."

"No, no, none of that," said Inez when Henrietta began to frown. "You'll be home with Muffin soon enough. Today I have you all to myself."

Inez was good company. Sometimes when business slowed down, she even read stories from a huge book of fairy tales. And they were all about the usual fairy-tale things of girls trapped in towers or lost in forests, but everything always turned out right in the end. In fact, the girls always ended up happily married and ruling a small kingdom of their very own and never eating fish stew or kidney pie ever again. Just hearing the stories gave Henrietta hope that her own situation might change, somehow, for the better.

"How's that going to happen?" the girl asks. "Princes don't walk into a bookshop."

"You never know," the mother says. "Everyone needs something to read."

A GIANT NAMED GUS

The job in Inez's store wasn't the only thing improving Henrietta's mood. Henrietta had a feeling that one day soon Arabella would be with her. And in the black bed, with cat whiskers tickling her cheek, Henrietta had a dream about her sister. The dream seemed more real to Henrietta than her waking life. She saw Arabella studying a map and slipping it into a secret box beneath her bed.

"That's amazing!" says the girl.

"It was," agrees the mother.

And soon Arabella had an amazing experience of her own. She met a giant named Gus.

"Oh, now you've gone too far!" says the girl. "If there can't be witches in the story, there can't be any giants."

"There could be witches, or wiccans, or whatever," the mother says. "There just don't happen to be. This is a true story from real life. I can't make up what didn't happen."

The girl frowns at her mother. "There are no giants in real life."

"Of course there are," says the mother. "It's an issue with the pituitary gland. You could look it up if you like. Or ask your teacher."

"So she met a giant?" asks the girl. "A real giant?"

"She did indeed," says the mother. "Only Arabella didn't realize at first that Gus was a giant because when she first happened upon him, Gus was lying down in the shade under a tree, reading a book with a canning jar of iced tea by his side. He looked tall, of course, but not as enormous as he did standing up."

"Did he say 'Fee Fi Fo Fum' and all that?"

"No. That story's already been told."

Gus liked to spend as much time outdoors as possible. His parents, who were of average height, had designed their house to accommodate their son's expanding frame. But they did not know at the time that Gus would grow so fond of trees and flowers, or that he would so often need to escape their harsh words and disappointment about their lives. The house felt cramped for Gus. And, although Arabella didn't know it, Gus's family blamed his height on none other than Priscilla Renfrew. They claimed she had put some sort of curse on Gus.

It started before Gus was even born. His parents went to see Priscilla in a play when they were dating. They were young and in love and much more interested in each other than they were in the play. And during the performance they started to whisper secrets and giggle. They were sitting in the front row, and their commotion seemed to throw Priscilla off. She stumbled over a few of her lines, and that was not like her at all. Afterward, as they were leaving the theater, Priscilla grabbed Gus's father by the sleeve.

"You'll pay for what you did to me today," she told him. She didn't say how, and she didn't say when, but she threatened them. Gus's father laughed in her face, and his mother wasn't worried either—not until the day, years later, when she found out she was pregnant with Gus. Then she remembered about Priscilla. She could still imagine Priscilla in front of them going on about how they would be sorry for what they had done. And suddenly she was terrified at the thought of what Priscilla might do to spoil their happiness.

For the rest of the pregnancy, she was afraid that something would be wrong with the baby. And, of course, they eventually found out that something was.

"But he's just different," the girl says. "Just tall. He could still live a perfectly good life."

"Well, yes," says the mother. "But being a giant is a terrible strain on your heart. Most of them die young."

"How sad!"

But Arabella didn't know any of this when she came upon Gus reading under the tree. She just saw his foot at first, his very large, bare foot lying there in the grass. Then her eyes traveled all the way up to his head, partially hidden by a copy of *A Gardener's Guide to Wildflowers*, which was one of his favorite books. The problem was that Arabella's own feet kept moving along with her eyes, and she was so shocked by what she was seeing that she tripped over Gus's foot, and he had to help her up. In a very deep voice, he asked if she was all right.

Then he asked, "You're afraid of me, aren't you?"

"Of course not," Arabella answered.

"Yes, you are," Gus insisted.

"Should I be?" Arabella asked.

"No, not at all. I'm sorry," Gus said. "I must be making a

terrible first impression. It's just that, you know, I get that a lot."

"What?"

"Abject terror. Trembling."

"Really?"

"No. I guess I'm exaggerating. But people are shocked sometimes. They tend to stare or say something stupid. They think I'm a lot older and much scarier than I really am."

"How old are you?" Arabella asked.

"I'm eleven. And not at all scary, in case you were going to ask."

"People get the wrong idea about me too," Arabella said. "Just because I'm blond . . ."

"And pretty," Gus added.

"Thank you," Arabella said with a blush. "Well, people talk to me like I'm dense."

"How annoying," Gus said.

"And I happen to be a straight-A student," Arabella told him.

Then, to Arabella's embarrassment, her stomach growled. Loudly.

Gus began to laugh, not unkindly, and that made Arabella laugh too.

"I'm terribly sorry," said Gus. "Where are my manners? My name is Gus."

"Arabella," she said, holding out her hand.

"You must be hungry, Arabella. Let's go inside. It's almost time for dinner, and you can meet my parents."

As they neared the house, Arabella could hear some boisterous singing.

"That's my mother," Gus said with an apologetic smile. "She likes opera."

"Oh," said Arabella. She felt she probably should have said more, offered some compliment, but it sounded like a cat whose tail had been pulled, and she doubted her ability to seem sincere.

"It's nice that she has a hobby," Arabella said after a long pause.

As they entered the house, Gus's mother was standing on a low stool in front of the sink. Her eyes were squeezed shut, her head thrown back. One arm was stretched forward, and the other was thrown across her substantial chest as she reached for a final high note. She opened her eyes when she heard them come in.

"Oh my!" she said, stumbling down off the stool. "Who do we have here?"

"This is Arabella," Gus said. "My new friend. I thought she might stay for dinner."

"Delightful! We're having pasta."

"She thinks we're in Italy," Gus whispered. "Let me show you the house."

Soon Gus's father joined them for the tour. The house was amazing, with high ceilings and large windows. Arabella told them right away how much she liked it.

"We designed it special," Gus's father said proudly. "Once we knew how big our boy would be."

"Sit down," his mother said. "Let's have something to eat."

She was an excellent cook and served the pasta with a wonderful salad and a lemony iced tea that Gus kept drinking from his canning jar. As they ate, they started discussing Arabella's journey. She felt so relaxed that eventually Arabella admitted she was on her way to see her sister.

"My parents sent her away," she explained. "To stay with my father's aunt. But I keep having terrible dreams, and I think she isn't happy. Maybe not even safe. So I have to go and find her."

"We dream all sorts of strange things, dear," said Gus's mother. "I'm sure she's fine. I bet she's doing something really lovely right this minute. Like eating an orange or having a nice nap."

But once Arabella started to give them details about her dreams, Gus and his family had to admit that the situation did sound dire.

"Aren't you afraid to go there?" asked Gus's father.

"Hush, Quentin. No need to frighten the girl, is there? Honestly, sometimes you don't have the sense—"

"If you would kindly let me finish *for a change*. I simply think—" said Gus's father.

"That's the whole trouble," his mother interrupted. "You don't stop to think."

"Let's go outside," whispered Gus. He was always embarrassed when his parents started to quarrel, and he knew from experience that once they started, it would go on for a while and could get very loud.

"Sorry about that," Gus said as they stood outside together in the green grass.

"Don't be silly," Arabella told him. "It isn't your fault."

But she found somehow that she couldn't quite look at him now.

"Perhaps I'd better be going," she said.

"I wish you could stay," Gus said. "We never get visitors, and it's been so interesting talking to you."

Arabella smiled at him. Inside, the loud voices continued.

"Well," Gus said at last, "perhaps you're right. I hate to send you off alone, though; do you want me to come with you?"

Now, the truth was that Arabella did want Gus to come along, but she was trying to be practical. Despite sharing her story with Gus and his family, she was still planning to keep a low profile—as behooves a runaway. And it isn't easy to be inconspicuous when you're traveling with a giant.

"Thank you," said Arabella, "but I think I should go alone. I'll be all right."

"Let me give you something," said Gus.

"He's going to give her a rabbit's foot," says the girl. "For luck."

"I've never understood why a rabbit's foot is good luck. It certainly wasn't lucky for the rabbit."

"Mother! Get on with the story."

"I was just going to say that Gus gave her a silver whistle."

"Here," said Gus as he slid the whistle onto a blue ribbon and tied it around Arabella's neck. "For safety. In case you get lost."

"I'm not sure if I should be more afraid of getting lost or of being found," Arabella said, and smiled. "But thank you."

They could still hear Gus's parents yelling at one another and throwing pots and pans around the kitchen.

Arabella gave Gus a sympathetic look. "Will you be all right?" she asked.

"Sure," he said. "This happens a lot."

So Arabella stood on her tiptoes; she grabbed Gus's hand and squeezed it.

"Goodbye, my friend," she whispered.

She realized now that Henrietta wasn't the only one who didn't have a very nice place to live. But she had a mission. And she decided to get on with it.

⇒ NIGHT FALLS ⇐

After she left Gus, Arabella soon reached a small, unfamiliar town. It was evening now, and the lights were beginning to come on in the houses. Through the windows she could see people settling in for the night: washing up dishes or stooping to pet a dog. Looking at them from the damp sidewalk was impossibly sad. A part of her began to wish that someone along the way had called her parents. Perhaps the woman who questioned her so closely at lunchtime had telephoned the police by now, and any minute her parents would be coming to collect her. That was what Arabella hoped. The truth was that Arabella was out in the wide world on her own. However much that kindly woman may have worried initially, she never did notify the authorities.

"So nobody is going to help her?" asks the girl.

"That's not what I said. As you recall, the police were already at the Osgoods' house."

Mrs. Osgood rested—propped up on pillows in her blue satin robe—on a couch in the center of the living room as the police explained that it was quite possible Arabella hadn't run away at all but had been snatched.

"What can we do?" Mrs. Osgood asked.

"Try not to worry, ma'am," said the chief of police. "My men are searching for her now with the dogs."

Mrs. Osgood gasped loudly at this.

"I'll post guards around the house. I'd expect a call, or a note, fairly soon if this is a kidnapping."

"I think I'm going to faint," said Mrs. Osgood.

"There must be something else we can do," Mr. Osgood exclaimed, but the police insisted they were doing all they could, and there was nothing left to do but wait.

Eventually, Mrs. Osgood fell asleep, with Muffin snoring softly on her lap. And Mr. Osgood paced the floor, worrying about Arabella. He was surprised to find himself thinking too of Henrietta. How was it possible that, without really meaning to, he had somehow given one girl away and lost the other? He stared out of the front window into the rainy night, where his own worried reflection hovered like a ghost.

"But they are going to find her, aren't they?" the girl asks.

"They were trying very hard," says the mother.

As the Osgoods waited, the search party was spreading out across the town. Police in yellow rain slickers followed the lead of their trained dogs. Parents and neighbors trailed along beside them, calling Arabella's name and aiming their flashlight beams into the darkness.

❧ A MODEST PROPOSAL ❧

While most of the town was in an uproar over Arabella's disappearance, there were a few people who were still blissfully unaware of what had transpired. Two of them were at that moment in the school's library: Mr. Northington, the assistant principal, and Rebecca Dewey, the school librarian.

"That is not her name!" says the girl. "That's the system they use in the library for organizing the books!"

"Well, it is a name as well. It is the name of the man who invented that system, and Miss Dewey happens to be related to him. That's why she went into library work in the first place."

"Oh. I guess that makes sense. But what were they doing in the library at night?"

"I'm sure Miss Dewey had more work most days than she could ever hope to finish," says the mother. "But in Mr. Northington's case, there was more to it than that."

In addition to being the school librarian, Miss Dewey was also (and more importantly) the object of Mr. Northington's affection. Once he noticed that she had decided to stay late at the school, he did the same, pretending to be extremely busy. He stopped by the library and asked very politely if he could take Miss Dewey out to dinner.

"Oh, Edward," she said. "That's sweet of you, and I am a bit hungry."

Her smile and the sudden use of his first name left Mr. Northington feeling slightly dazed.

"It's such a shame I have all this work to do this evening," she continued, pointing to the box of books she was unpacking.

"Well," said Mr. Northington, in his most authoritative voice, "I think it would be perfectly fine if you left the rest of that until tomorrow. As the principal, I—"

"Assistant principal," she gently corrected him.

"I would be glad to get some of the children to help you after school. In fact, I insist on it."

"That's kind," she said. "But I think it's best if I do it myself."

"Didn't she like him?" asks the girl.

"I think she did like him. Perhaps she just didn't realize it yet. And anyway, she didn't want to deal with all the gossip and the teasing from the children."

"I can understand that," says the girl. "Northington and Dewey sitting in a tree . . ."

"My point exactly."

Mr. Northington returned to his office, not yet completely prepared to give up for the night. "She did say she was hungry," he was thinking. Then he had an idea. If Miss Dewey would not go out to dinner with him, he would bring dinner to her. Rushing around the corner to a small gourmet cheese shop, he forced himself inside the door just as the proprietor was pulling down the front shade.

"We're closing," the man said.

"This is an emergency!" Mr. Northington cried.

"A *cheese* emergency?"

"A love emergency."

"Oh, Mother," groans the girl.

"Just listen," the mother insists.

Luckily for Mr. Northington, the shop owner was a bit of a romantic. He packed up a lovely picnic supper inside a large wicker basket and even tossed in some gold candlesticks (from the shop's front window), which Mr. Northington promised to return the next day. Northington took these treasures to the school. When he got back to the library, Miss Dewey was nowhere to be seen. Northington sighed and prepared to admit defeat. Then he saw a small slice of light coming from beneath her office door at the rear of the library. So, quickly and quietly he arranged his feast on one of the library tables.

Then he tapped on Miss Dewey's door and said, "I'm sorry to disturb you, but I've brought you a food, some food, a . . ."

Mr. Northington got tongue-tied around Miss Dewey quite often. He led her out of the office and gestured toward the food with a flourish.

"Shall we?" he asked.

Clearly, he had hoped to impress her with this spontaneous and gallant gesture.

So imagine his surprise when instead of swooning with joy, Miss Dewey began to inspect the food and said, "Pack that up at once!"

"But why?"

"Why? I don't allow anyone to *eat* in the library. And just look at what you've brought here: a sharp knife and tree nuts? In a school? Are you mad?"

"She does have a point," says the girl. "A lot of people are allergic."

"Miss Dewey was a very sensible young lady. You could have learned a lot from her."

"I'm sorry!" Mr. Northington cried. "Of course, you're right. As usual."

And though these words would seem to be music to any woman's ears, it took a bit to calm Miss Dewey down.

"It's—it's just . . . ," he stammered. "How else am I to get your attention? You don't notice me at all. You spend all your time talking to the children."

"Oh, Edward," said Miss Dewey.

"Mother!" exclaims the girl. "I thought you promised she was sensible."

"She didn't say it the way you think."

"Edward," she said, "is this your idea of how to attract a woman? By bringing her a hunk of cheese?"

"No," he mumbled, hanging his head.

"I'm a librarian, not a mouse," said Miss Dewey, maneuvering Mr. Northington toward the door.

"Will I see you tomorrow?" he asked hopefully.

"Mr. Northington," she reminded him. "You'll see me every day. I work here."

MISSING ARABELLA

For once, Henrietta was the only one who would sleep well. While her sister walked through the damp darkness of her first night on the road, Henrietta watched the rain slide down her bedroom window on Chillington Lane. She had gotten used to the strange room at Aunt Priscilla's. The cats, while not overly friendly, had stopped hissing and learned to tolerate their new companion, as cats will. And Henrietta, for her part, was trying her best to fit in at her strange new household.

She had spent the afternoon raking leaves in Aunt Priscilla's unruly back garden, scooping them into large piles that stood between the broken trellises and crumbling wooden archways. Priscilla's garden was nothing like the one at home, yet it still called to mind games of hide-and-seek with Arabella. Henrietta was lost in thought, remembering her sister, when Priscilla's voice startled her.

"Someone is here to see you," Priscilla announced from the back door.

And for one hopeful moment, Henrietta believed that her sister might step through the back door to join her in the ruined garden, that fond memories alone might be enough to make her materialize. Instead, Inez was there, holding a book under her arm.

"I think you need a warmer jacket," she said, by way of greeting. "Your cheeks are bright pink."

"I love it out here," Henrietta said. "I guess I miss my mother's garden."

"Well," said Inez, "when you're ready to come in and warm up, have a look at this."

And she handed her a new book. Henrietta opened it and sniffed the pages.

"New-book smell," Henrietta replied. "Almost as good as burning leaves."

"Burning leaves?" asks the girl by the fire. "Isn't that illegal?"

"Not in the old days," says the mother.

"That makes air pollution!" insists the girl.

"It probably does," says the mother. "But it smells wonderful."

"You'll like it even more when you have a chance to read it," Inez said fondly.

And they went inside to share some tea and some butter cookies Inez had brought in a small bakery box tied with string.

"You should offer your friend some soup," suggested Aunt Priscilla. "Your last batch wasn't half-bad."

"Is that a compliment?" asks the girl.

"Coming from Aunt Priscilla, it was high praise indeed," says the mother.

Then Priscilla excused herself for a nap and left Inez and Henrietta to their plate of cookies. (Neither one of them really wanted the soup.)

Henrietta was grateful for the snack. Though she tried to be a good sport, the food at Aunt Priscilla's was difficult to adjust to. She managed most nights to get away without consuming much by hiding the solid bits in her napkin and slipping some to the cats. The rest she swallowed as fast as she could, hoping to taste it as little as possible. The obvious downside was that Henrietta was often hungry.

Since she was now the chief cook and bottle washer at Aunt Priscilla's . . .

"The chief cook?" asks the girl.

"Just an expression," says the mother. "They were quite alone. Apart from the cats."

"And Inez," says the girl.

"Yes. Just this once, Inez. But she could stay for only a short time before she had to leave to reopen the shop."

Delicious as the butter cookies were, they weren't enough to fill Henrietta's stomach for a full day, and neither was the odd, thin stew they had for dinner. So later that evening, as Henrietta stood at the window watching the rain, she felt her stomach rumble. And she decided to slip down to the kitchen, where she began to rummage around, looking for anything she might be willing to eat. The grocery box that had been delivered to their door that day contained merely the usual, horrible ingredients for Aunt Priscilla's bizarre recipes. Snacks were hard to come by.

The kitchen was huge. Dried herbs hung from a pot rack, and there were many tall cabinets, but Henrietta never had much of a chance to investigate them; her time in the kitchen was always occupied by cooking or washing the seemingly endless stacks of dishes that formed by the sink.

This particular night, however, as her sister was looking for a place to rest and her parents were busy worrying about where Arabella was, Henrietta was enjoying a moment's peace.

"You're always saying you need one of those," says the girl.

"All mothers do."

Henrietta got hers because Aunt Priscilla fell asleep in front of the fire. And Henrietta climbed on a stool and opened a tall, creaky cabinet in the kitchen. There, beneath a soft film of dust, she found a small collection of spices, including her personal favorite: cinnamon. Henrietta grabbed the jar and was about to go to work when she glanced out the kitchen window and saw that the rain had started to turn to snow—the first, light, magical snowfall of the year was drifting down from the sky, outlining each branch in Priscilla's neglected garden. Without stopping for a coat, Henrietta went through the back door, tilted her head to the sky, and began to catch snowflakes on her tongue. She thought of all the times she and Arabella had made snow angels together, spreading their arms wide in the glistening white.

"Aunt Priscilla shouldn't miss this," she thought.

And she ran to wake Priscilla, rushing to her chair by the fire, and stopping only at the last moment when doubt overtook her. Priscilla must have sensed her presence, for she opened her eyes and said, "You're all wet!"

"It's snowing," Henrietta said. "Come and see."

And she grabbed Priscilla's gnarled hand and helped her out of the chair. Perhaps she was still half-asleep; perhaps she was just too startled to resist. But moments later Priscilla was standing at the threshold looking out at the snow. Because she paused there, Henrietta had to take her by both hands and tug. The momentum sent them spinning in a circle, arms locked, as snowflakes fell on their hair and eyelashes. The sound that came next was more like a small dog barking than anything human, and Henrietta would have been hard-pressed to identify it in any case because (she suddenly realized) she had never heard Priscilla laugh.

When she had finished, the world seemed still and silent in the way it only can during a snowfall. Priscilla drew a long breath and sighed.

"We should go in," she said.

"But it's so lovely," Henrietta protested.

Aunt Priscilla looked toward the house. When she turned her gaze back toward her niece, Henrietta could see that her expression had shifted. Aunt Priscilla looked uncomfortable.

"She's probably cold," suggests the girl.

"I think she felt nervous," explains the mother. "About being outside."

And just like that, the spell was broken. Priscilla returned to doze by the fire, and Henrietta went back to the kitchen alone to reclaim the little jar of cinnamon she had abandoned on the counter.

Every few minutes she would tiptoe back to see that Priscilla was still asleep. Finally she stepped too close in her inspection, and Priscilla's eyelids fluttered, then snapped open.

"What?" she asked.

"It's just me again," Henrietta told her, stepping back. "I didn't mean to startle you."

"Have you finished your chores?"

"Almost," Henrietta said.

"Then off to bed with you," Aunt Priscilla said.

Henrietta sighed.

"What's the matter now?" Priscilla demanded.

"Even if I go to bed," Henrietta said sadly, "I won't be able to sleep."

"Child, are you implying the room isn't what it ought to be?"

"No," said Henrietta with a catch in her voice. "I just don't like sleeping alone."

And as she stood there trying to explain it all to Aunt Priscilla, Henrietta remembered countless whispered conversations in the dark with her sister and the way they had to stifle their laughter sometimes so the grown-ups wouldn't hear. She remembered winter nights in flannel nightgowns and white kneesocks when they would tent their blankets and kick against them and watch the bright sparks of static electricity flash like indoor stars.

"You'll be asleep," Priscilla insisted. "It won't matter."

"I know," Henrietta said, a tear sliding down her cheek. "I guess I'm just missing Arabella."

"Oh," said Aunt Priscilla. And she patted Henrietta's hand with her stiff, bony fingers.

"Aunt Priscilla?" Henrietta asked, sniffing. "Would you like a bedtime snack?"

"Don't believe in them," Priscilla said firmly.

"Why don't you try it?" Henrietta asked.

"I suppose it can't hurt," Priscilla said. "Just this once."

So Henrietta returned to the kitchen to collect the cinnamon toast and brought it out to Aunt Priscilla by the fire. And they both fell asleep still tasting the gritty sweetness, happily unaware that it would be their last full night together in that house.

ARABELLA HAS A BIT OF A FRIGHT

As melancholy as it was to walk past the well-lit houses of the town, returning to the empty countryside was even worse. Without the streetlights to guide her, Arabella had no idea whether she was still on course. It wasn't her original idea or first choice to spend the night in the woods. That's simply where she found herself when she finally and for good ran out of energy.

The woods that night were terrifying and lovely all at once. The dark center of her new world. The rain had stopped, but the canopy of trees above her still dripped, and Arabella touched the wet leaves with her fingertips. Her thoughts kept turning to Henrietta, to the fateful day when Henrietta had been sent away, and she—despite her favored status—had done nothing to intervene.

Arabella wished now that she had set out to save her sister sooner—that she had defended her with words from the start. Then this whole lonely journey would not have been needed. But there was no going back. There was no going anywhere—tired as she was. She sank down onto the cool, wet earth beneath a tree and began to cry.

The moon above was clear and full; she could see its rippled reflection in the surface of the stream she had crossed. The wind blew. And in the distance she heard dogs barking and the muffled cries of people moving through the woods.

Were they coming for her? Were they there to bring her home?

Arabella shivered and touched the silver whistle around her neck. If she used it, they might find her. And she could be home, safe in her warm bed. Maybe that was what she should do. Maybe it had all been a mistake thinking that she could find her way to Henrietta all alone.

Arabella pressed the whistle to her lips, and the moon hung in the dark sky as she considered the possibilities. A tear traced its way along her cheek, and she let the voices fade away.

Henrietta needed her. Henrietta needed her, so Arabella would go to her.

Arabella settled herself at the base of a tree and pretended to be calm, until finally she really was calm enough to close her eyes and go to sleep.

The wind blew, and leaves skittered across the ground. But Arabella slept on—oblivious to all of it. Her head tipped against her shoulder, and her gold hair curtained her beautiful face. Until a loud, eerie call awakened her.

"Whoo, whoo!"

She jumped to her feet, trying to remember where she was.

"Whoo, whoo!" came the cry again.

Now she was wide awake, and it took only a moment for Arabella to spot the owl's yellow eyes in the dark. Its head swiveled toward her with alarming speed. Arabella yelped and crouched down low to watch the owl. She clutched the silver whistle Gus had given her. As her hand closed around it, the owl took flight—a flurry of wings

in the darkness. Then all around her was quiet again. Too quiet. So quiet that she could hear everything: small birds trilling and branches snapping. Earlier she had been afraid of being alone in the woods. Now Arabella realized that she was only one among many. There were creatures all around her. She even thought she saw a firefly in the distance, though she knew those were long gone, like the warm air of summer.

"I don't like it," says the girl.

"What?"

"Her being out there all alone. I wish the silver whistle were magic."

"Well," says the mother, "having it did make her feel more sure of herself—even though she didn't use it. And whatever makes you feel safe, whatever gives you confidence, there's a kind of magic in that."

In fact, Arabella was now as curious as she was frightened. She watched the little light in the distance and realized that it didn't wink on and off as a firefly would, but held steady, like a night-light. She tiptoed toward it, through the damp leaves and fallen twigs. It seemed a great distance away because she was moving so slowly. With each step, she could feel her heart beating against her chest. It was a candle she saw—a candle planted in white sand inside a glass canning jar.

"Where have I seen that jar before?" Arabella wondered.

Shadows were everywhere, and she thought she heard something large and alive moving toward her. Arabella took a deep breath.

"She screamed!" shouts the girl.

"No," says the mother.

She smiled and ran forward. She threw her arms around him and said his name.

"Gus."

TOGETHER—ALL ALONE

"You followed me," Arabella said softly.

"I couldn't help it," Gus replied. "It was so brave of you to set out on your own."

Arabella looked around at the dark woods, at the small candle Gus had lit. It all seemed so much more manageable now that he was here.

"Thank you," she told him, feeling suddenly shy with gratitude.

And they nestled in together beneath the falling leaves. Gus gave her his jacket, which was huge and warm.

"You'll be too cold to sleep now," she protested.

"No," he said. "I can't sleep anyway."

"Then I'll keep you company."

They rested there in the glow of the candle, and the noises all around them seemed softer now—less frightening. Time eased by, and the silence between them was the comfortable kind between friends.

"Are you awake?" she couldn't help asking.

"Entirely."

"Do you think I'll find her, Gus? Or should I just go home?"

"You have to find her. Anyway, she's not very far away. She never was. It just seems that way because you've never been on your own before."

"Have you?" she asked.

"Of course not," said Gus. "I'm only eleven."

Arabella reached out to touch his hand. "I keep forgetting," she said. "Sorry."

"It's okay," he assured her. "Sometimes I wish I were on my own."

Arabella wondered if he was thinking of his parents. She remembered their loud fight as she said goodbye to Gus.

"My family's not perfect either," she told him. "They never should have sent her away. My sister. And it's really all my fault too."

Though Gus couldn't see it, Arabella's face had clouded over.

"Don't be too hard on yourself," Gus said. "It's difficult to refuse when everyone lets you have your way. People do the same thing to me."

"I suppose," Arabella said.

"Everyone forgets to be fair sometimes," Gus said.

"Mother," says the girl. "Do you think Arabella's mean?"

"No," says the mother with a smile. "I think Arabella is changing."

Arabella grew quiet, thinking. At last, she slept, sure that when morning came, they would find their way to the road, the road that would eventually lead to Henrietta.

❧ ESCAPE ❧

With Gus by her side, Arabella felt entirely safe. Yet Gus was not the only one who was following Arabella on her journey. The police had set out hours earlier with dogs and flashlights and more volunteers than they really wanted. Finding nothing as the night wore on, the civilians turned back and went home to sleep in their warm beds, their fatigue winning out in the end, despite their best intentions. Only the chief and a few of his senior officers remained; they were determined to press a bit farther into the woods before giving up for the night. And Gus, a light sleeper under the best of circumstances, woke to the sound of their approach.

"Arabella!" he whispered, nudging her awake. "Get up! Someone's coming."

The rustling was louder now. They heard one of the dogs bark.

"Hurry," Gus urged. "We can't waste any time. We have to get across the stream."

"The stream?" Arabella asked.

"It's the best way to lose the dogs," Gus said.

He grabbed her hand; she grabbed her bookbag. They were off.

"How deep is it?" Arabella asked as they reached the edge of the stream.

Gus had already waded in, and he turned back to face her. "What?"

"Gus," she said, her voice trembling just slightly. "Have I mentioned that I don't know how to swim?"

"Here," he said, crouching at her feet. "Get up on my shoulders."

Now, the truth was that Arabella was also a bit afraid of heights, but this didn't seem the best time to mention it.

"Hang on!" Gus ordered as he plunged back into the water and began to walk downstream.

The sky had clouded over, and a light snow started to fall. They could still hear the dogs barking in the distance when they climbed out onto the bank, damp and missing one shoe (Arabella's). But gradually the sound faded, the flashlight beams swung away from them, and Arabella's pounding heart began to slow.

"Gus," Arabella whispered. "Do you think they're gone?"

"Absolutely," Gus assured her. "It's just us."

And so it was—just the two of them in the quiet, snowy woods.

MR. NORTHINGTON ON THE CASE

That next morning, as Arabella and Gus were dusting themselves off in the chilly woods, Mr. Northington arrived at the school bright and early as usual. His failed attempt at a picnic dinner had left him feeling far too embarrassed to stop by the library for his customary chat with Miss Dewey. Instead, he went straight to Principal Rothbottom's office, where he learned all about the missing Osgood girl.

"Have they found her?" Northington asked.

"Not yet," said Principal Rothbottom wearily. "They searched last night with no luck. Anyway, they aren't even sure what has happened. She may have been kidnapped for all we know, though there's been no note."

"Kidnapped?" Northington asked. "Does the family have that kind of money?"

"I suppose they do," said Principal Rothbottom impatiently. "But that's hardly the point. The girl's safety is the issue."

"Of course," said Northington, beginning to daydream.

"Northington!" yelled Principal Rothbottom. "Are you listening to me? I'll need you to interview the children. Find out if any of them know anything."

• • •

So Northington spent the morning asking the children if they had any idea where Arabella might be. Of course, most of them were genuinely unaware of her whereabouts, and they were able to tell the truth quite easily. But then there were the children in Arabella's own class, and they knew full well what Arabella had done. They had helped her do it.

At recess, Brendan Crowhurst gathered everyone together on the playground for an emergency meeting.

"Listen," he said. "Nobody says a word about what really happened, or we're all in trouble!"

"*You* listen!" said Lacey. "The police were at my house yesterday asking all sorts of questions."

"The police!" Eliza Sneedle exclaimed.

But Brendan silenced her with a look.

"My dad was out last night with the search party, and he says they think she might be lost in the woods," said another boy. "They're going back today to keep looking."

"Let them!" yelled Brendan.

"You're too loud," said Lacey. "The teachers will hear."

"I say we didn't really have anything to do with this," Brendan said, puffing out his chest and daring them to disagree. "We didn't make her leave."

"We tricked Miss Brittlewhite," Eliza insisted.

"So?"

And nobody could really argue with that, as cruelty toward substitute teachers is a right of childhood.

"Really?" asks the girl.

"Of course not," says the mother. "But there's little that can stop it."

Eventually, of course, Brendan Crowhurst had his way, and everyone agreed that it was too late to tell the truth now. They would keep their secret and wait to see what happened.

"What did happen?" asks the girl.

"That's what I'm getting to," says the mother.

Later that morning, Principal Rothbottom announced that he planned to leave for an early lunch. He instructed Mr. Northington to call the Osgoods and update them on the school's investigation.

"I'll do better than that," said Mr. Northington. "I'll visit them myself."

"Good idea," said Principal Rothbottom, secretly hoping he would not come to regret it. "The personal touch."

"Close the door, will you?" Northington asked, smiling as the principal left. Then Northington pulled a sandwich out of his bottom drawer and nibbled on it as he reviewed the list of students he had yet to interview. An hour later, as he was leaving to visit the Osgoods, Northington brushed past a tearful Miss Dewey outside the teachers' lounge, where Arabella was now the only topic of conversation.

"It's awful, Mr. Northington, isn't it?" Miss Dewey asked. "That poor girl."

"You're not to worry, Miss Dewey," he said, squaring his shoulders. "I'm certain we'll find her. I give you my word."

"Thank you," she said, squeezing his hand. "I know we can count on you. Well, I must get back."

Mr. Northington stared at her. She was even more beautiful with her deep brown eyes swimming with tears. Mr. Northington continued to stare while Miss Dewey looked from his face to her own hand, which was still caught in his.

"Oh!" he said, startled. And he dropped her hand quickly. "Yes. Yes, of course."

Then Northington hurried away—remembering, after a few moments, that he was headed to the Osgoods.

"Do you think he can really find her?" asks the girl.

"Well, he has a powerful motive to try," says the mother.

"Miss Dewey?"

"Exactly."

❧ THE MISSING POSTER ❧

When Northington arrived at the house, the living room was crowded; he entered quietly when Rose let him in, and he took in the scene. Mrs. Osgood was wringing her hands and asking "What will we do?" over and over again. Rose offered tea to everyone while Mr. Osgood—looking completely exhausted—consulted with the police.

"We found no trace of her in the woods last night," the chief of police was saying. "And usually at this juncture we would be receiving a note from the kidnappers threatening to kill the, ah, the victim, kidnappee—"

"Kill?" shrieked Mrs. Osgood.

"It's just what they say, ma'am. You know, if you don't send the money, blah, blah, blah . . ."

"What?"

"You'll find her body, blah, blah, blah . . ."

"Please!" yelled Mr. Osgood. "You are frightening my wife."

Standing in the corner, Mr. Northington admired Mr. Osgood and thought how wonderful it would be to protect Miss Dewey so gallantly.

"My point, Mrs. Osgood," said the chief of police, "is that we have no ransom note. Therefore I have to conclude that your daughter wasn't kidnapped for ransom at all. So there's nothing to be upset about!"

He smiled.

"Oh," said Mrs. Osgood in a small voice.

Mr. Osgood sighed. "I am delighted to hear she hasn't been kidnapped. But as you can see, she isn't here either! We still have a rather large problem."

"Yes?" asked the chief.

"Where *is* she?" asked Mr. Osgood, exasperated.

The chief shrugged. "Ran away? Drowned in the river?"

"Oh no!" yelled Mrs. Osgood. "Oh dear, oh dear, oh dear!"

"Perhaps I can help," said Mr. Northington, stepping forward.

"Who are you?" asked the Osgoods.

Mr. Northington introduced himself, with handshakes all around, and explained that he was conducting a thorough investigation (he loved those words) into Arabella's disappearance on the school's behalf.

"As well you might be!" snapped Mrs. Osgood. "Since you were the ones who lost my girl in the first place."

"We don't know that, dear," said Mr. Osgood.

"But we are prepared to find her," said Mr. Northington. "And I, for one, think the first step should be . . ." He paused and looked desperately toward the chief of police.

"A missing poster!" the chief of police shouted. "Send for the sketch artist!"

"Nonsense," said Mrs. Osgood. "I'm an artist myself. And nobody knows a child better than her own mother."

She sniffed and sent Rose running for her art supplies.

"Yes," said Mr. Osgood. "We can do the poster. Leave it to us."

As Mrs. Osgood was busy sketching, the chief said, "I think we should offer a reward."

"The school would be glad to assist," Mr. Northington said. "Perhaps a carnival, to raise money."

"That's ridiculous," said Mr. Osgood. "We haven't got that kind of time."

"A penny drive?"

"A penny drive! How will that help?" Mr. Osgood yelled. "We need to offer a substantial and immediate reward."

"He's right," the girl says.

"Well, pennies do add up, as I keep trying to tell you," the mother says. "But, of course, pennies weren't enough,

128

and what the Osgoods had themselves wasn't enough, and eventually they decided to turn to the only person they could think of who might be able to help. Can you guess who it was?"

"Miss Brittlewhite."

"No. Of course not. Teachers never have any money."

"The police?"

"They were doing all they could. No, the Osgoods decided that as difficult as it would be, they would need to speak to Aunt Priscilla about donating the reward money."

"She's got to help us," Mrs. Osgood said.

"My dear, she may not have that kind of money at hand."

"Nonsense!" Mrs. Osgood shouted. "Let her sell that giant emerald ring she wears or offer it as a reward."

"Emerald?" asked Mr. Northington.

"Wait," says the girl. "Aunt Priscilla is rich?"

"Quite."

"But she lives in such squalor!"

"Nice word," says the mother.

"How's the sketch coming?" asked the chief of police.

"Nearly finished," said Mrs. Osgood, a note of pride in her voice.

"And I've typed the message to paste beneath it!" said Mr. Osgood, rushing in from his study.

"What's this supposed to be?" asked the chief, staring at the drawing.

"Why, it's Arabella! And quite a good likeness, if I do say so myself."

"Why are her ears on top of her head?"

"Those aren't her ears, you fool. That's a bow in her hair. Anyone can see that."

The chief sighed and reached for the note Mr. Osgood was handing him.

"What's that supposed to say?" he asked, looking down at the note.

,oddo,mh hot;/ Stsnr;;s Pdhppf/ Trestf pggrtrf.

"Oh, doe, hot stersen, trest oh gert? Ogre? Hot star? Ogre person?"

"This isn't charades!" yelled Mr. Osgood. "Clearly it says: 'Missing girl. Arabella Osgood. Reward offered.'"

"You moved your hands again!" Mrs. Osgood yelled at her husband. "You're a terrible typist. Where are your spectacles?"

"I think we'll take it from here," said the chief of police.

🌿 THE UNEXPECTED VISITORS 🌿

Aunt Priscilla, you see, had piled up quite a fortune during her days as a famous actress, though you would never know it to look at her house. And she certainly wasn't spending it on gourmet meals. In fact, she wasn't spending much of it at all. Still, the Osgoods knew it would be hard to get her to part with any of it even in such extreme circumstances as these. But they had to go to Aunt Priscilla in person and make their case. And they had to do it right away because, though none of them had given a moment's thought to visiting Henrietta, they were desperate to do all they could for Arabella. So they piled into the Osgoods' car: Mr. Osgood,

Mrs. Osgood, Rose, Principal Rothbottom (who had joined the group after lunch), Mr. Northington, the chief of police, and Mrs. Osgood's lapdog, Muffin.

"Isn't that too many people for one car?" asks the girl.

"Yes. They decided it was. They asked Mr. Northington to get out."

"How rude!" says the girl.

"Well," says the mother, "the car was becoming noisy. Muffin was barking, and Mrs. Osgood, in her satin robe, was sniffling loudly."

"She still isn't dressed?"

"They tried to make her, but she refused, and they were in a hurry, so they just threw a blanket round her shoulders. I used to do it with you all the time when you were younger."

They left Mr. Northington behind and resettled themselves for the trip. As soon as they started off, Mr. Osgood was discussing strategy with the chief of police, Principal Rothbottom was saying over and over again how terribly sorry he was that this whole thing had happened in the first place, and Muffin, of course, was still barking loudly and nipping at the chief of police's ankles. They went along that way down a half dozen country roads, disturbing the residents of the nearby small towns, including Gus's parents, who had just taken up their loud fight right where they had left off yesterday and were too engrossed in it to notice that Gus was missing.

At last they came to Aunt Priscilla's house. They pulled into the driveway in a huge rush, barking and weeping and tooting the horn. Henrietta heard the noise from the kitchen and ran to the front window just in time to see her father's car pull into the driveway. So many people tumbled out of it that she had a hard time identifying everyone at first. Some of the voices were familiar, of course, and in the mix she heard the voices of both her parents. A huge rush of relief and joy filled her heart because she imagined that they had come to retrieve her.

"That's too sad," says the girl. "She's getting her hopes up for nothing."

"Don't be such a pessimist," says the mother.

Henrietta watched as the group made their way to the door, but she didn't dare answer it once she caught sight of the police. And, after all, it was still Aunt Priscilla's house. Henrietta ran instead toward her room, stopping at the top

of the stairs when curiosity got the better of her. Priscilla, for her part, was leisurely petting a cat (the one they now called Professor Wiggles) and considering making a late lunch of the cold fish soup they had eaten the night before for dinner.

"Not the soup again! And cold! That's even more disgusting."

"No. I think it was actually a bit better cold."

"Cold soup?"

"Listen, there are lots of cold soups. Gazpacho, vichyssoise . . ."

"Mother!"

"Well, it really doesn't matter anyway because when Priscilla heard the racket outside, she forgot all about the soup and rushed to the door. She wasn't keen about the outside world even when it kept to itself, so you can imagine how she felt about it knocking on her door uninvited."

"But they're her family."

"True enough, but she wasn't the sort of person with a lot of family feeling."

Aunt Priscilla went to the door and put her eye to the peephole, but she couldn't see a thing. Unfortunately, Mr. Osgood was doing the same thing on his side of the door, and they really weren't getting anywhere. Mrs. Osgood was taking matters into her own hands and had started to push through the dense bushes in front of the house in order to peek in the front windows. And they might have stood there all day if the chief of police hadn't fought his way to the front and started banging on the door with his nightstick.

"Open up!" the chief of police commanded.

From her side of the door, Aunt Priscilla took a step back and demanded to know who it was.

"It's Osgood, Aunt Priscilla," yelled Mr. Osgood.

"Osgood, you can't speak to me that way!"

"That wasn't me, Aunt Priscilla. That was the chief of police."

"Police?"

"Don't panic her," advised the nanny.

"I'll explain everything," Mr. Osgood promised, "if you'll just open the door. Please. It's a dire emergency."

"He doesn't really have to say that, does he? Dire and emergency. If it's—"

"Some people are prone to exaggeration, I suppose," says the mother.

"Like Mr. Northington and the cheese emergency?"

"Indeed."

Eventually, Aunt Priscilla unbarred the door. It took some doing because she had an amazing number of locks on it. It was more like a safe at the bank than a front door, really.

The chief of police was most impressed. "She certainly has gone to pains to secure the perimeter."

✥ AUNT PRISCILLA TO THE RESCUE? ✥

At last they were all inside Aunt Priscilla's front parlor, which was dusty and dark, even during the day. There had never been this many people inside Priscilla Renfrew's house at one time, and the cats were completely discom-bobulated by the commotion. They gave out little yowls and scurried for the corners of the rooms, where they crouched behind plant stands and coat racks and hissed loudly. Aunt Priscilla, being quite unused to company, wasn't sure how to act. She didn't do the usual things, like offering them a seat or putting on a kettle so that they all might have some tea. They had to take matters into their own hands, and they did. Principal Rothbottom took off his jacket, cleared some space on the crowded furniture, and asked Priscilla if he might open the drapes. She frowned, then sighed heavily.

"If you must," Priscilla said.

"That's rude!" says the girl.

"Well, consider the source," says her mother.

And Rose, the nanny, said, "We're all a bit chilly. Do you suppose we might have a cup of tea? I'd be glad to assist if you'd show me. . . ."

Aunt Priscilla just pointed one bony, bejeweled finger toward the kitchen door.

Mrs. Osgood, who was not about to help in any way, just drew her blanket around her shivering shoulders and looked aggrieved.

"Aggrieved?"

"Let's see," says the mother. "It's sort of a cross between sad and put out."

"Oh," says the girl.

Mr. Osgood rushed to find his wife a place on the sofa. "Sit down, my dear," he said.

She did, and a cloud of ancient dust puffed up all around her, causing a fit of coughing. They had to call out to Rose in the kitchen to bring some water.

The chief of police, who was pacing in front of the fire, was eager to get things started. "We're here," he said, "on a matter of urgent business."

Now this was very confusing to Henrietta, who was still hiding at the top of the stairs. Henrietta believed that her parents had come to take her home and would at any moment ask to see her or even, overtaken by grief and regret, come rushing up the stairs to find her. But that didn't seem to be what was happening. She stood at the top of the steps— leaning forward to be sure to hear every word—and these last words about urgent business were most alarming. Suddenly she was afraid that she was in trouble of some sort, but what sort of trouble could be bad enough to bring the police? True, she had entertained some very nasty fantasies about Aunt Priscilla since she came, but they couldn't put you in jail just for those, could they?

Downstairs, the chief of police was saying, "Miss Renfrew, I'll come straight to the point. A situation has developed, an emergency, really. And though we hate to bother you with it, as it really isn't any of your affair, nevertheless, we feel, after careful consideration of all the facts and pondering the possible outcomes and examining every prudent contingency, it is our considered opinion that—"

"Oh, for pity's sake!" yelled Mr. Osgood. "Come to the point."

"She's missing!" sobbed Mrs. Osgood. "Our girl is gone!"

"Nonsense," said Aunt Priscilla. "She's around here somewhere. Out in the kitchen probably."

"*No!*" yelled the Osgoods.

"I should think so. I sent her there myself to make the soup and feed the bat."

"Oh, not *that* girl," said Mrs. Osgood. "Not Henrietta! We're talking about Arabella!"

Well, at the top of the stairs, Henrietta was a mass of conflicted emotion. She was surprised and alarmed, most of all, to hear that her twin was missing. She felt a small thrill, after such a long time, to hear her own name on her mother's lips, even in passing. And mixed with it all was the familiar disappointment that this current conversation, this urgent visit, this huge fuss, like everything else in her life, was not about her but about the only one who really mattered: her sister, Arabella.

"You've simply got to help us," Mrs. Osgood was saying now, sniffling into a handkerchief.

"We wouldn't have come," Mr. Osgood added, "if there were any other way."

"Well, I fail to see how I can be of any help," said Priscilla. "Clearly it's a matter for the police, and you seem to have brought the police here with you. Perhaps if they went out and started looking for the girl instead of pounding down my front door and bursting into my house uninvited, we might get somewhere."

"We've done our best, ma'am," said the chief of police. "We've tried to find her. But the longer she's gone the less likely that is."

"What?" yelled Mr. Osgood.

"Statistically speaking."

"But Arabella is not a statistic," says the girl.

"Of course not," says the mother. "That's why everyone is trying very hard to help her."

"The point is," said Mr. Osgood, "the police feel we need to offer a reward. A rather considerable sum."

"Then do it," snapped Priscilla.

"We haven't got it," admitted Mr. Osgood. "Not as much as we need."

"Go to the bank. Ask for a loan. Isn't that what people do when they run short? For pity's sake, you're a banker. Why would you come running to me for money?"

"Miss Renfrew," said Rose, drawing her aside and speaking softly, "the Osgoods, well, I'm sure they would find it terribly hard to say this to anyone, but they live a bit beyond their means, and so, you see, really, truly, just at the moment, they are a little low on cash. And we thought, naturally, since your great wealth and fame must have left you with quite a bit of savings, that you might, just this once of course, part with a little of it for the safety and welfare of your niece."

Well, Priscilla was quite torn at this point. On the one hand, she was flattered that the nanny had made reference to her being a wealthy and world-famous actress. On the other hand, Priscilla was quite protective of her store of riches. After all, she wasn't acting anymore, and whatever she had would have to last her for the rest of her life.

"We wouldn't ask," said Mrs. Osgood. "But I'm terrified she could be gone for good. She may be in serious danger."

"But she's not," says the girl.

"True. But mothers tend to picture the worst. Always remember that when it's time to call home."

Henrietta was a bit of a worrier as well, and this last proclamation was too much for her. Listening at the top of the stairs to the shocking news that she might never see Arabella again, Henrietta began to feel ill. First her head felt light; then she slumped against the wall and tumbled all the way down the stairs into the living room, landing on a few of the cats along the way and setting them howling.

GUS IN DISGUISE

Although her life was not really in imminent danger, Arabella did have troubles of her own. For one thing, she was missing a shoe. For another, she was cold, damp, and completely exhausted. But physical discomfort was really the least of her worries. No, what really troubled Arabella most was the thought that they were still being followed.

"Gus," she asked as they walked along, "do you think they'll come back? The men from last night?"

"The police?"

"The police! Is that who they were?"

"I imagine so. Who did you think they were?"

"I don't know. Robbers?"

Gus laughed. "Who would they be robbing in the middle of the woods? Bunnies and squirrels? No. They're searching for you."

"I thought they might be. But why the police?" Arabella asked. "I'm just trying to find my sister. I'm not a criminal."

"You disappeared. Your parents must be worried sick. They probably called the police right away."

Arabella stopped walking. She sat down on the ground and covered her face with her hands.

"Oh, Gus," she said, "I've made a mess of everything! All I wanted was a chance to see Henrietta again. And now I've upset everyone. And I don't even know if we're going the right way. I had a map, but it got all wet and smudgy."

She pulled it out of her pocket and thrust it toward Gus, who examined it for a moment.

"I think I can get us there," he said.

"Really?"

"Yes, but . . ."

"What?" she asked. "Tell me."

"Arabella, I can't promise that we won't get caught. We're out in broad daylight now. Someone may see us, you know."

"There must be something we can do," Arabella insisted. "Maybe we could disguise ourselves."

"Maybe," Gus said. "I have an idea."

"What's he going to do?" asks the girl.

"I can't tell you that," says the mother. "It'll spoil the surprise."

"You know I hate surprises," says the girl. "Out with it."

"Well, it just so happened the morning was a breezy one, and they were hoping to find some laundry hanging out that they might be able to borrow."

"Borrow? You mean steal, don't you?"

"No need to get hysterical," says the mother. "They didn't find any."

The day was too cold for hanging laundry on the line. They did, however, spot a wonderful porch with a number of coats and hats hanging on hooks near the door.

"We can't take those!" Arabella whispered to Gus. "Just give me your jacket again."

"It's too wet!"

"I'm not stealing," said Arabella.

"We need them!" Gus said. "You can bring them back later."

"Will they bring them back later?" asks the girl.

"Of course not," says the mother. "But at least they had good intentions."

While Gus hid behind the nearby fence, Arabella darted onto the porch and scooped up an armful of clothes.

"Here," she said, offering Gus a wide-brimmed straw hat with a pink flower.

"I can't wear this!" Gus said.

"Don't be so fussy. It's perfect. It will cover your face. Nobody will know it's you. Here, put this on too," she said, handing him a fuzzy pink cardigan.

"I'll look like my grandmother!" Gus said.

"I thought we agreed that we needed disguises."

"I never said you could dress me as a girl!" Gus said.

"Please!" Arabella said. "I'm in a lot of trouble, and you said you would help."

Gus glared at Arabella for a long moment before he slipped his arm into the pink sweater and pulled on the too-tight hat.

"At least it's warm," he muttered.

"You look very nice," Arabella told him, trying not to smile as she wrapped herself up in a large shawl.

A CASE OF MISTAKEN IDENTITY

Though Gus thought he knew where they were going, they didn't seem to be getting there very quickly. As the day wore on, Gus and Arabella continued trudging forward on weary limbs. And despite his naturally long stride, Gus was having as much trouble as Arabella, who had kicked off her remaining shoe and was now traveling in her stocking feet. In fact, Arabella noticed, Gus seemed to be limping.

"Are you all right?" she asked him.

"I'm fine," he said at first.

"Gus, you can hardly walk," Arabella said.

"It's my joints," he said. "Comes with the territory."

"The territory?"

Gus gestured from his waist toward his toes, pointing out the length of his leg.

"Oh," she said. "I'm sorry. I never realized. Let's rest."

And so they sat for a while.

"It's good of you to help me," Arabella said.

"Well, I know how much you must miss your sister. I'm sure your parents do too in their heart of hearts. Not to mention her friends."

"Oh, Henrietta doesn't have any friends. Just me."

"Oh," said Gus, and his face fell.

"She doesn't mind much," said Arabella. "I play with her when I have time."

"When you have time?" Gus asked.

"Well, all the time," Arabella said, though she felt as she said it that it wasn't completely true.

Gus pulled himself to his feet. "Let's get going."

"Wait, Gus, are you mad at me?"

He shook his head.

"Yes, you are," Arabella insisted. "You disapprove."

"Arabella," he said. "You are who you are. I can't expect you to understand how things are. For people like Henrietta. And me."

He mumbled the last two words, but, of course, his voice was still loud, and Arabella could hear him clearly.

"Then tell me," Arabella said.

"Tell you what?"

"What it's like to be you."

"Lonely," said Gus.

And the word sliced through the air and silenced her. And then they walked along for a long time without talking at all until they found themselves at the edge of a park, where Arabella saw a chance to rest. She took a seat on a park bench, and Gus sat down beside her. They scarcely moved for so long that they both fell sound asleep.

"Do you think that Gus is really mad at her?" asks the girl.

"Perhaps," says the mother. "But I suspect he'll get over it."

"Maybe he doesn't like her anymore," says the girl.

"I doubt that," says the mother. "Gus is a true friend, and true friendship is a sturdy thing."

When she awoke, Arabella felt much better—even though she was quite hungry. She and Gus grabbed some apples that had fallen from a nearby tree and ate them in huge, grateful bites, wiping the juice on their sleeves. It gave them enough energy to continue, which was fortunate because Arabella was much closer to her sister than she realized.

Walking down the next block, they came to a bookshop

and decided on impulse to stop there and ask for directions to Aunt Priscilla's house. Gus waited outside to keep watch and sent Arabella in on her own.

"Excuse me," Arabella said, smiling at the woman behind the counter.

"Why, Henrietta, I wasn't expecting you until next week," the woman said. "How lovely to see you, and in such fine spirits too! I don't think I've ever seen you smile like that."

"Henrietta!" said Arabella. "You know Henrietta?"

Now the shopkeeper was most confused. "You aren't . . . ," she said slowly.

"I'm her sister, her twin sister," Arabella explained.

"Oh my! Yes, of course. The one she sent the note to," said Inez.

"How do you know about the note?" Arabella asked.

"She was here when she wrote it," Inez said. "And I helped her mail it."

"Thank you!" Arabella said, throwing her arms around Inez.

Then Arabella stepped back and looked up at Inez, blushing with embarrassment for being so impulsive. "I know we just met, but maybe you could help me too. I want to go and see her, but I'm not sure I can find my aunt's house."

"Of course," said Inez. "Come with me."

Inez took Arabella into the back of the shop, where she drew a map of the town.

"It's quite a long walk," Inez said, glancing at Arabella's shoeless feet. "Why don't you rest a bit before you continue?"

"I have a friend waiting," said Arabella, gesturing toward the front of the shop.

Inez peeked out the front window. "So you do," she said, commenting not at all on Gus's size or his outfit. "Let's ask him in."

Arabella agreed. And the three of them sat in the back of the shop, snacking on cookies and studying the map Inez had drawn for them. They saw at once that they had taken an overly long and roundabout route to cover the distance they had traveled so far.

"Well," Inez said, "however far you've strayed off course, the main thing is that you've come all this way to visit. And Henrietta will be thrilled to see you."

It didn't seem accurate to call running away a visit. But it didn't seem prudent to correct her either. So Arabella just smiled again, and she and Gus thanked Inez for the food and the new map. Then they gathered their things and went out of the shop.

"We'll be there before you know it," Gus said.

Arabella smiled and nudged him. "Lead the way," she said.

❧ MORE BAD LUCK FOR HENRIETTA ☙

Of course Henrietta had no idea that Arabella—far from being in any danger—was actually snacking on cookies with Inez. Henrietta had just been told that her sister was in grave danger. And after hearing this news, Henrietta, you will recall, collapsed in a heap at the bottom of the stairs, landing right in front of her nanny. Rose knelt down to examine her.

"Oh dear," said Rose. "She's fainted. We'd better get her some water."

"This is just like her," said Mrs. Osgood. "To be a bother at the worst possible moment when we're in the middle of something important. Just drag her over to the corner before someone trips on her while we sort this out."

"Yes," said Mr. Osgood. "We have no time to lose. Arabella may be in grave danger!"

"This is enough!" yelled Priscilla. "Clear out, all of you. Get out."

"You can't mean that," said Mrs. Osgood.

"But we've come to no conclusion," said Mr. Osgood.

"I think she wants us to go," said Rose.

"But you haven't asked her!" said Mrs. Osgood, elbowing her husband.

"I've asked her, my dear, and Aunt Priscilla has declined. She isn't going to supply the money."

"Not the money!" Mrs. Osgood yelled. "The ring!"

"The ring?" asked Aunt Priscilla.

"Yes!" said Mrs. Osgood. "The police think we should offer it as part of the reward."

Aunt Priscilla stood up and pointed at the chief of police, the emerald ring in question glinting on her finger. "If he thinks I'm giving up this ring, he is sadly mistaken!"

"She was the one who mentioned it first," said the chief of police, pointing at Mrs. Osgood.

"All they're doing is wasting time blaming each other," says the girl.

"Yes. They're being rather childish."

"That's not even a fair word, really. When you think about it," says the girl.

"Point taken," the mother replies.

Mrs. Osgood had started to cry again. She was beside herself at Aunt Priscilla's unwillingness to part with anything that might bring about Arabella's safe return.

"How can you be so selfish?" she demanded. "Have you no feelings at all?"

"You don't know what you're asking," Priscilla told her. "This ring is quite valuable. It's not some trinket."

"Valuable?" Mrs. Osgood said. "Valuable? What price would you set on Arabella's safe return?"

"Do you really think she isn't coming back?" asked a small voice from a corner of the room. And they all turned to see that Henrietta—while still very pale—had recovered enough to sit up and join the conversation. In fact, she stood up and walked on shaky legs toward Aunt Priscilla's chair. Henrietta picked up Aunt Priscilla's spotted, gnarled hand and studied the glittering emerald ring.

"I know it means a lot to you," she said. "Almost as much as my sister means to me."

The two locked eyes, and everyone in the room was absolutely quiet, waiting.

Finally Henrietta broke the silence. "Please?" she asked.

"Oh, all right!" said Priscilla, shrugging off Henrietta's immediate and urgent embraces.

"Thank you, Aunt Priscilla!" said Henrietta. "Thank you!"

The Osgoods were amazed at Priscilla's assent. They stood speechless for a moment, taking in the odd sight of their daughter Henrietta lifting and kissing Priscilla's gnarled hand.

"Here," said Priscilla at last, reaching to remove the emerald ring from her finger. She slid and twisted, but the ring would not clear her (rather large) knuckle.

"Let me help," said Mr. Osgood, grabbing her hand and pulling with all his might.

"Don't be so rough," said Henrietta.

"That's not going to work," said Mrs. Osgood. "Take her to the kitchen and use some soap."

They decided to try it, but they failed—miserably. Time was ticking by.

"We should cut it off," said the chief of police. "No time for half measures."

"Her finger?" says the girl.

"Of course not. That would be barbaric. No, he meant they could cut through the band to get the ring off."

"But that would ruin it," says the girl.

"That was the problem."

159

"Don't break it!" Mrs. Osgood was yelling.

By now the ring was wedged tightly on Priscilla's finger, and it wouldn't move in either direction.

"Her finger doesn't look right," said Rose. "I think we should take her to the doctor."

"Good thinking," said Principal Rothbottom.

"Maybe they can get it off," said the chief of police.

"I am *not* leaving this house!" said Aunt Priscilla.

"But she went out with Henrietta," says the girl.

"True," says the mother. "But until that night in the snow, Aunt Priscilla had not left that house in years. Going out was no small thing for her."

When Priscilla refused to leave the house, the room exploded in noise as everyone assembled began to yell at once about how urgently they needed her cooperation.

"My girl!" Mrs. Osgood yelled.

"It's getting late," the chief of police warned.

"Aunt Priscilla!" Mr. Osgood yelled.

Then, as they all fell silent for a moment, it was Henrietta who said the two words that finally moved Priscilla out of her chair.

Henrietta looked at Priscilla and said softly, "You promised."

"All right," Priscilla said, "let's go."

She wrapped herself in a dark cape . . .

"Like a witch," says the girl.

"She was terrified, really. Would a witch be terrified? She was pale and trembling when they got her into the car. She could hardly speak to tell them where to go. Sometimes she would just lift a finger and point."

"Couldn't Henrietta help?" asks the girl.

"She might have known the way," says the mother, "if they had remembered to invite her along."

The sad truth was that in their rush to help Arabella, they had forgotten all about Henrietta—as usual. So she was left behind and spent the evening as she always did—alone. Too tired to finish her chores and exhausted with worry, she passed out in front of the fire. In fact, she had pulled her chair a tad too close to the flames because a spark landed on the edge of her sweater, and she woke just in time to see it starting to burn. She jumped up, of course, screaming, and swatted at the flames with a newspaper.

"That's not what you do!" says the girl. "Stop, drop, and roll. Didn't they teach her anything in school?"

"Well, dear, she's missed quite a bit of school, and she's been spending her time cooking hideous food and reading fairy tales at the bookshop. You don't learn much that way."

But eventually Henrietta realized, even in her panic, that she could just slip out of her sweater, and she did. The bad part was that it really was burning now, not just the sweater but the chair and then the room. And so, not thinking clearly, Henrietta rushed back up the stairs toward her room.

"No!" yells the girl. "Now she's trapped."

"Exactly," says the mother.

MR. NORTHINGTON
JOINS THE SEARCH

While Henrietta was contemplating her doom, the adults in charge were busy with other things. The Osgoods, accompanied by the chief of police, the nanny, and the principal, were driving Aunt Priscilla to the hospital so her ring could be removed. And Mr. Northington, having been left behind at the start, had just completed a long day of interviewing students. He had twisted as many arms as he could, trying to learn the truth of Arabella's whereabouts.

"That's not allowed!" shouts the girl.

"Just an expression," the mother says. "No cause for alarm."

Now Northington was riding through the town, on the front half of his parents' old tandem bicycle, putting up the missing posters. As he rode, he pictured another sort of ride, one in which Miss Dewey was perched on the seat behind him, laughing at his jokes and whispering in his ear.

"That's not going to happen," says the girl.

"Love had made him optimistic," says the mother.

He thought of the missing girl as he rode. And he remembered Miss Dewey's tearful thanks to him for promising to rescue her. Suddenly Mr. Northington could see it all in his mind's eye: He would rescue the little girl, return her to her parents, collect the reward money (and the emerald ring Mrs. Osgood had mentioned). Then Miss Dewey would be his. How could she resist him? A hero who had rescued a little girl, a newly wealthy man with a beautiful ring to offer? The principal of her school.

"Assistant principal," says the girl. "And Miss Dewey isn't even his girlfriend yet."

"True. He was getting a bit ahead of himself."

But once he saw it all clearly, Northington knew that he was doing the wrong thing. Why should he hang these missing posters all over town so that anyone might find Arabella and earn the reward? True, the sketch didn't much resemble the girl (Mrs. Osgood wasn't much of an artist), but Mr. Northington didn't fancy any competition.

He retraced his steps and undid his work—pulling down the missing posters as fast as he could. As he was removing the last one, he saw one of the students he had interviewed earlier that day. A girl. What was her name? Elmira? Elvira?

"Eliza!" says the girl.

"Indeed."

"Oh no," says the girl.

"You there!" said Mr. Northington. "Come here a moment."

Eliza's mother had sent her to the store to buy some milk, and she was expecting her to return directly. Eliza was not to stop to speak to any strange men along the way. But, of course, she recognized Mr. Northington from school. If he had asked her to stop in the hallway of the school, she would have done so immediately. But outside the school, she hesitated.

"Little girl!" Mr. Northington said. "I'd like to speak to you."

Reluctantly, Eliza went over to him.

"We spoke earlier," Mr. Northington said. "About this Arabella Osgood business."

"Yes," said Eliza, remembering her promise to say nothing.

"You know the police are involved now, don't you?"

"I've heard that," Eliza said.

"And I bet a bright young lady like you might know something about it too," Northington said.

"I can't really talk now," Eliza told him. "I told my mother I'd hurry back."

"Oh, but this will only take a minute," Northington said. "Eliza, don't you think your mother would want you to do the right thing?"

Eliza looked down and studied her shoes, unsure of what to do.

"I think you know the answer," Northington cajoled.

Eliza, who prided herself on always knowing the answer, who spent the bulk of each school day with her hand stretched skyward in a constant, desperate bid to be called on, could take it no longer.

"She's on her way to her aunt's house!" Eliza yelled.

It was such a relief to say it finally that Eliza forgot for the moment all the promises they had made to Brendan Crowhurst.

"Her aunt?" Northington asked. "Priscilla? That's right! Priscilla . . ."

"Renfrew," said Eliza. "R as in 'rapid,' e, n, f, r, e, w. Renfrew."

"What?" asks the girl.

"Spelling bee champion," explains the mother.

"Good girl," said Mr. Northington as Eliza rushed away as fast as her legs would carry her.

 A MISHAP

Northington was delighted by what Eliza Sneedle had divulged. He set out to find this Aunt Priscilla right away.

"Renfrew," he repeated aloud to himself as he rode.

"But he doesn't know where he's going!" says the girl.

"True," says the mother. "But sadly that wasn't enough to stop him."

"Renfrew," he said as he pedaled. "Ha, ha! Renfrew."

Mr. Northington was as excited as a child with a new toy. And his joy caused him to do something he definitely should not have done: he raised his hands off the handlebars.

He followed each twist and turn in the road, enjoying every bounce and bump, secure in the knowledge that he could locate Arabella and return as a hero who would win Miss Dewey's heart. And so, his mind was elsewhere and the sun was shining when he swerved off the road and crashed the bicycle into a large bush, jostling a low-hanging nest of wasps and unleashing their fury. Northington hopped off the tandem bike and began to run, still twisting and turning, with a cloud of angry wasps buzzing around his head.

"Was he stung?" asks the girl.

"Yes. Poor hapless fellow. He was," says the mother. "Repeatedly."

They chased and stung him until he fell to the ground.

"Was he still saying 'Renfrew'?"

"He was trying," says the mother.

"I shouldn't laugh," says the girl.

Northington's face and eyelids began to swell. His tongue puffed up in his mouth.

"Oh no," he tried to say. "Oh no," he tried again.

Northington wobbled away on his dented bicycle, which now swerved all of its own accord.

"I think I need a hothpital," he said to the first passerby he met.

AT THE HOSPITAL

And so it happened that Mr. Northington arrived at the hospital with his emergency just before the Osgoods got there with Aunt Priscilla and her swollen knuckle.

"Name?" asked the clerk at the admitting desk.

"Nothing-hon," he replied, his tongue now as thick as a sausage.

"Sir, everyone has a name," the clerk said sharply (she was used to dealing with the uncooperative and under-informed). "And I need yours."

"Nothing-hon," he repeated with great effort.

"My name, for example," said the clerk, "is Mrs. Sandsbury. Not hon. Not honey. Mrs. Sandsbury."

Mr. Northington, hugely frustrated by this point, stamped his foot like a balky horse.

"Perhaps you intend to spell it out," suggested Mrs. Sandsbury with a sigh.

Just then the front door opened and the Osgoods came through, trailing their nanny, Principal Rothbottom, the chief of police, Aunt Priscilla, and an overexcited, yipping Muffin.

"What's a yipping muffin?" asks the girl.

"Mrs. Osgood's little dog. Muffin."

"Oh," says the girl. "That wasn't what I was picturing. Now I feel silly."

Though Mr. Northington was having great difficulty identifying himself, Principal Rothbottom and Mrs. Osgood recognized him at once.

"There's that ridiculous fellow from the school," she said. "What's the matter with him?"

"It looks as though he's having some sort of a fit," Mr. Osgood suggested.

Muffin, drawn to the movement of Mr. Northington's stamping foot, clamped onto his ankle with her pointed little teeth.

Mrs. Sandsbury sighed heavily and called out for a wheelchair.

"Who is the owner of this dog?" Mrs. Sandsbury demanded.

"Mrs. Osgood," said the principal. "I believe that's your dog. Muffin."

Mrs. Osgood, who normally was quick to claim her prized pooch, looked around at the others as if expecting them to answer. "Dog?" her face seemed to say. "What dog?"

"We do not allow animals inside the hospital," said Mrs. Sandsbury as Muffin chased after the yowling Mr. Northington and disappeared behind a curtain.

"This is a madhouse!" Aunt Priscilla exclaimed. "Take me home."

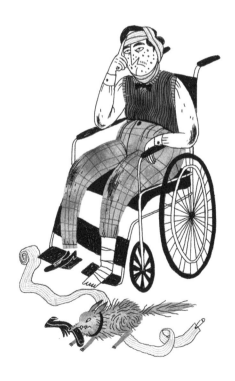

"We have to get the ring off first," said Mrs. Osgood.

"*Next!*" Mrs. Sandsbury yelled.

"We're next!" Mrs. Osgood yelled back.

She grabbed Aunt Priscilla by the hand, dragged her to the admitting desk, and thrust her hand toward the clerk.

"We need to get this taken off," she announced.

"What did you have in mind?" asked Mrs. Sandsbury sarcastically. "Just a few fingers or the whole hand?"

Mr. Northington was wheeled back out then, his head and ankle bandaged, his face dotted with the heavy white cream that had been used to treat the stings.

"Could he talk again?" asks the girl.

"Not well," says the mother. "Yet he still had plenty to say."

As Priscilla was checking in at the desk, Northington overheard her name, and his ears perked up. He turned to the nurse who was walking him out.

Still struggling to speak with his swollen tongue, he asked, "Is that Prithilla Renthrough?"

"I shouldn't say," whispered the nurse. "But yes. She was quite famous back in the day. Nobody in town has seen her for years."

Then Mr. Northington spotted the Osgoods and the chief

of police he had met at the Osgoods' house. He rushed over to tell them what he knew.

"I know thomthing!" he shouted.

They all turned to look at him, and he was quite a sight: his hair was in disarray, his cheeks were swollen, his eyes were a watery red, and his bandaged tongue lolled partway out of his mouth as he spoke. At his feet, Muffin was nibbling on his bandaged ankle. But Mr. Northington was undeterred.

"I know where thee ith!" he shouted. "Anthabella!"

"He knows where she is!" shouted Mrs. Osgood.

And he pointed at Aunt Priscilla, who was being led out by another nurse.

"Thee's on her way to *her* howf. To Aunt Prithilla's."

"That's ridiculous," said the chief of police. "We've all just come from there, and Arabella was not with us."

"Just the other one," Mrs. Osgood sighed. "Just Henrietta."

"Henrietta!" Mr. Osgood said, realizing for the first time that they had forgotten all about her.

"Henrietta!" says the girl. "You never told me. What happened to Henrietta?"

177

ARABELLA HESITATES

Henrietta was in a panic. As soon as the fire started, she ran to her room and slammed the door. She went to the window and tried to open it, but it was stuck. She was desperate to get the window open somehow, but there was nothing in the room she could think to use. Finally she was so terrified that she decided to kick out the glass. Then she stood at the window screaming for help as loudly as she possibly could.

What Henrietta didn't know, what almost no one knew at the time, was that Arabella was very near. In fact, Arabella and Gus had arrived at Aunt Priscilla's earlier and left again.

"What?" says the girl. "Why would they do that?"

"They had good reason," the mother replies.

The first time they arrived, they could hear the chief of police pounding on Aunt Priscilla's door from almost a block away. They froze in their tracks and crept forward slowly, doing their best not to be seen, which in Gus's case (as you can imagine) was a real challenge. As they got closer, they could make out voices and even words: "Aunt Priscilla" and "police."

"Wait here," Arabella said to Gus.

"Don't be ridiculous. I can't let you go over there alone."

"They'll see you," Arabella said.

"Good point," says the girl. "It's hard to miss a giant in a fuzzy pink sweater."

"True."

And that's why Arabella crept forward all alone just in time to see her parents, her nanny, her principal, and the chief of police enter the house on Chillington Lane without her.

Arabella could not believe her eyes. She turned on her heel and flew back to Gus.

"My parents are there!" she yelled. "And the police!"

"Calm down," said Gus.

"But what are they doing there? Do you think they're having Henrietta arrested?"

"Arrested?" laughed Gus. "Of course not! What for?"

"Then why?"

"I warned you before," said Gus. "They're probably looking for you."

As soon as he said it, Arabella knew Gus was right.

"I can't believe it," she said, tears welling in her eyes. "I've come all this way."

"I know," said Gus.

"Gus, I'm in big trouble. The police!"

"Let's just see if we can find out what's going on," said Gus.

And so they walked the rest of the way to Aunt Priscilla's house, hoping that nobody would spot them.

"Didn't anyone see?" asks the girl.

"No."

"Wouldn't they?"

"Nobody did. Not a soul. They were all alone. All alone in a world of very unobservant grown-ups."

"I know the feeling," says the girl.

Gus and Arabella reached Priscilla's house and tiptoed toward the front window. They desperately wanted to peek inside so they could figure out what was going on, but the curtains were pulled tight. They stood and stared at them helplessly for a few long moments, and then suddenly the curtains sprang apart. And Gus leapt to one side and Arabella to the other, like actors waiting in the wings at opposite ends of a stage. Through the window, Arabella could see her mother crying and the chief of police pacing the room.

"What are they saying?" Arabella whispered to Gus.

"I can't hear a thing. Just that little dog barking."

"That's Muffin," Arabella whispered.

They watched as the adults inside the dimly lit living room waved their arms and changed positions. Then there was a loud noise, and an alarming thing happened.

"What?" asks the girl.

"Don't you remember?" asks the mother. "Henrietta fell down the stairs."

Imagine how hard it was for Arabella. She had made such a long journey to see her sister, and at last she had arrived, but she could not go inside to help her. Fortunately, Rose went to check on Henrietta, and shortly Arabella could see that her sister was all right. Arabella watched through the window as Henrietta approached the old woman.

"That must be her," she whispered to Gus. "That must be Aunt Priscilla."

Arabella was surprised Priscilla didn't look as scary as she had expected; at any rate, Henrietta didn't seem to be afraid of her. In fact, Henrietta was hugging the old woman. And then Priscilla began to pull at her hand. And then they all huddled around her, and there was more muffled yelling, as well as furious barking from Muffin.

"What are they doing?" Arabella whispered.

Gus shrugged, but then a second later he grabbed her hand. "They're coming toward the door!" Gus yelled. "Run!"

"They just left her there?" asks the girl. "After all that?"

"No," says the mother. "But they didn't want to get caught. They needed a plan."

Arabella and Gus ran across the street and hid behind a bush.

182

"They hid?"

"Yes, dear."

"Behind a bush?"

"Yes, dear."

"A giant was able to hide behind a bush."

"It was a large bush."

"Even so."

"It was getting dark, you must remember."

"Even so!"

"Well, they were all quite focused on getting Aunt Priscilla to the hospital. They considered it . . ."

". . . an emergency," says the girl with a sigh.

Gus and Arabella hid and watched the Osgoods and Rose and the chief of police and Principal Rothbottom and Aunt Priscilla pile into the car and head off, not understanding a bit of what they were seeing. Then they debated for a long while about what to do.

"Go," Gus said. "You've gotten this far. Now's your chance."

"What if they come back?" Arabella said.

"I'll keep watch for you," Gus told her.

"I don't know," said Arabella, hesitating.

"Arabella," said Gus sternly. "You can't lose heart now. Think how happy Henrietta will be to see you."

Arabella knew that he was right, but it took some time and a short walk for Gus to convince her.

"Please go with me," Arabella said when they returned, "to make sure they are gone."

And so they went together. And halfway back they saw and heard something that ended all hesistation: smoke was billowing out of Priscilla's house, and they could hear Henrietta yelling for help.

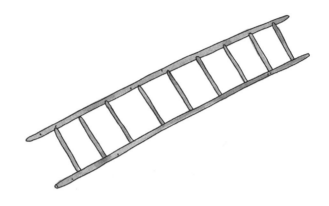

A RESCUE AND A REUNION

Arabella ran toward the house, calling out her sister's name and assuring her that she would save her. Arabella ran so fast, her lungs burned until she was, at last, standing beneath a huge arched window. Henrietta stood above her, framed in broken glass. They were both crying by now.

"It's going to be all right, Hen," Arabella assured her sister. "But you need to jump."

"I can't," said Henrietta. "I'm too scared."

They argued for a while, screaming back and forth: jump, I can't, jump, I can't, and so on. And it might have all ended very badly except for the fact that Gus was there to save the day.

"How?" asks the girl.

"How what?"

"How did he save the day, of course! Did he convince Henrietta to jump into his arms and escape?"

"No! He was tall, but not as tall as a house. He found a ladder and used that. Just as anyone else would."

"What about the house?"

"Well, honey, Gus was resourceful and brave, but he wasn't a firefighter, I'm afraid."

Henrietta, trembling, descended the ladder. At the bottom, Arabella was waiting. The girls threw their arms around each other, and Henrietta could feel her sister's tears dampening her neck.

"Don't cry," Henrietta told her. "It's all right now."

"Oh, Hen," Arabella said. "What have I done? This is all my fault."

"But you saved me, Bella!" Henrietta said. "I can't believe you're here."

"Of course I'm here. I had to find you."

"I hate to interrupt," Gus said, his deep voice startling them. "But I think we'd better go."

The house was fully in flames now, and the smoke was beginning to make them cough. Just then they heard the first fire truck come roaring toward them. A crowd began to form on the street.

"Stand back!" the firefighters yelled as they jumped off the truck.

"Aunt Priscilla's house!" Henrietta said sadly.

"The firefighters will do what they can," Gus said.

"Do you think they can save it?" Henrietta asked.

"I'm afraid it isn't likely," Gus answered.

"But where will we go?" asked Arabella.

Henrietta thought for a second and then suggested that they go to the bookshop.

"I know where Inez hides the spare key," Henrietta said. "And under the circumstances, I don't think she'll mind a bit if we let ourselves in."

. . .

Then they set off. Arabella, remembering her manners at last, introduced Gus to her sister. And Gus lifted the girls onto his shoulders and carried them all the way to the bookshop, where he gently set them down.

"I know this place!" Arabella exclaimed. "The woman who owns it helped me find you."

"I'm not surprised," said Henrietta. "She's been really kind to me."

Henrietta found the key and let them in, leading them through the soft darkness toward the back of the shop to Inez's office.

"Here," said Henrietta, handing the electric kettle to Gus. "Fill this, please, and I'll get us some cups for tea."

When Gus had walked away, Henrietta ran her fingers through her sister's too-short bangs.

"I'm sorry," she whispered.

"Me too, Hen," said Arabella.

Though they had spent their whole lives talking to each other, neither of them knew what else to say at that moment. So Henrietta lifted the dish of peppermints Inez kept on her desk and offered it to Arabella.

"Want one?" she asked.

"It's better than fish soup," Arabella said.

"How do you know about that?" Henrietta asked.

"I'm your sister, silly. I know everything about you."

When Gus returned, he found the girls smiling at one another, their faces so alike that he had to stop himself from staring.

They talked for a while longer until they grew sleepy and decided they should turn in for the night. The twins slept on the sofa, with their heads at opposite ends. Gus took off his sweater and threw it over them. They were warm and comfortable there and almost completely happy, because they were together again. Of course, it was hard not to worry about what would happen in the morning and whether they would be in trouble for running away or would be blamed for the fire, but it had been a very long day. And now they were able to forget it all for a while, just shut it out and close their eyes.

Gus had a harder time falling asleep. He was too big for the desk chair, and had to sit on the floor, and even then the only way he could stretch out his very long legs was to prop his head in the corner of the room and unfold his legs diagonally between the couch and the desk. Once he had arranged himself, he still couldn't rest because he was cold. Very cold. And then he got the idea to take down one of the drapes that hung on the window behind the desk. The drapes were made of green velvet, and they were warm and soft, the perfect blanket. And so, finally, they all fell asleep in the back office of the bookshop, their dreams as lovely as the stories in the books that surrounded them.

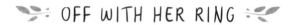 OFF WITH HER RING

While Gus and the girls were busy with the fire at Aunt Priscilla's, Aunt Priscilla herself was in an examining room at the hospital, waiting for the doctor who would remove the emerald ring from her swollen finger.

"Do we have to cut it off?" Mrs. Osgood kept asking the nurse who was taking Priscilla's temperature. "Nobody's going to want it if it's damaged."

"Oh, it has to come off," the nurse insisted. "And right away. People lose a digit this way all the time."

"A digit?" asks the girl.

"A finger," says the mother.

"Please tell me you're kidding," says the girl.

"I can hear you!" said Aunt Priscilla. "Stop nattering and go get the doctor!"

"The doctor will be here in a moment," said the nurse just as the doctor walked in.

"Well. Miss Larchmont," said the doctor with a smile. "Let's get you ready for surgery!"

"Surgery?" said Aunt Priscilla. "I'm not having surgery!"

"Now, now, Miss Larchmont, there's no need to be nervous. You'll feel much better once we remove that appendix, believe you me."

"The ring!" yelled Mrs. Osgood to the nurse. "Tell him about the ring."

"Miss Larchmont's ring—" the nurse began.

"My!" said the doctor. "I think that's the largest emerald I've ever seen."

"My name is not—" began Priscilla, who was suddenly interrupted by barking.

"Bad dog!" yelled Mrs. Osgood. "Muffin, come here!"

"You need to get that dog out of here," said the nurse. "We need to concentrate on Miss Larchmont now."

"*Stop!*" yelled Priscilla. "There is nothing wrong with my appendix, and my name is not Miss Larchmont!"

"I don't understand," said the doctor. "Where is Miss Larchmont?"

"Over here," said a voice from the next curtained cubicle.

"Excuse me," said the doctor, backing out of the exam area and entering the one next door.

"Well, Miss Larchmont!" they heard him say. "Let's get you ready for surgery!"

Aunt Priscilla rolled her eyes.

"Did they ever take the ring off?" asks the girl.

"They most certainly did. Another doctor came in at last and tended to Aunt Priscilla."

"That's good," says the girl.

"It was," says the mother. "Though the whole thing was a little hard on Miss Larchmont."

"Miss Larchmont?"

Over on her side of the curtains, Miss Larchmont was terribly nervous about her impending surgery, and unfortunately she had nothing better to do while she waited than to eavesdrop on what was happening to Aunt Priscilla.

"Let me see your finger," she heard the doctor say. "My, that is swollen. Don't worry. We'll have this cut off in no time."

"Please don't lose it!" Aunt Priscilla said.

"Of course not," said the doctor. "We'll put it in a bag so you can take it home with you."

"Nurse!" yelled Miss Larchmont. "I think I'm going to be sick."

Grinding sounds began in Aunt Priscilla's room.

"There you are," said the doctor. "Nothing to it, really."

"Nurse!" yelled Miss Larchmont. "I think I'm going to faint!"

✎ THE TRUTH COMES OUT ✎

In the waiting room, Mr. Osgood had begun to pace the floor, a worried crease forming in his brow.

"Relax," Mrs. Osgood told him. "Someone is bound to find Arabella any moment. The sketch I created looks just like her."

"If I may interrupt," said the chief of police, "I think we're going to need to redo those posters a bit."

"Why?" asked Mrs. Osgood. "I think they're perfect."

"We never listed the amount of the reward," said the chief. "And we need to mention the emerald ring. In fact, as long as we're making new posters, perhaps you have a photo of Arabella we might use?"

Mrs. Osgood glared at him, incensed at the implied criticism of her artistic ability.

"Or," said the chief, eager for any excuse to separate himself from Mrs. Osgood, "perhaps the school has something."

Meanwhile, Principal Rothbottom was proclaiming his innocence to an elderly couple.

"I mean, clearly the school is not at fault. But that's how it is these days! Parents expect the schools to practically raise their children for them. Never mind that they don't even bother keeping track of where said children are at any given hour of the day. . . ."

"Excuse me," said Mrs. Sandsbury. "Perhaps it would be better if you waited for their translator to arrive."

"Translator?" asked Principal Rothbottom.

"Yes. It might be best. Unless you speak Chinese."

"Oh," said Principal Rothbottom.

"You mean they didn't understand what he was saying?" says the girl.

"Not a word," says the mother.

"If you'll excuse me," said Rose to Mrs. Osgood, "I'd like to freshen up a bit." And she hurried away to the restroom to straighten her skirt and smooth her hair, because she hated to look a mess, and besides, the doctor was a very attractive fellow.

Unmoved by all the fuss, Mr. Osgood was quietly staring out the window, wondering where Arabella was and wishing that Aunt Priscilla would emerge soon so that they could take her home and check on Henrietta.

"Poor Henrietta," he thought guiltily. "We've forgotten you again."

"He misses her!" says the girl.

"I believe he was beginning to," says the mother.

He even went up to his wife and said, "I'm heading back to Priscilla's. We shouldn't have left Henrietta there all alone."

"She'll be fine," said Mrs. Osgood. "She's a very sensible little girl."

"Sensible?" asked Principal Rothbottom, butting into the conversation. "Mr. Stilton-Sterne informed me that the girl had attacked her sister with a pair of scissors."

"Well . . . ," said Mrs. Osgood.

"That's what you said in your note to the school," said Principal Rothbottom. "That Henrietta had attacked her sister. Disfigured her, I believe."

Aunt Priscilla emerged at that moment—newly ringless—

from the curtained room. "Osgood, you sent a violent criminal to live with me?"

"Of course not!" yelled Mr. Osgood.

"A violent criminal?" asked Rose, who had just returned. "Who's a violent criminal?"

"The Osgood girl," said the chief of police. "Why were we not informed of this alleged assault?"

"It wasn't that way!" said Mr. Osgood. "My wife was upset when she wrote that note."

"No good covering up for the girl," said the chief of police. "Best to come clean now."

"Are they talking about her bangs?" Rose asked Mrs. Osgood.

"I believe they are," said Mrs. Osgood.

She looked strange. If Rose hadn't known her better, she would have sworn that Mrs. Osgood was blushing with embarrassment.

"Now, now," said Rose, as if she were scolding children. "Stop this at once! Henrietta's no monster. I've helped raise her myself. I ought to know. She feels awful about cutting her sister's bangs."

"Cutting her bangs?" they all asked in unison.

"Why, yes. Isn't that what you're all talking about? She cut Arabella's bangs, and that's why—"

"Are you telling me," asked Aunt Priscilla, nearly trembling with rage, "that this *whole thing* was started by a *bad haircut*?!"

"Well," said Mrs. Osgood quietly, "it's possible that I may have overreacted."

TWO GIRLS MISSING

"Aunt Priscilla," said Mr. Osgood in his most soothing voice, "let us take you home."

Aunt Priscilla, relieved as she was to have the ring off and her hand returning to normal, was in no mood to be taking orders from her nephew.

"Osgood," she said, "I have no intention of getting back into that car with the pack of you and that yippy little dog."

"Well, we can't leave you here," said Mr. Osgood. "After all you've been through."

"Osgood," said Aunt Priscilla. "I've been taking care of myself for years. I see no particular reason why I should stop right now."

Aunt Priscilla insisted that she would take a taxi home because she needed her beauty sleep and the whole thing had, after all, already been a horrible strain and inconvenience. And, in the end, they didn't even apologize for disturbing her and crashing into her house and coercing her out of her most prized possession, which Mrs. Osgood snatched just as they dashed out the door. Worse yet, in their haste they forgot Muffin, and Aunt Priscilla, sighing, had to grab the little dog and keep it with her.

. . .

"What happens next?" Mrs. Osgood asked as they drove away from the hospital.

"I thought we agreed to stop back at Priscilla's and check in on Henrietta before we head home," said Mr. Osgood.

"I'm sure she's fine," said Mrs. Osgood.

"It's on the way," said Mr. Osgood.

"That's what you always say!" said Mrs. Osgood, her exasperation evident to everyone in the car.

"Oh dear," whispered the nanny to the principal in the backseat.

"Precisely why I never married," the principal whispered in reply.

"I think we should check on the girl," said Principal Rothbottom in his most authoritative voice.

"Did he think something was wrong?" asks the girl.

"Not really. But who wants to listen to married people argue? Particularly when you're trapped in a car with them."

Now, the Osgoods enjoyed bickering as much as any long-married couple, but it had been a tiring day, and even Mrs. Osgood was beginning to feel a bit ashamed of leaving Henrietta behind. So at last they drove to Aunt Priscilla's house to check on Henrietta. Well, perhaps it would be more accurate to say that they drove to the spot where Aunt Priscilla's house used to stand. By the time they got there, the fire department was dousing the last of the flames.

"Henrietta!" screamed Mrs. Osgood, jumping from the car. "My baby!"

"Now she's concerned?"

"Well, she is the girl's mother."

"And she probably did feel a little guilty," says the girl.

"Mothers always do," says the mother.

"Are you the owners?" asked a firefighter.

"No," answered Mr. Osgood. "My aunt."

"Well, sir," the firefighter said. "I'm afraid the news is not good. The neighbors heard someone calling for help, but all we've been able to find is this."

And the firefighter held up one scorched shoe—a shoe far too small to belong to a grown woman.

Mrs. Osgood took one look at it and a single word escaped her lips: "Henrietta." Then she fainted into Mr. Osgood's arms.

❧ HOME ALONE ☙

The Osgoods were distraught, dazed by their misfortune.
Two girls missing. And this last one—they had to admit—
seemed entirely their fault. They had, after all, left the girl
completely unattended.

"That man at the hospital . . . ," Mrs. Osgood said.

"Northington?" asked Principal Rothbottom.

"He was trying to tell us where Arabella is."

"I'm sure he has no idea," said Principal Rothbottom.

"Besides, my dear," said Mr. Osgood sadly, "he seemed to
think that Arabella was here."

"Then it's really true. She's . . ." Mrs. Osgood, unable to finish, began to wail anew.

"You must get hold of yourself, ma'am," said the firefighter. "We aren't certain of anything yet. Our investigation is just beginning. Why don't you go home and get some rest?"

And as soon as he said it, they knew he was right. They had done all they could for one day, and so they headed home.

"That's sad," says the girl.

"It was," agrees the mother.

"And they didn't even wait for Aunt Priscilla to get home," says the girl.

"As usual," says the mother, "they were a bit too focused on themselves."

In all their panic over the twins, they had forgotten poor Priscilla, or at least left her to fend for herself. They piled back into the car, where they were all finally quiet on the ride to the Osgoods'. When they got home, the house looked lovely in the moonlight. It was a beautiful home, but empty now of the children who belonged there.

"We will find them," Mr. Osgood whispered to his wife as they waved goodbye to the principal and the chief of police and let themselves in through the front door.

"I guess you won't be needing me tomorrow," the nanny said.

"Nonsense," said Mr. Osgood. "Go and get a good night's sleep. We'll expect you bright and early."

 WIDE AWAKE

The Osgoods had a troubled, fitful sleep that night, exhaustion competing with worry. If only they could have known how cozy and safe their girls were—asleep in the bookshop—they would have smiled and rested. Instead, they tossed and turned and kept waking, expecting the morning, only to find that the most horrible night of their lives still had not ended.

And Mr. Northington—similarly ignorant of the girls' whereabouts—was also wide awake. When the Osgoods scoffed at his announcement that Arabella was heading to her aunt's house, Northington nearly gave up hope. He left the hospital and collected his dented tandem bicycle and began to pedal toward home, dejected.

"It's going to take me forever to get home, tired as I am," he thought. "Even if I don't dawdle."

And as soon as he had that thought, another struck him like a thunderbolt.

"That's it!" he shouted out loud to no one. "U-weeka!"

"What's wrong with him?" asks the girl.

"Nothing at all," says the mother. "Quite the contrary. He's had an epiphany."

"Like a seizure?"

"No, like a sudden realization."

Mr. Northington—despite his many limitations—had devoted many years to working with children. And much of that time had been spent trying to hurry them along in one way or another. He had prodded slow eaters to finish their lunches, rounded up stragglers who stuck to the edges of the playground after the bell had rung, and hustled the last few remaining children out of the school building at the end of each day, marveling at the trail of dropped homework papers they left in their wake. Northington knew how slow children could be, moving through the world on those smallish legs, constantly distracted by every rock and stick. And that is why Northington also knew—with complete certainty—that Arabella might still be on her way to Aunt Priscilla's house.

"Was she?" asks the girl.

"No," says the mother. "By the time Mr. Northington was having his . . ."

". . . epiphany . . ."

"Yes. Very nice. By then Gus and Arabella had already come and gone from Aunt Priscilla's."

And by the time Mr. Northington located Chillington Lane—a process that was greatly slowed by his garbled pronunciation—Gus and Arabella were huddled at the end of Priscilla's street, trying to determine if it was safe to go back and visit Henrietta. Northington was so excited when he spotted Arabella that he nearly fell off his bike. Arabella, on the other hand, was preoccupied with her conversation with Gus and didn't even notice him. So Northington was able to prop his bike against a tree and hide.

"He hid behind the tree?"

"He was a tall, lanky fellow," says the mother. "Picky eater as a child."

It was hard to see Arabella, clearly hidden as she was by that huge girl (or was it a woman?) in the floppy straw hat. But Northington studied the scene from his hiding spot. He wanted to grab Arabella immediately and order her onto the back of the rickety tandem bicycle to take her home, where he would be rewarded and welcomed as a hero. But that huge friend of hers looked like trouble. And so Northington hesitated.

"He was afraid of a girl?" asks the girl.

"Well, it wasn't *really* a girl, was it? It was Gus."

"In a stolen hat."

"Anyway," asks the mother, "aren't you the one who's always saying girls are just as tough as boys?"

"Continue," says the girl.

"You've come this far," Northington heard Arabella's huge friend say.

And soon Gus and Arabella were heading past him down the road. Northington followed on foot, running in short spurts behind them, concealing himself at every opportunity behind bushes and trees and lampposts.

"Lampposts?" asks the girl.

"Rather ineffective, I must admit."

But Gus and Arabella were too distracted by the fire and Henrietta's cries for help to notice anything else. Northington watched from across the road as the Osgood girls yelled to one another. He saw Gus prop the ladder against the house. He saw the fire trucks arrive. Throughout it all, he knew that he ought to move. He was the adult, and they— possibly even that huge creature in the hat—were children.

"Why didn't he help them?" asks the girl.

"He was afraid," says the mother. "And unsure of what to do."

"But he's the principal!" says the girl.

"Assistant principal," reminds the mother. "And the truth is that the people in charge are often afraid and uncertain."

"So he did nothing?"

"No. As they left, he followed them. After all, he made his living being suspicious about what children might be up to."

Northington followed them to the bookshop. He watched them enter, then wrote down the address in a small notebook he always kept in his back pocket to record the names of children who needed to be sent to Principal Rothbottom's office. Then, as Gus and Arabella and Henrietta settled in to sleep, Northington pedaled home under the full moon, secure in the knowledge that by morning he could reveal all to the Osgoods and the police. He would be a hero. Miss Dewey would be unspeakably impressed by his gallant rescue of the missing girl. Exhausted as he was, he forged ahead, imagining a ceremony at which the mayor pinned a medal to his chest as Miss Dewey sat clapping in the front row.

PRISCILLA RENFREW MEETS HER MATCH

Like all the others, Aunt Priscilla had had a very long night. She had been accosted by relatives, had surrendered her precious emerald ring, and had been abandoned at the hospital with Muffin, who was clearly the world's most troublesome little lapdog. And the worst was yet to come. As there was only one cab driver in town, and a rather unreliable one at that, Priscilla waited for hours, dozing in the hospital lobby. Finally she decided to walk back home, carrying the whimpering Muffin in her arms.

"Couldn't she just say a spell and transport herself there?" asks the girl.

"Or fly there on a broom, right?" asks the mother.

"Yes."

"How many times must I tell you that she's not a witch? She had to walk. And it was very slow going too because she's an older woman."

"Poor Priscilla," says the girl.

Aunt Priscilla walked a very long time; the sun began to come up. And at some point she saw a fire engine stopped at a red light. She decided to ask them if . . .

"Stopped at a red light?" asks the girl.

"Well, they were on the way back from the fire, dear. No need to run red lights at that point, is there?"

Priscilla asked them if they might give her a ride home, and they said they were sorry but they were going the other way.

"We're on our way back from a house fire," they said. "Big gray Victorian at the end of Chillington Lane."

"Gray?" asked Priscilla, her voice starting to shake.

"Yes. Shame it burned down; we tried our best. Worst part is we couldn't find the old woman who lives there. Everybody says she hasn't left the house in years, and of course that leaves us to imagine. . . . Well, nobody's exactly crying big crocodile tears about losing her, though, if you know what I mean."

Priscilla had turned pale.

"Ma'am?" asked the firefighter. "Are you okay?"

Of course Priscilla recognized the description of herself and her house. She thought for a moment about bursting into tears, but that wasn't her way. So, instead, she turned toward the firefighters and pointed a long, crooked finger at them. Then she began to shout.

"You fools! You incompetent fools! Are you trying to tell me that the first time in . . . in a *very* long time that I have left my house, the pack of you have managed to let it burn to the ground?"

"Sorry, ma'am," the firefighter yelled down to her from the engine's cab.

"We have to get going. Need to check in at the station," added his partner, who was driving.

Then they switched on the siren and sped away.

"But it wasn't an emergency anymore," says the girl.

"I think they really wanted to get away from her," says the mother.

"Poor Priscilla."

She was a pathetic sight. "Stop!" she was yelling. Also "You will pay for this!" and other threatening things. They really didn't hear much of it, given their loud and hasty exit. Eventually, Priscilla's noisy and hostile complaints trailed off to a pathetic whimper. She sat down at the edge of the dusty roadway on the curb, where she did, finally, and perhaps for the first time in her life, begin to cry.

"Why me?" she wailed. "Why me? I'm a good person!"

"She really is," says the girl to her mother. "She did give up the ring to save Arabella."

"She did indeed," says the mother.

Priscilla cried and muttered loudly about how this is what happened to you when you spent your time trying to help distant relatives, and wasn't it enough that she had taken in Osgood's daughter, who (though she really wasn't as bad as she had seemed at first) was no help around the house and couldn't even cook a simple meal. And now, because of the other one, she was away at the wrong moment and had lost everything. *Everything.* It was simply too much. Even their ridiculous, noisy little dog had abandoned her. It was, at that moment, fading off into the distance, still running, barking, following the fire engine.

Then Priscilla had an even darker thought.

"Henrietta!" she cried. "Henrietta was in the house! Oh no!" And she covered her face and sobbed.

She was weeping and muttering Henrietta's name when she felt a tap on her shoulder and heard a small, timid voice ask her, "Aunt Priscilla? Aunt Priscilla, are you all right?"

Aunt Priscilla jumped up at the sound of Henrietta's voice. Her eyes grew wide as if she were seeing a ghost. She reached out and pinched Henrietta's arm.

"Ouch!" Henrietta yelled.

"Oh, good!" cried Priscilla. "You're real."

"Of course I'm real," said Henrietta. "We came to check on you."

Arabella and Henrietta and Gus had gotten up early that morning, and finding that they were too hungry to make a breakfast of tea and peppermint candy, and feeling guilty that they had not stayed long enough to see what had happened to Priscilla and her burning house, they had decided to walk back to find out.

"You must be the sister," Priscilla said, pointing at Arabella. "You, young lady, have been the cause of quite a lot of trouble. Aren't you supposed to be missing?"

"All I wanted was to find my sister," Arabella said. Arabella explained the long journey she had made to find her twin.

"So you're a runaway!" Pricilla shouted. "A runaway!

I might have known. And I've gone to all this trouble to try to help you when you didn't need help. When what you *needed* was to be severely punished. And you shall be; I can promise you that!"

"Miss Renfrew," said Gus. "If I may be so bold as to interrupt . . ."

"He's very polite, isn't he?" asks the girl.

"He's a gentle giant," replies her mother.

Gus went on to explain, in the mildest possible terms, that Priscilla had other problems; for example, her house had burned, right to the ground.

"I know that!" yelled Priscilla. "Do you think I need you to come along and explain it all to me? If I hadn't been out of the house, running to the hospital after nearly destroying my hand to give up valuable property to help find nieces who aren't really missing, who deserve to be *throttled* . . ." And then she stopped. "I'm so confused," she said. And she burst into tears again.

Henrietta felt sorry for Priscilla, in spite of all the horrible food and the drafty, creepy bedroom. Gus felt even worse, and he gathered her up and carried her the rest of the way in his arms as you would carry a tired and cranky child off to bed. He didn't put her down until they reached her house. Or, to be more exact, the place where her house had been. What was left was a still-smoking pile of rubble and a few crumbling, blackened walls. Black cats were wandering through the sooty debris, mewing.

"Oh dear," said Priscilla when she saw it. "Oh dear, look at this. Look at this!"

And the four of them did just that: stood there with mouths hanging open, wondering what to do next.

☙ THE RETURNING HERO ❧

Mr. Northington, who had arrived home in the wee hours of the morning, was up early after a short nap. He knotted his tie, carefully combed his sparse hair, and presented himself at the Osgoods' front door at an inappropriately early hour. Mr. Osgood, the only member of the household who was awake, seemed confused to see him there.

"Yes?" he said, opening the door just a crack.

Mr. Northington smiled widely and patted himself on the chest. "Excellent news, Mr. Osgood!" he said, entirely too loudly. "Excellent news! I know where they are."

Mr. Osgood was trying to recall who this lunatic on his

front steps was. "Oh, yes," he said. "Mr. Northington. From the school."

"At your service," said Mr. Northington.

"Listen, Mr. Northington," said Osgood, "I don't mean to be rude, but my wife and I have been through quite an ordeal and—"

"Visitors?" asked Rose sleepily as she joined Mr. Osgood in the doorway. "Would you like some tea?"

"Yes!" said Northington.

"No!" said Mr. Osgood.

"What's all the shouting?" asked Mrs. Osgood, descending the stairs in her blue robe, wiping sleep from her eyes.

"She's never getting dressed, is she?"

"That was really the least of her worries," says the mother.

"Mr. Northington, I think it would be best—" Mr. Osgood tried again.

"The man from the hospital!" Mrs. Osgood shouted. "Let him in!"

"Tea?" asked Rose.

"Yes!" said Northington, smiling.

"No!!" said Mr. Osgood.

But Rose was already leading Northington into the

living room. "We're so grateful," she was saying, "for any help we can get."

"Whatever I can do to assist," said Northington, gazing into Rose's (very blue) eyes.

"Do you know anything?" Mrs. Osgood asked. "About either of my girls?"

Northington cleared his throat and settled back into a lovely wingback chair; he was just about to answer when the doorbell rang again.

"Excuse me," said Mr. Osgood.

By now there was quite a ruckus outside. Through the Osgoods' front window, Northington spotted a clump of newcomers on the front porch. Principal Rothbottom and the chief of police stood nearly shoulder to shoulder with a smallish child squirming between them. As Mr. Osgood opened the front door, the chief of police was yelling, "We'll take this from here, Rothbottom."

"Unhand her," Principal Rothbottom was saying.

"Arabella!" Mrs. Osgood exclaimed, dashing toward the door.

In another moment, all of them had tumbled into the Osgoods' living room.

"That's right!" said the chief of police proudly. "We've found her! We've found your girl!"

"What?" asked Mr. Northington. "No! *I've* found her! I have the address right here!"

Mrs. Osgood, who by now had pushed her way through the crowd and grabbed the small personage in question, screamed, "You *absolute idiots*! That's not Arabella! That's not Henrietta either!"

"Are you sure?" asked the chief of police. "She looks just like the sketch."

"Oh, for pity's sake," said Rose. "Hand me that child. What's your name, love?"

"Waaaaah," sobbed Eliza.

"Wanda?" guessed the chief of police.

The nanny rolled her eyes. "Give us a moment, would you?" she asked.

"Eh, eh, eh," heaved Eliza, who was beginning to hyperventilate.

"Elmira!" yelled Mr. Northington. "I'm certain her name is Elmira."

"Elvira," corrected Principal Rothbottom.

"There, there, calm down, dear. Just breathe," said Rose. "Why don't you come and sit down, and we'll get you some tea and a biscuit."

"A biscuit!" snorted Mrs. Osgood. "Look, you, if you know anything about this, you better start talking."

Eliza sniffed and said, "My name is Eliza Sneedle, and I've only come to say that I'm sorry. We never should have done it."

"Done what?" Mrs. Osgood asked.

And Eliza started to weep again so loudly that it was left to Principal Rothbottom to explain how the children had concealed Arabella's absence by answering for her during roll call that fateful day.

"I knew that!" yelled Northington. "I'm the one who told you that! I have interviewed this child extensively and—"

"Northington," said Principal Rothbottom, "kindly let me handle this."

"So this really isn't your daughter?" asked the chief of police.

"*No!*" said the Osgoods in unison.

Then the room grew quiet for a second, and Northington seized his opportunity. Drawing himself up to his full height and raising one finger up in the air, he loudly proclaimed once more, "I know where the Osgood girls are!"

But his words were drowned out by the sound of a siren as a fire truck screeched to a stop in front of the house. And when the front door opened a third time, Henrietta, Arabella, and Gus stepped through.

"But how?" asks the girl.

"The firefighters had returned to check the scene, and they offered them a ride home."

"Poor Northington," says the girl.

"Poor Northington," the mother agrees.

But even Northington was moved by the girls' reunion with their parents. Mrs. Osgood rushed to the door and threw her

arms around both daughters. For once, she was at a loss for words.

"I'm glad to be home," said Henrietta.

"Can she stay?" asked Arabella.

"Of course," said Mrs. Osgood softly. "This is where she belongs."

And Mr. Osgood smiled and patted their heads.

"I can't find my handkerchief," said the chief of police.

"You can't find anything," said Mrs. Osgood, but she was smiling now, and the edge was gone from her voice.

The room grew so quiet then that they were all startled to hear a soft knock on the door.

"Who can that be?" asked Mr. Osgood. "The whole town is already here."

"Inez!" said Henrietta, pushing toward the door as soon as she spotted her friend. "I'm so glad you came!"

"Well," said Inez, "once I heard about the fire, I had to make sure you were okay. I wanted you to know Aunt Priscilla has decided to stay with me for a while."

"How good of you to come and tell us," said Mr. Osgood.

"How could I stay away?" She smiled. "You know how I love a good story."

A FRESH START

Sometimes a disaster is just a disaster, and nothing good can be said about it. But sometimes a disaster is an excuse for a fresh start. And that was the case for the Osgoods and Aunt Priscilla and all the others.

The next morning, while Mr. Osgood prepared to leave for the office, Mrs. Osgood sat down at her desk to write a note to Principal Rothbottom. This is what it said:

. . .

Dear Principal Rothbottom,

Please excuse my daughters' recent absence from school. We appreciate anything you can do to help the girls catch up on their studies.

Sincerely,
Mrs. Osgood

"They must be so far behind!" says the girl.

"They were. But fortunately Miss Dewey offered to tutor them in the library and help them compensate for the missing work. In fact, the girls, with some help from Miss Dewey, created a scrapbook of their travels to make up for the assignments they missed in school."

"Did they get extra credit?"

"Of course not! They had skipped homework and behaved badly here and there. But really it was a lovely book, with a pale blue cover and ivory pages. All hand-stitched. The girls asked Inez to help illustrate. Here, let me show you."

"It's beautiful," says the girl. "They must have been so proud."

"Children are capable of amazing things," says the mother.

"How good to hear you admit that," says the girl. "But, Mother . . ."

"Yes?"

"Where did you get it?"

"From your grandmother, of course. When they were done making it together and had read it many nights at home, Arabella and Henrietta gave it back to Miss Dewey."

"You mean Miss Dewey was . . ."

"Your grandmother, dear. Dewey was her maiden name—before she married. She added the book to the library. In fact, it was her favorite story there. And when she retired, she took it with her and gave it to me. It's yours now, if you want it."

"Really?" asks the girl, taking the pale blue book in her hands.

"Of course," says the mother.

"How did the story end?" asks the girl. "For the others?"

Well, Aunt Priscilla didn't weep forever about the fire. It was a huge loss, of course. All her familiar surroundings were gone. And the cats, disloyal creatures in the end, wandered away and never returned. And, of course, there was the expense.

"Didn't she have insurance or something?"

"That would have been handy, but no," says the mother.

"But she still had her fortune, right?"

"Well, it had dwindled over the years. But she did have her emerald ring. Until she had to sell it."

"How awful!" says the girl.

"Not really," the mother says.

In fact, the fire was in some ways the best thing that could have happened to Priscilla. After all, there's no better cure for fearing the world than having your house burn down. It rather forces you outside and back into life. And that is what happened with Aunt Priscilla Renfrew. Once she had ventured outdoors, she underwent an almost magical transformation; everything about her life began to change. She found a new place to live, of course—a small cottage near the center of town. And for the first time, she came to know her neighbors. She even discovered that some of them, like Inez and the goat tender Arabella had met, knew of her former glory on the stage. With their encouragement and support, and the money she got from the ring, Priscilla eventually opened up the Emerald Theater, where she staged plays and gave acting lessons. The Osgood sisters visited in the summers and helped with larger productions in exchange for voice and acting lessons from their aunt, who never asked either of them to cook.

"What about Gus?" asks the girl.

"I was just getting to him," replies her mother. "Gus returned home to find that his parents had decided to get a divorce."

"That's not a very happy ending," protests the girl.

"Well, sometimes that's the happiest ending that's possible."

Gus lived with his mother for a few years until he was old enough to venture out on his own. Then he left the nest and joined the circus. In fact, he rose through the ranks, or the rings, or whatever, until he was the ringmaster. It was quite good publicity for the circus, having a giant for a ringmaster,

and finally Gus felt that he had a place in the world that was large enough, so to speak.

"And the Osgoods?"

"Well, the first problem they had was to find a new nanny. Rose left to marry Mr. Northington within a month of the girls' return."

"Mr. Northington! But he was in love with Miss Dewey!"

"He was. But he and Rose began to talk after school each day when she came to collect the Osgood girls. And soon Rose proved a more appreciative audience for Mr. Northington than Miss Dewey had ever been."

"That's so fickle!" protests the girl.

"You should be happy for him," scolds the mother. "He finally had someone to ride with him on that tandem bicycle!"

"And Henrietta and Arabella?"

"Well, they went back to being sisters. And not just sisters, but best friends."

"Your sister can't be your best friend," says the girl.

"I beg to differ," says the mother. "Your sister can always be your best friend. After all, you have each other for your whole lives."

After their misadventure, Henrietta and Arabella got along a good deal better than they ever had before. By running away, Arabella had proven two things: that she loved her sister deeply and that she was not always perfect. And Henrietta had been missed during her time away and was therefore truly treasured when she returned.

HOME AT LAST

And so it ends, in front of the fire, the story of two twin sisters and the adventures they shared with their parents, their aunt Priscilla, and their good friend Gus. The girls lived happily together in a lovely country house with a beautiful garden, where yellow roses perfumed the air. You can see them there, through the huge arched window, their heads bent close together in the lamplight, reading. It is a story of their own creation, full of the magic and misadventure of their lives.

ACKNOWLEDGMENTS

Many thanks to two early readers, Karen DeBrulye Cruze and Gay Lynn Cronin, talented writers and librarians, for getting me started. I am beyond grateful to my amazing agent, Miriam Altshuler, for her wise, skilled, and patient guidance at every stage of this book.

I am indebted as well to Michelle Frey, my kind and gifted editor at Knopf, and to everyone on the Knopf team, including Katrina Damkoehler, Artie Bennett, and Patricia Callahan.

And many thanks to Júlia Sardà for her beautiful illustrations.

I am grateful to my family for their enthusiasm and support. Michael, Liz, Bob, Judy, Eileen, Nick, Mary, and Kerry, you are the best siblings and in-laws on the planet.

Finally, and most importantly, I want to thank my husband, Gerry, and our sons, Sean and Jack, whose love and confidence in me make all things possible.

ABOUT THE AUTHOR

Kathryn Siebel teaches humanities at Billings Middle School in Seattle and works with elementary school students at the Green Lake School-Age Care Program. She has worked in educational publishing and as an English teacher and librarian and has an MFA from the Iowa Writers' Workshop.

Kathryn lives with her family in Seattle. *The Trouble with Twins* is her first novel. You can find out more about Kathryn at kathrynsiebel.com.

ABOUT THE ILLUSTRATOR

Júlia Sardà is an illustrator with a background in fine and graphic arts. She has also worked as a colorist in a studio affiliated with Disney/Pixar. Today she mostly does illustration for children's books, including some of her own childhood favorites: *Alice's Adventures in Wonderland*, *The Wonderful Wizard of Oz*, and *Charlie and the Chocolate Factory*.

Júlia lives in Barcelona, Spain. You can find out more about her work at juliasarda.com.

THE
UNITED STATES
CONSTITUTION

THE
UNITED STATES
CONSTITUTION
Questions and Answers,
Second Edition

John R. Vile

ABC-CLIO

Santa Barbara, California   Denver, Colorado   Oxford, England

Copyright 2014 by ABC-CLIO, LLC

All rights reserved. No part of this publication may be reproduced, stored in
a retrieval system, or transmitted, in any form or by any means, electronic,
mechanical, photocopying, recording, or otherwise, except for the inclusion of
brief quotations in a review, without prior permission in writing from the publisher.

Library of Congress Cataloging-in-Publication Data
Vile, John R.
   United States Constitution : questions and answers / John R. Vile. — 2nd ed.
       pages cm
   ISBN 978-1-61069-571-8 (hardback) — ISBN 978-1-61069-572-5 (ebook)
1. Constitutional law—United States. 2. Constitutional law—United States—
Miscellanea.   I. Title.
   KF4550.V553 2014
   342.7302—dc23   2013029941

ISBN: 978-1-61069-571-8
EISBN: 978-1-61069-572-5

18 17 16 15 14   1 2 3 4 5

This book is also available on the World Wide Web as an e-book
Visit www.abc-clio.com for details.

ABC-CLIO, LLC
130 Cremona Drive, P.O. Box 1911
Santa Barbara, California 93116-1911

This book is printed on acid-free paper ∞
Manufactured in the United States of America

To Moffett, Lynne, Andrew, Kathleen and Sallie and
to the memory of Mr. and Mrs. Hubert Luther
"Bud" Roller and Kathleen Hamrick Roller

Table of Contents

Introduction

I have now been teaching the U.S. Constitution to college students for more than thirty years, and, in these years, my appreciation for the document and its principles has deepened. It is exciting to live at a time when there are more books, articles, and casebooks on the Constitution than there have ever been. At the same time, I am somewhat troubled by the seemingly widespread, if somewhat contradictory, views that the Constitution is so enigmatic as to mean anything readers want it to mean, that it is no longer relevant to current political discourse, or that it is accessible only to experts with political science or law degrees.

In 1828, Arthur J. Stansbury authored *An Elementary Catechism of the Constitution,* which he designed to educate boys (at the time it was uncommon for girls to attend school) about the U.S. Constitution. As his title suggested, Stansbury was a pastor who had decided to adopt the question-and-answer format, which had long been used to teach religious doctrine, via catechisms, to the teaching of the Constitution.

A number of subsequent writers continued Stansbury's method of teaching the U.S. Constitution through a series of questions and answers. They included John Hart, who authored *A Brief Exposition of the Constitution of the United States for the Use of Common Schools* in 1845; John Wilford Overall, who wrote *A Catechism of the Constitution of the United States* in 1896; and Sol Bloom, who included a set of questions and answers in a book that he oversaw as head of the U.S. Sesquicentennial Commission in 1937. I first published my own set of questions and answers in 1998, before I was aware of most of my predecessors who had adopted a similar method. At the time, the closest analogy to my method that I contemplated was that of "trivial pursuit," although I emphasized that I did not then, nor do I now, think that answers to constitutional questions are inconsequential!

Stansbury's book was easy to read and remarkably free of errors, and his question- and-answer approach has withstood the test of time (See Vile, 2013). Moreover, it combined a sense both for the importance of learning constitutional facts and for the potential impact of such knowledge on good citizenship. Still, apart from nostalgia for a simpler time, it seems odd to see that Stansbury's work, which was written less than 50 years after the Constitution was written, has regained popularity as an educational tool in the 21st century. Why? Because it was written prior to the Civil War, the Reconstruction Amendments, the death or impeachment of any sitting president, the application of most provisions of the Bill of Rights to the states, the Progressive Era, the advent of women's suffrage, the New Deal, modern decisions respecting the right to privacy, and a host of other developments that have substantially impacted contemporary understandings of the document. Although Stansbury's work can give a relatively good view of what the Constitution meant in 1828, it says nothing about amendments and interpretations that have followed.

I have continued to chronicle such developments in my *Companion to the U.S. Constitution and Its Amendments,* which is now in its 5th edition, and in *Essential Supreme Court Decisions: Summaries of Leading Cases in U.S. Constitutional Law,* which will soon be in its 16th, but after the revival of interest in Stansbury's work, it also seemed propitious to revise my own earlier set of questions and answers. Like the first edition, this edition is designed to appeal to general readers, to a wide variety of reference libraries, and to high school and college students. I further hope to appeal to those who continue to admire Stansbury's approach but who recognize that U.S. constitutional development did not end either in 1828 or in 1998 and that an important element of good citizenship is that of keeping up with changes.

Because it has been 15 years since the first edition, the changes in this book are more than cosmetic. In addition to adding updates for the last 15 years, I have thoroughly reviewed and revised both the questions and the answers so that they are easier to understand. Although most of the original content was accurate, I have made stylistic changes on almost every page that I believe will make this volume more readable. I have not been an idle writer over the last 15 years, and I believe that many of the lessons about writing that I have learned during this time have produced a far better book. The organization is nearly identical, but I did decide to break the discussion of the Bill of Rights into two chapters (one focused chiefly on the First Amendment) that I think will make the text more accessible to readers.

Although I have looked for facts that will make the reading entertaining, I have continued to emphasize constitutional concepts like separation of powers, enumerated powers, federalism, and checks and balances that the Constitution does not always specifically name. In contrast to Stansbury (albeit consistent with catechism that focus on chapters and verses), I have also continued to emphasize how the Framers organized the Constitution and where they listed various provisions. The introductory chapter of this book addresses the Declaration of Independence and other constitutional foundations. As readers comb through the rest of this book, they will be proceeding through the various sections of the document from beginning to end. Accordingly, I believe that conscientious readers will emerge not simply with heads full of facts but also with a fairly complete understanding of the document. As in my *Companion,* although I reference a number of important Supreme Court decisions and other historical developments, I have attempted to keep the primary focus on the Constitution itself and not on what commentators and courts have said about it. To this end, I would especially encourage readers to examine and consult the text of the Constitution, which I have included as an appendix to this book. Other appendices include the Declaration of Independence and the Articles of Confederation, charts on each of the three branches of the national government, and a chart on the states that compose our federal system.

I have attempted to compile a thorough list of questions and answers, but I am sure that I must have omitted some that interest readers. Accordingly, I welcome correspondence or e-mail (john.vile@mtsu.edu) from readers who think of additional questions that they would like to have answered or that they think should be added to future editions of this work. As is the case with my earlier books, I owe special thanks to my loving wife and twin daughters, to students in my American government, constitutional law, and mock trial classes, to my supportive colleagues at Middle Tennessee State University (and especially the Honors College where I now work), to MTSU's ever patient and ever supportive librarians, and to my editors, especially Barbara Rader, who helped with the first edition, and Denver Compton, who helped with the second. I dedicate this book to a long-time friend and his family, whose continuing association I still highly value.

BIBLIOGRAPHY

Sol Bloom. "Questions and Answers Pertaining to the Constitution," *The Story of the Constitution.* Washington, D.C.: United States Constitution Sesquicentennial Commission, 1937, pp. 162–178.

John S. Hart, *A Brief Exposition of the Constitution of the United States for the Use of Common Schools.* Philadelphia: E. H. Butler & Co., 1871.

John Wilford Overall. *A Catechism of the Constitution of the United States of America. With Sketches of the Constitutional and Ratifying Conventions; and Valuable Personal, Historical, Political and Legal Information, Criticism and Interpretation.* Adopted to Students and Statesmen. New York: The Author 1896 [1895].

Arthur J. Stansbury. 1828. *Elementary Catechism on the Constitution of the United States for the Use of Schools.* Boston: Hilliard, Gray, Little, and Wilkins, 1828.

John R. Vile. "Of Catechisms, Religious and Constitution," Introduction to Stansbury's *Elementary Catechism on the Constitution of the United*

States for the Use of Schools. Clark, NJ: The LawBook Exchange, 2013.

John R. Vile. 2012. 5th ed. *A Companion to the United States Constitution and Its Amendments.* Lanham, MD: Rowman & Littlefield.

John R. Vile. 2014. *Essential Supreme Court Decisions: Summaries of Leading Cases in U.S. Constitutional Law.* 16th ed. Lanham, MD: Rowman & Littlefield.

Chapter 1

Foundations and Purposes of the United States Constitution

AMERICAN CONSTITUTIONALISM AND ITS MOST BASIC PRINCIPLES

What is a constitution?

When Americans think about a constitution, they typically think of a written document, unchangeable by ordinary legislative means, which outlines the major institutions of government, distributes and divides governmental powers among such institutions, and outlines basic protections for individual rights.

Do all countries have a constitution?

All governments except perhaps for those in a state of anarchy, or chaos, have a way of doing things, but not all have a single written document, like the U.S. Constitution, that serves as a guide to these practices and that can serve as a basis for legal action in cases where governments violate such guidelines.

What are the alternatives to a written constitution?

Leaders of dictatorial governments may prefer to operate solely according to their own wills rather than to be bound by a commitment to established procedures, but even democratic governments may not rely on a written constitution like that in the United States. The British government, for example, has what is known, not altogether accurately (since it is based in part on written documents), as an "unwritten" constitution. Britain has established relatively clear procedures for adopting laws, calling elections, and the like, but these are recognized as established customs and usages, or scattered in a variety of laws and decisions, rather than embodied in a single written document like the U.S. Constitution. Moreover, the English system operates according to the principle of parliamentary sovereignty, whereby whatever the established customs and usages may be, there are no fixed constitutional limits on the powers of the national legislature, or parliament.

A sketch of Independence Hall, the statehouse of Philadelphia, in 1778. (Library of Congress)

In recent years, however, even Parliament's rights have been subject to restraints connected to Britain's participation in the European Union.

What are the primary advantages of a written constitution?

Like other laws, if constitutions are well constructed, they can serve to guard against arbitrary actions by providing for future contingencies with relatively fixed rules of procedure. Constitutions are especially important in federal systems of government that divide power between a central government and various state governments. If a constitution spells out individual rights, it may also serve to keep such rights more clearly in view of the people and to provide language whereby existing institutions of government, especially the courts, may enforce such rights.

Are there any disadvantages of a written constitution?

Obviously, any constitution may contain flaws. These flaws become more critical the more difficult constitutions are to change. Moreover, citizens may also gain a false sense of security from seeing guarantees on paper that may or may not be enforced in practice. For the most part, the U.S. Constitution eschews highly aspirational constitutional language for specific restraints (such as the First Amendment provision stating that "Congress shall make no law respecting an establishment of religion"), which can be enforced in judicial proceedings.

Other than outlining, distributing, and limiting governmental powers, what other significance do written constitutions have?

Over time, a Constitution, like a flag, can acquire value as a unifying symbol. Some have argued that in a nation like the United States where there is no monarch, such symbols are especially important. Commentators have observed that there may be tension between the use of the Constitution as an instrument of government and its use as a symbol of nationality.

What was the world's first written Constitution?

It is difficult to answer this question with certainty. In some respects, the colonial charters of government that the kings issued to the American colonies resembled constitutions and served as a type of model for later constitutions; so too, the Pilgrims signed a type of constitutional prototype called the Mayflower Compact, which was based in part on Old Testament ideas of a covenant, prior to disembarking from their ship. During the reign of Oliver Cromwell in England, Parliament debated a Constitution, or Instrument of Government, but it never put it into effect. Most American states wrote constitutions at the time of the American Revolution, and the national constitution later imitated many of their features.

What is the world's oldest written constitution that is still in force?

The United States Constitution, written in 1787, is the oldest such national document. The constitution of the state of Massachusetts, written in 1779 (John Adams was a major contributor), is a few years older, but it has also been amended far more frequently (twice by conventions).

What kind of government did the U.S. Constitution establish?

One can describe this government through a variety of terms. These include democracy, constitutional government, and republican government. Political scientists also sometimes describe the American system as a presidential system of government. From an economic perspective, the system also emphasizes free enterprise.

What is a democracy?

The term "democracy" refers to government in which the people rule. Classic philosophers identified three forms of good government (kingship, aristocracy, and democracy) and three forms of bad government (tyranny, oligarchy, and mob rule). A kingship was a government in which a single individual ruled on behalf of his or her people; in a tyranny, a single individual ruled in his or her own self-interest. An aristocracy was a government in which a group of wise individuals ruled on behalf of the public good; in an oligarchy, a group of individuals (oligarchs) ruled on behalf of their own interests. Democracy was a government under which the people ruled for the common good; in mob-rule situations, such people were guided instead by their own passions.

Does the United States Constitution establish a pure democracy?

No, it does not. In explaining the nature of the new government in *Federalist* No. 10, James Madison, one of America's most astute political theorists, distinguished the American government from a pure democracy in two respects. First, he noted that the United States established a representative democracy rather than a direct democracy. At the national level, at least, citizens do not vote directly on legislation that affects them; rather they vote for representatives who vote on their behalf. Second, and largely as a consequence, a republic can cover a larger land area than can a democracy. A democracy has to be small enough for all citizens to assemble in a single place. By contrast, in a republic, citizens can elect a limited number of representatives who assemble on their behalf.

Some democratic theorists, most notably the Baron de Montesquieu of France (1689–1755), argued that governments covering large land areas were necessarily despotic. Madison, partially drawing from arguments developed by the English philosopher David Hume (1711–1776), argued that republican governments could maintain democratic ideals even in large nations. Indeed, Madison believed that elected leaders who specialized in government would have greater wisdom in deciding on legislation than the people themselves.

What is a republic?

When asked what kind of government the new Constitution established, Benjamin Franklin reputedly said, "A Republic, if you can keep it." Similarly, the pledge of allegiance to the American flag contains the words, "and to the republic for which it stands."

A republic uses a scheme of representation. The idea of republican government may also carry with it various ideas connected with the idea of citizen participation and virtue. There is continuing debate on the degree of virtue that is required for the effective operation of such governments and the degree to which institutional structures can channel even selfish human behavior to constructive purposes.

What is constitutional government?

It is one that emphasizes the rule of law. Such a government is typically democratic, but it generally attempts to balance the idea of majority rule with that of minority rights. Such governments may also be called free governments.

What is a presidential system of government?

This is a government, like that which the U.S. Constitution established, in which the chief executive, or president, is elected independently of the legislature. Many democratic governments, England being the premier example, operate according to a parliamentary system. Under such a system, the head of the majority party in the legislature (there designated as the Parliament) is automatically the prime minister, or head of the government. By contrast, in the system created by the United States Constitution, it is possible to have divided government under which the head of the government, the president, is from a different party than the majority of the members of one or both houses of Congress.

What is a system of free enterprise?

It is a capitalist system, which is bolstered by the protections for property in the U.S. Constitution, in which private individuals own most key industries (banking, mining, transportation, communications, and the like) and employ their own workers. By contrast, in socialistic nations, which are generally democratic, and in communist nations, which are governed dictatorially, the government owns most key industries, and their workers are thus governmental employees. Advocates of socialistic systems believe that they help equalize wealth. Proponents of free enterprise systems believe that they stimulate greater individual effort and national economic growth. The U.S. welfare system buffers some of the perceived negative consequences of private enterprise. Thus some individuals refer to the current U.S. economic system as a "mixed system."

What are the major sources of the political thought of those who authored the Constitution?

The Framers drew from a variety of sources. These included classical liberalism, republicanism, Scottish common-sense philosophy, British common law, and Christianity. Differing Framers would have been subject to differing degrees of influence from these and other sources.

What is classical liberalism, and what ideas did the Framers borrow from it?

Classical liberalism is the philosophy that the English theorist John Locke (1632–1704), the author of the *Second Treatise on Government;*

and the French philosopher, the Baron de Montesquieu (1689–1755), the author of *The Spirit of the Laws*; and others articulated. This philosophy stressed the importance of a social contract, government by consent, and a system of checks and balances. This philosophy also emphasized that government was primarily instituted to protect individual rights such as life, liberty, and property. This view of natural rights was at least indirectly tied to earlier ideas of natural law; that is, the view that written law was subject to certain commonly recognized moral restraints. The Declaration of Independence also reflects many of the main ideas of classical liberalism.

What is republicanism, and what ideas did the Framers borrow from it?

This view, which scholars have traced back to Niccolo Machiavelli (1469–1527) and other Italian theorists and through the opposition political party, the Whigs, in England—most notably John Trenchard and Thomas Gordon, the authors of *Cato's Letters* (first published between 1720–1723)—stressed the need for citizen participation and virtue and emphasized the corrupting influence of power and the need to guard against governmental abuses.

What was Scottish common-sense philosophy, and what ideas did the Founders borrow from it?

Scottish common-sense philosophy was the view of such Scottish thinkers as Francis Hutcheson (1694–1746), Adam Smith (1723–1790), whose *Wealth of Nations* was first published in 1776, and David Hume (1711–1776), who wrote numerous political essays that tended to emphasize the importance of common-sense understandings and the universal possession of the moral sense. Hume, whose views on the subject appear to have influenced James Madison, especially emphasized the importance of controlling factions.

What was British common law?

Common law was the system of judge-articulated law that had developed in England and had been subsequently transported (with modifications appropriate to the new situation) to the New World. Many of the Founding Fathers were lawyers who were familiar with the common law system. The primary expositors of English legal concepts were Sir Edward Coke (pronounced as "Cook," 1552–1634) and Sir William Blackstone (1723–1780); such commentators often professed to find the origins of English liberties in the Magna Carta of 1215 and in other ancient documents and agreements. The British common law system put substantial emphasis on ideas of the rule of law and procedural fairness that later found their way into the Bill of Rights.

How did Christianity influence the authors of the U.S. Constitution?

Although some were professed Deists, most delegates to the Constitutional Convention were at least nominal Christians, and some (Roger Sherman and Oliver Ellsworth of Connecticut and Richard Bassett of Delaware, for example) were well known for their faith. Christianity had spread the idea of human equality and liberty and had stressed the importance of justice. In addition, most of the Framers were familiar with the Bible, and many drew their lessons about both the flaws and sacredness of human nature and about personal ethics from this document. By the same token, many of the Framers were strongly committed to the idea of religious liberty, which they thought the separation of church and state helped to secure.

Did political theory or practical experience influence the U.S. Framers more?

Both were important, although the second probably predominated. The Framers had especially learned from the experiences under the Articles of Confederation, which they hoped to use the new Constitution to correct.

Many commentators have distinguished the practical work of American revolutionaries (including those who wrote the Constitution) from those of later French (1789) and Russian (1917) Revolutionaries who tended to view the world more abstractly and were not always as politically experienced.

What are some of the major principles of the U.S. Constitution?

Among these principles are the ideas of the rule of law, separation of powers, checks and balances, enumerated powers, federalism, liberty, and equality.

What is the rule of law?

The rule of law provides that rules of fixed procedure—such as those found in the Constitution—will govern contingencies rather than having them decided on an ad hoc basis. In the United States, no individual, including the one who holds the highest office, is above the law. The United States also recognizes a certain hierarchy of laws, whereby the Constitution is supreme to, or paramount over, any conflicting state or federal laws. The Constitution might thus be referred to as fundamental or supreme law. The idea of supreme law partly captures an idea, common among the American Framers, that there is a higher law, often associated with principles of justice implicit in natural law.

What is separation of powers?

Because they believed that all individuals with power are tempted to abuse it, the American founders regarded a system concentrating all powers in a single individual or institution to be the very essence of tyranny. They therefore decided to divide the powers of government among different institutions that would share powers. The central division of power at the national level is among the three branches of government—the legislative, the executive, and the judicial branches.

What are checks and balances?

This concept is closely related to that of separation of powers. The Framers expected each branch of government to protect its own power, thus preventing any one branch from gaining a monopoly of power that might result in tyranny. To cite but a few examples, Congress can only adopt a law if the president signs it, or if both houses adopt such legislation over such a veto by two-thirds majorities. Courts can review the meaning and constitutionality of laws that come before them in cases. Most presidential appointments are subject to Senate confirmation. In such cases, one branch of government has the possibility to check improvident or unjust acts of another branch.

What are enumerated powers?

These are powers that are specifically listed. The Framers sought to limit the domain of the national government, especially Congress, by designating the powers (chiefly in Article I, Section 8) that it could exercise. Such powers may, however, allow Congress to exercise certain implied powers (congressional investigations, for example) that are tied to the effective exercise of such powers.

What is federalism?

As the chapter on Article IV of the Constitution will show in greater detail, federalism is a governmental system that divides powers between a national government and various subgovernments, each of whose continuing existence is guaranteed and each of which has its own constitution.

What is liberty?

Liberty is another word for freedom. The preamble to the Constitution indicated that one of its purposes was "to establish the blessings of liberty." The notion of liberty is connected to the idea of the rule of law. Thus, classical theorists and the American founders both sometimes distinguished liberty from license. They created what is sometimes called "ordered liberty." A system that is free does not exempt citizens from all laws with which they may disagree; rather, it ensures citizens that they will, through voting and speaking, have the opportunity to influence such laws.

What is equality?

Equality is the principle of treating similarly situated individuals in similar fashions. In the Declaration of Independence, Thomas Jefferson asserted that "all men are created equal" and that all were entitled to equal rights. This principle is arguably implicit throughout the U.S. Constitution but especially in the equal protection provision of the Fourteenth Amendment, which the states ratified in 1868.

Did the authors of the Constitution intend to create a system of complete equality?

At the time the Constitution, African Americans, women, and other minority groups did not have the same legal rights that they have today, and the Constitution did not immediately change this.

Moreover, even when it came to white males, most of the Framers would probably have distinguished between equality of opportunity and equality of result. Clearly, the law needs to treat individuals fairly regardless of social status or income. Similarly, the system established by the Constitution makes many attempts to give individuals equal opportunity—the nation's commitment to public education is one indication of this. Equal opportunity is probably more of an ideal than an achievable goal.

In any case, equality of opportunity does not guarantee an equality of outcomes. Individuals who are more attractive, luckier, wittier, more brilliant, more adept at social interaction, better able to make friends, or better gifted with supportive or wealthier families or communities, often achieve more than other citizens who lack such advantages. Although governments might want to moderate extremes of wealth or poverty, most do not aim for complete equality of outcomes.

THE COLONIAL BACKGROUND

How did the United States begin?

The United States began as thirteen colonies settled on the North American coast, most of which were originally settled by, and all of which eventually came under the jurisdiction of, Great Britain. The colony in Virginia dated to 1603 and that of Massachusetts to 1620. The Spanish had established earlier settlements in the area that is within Florida today, as well as in Central and South America. The French established a colony in modern-day Canada, which France later ceded to the British after the French and Indian War.

Did Britain control all affairs in the thirteen colonies?

No, the colonies were so far distant from Britain that they had to make many decisions on their own. Virginia created a legislative body, known as the House of Burgesses, in 1619. Individuals on the *Mayflower* signed a document of mutual responsibilities (the Mayflower Compact) before they disembarked from the ship. The British appointed governors who could veto some colonial acts, but Britain exercised a policy known as "salutary [beneficial] neglect" during much of the early years. This lasted until about 1763.

What happened to change that policy?

Britain was engaged in a worldwide conflict with France that Americans usually referred to as the French and Indian War (1754–1763). Although the colonies bore many of the casualties, the British paid for much of the financial costs. At the end of the war, the British Parliament (its legislature), which considered itself to be sovereign (having ultimate authority in both the home country and the colonies), decided that the colonies should share in taxes to pay for the war, and it began to enact taxes on paper, tea, and other commodities.

How did the colonists react?

Citing the principle of "no taxation without representation" that they traced back to the Magna Carta of 1215, the colonists asserted that Parliament had no right to tax them if they did not elect delegates there.

How did the British respond?

They argued that the colonists remained English citizens and that, as such, Parliament virtually represented them even though they did not elect delegates.

And how did the colonists respond?

The colonists certainly wanted to have the rights of Englishmen and the protection of the Crown against foreign invaders, but they traced this citizenship not to allegiance to the Parliament but to the king who had issued most of their charters and to whom they appealed for redress.

How was this issue resolved?

The Americans and British never resolved this peacefully. Parliament continued to enact taxes, the colonists resisted them, and as conflicts developed between the colonists and British troops, the British sent more troops, which further heightened the problem, as in the tragedy often called the Boston Massacre. The colonists called a Stamp Act Congress in 1765 to resist British taxation and again in 1775 and 1776 with the First and Second Continental Congresses. In these meetings, colonists began to recognize that they had common problems.

THE DECLARATION OF INDEPENDENCE

When did fighting between Great Britain and the American colonies begin?

It began with the battles of Lexington and Concord in Massachusetts in April of 1775. Even after fighting began and Congress appointed George Washington to lead colonial forces, many of the colonists hoped for reconciliation with Great Britain. A publication of January 1776 helped push the colonists toward independence.

What was this influential publication?

Thomas Paine, a British-born immigrant, wrote a book titled *Common Sense* that argued that the time for independence had arrived and that further association with Great Britain would simply involve the colonies in further wars and destroy their liberties. Paine also made a strong case against the practice of hereditary succession by which the throne passed from parent to child with little regard to the child's fitness.

Once Paine published his book, did the Congress take the lead in declaring independence?

Not exactly. Many members, most notably John Dickinson, who ultimately refused to sign the Declaration, hoped for conciliation with the British. Numerous states sent petitions to Congress asking Congress to act before it actually did so.

When did a member of the Second Continental Congress first introduce the resolution for independence from Great Britain?

Virginia's Richard Henry Lee first introduced such a resolution on June 7, 1776.

Did Richard Henry Lee introduce any other resolutions at this time?

Yes, he also introduced resolutions for a new form of government and for alliances to help pursue war against Britain. At the time, many delegates considered these two issues to be more important than the writing of the Declaration of Independence.

Which five men did Congress appoint to the committee responsible for writing the Declaration of Independence?

Thomas Jefferson of Virginia, John Adams of Massachusetts, Benjamin Franklin of Pennsylvania, Roger Sherman of Connecticut, and Robert Livingston of New York all served on this committee.

Engraving of artist John Trumbull's, *The Declaration of Independence*, which was painted in the decades after the American Revolution. Among the signatories of the document portrayed in the painting are the five members of the drafting committee, John Adams, Roger Sherman, Robert R. Livingston, Thomas Jefferson, and Benjamin Franklin standing before a seated John Hancock. (Library of Congress)

Of the individuals who served on the committee to draft the Declaration of Independence, who was the most influential?

Thomas Jefferson did most of the drafting, and Franklin and Adams made some minor emendations. However, the Second Continental Congress made substantial changes in Jefferson's document, cutting it by almost one-fourth and polishing much of its language.

At the time his fellow delegates selected Jefferson to write the Declaration of Independence, what did fellow delegates know about him?

They probably best knew him for having written *A Summary View of the Rights of British America* in which he had outlined the colonists' case against Britain. Although he was not a very powerful speaker and thus said very little at the Second Continental Congress, he was a diligent worker on committees. Jefferson had not originally been appointed to the Second Continental Congress but had come as a replacement for Virginia's governor, Peyton Randolph.

Did Jefferson copy the Declaration from any previous documents?

No, he indicated that he did not plan for the Declaration to express novel principles but rather the "common-sense" of the subject as the colonists understood it. He appears to have drawn fairly heavily from the natural rights philosophy of his day. He may also have drawn from the Scottish common-sense philosophers.

In her book *American Scripture,* historian Pauline Maier documents that many states and localities had previously adopted their own declarations of independence. These, like the earlier English Declaration of Rights and the Virginia Bill of Rights, appear to have served as models for Jefferson's draft of the Declaration of Independence.

What was the purpose of the Declaration of Independence?

The Declaration was designed to justify the colonists' decision to separate from Great Britain and articulated principles that could unite them. It did not establish a new form of government. This was the work of the Articles of Confederation and the United States Constitution.

What title did Congress give to the Declaration of Independence?

It described it as "The Unanimous Declaration of the Thirteen United States of America." This unanimity was not complete on July 4th but on July 19th, when news of New York's approval of the Document, given 10 days earlier, reached Congress.

What are the opening words of the Declaration of Independence?

The document begins with the words, "When in the course of human events . . . "

The Declaration of Independence refers to certain "self-evident truths." What did it mean by that term?

Such truths are designed to serve as fundamental axioms, or first principles, of government.

What is the first such truth that the Declaration mentions?

Its first affirmation is that "all men are created equal."

By designating "men," did the Declaration intend to exclude women?

Today, the terminology of the Declaration of Independence is not "politically correct." It appears, however, that the Declaration used the term "men," as was common at the time, so as to include members of both sexes (who would, not, however, have been equally entitled to participate in governmental affairs).

In what way does the Declaration of Independence assert that men are equal?

It indicates that, having a common Creator, they are entitled to the same rights.

What specific human rights does the Declaration of Independence list?

It mentions the rights of "life, liberty, and the pursuit of happiness."

What adjective does the Declaration use to describe these rights?

It describes them as unalienable.

What does unalienable mean?

The term refers to that which inheres in the nature of a thing and cannot be legitimately forfeited, or alienated. By the Declaration's analysis, individuals possess rights by virtue of being human beings created by God and not by grace of any government. Thus, since God intended for men to be free, they cannot sell themselves into slavery.

What is the "pursuit of happiness"?

The Declaration of Independence does not specifically define the pursuit of happiness, perhaps indicating that different individuals will perceive happiness differently. Classical philosophers argued that most individuals sought happy lives. The "pursuit of happiness" is a broader term than "property," the protection of which many contemporaries regarded as a key function of government.

By using the term "pursuit of happiness," Jefferson may also have muted questions that later emerged with the writing of the Constitution as to whether slaves were considered to be property or persons.

According to the Declaration of Independence, what serves as the foundation of governments?

According to the document, which reflected English social contract or liberal thinking, such governments rest on "the consent of the governed." By contrast, many monarchs of Jefferson's day followed England's James I (1566–1625) in proclaiming that they ruled by "divine right"; that is, by God's will and choosing.

According to the Declaration of Independence, what is the chief purpose of government?

Its chief purpose is to secure individual rights.

According to the Declaration of Independence, what should people do when they find that their governments are not protecting individual rights?

They have the right, indeed the duty, to overthrow the existing government and establish a new one.

According to the Declaration of Independence, under what circumstances may a people engage in revolution?

The people should not engage frivolously in such revolution but only if a long series of abuses demonstrates an intent on the part of existing governors to rule despotically or dictatorially.

In referring to British abuses, which English leader does the Declaration of Independence have in mind?

It focuses on the English King (the unnamed George III [1738–1820]). Most colonists had already rejected the idea of parliamentary sovereignty, leaving their ties to the king the only ones still needing to be broken for America to be independent.

How many charges does the Declaration of Independence level against the English king and his associates?

It lists about twenty-five such accusations. This part of the Declaration of Independence, which is the longest and least-cited portion of the document, reads much like a legal brief or extended argument.

What are the chief accusations that the Declaration leveled against the king?

Many of the charges accused the king of denying self-government to the colonies. Others deal with alleged abuses of the criminal justice system. Still others relate to war atrocities that had occurred in the wake of fighting at Lexington and Concord.

Does the Declaration of Independence mention slavery?

It does so only indirectly when it accuses the king of exciting "domestic insurrections among us. . . ." Jefferson's draft of the Declaration also condemned the king for introducing slavery into the New World, but Congress deleted this condemnation, perhaps more sensitive than Jefferson of the irony of slaveholders (including Jefferson) blaming the king for this institution.

What are the closing words of the Declaration of Independence?

It ends with the words, "And for the support of this declaration, with a firm reliance on the protection of Divine Providence, we mutually pledge to each other our lives, our fortunes, and our sacred honor."

Is the reference in the last paragraph the first time the Declaration mentioned God?

No, the Declaration also mentions God in the first paragraph.

On what day did the Second Continental Congress adopt Richard Henry Lee's resolution for independence?

It adopted the resolution on July 2, 1776.

On what day did Congress accept the Declaration of Independence as an explanation of the former colonists' decision?

It did so on July 4, 1776, the day that the nation now celebrates as Independence Day. The end of the Document incorporates the resolution for independence that Richard Henry Lee had introduced on June 7th.

How many words does the Declaration of Independence contain?

1,337

Who signed the first printed copy of the Declaration of Independence?

It appears that John Hancock, the president of the Second Continental Congress, and the secretary, Charles Thomson, signed the first printed copy on July 4, 1776.

Who copied the Declaration of Independence on parchment in a form appropriate for signing?

Timothy Matlack of Philadelphia so "engrossed" the document.

When Matlack engrossed the Declaration of Independence for signing, how many pages did it occupy?

The entire document, including the delegates' signatures, fit on a single page.

When did delegates sign the Declaration of Independence?

They signed over a period of months beginning in August 2, 1776, and continuing at least through November 4, 1776 (possibly as late as January 1777) rather than at a single sitting, as is often portrayed in paintings, as, for example, that by John Trumbull, which is portrayed on the back of the two-dollar bill.

How many individuals signed the Declaration of Independence?

Fifty-seven signed; these included fifty-six delegates and Secretary Charles Thomson.

Which state supplied the most signers of the Declaration of Independence?

Pennsylvania did. It had nine signers. Virginia was next with seven.

How many future U.S. presidents signed the Declaration of Independence?

Two did, namely Thomas Jefferson and John Adams.

Whose bold signature, which heads the others on the Declaration of Independence, has become a standard expression?

John Hancock's has. It is common to tell someone to sign their John Hancock on a document.

Why did Hancock list his signature separately on the Declaration of Independence rather than with those of other delegates from Massachusetts?

Hancock signed not simply as a delegate from Massachusetts but also as president of the Second Continental Congress that endorsed the document.

Who did Congress commission to make the first printing of the Declaration of Independence?

It gave this job to John Dunlap, a Philadelphia printer.

How do we know that Jefferson regarded the Declaration of Independence as one of his primary accomplishments?

Along with writing the Virginia Statute for Religious Liberty (helping to establish separation of church and state in the state) and founding the University of Virginia, he asked that the tombstone at his home at Monticello list his authorship of this document. Interestingly, Jefferson did not list his service as president of the United States.

Jefferson also made a point to send his friends his version of the document rather than the one that the Second Continental Congress adopted.

How many of the individuals who signed the Declaration of Independence later supported the U.S. Constitution?

Garry Wills (*Inventing America*, p. 353) says that "thirty of the forty-three living Signers supported the Constitution."

THE ARTICLES OF CONFEDERATION

Was the United States Constitution the first constitution for the United States?

No, it was not. Prior to the current Constitution, the thirteen former colonies had allied together under what was known at the Articles of Confederation.

When were the Articles of Confederation written?

They were written and revised in 1776 and 1777, near the beginning of the Revolutionary War.

Who authored the Articles of Confederation?

John Dickinson of Delaware, who had been known as the "penman" of the Revolution, was the chief author of the Articles. The Second Continental Congress substantially revised his document. North Carolina's Governor Thomas Burke was especially influential in seeing that the Articles recognized the continuing sovereignty of the states.

When did the states ratify the Articles of Confederation?

The Articles required ratification by all thirteen states. The last state to ratify, Maryland, did not do so until 1781. As a state with no western land claims, Maryland had refused to ratify the Articles until other states with such claims relinquished them.

How did the states ratify the Articles of Confederation?

They did so by authorizing their representatives in Congress to sign the document on their behalf; by contrast, conventions within the states ratified the Constitution of 1787.

How many articles did the Articles of Confederation contain?

It contained thirteen.

Where did the Articles of Confederation concentrate powers?

It concentrated such power in the states. Article II of the Articles specified that "[e]ach state retains its sovereignty, freedom, and independence, and every Power, Jurisdiction and right, which is not by this confederation expressly delegated to the United States, in Congress assembled." The Articles themselves refer to a "league of friendship" among the states.

Who handled the collective affairs of the states under the Articles of Confederation?

Congress, which often acted through committees, did so.

How did the Congress under the Articles of Confederation represent states?

Each state could send from two to seven delegates, but each state had an equal vote.

How many chambers were there in the Congress under the Articles of Confederation?

There was only one. Scholars thus classify this body as a unicameral Congress (a bicameral Congress would have two houses).

How long did members of the Congress of the Articles of Confederation serve?

They were appointed in a manner specified by each state legislature for one-year terms. However, states had power to recall delegates, a power they do not exercise today. Moreover, the Articles prevented delegates from serving for any more than three years in any six-year period.

What kind of powers did the Congress under the Articles of Confederation exercise?

Its powers mostly related to foreign affairs and were much less comprehensive than those of the current Congress. When it came to critical matters, the Articles required the consent of nine or more states. Moreover, on key issues such as raising armies and taxation, the Articles limited Congress's power to requisitioning the states, and Congress depended on their responses.

Did the Articles of Confederation prove effective?

The Articles had a number of successes, including victory in the conflict with Great Britain and adoption of legislation relative to the Northwest Territory, which Congress adopted during the meeting of the U.S. Constitutional Convention of 1787. Modern scholars, however, are more likely to remember the Articles for their failures than for their successes.

What were the chief defects of the Articles of Confederation?

The national government was too weak. Apart from the president of a "Committee of States" that met when Congress adjourned, the Articles had no effective executive authority; a national judiciary was also lacking.

Generally, congressional powers were inadequate—for example, Congress had no power to control interstate commerce, and states coined their own money. Congress could make recommendations on matters of defense and finance, but it depended on the states for enforcement of such recommendations, and states, ever jealous of their powers and prerogatives, were not altogether cooperative.

What problems did the Articles of Confederation encounter?

Rivalry among the states led to economic decline; there was fear that the national government was not strong enough to survive threats to the Union; other nations, who saw that America was unable to get the British to remove their troops from the Northwest Territory, as the Treaty of Paris that had ended the Revolutionary War had specified, did not treat the nation with respect.

Was it possible to amend the Articles of Confederation?

The Articles had an amending mechanism, but it required all the states to ratify such proposals before they went into effect.

How many such amendments did the states adopt during the duration of the Articles?

Congress proposed a number of amendments, most relative to raising revenue, but the amending mechanism was so wooden that the states did not unanimously ratify any of them.

THE WRITING OF THE UNITED STATES CONSTITUTION

Who wrote the United States Constitution?

The Constitution was a collective effort that grew out of a constitutional convention.

Who called the Convention?

Delegates to the Annapolis Convention issued the call for a meeting "to take into consideration the situation of the United States, [and] to devise such further provisions as shall appear to them necessary to render the constitution of the Foederal [*sic*] Government adequate to the exigencies of the Union. . . ." Congress subsequently invited states to send delegates to such a convention.

What was the Annapolis Convention?

The Annapolis Convention was a meeting held in Annapolis, Maryland, in September of 1786 to discuss common problems of commerce and navigation among the states. Delegates from Maryland and Virginia who had met at George Washington's house, Mt. Vernon, in the spring of 1785, to discuss problems between the two states in regard to navigation on the Potomac River, had suggested this meeting.

How many states sent delegates to the Annapolis Convention?

Delegates from five states attended. The states were New York, New Jersey, Pennsylvania, Delaware, and Virginia.

Guards stand by as visitors view the first exhibit of the entire United States Constitution in Washington, D.C., on September 17, 1970. (National Archives)

How many of the delegates to the Annapolis Convention attended the Constitutional Convention that followed?

Seven did. These included John Dickinson who had served as chairman of the Annapolis Convention; James Madison, often called the "Father" of the Constitution; and Alexander Hamilton, who was influential in using the Annapolis Convention to call for the Philadelphia Convention.

Why did more states send delegates to Philadelphia than to Annapolis?

Shays' Rebellion, a taxpayers' rebellion that broke out in Massachusetts in the winter of 1786–1787, helped convince some states that the government might be facing a crisis that required it to have greater powers. Moreover, Congress adopted a resolution urging states to attend, thus providing legitimacy to what might otherwise appear to be an illegal body.

Where did the Constitutional Convention meet?

It met at the State House (also known as Independence Hall) in Philadelphia, the same site where Congress had proposed the Declaration of Independence and the Articles of Confederation.

In what year was the Constitutional Convention held?

It was held in 1787. This was 11 years after the writing of the Declaration of Independence. In 1987, the United States celebrated the bicentennial of the Constitution.

THE DELEGATES

How many delegates did states choose to attend the Constitutional Convention?

They chose 74 delegates.

How many delegates attended the Convention?

Fifty-five delegates attended the convention.

What was the racial and gender makeup of the delegates to the Convention?

At a time when women and blacks did not have the right to vote, it is not surprising to find that all the convention delegates were white males.

Who chose the delegates to the Constitutional Convention?

Their state legislatures did.

Which state's delegation to the Constitutional Convention did not arrive until late July?

New Hampshire's two delegates did not arrive until this time.

Which state had two of its three delegates leave on July 10th?

New York did. Robert Yates and John Lansing both left the Convention, whose centralizing tendencies they opposed. New York's other delegate, Alexander Hamilton, was absent from the Convention during most of July and August, but he did return in September and signed the document.

How many future presidents attended the Constitutional Convention?

Two did. They were George Washington, who would serve as the nation's first president, and James Madison, who would serve as its fourth. Both played critical roles at the convention. Washington served as the convention's president, and Madison contributed to the Virginia Plan, debated almost every issue that came before the body, and kept meticulous notes of the Convention's proceedings.

John Adams, who would serve as the nation's second president, was an American diplomat in England, and Thomas Jefferson, who would be the third president, was an American diplomat in France. James Monroe, the nation's fifth president (and the last president from the Revolutionary generation), did not attend the Convention and actually joined forces with the Anti-Federalists at the Virginia Ratifying Convention in opposing constitutional ratification.

Which convention delegate did James Monroe defeat when he ran for president in 1816?

He defeated Rufus King of Massachusetts.

How many future vice presidents attended the Constitutional Convention?

Elbridge Gerry of Massachusetts was the only one; he would serve as vice president under James Madison, another Convention delegate. Gerry defeated Jared Ingersoll, a convention delegate from Pennsylvania, for the vice presidential post.

How many future justices of the U.S. Supreme Court signed the Constitution?

Five did. They were: William Paterson (NJ), who served from 1793–1806; James Wilson (PA), who served from 1789–1798; John Blair (VA), who served from 1789–96; John Rutledge (SC), who served from 1789–91; and Oliver Ellsworth (CT), who served as chief justice from 1796–1800. Ellsworth was one of the delegates who was not present when the Constitution was signed.

Who was the oldest delegate who attended Constitutional Convention?

Benjamin Franklin, of Pennsylvania, who was then 81 years of age, was the oldest. Franklin had also been the oldest person to sign the Declaration of Independence 11 years earlier.

Who was the youngest delegate at the Constitutional Convention?

Jonathan Dayton, of New Jersey, then 26 years of age, was the youngest, although Charles Pinckney of South Carolina (age 30) apparently did not correct misimpressions that he was.

How many of the 55 delegates who attended the Constitutional Convention had signed the Declaration of Independence?

Eight had.

What was the average age of the delegates to the Constitutional Convention?

The average age of the delegates was about 43.

How many of the delegates to the Constitutional Convention had engaged in some kind of military duty?

About 30 of them had so served, most in the Revolutionary War. Such individuals (Washington in particular) often had a more continental perspective than those who had not so served.

How many of the delegates to the Constitutional Convention had held some previous public office?

All 55 of them had some prior public service. Historian Clinton Rossiter has asserted that "[n]o gathering of the leaders of a newly independent nation at any time in history has had more cumulative political experience than the Convention of 1787" (*The Grand Convention,* p. 144).

How many of the delegates to the Constitutional Convention had served in Congress?

Forty-two had. In addition, three had sat in the Stamp Act Congress, and seven had served in the First Continental Congress.

What professions predominated at the Constitutional Convention?

Most delegates were lawyers, planters, merchants, or businessmen. All had some political experience, and a few—James Madison, for example—qualified as lifelong politicians.

How many of the convention delegates identified themselves as Roman Catholics?

Thomas Fitzsimons of Pennsylvania and Daniel Carroll of Maryland were both Catholics.

Which delegate to the Constitutional Convention had been trained as a cobbler?

Roger Sherman, of Connecticut, had been so trained, but he subsequently wrote almanacs, became a judge, and held numerous political offices.

To which political party did a majority of the delegates to the Constitutional Convention belong?

There were no officially recognized national political parties in the United States when the Constitutional Convention met.

How many of the delegates to the Constitutional Convention had attended college?

About 25 had done so.

Which American college was best represented (in terms of former students) at the Constitutional Convention?

The College of New Jersey (now Princeton University) was. Convention delegates who had attended the College of New Jersey included Oliver Ellsworth of Connecticut, William Paterson, William Churchill Houston, and David Brearly (nondegree) of New Jersey, Gunning Bedford of Delaware, Luther Martin of Maryland, James Madison of Virginia, and William David and Alexander Martin of North Carolina.

What other American colleges had three or more graduates in attendance at the Constitutional Convention?

Four Virginia delegates, George Wythe, James McClurg, John Blair, Jr., and Edmund Randolph; one Maryland delegate, John F. Mercer; and one Georgia delegate, William Pierce Jr., had all attended the College of William and Mary. George Wythe was later a professor there.

Connecticut's William Johnson, New Jersey's William Livingston, Pennsylvania's Jared Ingersoll, Jr., and Georgia's Abraham Baldwin had all attended Yale. In addition, Yale University had awarded Connecticut's Roger Sherman an honorary Masters of Law degree, and Oliver Ellsworth, also of Connecticut, had studied there for one year before transferring to the College of New Jersey.

Rufus King, Elbridge Gerry, and Caleb Strong, all from Massachusetts, had graduated from Harvard.

What, if any, other American colleges had graduates at the Constitutional Convention?

King's College (now Columbia) and the College of Philadelphia (now the University of Pennsylvania) also had graduates in attendance.

Which, if any, foreign universities had delegates to the Constitutional Convention attended?

Charles C. Pinckney of South Carolina had attended Oxford University, and James Wilson of Pennsylvania had attended St. Andrews. At least two delegates had also studied law at the London Inns of Court.

Most delegates to the Constitutional Convention had been born in the thirteen colonies. Which nation supplied the next highest number of delegates?

Ireland, which served as the birthplace of four delegates, supplied the next highest number of delegates.

Which four delegates to the Constitutional Convention were born in Ireland?

New Jersey's William Paterson, Pennsylvania's Thomas Fitzsimons, Maryland's James McHenry, and South Carolina's Pierce Butler were all born in Ireland.

Which delegate to the Constitutional Convention was born in Scotland?

James Wilson of Pennsylvania was.

Which delegates to the Constitutional Convention were born in England?

Robert Morris of Pennsylvania, often known as the "financier of the Revolution," was born in Liverpool. Once known as the richest man in America, he died bankrupt. North Carolina's William Richardson Davie was also born in England.

Which delegate to the Constitutional Convention was born in the West Indies?

Alexander Hamilton of New York was born on the West Indies island of Nevis. In addition to being foreign born, Hamilton was an illegitimate child of a Scottish father and a French mother. John Adams, a Federalist rival, once derogatorily referred to Hamilton as "a bastard brat of a Scotch peddler."

What do all the delegates to the Constitutional Convention who were born abroad have in common?

All were born in what is now Great Britain or in her colonies.

Which delegate to the Constitutional Convention had first proposed a plan of Continental Union in 1754?

Benjamin Franklin of Pennsylvania had proposed the so-called Albany Plan of Union at that time. Franklin suffered from gout and had to be conveyed on at least one occasion to the convention in a special contraption that was carried by prisoners.

Which delegate to the Constitutional Convention later helped found the Federalist Party?

Alexander Hamilton of New York did. George Washington is also often regarded as a Federalist, although he professed to be above parties.

Which delegate to the Constitutional Convention later helped found the Democratic-Republican Party?

James Madison of Virginia did. The other founder of this party, who opposed the Federalist Party, was Thomas Jefferson.

Which two delegates to the Constitutional Convention were second cousins?

General Charles Cotesworth Pinckney and Charles Pinckney, both of South Carolina, were so related.

Which delegate to the Constitutional Convention taught law to Thomas Jefferson?

Virginia's George Wythe, who later died of poisoning by his nephew and heir, did.

Which delegate to the Constitutional Convention was the nation's first attorney general and its second secretary of state?

Virginia's Edmund Randolph, the state governor who introduced the Virginia Plan at the Convention, was the nation's first attorney general and its second secretary of state.

Which two Pennsylvania delegates to the Constitutional Convention gave the most speeches there?

Gouverneur Morris and James Wilson did.

Who refused to attend the Convention, professing that he "smelt a rat"?

Virginia's outspoken orator and states' rights advocate, Patrick Henry, made this statement. He was a prominent Anti-Federalist who opposed the Constitution in the Virginia Ratifying Convention.

Which delegate at the Convention later had his name used for the practice of fashioning an oddly shaped political district in order to gain an electoral advantage?

Elbridge Gerry of Massachusetts did. The practice of configuring a political district so as to give an electoral advantage to one's friends is called gerrymandering. At a time when Gerry later was serving as governor, a cartoonist attributed a salamander-looking district to Gerry and called it a gerrymander. The name stuck and is still in use today.

How many delegates to the Constitutional Convention were slave owners?

According to historian Mel Bradford, who has written a book dealing with the lives of the delegates, "As many as thirty-five of the fifty-five Framers were slave-holders."

Which of the delegates to the Constitutional Convention had a wooden leg?

Gouverneur Morris of Pennsylvania, who had lost his leg in a carriage accident, did.

Which delegate to the convention proclaimed, "I would have lost this hand before it should have marked my name to the new government."

Virginia's George Mason, who had authored the Virginia Declaration of Rights and was especially concerned about the omission of a bill of rights in the national Constitution, made this statement.

Which Convention delegate, a former aide-de-camp to George Washington, became the first secretary of the Treasury in the Washington Administration?

New York's Alexander Hamilton did.

Which two delegates who signed the Constitution had also signed both the Declaration of Independence and the Articles of Confederation?

Roger Sherman of New Jersey and Robert Morris of Pennsylvania had.

Of the delegates who attended the Constitutional Convention, who survived the longest?

James Madison, who was 36 at the time of the Constitutional Convention, died in 1836 at the age of 85. Ironically, the physically diminutive Madison, who was only five feet four inches tall (some accounts say five feet six) and weighed less than a hundred pounds, was somewhat of a hypochondriac who suffered a nervous breakdown in his college years at Princeton, had epilepsy, and had not been expected to live long.

THE PROCEEDINGS

How many states sent delegates to the Constitutional Convention?

Twelve did. Rhode Island did not send any representatives. Delegates sometimes dismissively referred to the state as Rogues Island, because it had adopted financial policies that they thought unduly favored debtors.

When did the Convention meet?

It met from May through September of 1787. The convention had been scheduled to meet on May 14, but there was not a sufficient quorum for business until May 25.

How were states represented at the Convention?

States sent from two to seven delegates. Each state had a single vote.

How did the delegates choose this method of representation?

This was the system of representation that was used under the Articles of Confederation.

Who did the delegates select as president of the Constitutional Convention?

The delegates unanimously selected George Washington, then best known for his role in leading American forces during the American Revolution, as their president. Washington and Franklin were the two men at the Convention with the most widely known reputations. Franklin was, however, in poor health (he suffered from gout), making Washington the obvious choice.

What role did Washington play at the Constitutional Convention?

Washington is recorded as having given only a single speech at the beginning of the Convention and as having introduced a modification of the Constitution near the end of the proceedings. His presence at the Convention was important to the eventual public acceptance of its deliberations. In addition, the common belief that he would serve as the nation's first president influenced deliberations and led to a stronger presidency.

Were votes taken at the Constitutional Convention final?

No, the delegates specified that votes could be retaken. In addition, they specified that votes would not be recorded under individual names. Both rules were adopted to encourage flexibility and compromise.

Did the public have significant input into the Constitutional Convention?

The public was aware that such a convention was being held, and, at least indirectly, they had selected representatives through their state legislatures. However, the delegates kept convention proceedings secret to discourage partisanship and potential mob actions within the city of Philadelphia (the Second Continental Congress once moved to New Jersey to avoid such activity).

Who was the Convention's official secretary?

Major William Jackson of Philadelphia was. Jackson's notes were quite sketchy, mostly consisting of recorded votes.

What is the primary source of information about the proceedings at the Constitutional Convention?

The primary source of information comes from notes that James Madison took of the convention proceedings. These can be supplemented with recollections of various participants and notes and letters that they took during the Convention. Historian Max Farrand collected these writings in a four-volume work titled *Records of the Federal Convention of 1787*, which James H. Hutson supplemented with an additional volume in 1987. Writings by the supporters and opponents of the Constitution also cast considerable light on the controversies of the day.

When did James Madison's extensive notes of the Convention become available?

After his death in 1836, Dolley Madison sold his notes to the U.S. government for $30,000. These were first printed in 1840.

To what extent should contemporary interpreters base understandings of the Constitution on James Madison's notes and other convention records?

This is a matter for dispute. Some proponents of "original intent" think that such records are fairly authoritative for settling contemporary controversies. Others think that the "original intent" of the authors of the document—not then available to the general public—was less important than the "original intent" of those who ratified the document. Still others argue that the language of the Constitution should speak for itself or that the Constitution should be interpreted with contemporary needs in mind rather than according to the intention of those who formulated and/or ratified it. Often these are the kinds of issues that the Supreme Court has to resolve. Notably, individuals who attended the Convention themselves disagreed about its meaning.

What occupied the Constitutional Convention during its opening weeks?

A plan proposed by Edmund Randolph as governor and head of the Virginia Delegation led off the deliberations. Scholars typically refer to this plan as the Virginia Plan.

Who authored the Virginia Plan, which served as the basis for opening deliberations at the Constitutional Convention?

Although a number of delegates probably had a role in the plan, James Madison is believed to be the plan's primary author. Madison had spent months prior to the Convention reading works of political theory and writing essays on the weaknesses of prior confederations and the vices of the existing political system.

How did the Virginia Plan compare with the system of government under the existing Articles of Confederation?

The Virginia Plan proposed giving the national government significantly expanded powers.

How many branches of government did the Virginia Plan propose?

In contrast to the Articles of Confederation, in which Congress was the only real branch of government, the Virginia Plan proposed three branches—legislative, executive, and judicial.

How did the Virginia Plan propose representing states in Congress?

It proposed that states would be represented in both houses of Congress according to population. Not only did this comport well with democratic theory, but it also favored a populous state like Virginia, which at the time included today's West Virginia and Kentucky, and which accordingly had more residents than any other state.

Did the Virginia Plan propose any unique institutions?

In comparison with the Articles of Confederation, much that the Virginia Plan proposed was novel. One institution that the Virginia Plan proposed that did not make it into the final Constitution was a Council of Revision.

What was the proposed Council of Revision?

It would have consisted of members of the executive branch and the judiciary, who would have had power to veto state and federal laws. Although the Constitution never incorporated this specific institution, the presidential veto and the institution of judicial review (whereby courts can invalidate legislation deemed to be unconstitutional) arguably embody some elements of this mechanism.

Did the delegates to the Convention offer any alternatives to the Virginia Plan?

Yes. The most important alternative was the New Jersey Plan, which William Paterson of New Jersey introduced after about two weeks of debate.

How did the New Jersey Plan compare to the Virginia Plan?

Partly because the New Jersey Plan followed weeks of discussion of the Virginia Plan, it incorporated a number of elements—including a stronger (albeit unicameral) Congress, and a national government with three branches—that the Virginia Plan contained. The New Jersey Plan also recognized that the new national government would have to be stronger than that under the Articles of Confederation.

What was the central difference between the Virginia and New Jersey Plans?

Whereas the Virginia Plan proposed that representation in both houses of Congress should be according to population, the New Jersey Plan proposed that each state should continue to have the equal representation in the legislature that it already had in the Articles of Confederation. As one of the less populous states, New Jersey would have profited from continuing this system of representation just as Virginia would have profited from the system of proportional representation that it proposed.

How did the delegates resolve this dispute between the proposal for representation in the Virginia Plan and the proposal for representation in the New Jersey Plan?

Under a plan that the Convention eventually accepted, states would be represented according to population in the House of Representatives and equally in the Senate.

What is the name of this compromise?

It is called the Connecticut, or Great, Compromise. Without it, it is doubtful that the Constitution would have been accepted.

Which delegate proposed that the delegates at the Constitutional Convention should begin each day with prayer?

Benjamin Franklin did. He introduced this proposal during the time of bitter debate over how states should be represented.

Did the Convention adopt the proposal?

No, delegates feared that the public might sense the dissention within the body if it began to bring in a clergyman each day.

In addition to state representation, what were other major points of controversy at the Constitutional Convention?

A number of disputes related to the taxation and representation of slaves. The Northern states wanted slaves to count for purposes of taxation but not for purposes of representation, and, not surprisingly, a number of Southern states wanted exactly the reverse. Eventually, delegates resolved this controversy by the three-fifths compromise, which provided that slaves would count as three-fifths of a person for both purposes.

There was also controversy about how long slave importation could continue. Eventually, the Convention granted Congress power to regulate this trade, but only after the year 1808.

Other than state representation and slavery, were there other points of controversy at the Constitutional Convention?

Almost every proposal introduced at the convention resulted in some controversy, and the Constitution has been correctly referred to as "a bundle of compromises." A major point of contention centered on the selection of the president. Eventually, the Convention settled on an electoral college mechanism that provided that individuals who selected the president would not be affiliated with Congress. In an imitation of the Great Compromise between the most populous and least populous states, delegates provided that such electors would be apportioned according to the number of representatives and senators that each state possessed.

Why didn't the delegates simply provide for direct popular election of the president?

Some were concerned that ordinary individuals would be unfamiliar with those from out of state. There were no computers to count votes in an expeditious fashion. Moreover, many delegates were wary of direct democracy and thought that it was better to "filter" popular opinion through electors rather than allowing the public to vote directly on such matters.

What were the primary motives of those who attended the Constitutional Convention?

This is the subject of continuing scholarly dispute. Certainly, many delegates believed that the existing government under the Articles of Confederation was not strong enough to govern the nation or to represent the nation in foreign affairs. In the wake of Shays' Rebellion, many were also concerned about the ability of states to protect themselves from domestic insurrections and about the ability of the national government to provide for economic stability and growth.

Some have attributed the actions of the Framers to personal economic motives. Early in this century, historian Charles Beard wrote a book titled *An Economic Interpretation of the Constitution of the United States* (1949) in which he tried to show how supporters of the Constitution generally stood to gain financially from the government it established. His thesis has not held up particularly well under close scrutiny.

Undoubtedly, delegates had mixed motives. Most delegates conscientiously attempted to represent both the interests of their states and regions and the nation as a whole. It is doubtful if any contemporary group could lay any better claim to statesmanship than could the Founders.

Who is recorded as making the last comment at the Constitutional Convention?

According to James Madison's notes, the venerable Benjamin Franklin, who made note of a sun that was painted on the back of Washington's Chippendale chair at the front of the room, observed that artists had found it difficult to distinguish between a rising and a setting sun, but he had concluded that the sun was rising on a new day for America.

On what date did the delegates sign the Constitution?

They signed on September 17, 1787.

How many delegates signed the Constitution?

Thirty-nine (one by proxy) of forty-one delegates who remained at the Convention on September 17, 1787, signed the document.

Which delegates who remained on September 17 refused to sign?

Elbridge Gerry (MA), Edmund Randolph (VA), and George Mason (VA) all were present but refused to sign.

Which newspaper was the first to publish the Constitution?

The *Pennsylvania Packet* published it two days after it was signed. It took all four pages of the paper, which did not publish any other news on that day.

RATIFICATION OF THE CONSTITUTION

What provision did the designers of the Constitution make for its ratification?

The delegates to the Convention specified that it would go into effect among ratifying states when conventions in 9 or more states (two-thirds of the 12 that had attended the Convention) gave their consent.

Did this follow procedures set out in the Articles of Confederation?

No. The Articles had provided that Congress would propose amendments subject to the unanimous ratification of state legislatures.

Why did the delegates to the Convention propose a different method?

They thought that conventions were more closely tied to popular will than were state legislators (who had been chosen primarily to enact ordinary laws), and they wanted to ground the new Constitution, which they wanted to serve as fundamental law, in popular consent. Delegates realized that state legislators would be losing power vis-à-vis the new Congress, and they wanted the new constitution to have a good chance for adoption. Since Rhode Island had not even sent delegates to Philadelphia, it seemed especially unlikely that it would initially give its consent.

Did everyone in America support the new Constitution?

Far from it! The nation divided into Federalists, who supported the new document, Anti-Federalists, who opposed it, and others who attempted to ascertain whether the proposed Constitution was better than the existing government under the Articles of Confederation.

Where did the term "Federalist" originate?

Originally, contemporaries called the government under the Articles of Confederation a federal government. The proponents of the new Constitution, who argued that it was "partly national" and "partly federal," took some of the sting out of opponents' arguments by claiming the federal moniker for themselves. Similarly, by designating their opponents as "antis," Federalists were able to stress that they were advocating a more positive solution.

What were the primary advantages of the Federalists?

Federalist leaders emerged from a summer of intense secret negotiations in which they understood the rationale for existing compromises better than those who had not attended. Federalists were proposing a positive remedy for the perceived weaknesses under the Articles of Confederation. They touted the prestige of individuals like George Washington and Benjamin Franklin who had attended the Convention. They further had the support of financial interests who thought that political stability would foster economic growth and development, and they had strong support among leading newspapers throughout the former colonies.

What were the primary concerns of the Anti-Federalists?

Many were very protective of states' rights and of their own places within existing state governments. Some thought that it would be impossible to establish republican government over such a large land area as the United States. Others feared that judges, senators, or even the newly created presidency might form an oppressive aristocracy. Finally, many thought that the new Constitution should include a bill of rights specifically protecting individual citizens against the powers of the new national government.

How did the Federalists/Anti-Federalist debate proceed?

Each side attempted to elect proponents of its views to the state ratifying conventions, and published newspaper articles and pamphlets arguing for their respective positions.

What was the quality of this discourse?

On the whole it was quite high. Federalists had an advantage in the eastern cities where the press was most powerful, and both sides sometimes appealed to prejudices, as when, at the Virginia Ratifying Convention, Anti-Federalist Patrick Henry said that the new Constitution threatened the continuing existence of slavery, and when former delegates from South Carolina and Georgia assured their constituents that the new Constitution protected the institution of slavery. Still, numerous collections of Federalist and Anti-Federalist essays indicate that many of the arguments for and against the Constitution were quite sophisticated.

What is the best-known work that emerged from these debates?

A series of 85 articles, originally published in New York newspapers and then collected as a book called *The Federalist*, remains a leading exposition of Federalist principles.

Who authored these essays?

Alexander Hamilton (NY), James Madison (VA), and John Jay (NY) authored the essays under the pen name of Publius, a Roman statesman. Since they had attended the Constitutional Convention, Hamilton and Madison had some inside information. John Jay, who had not attended, mostly addressed issues of foreign policy.

What are the best known *Federalist* essays?

The most famous is *Federalist* No. 10 in which James Madison sought to refute Anti-Federalist fears that government was unsustainable over a large land area by arguing that a larger nation could actively promote such government by moderating the vices of factions. In *Federalist* No. 78, Hamilton further argued that the new Constitution would not elevate judges over others but that the exercise of judicial review of legislation would elevate the new constitution over all.

What were the results of the Federalist/Anti-Federalist debates?

In time the states ratified the Constitution. It initially went into effect without the participation of North Carolina and Rhode Island. Federalists refused to allow for the "conditional" ratification of the document (the vote by the conventions was all or nothing), but they did allow conventions to propose recommendatory amendments.

Did these recommendations have any effect?

Yes, in time they became the basis for the first 10 amendments to the Constitution, which contemporary scholars call the Bill of Rights. Congress designed these amendments specifically to protect individual rights against the new national government.

THE PREAMBLE TO THE CONSTITUTION

What is the name of the opening paragraph of the Constitution?

Scholars typically call this the preamble, although the Constitution does not specifically use this designation.

Does the preamble grant any powers to, or provide any specific limits on, government?

No.

How does the preamble of the U.S. Constitution differ from those of contemporary state constitutions?

Many such constitutions began with a bill or declaration of rights and with a reference to the general ends of government.

What are the opening words of the preamble (and, thus, of the Constitution)?

They are "We the People of the United States."

How does the wording of the preamble of the U.S. Constitution differ from that of the Articles of Confederation?

The preamble to the Articles listed each of the states by name.

Under the Constitution, are the people sovereign?

The Constitution does not specifically use the word "sovereignty," which many European theorists had used to describe the ultimate authority within a governmental system. The concept of sovereignty is not as easily applied to a system like that in the United States, which uses a system of divided and separate powers. However, the people, at least when exercising their power through the amending process, come closest in the American system to exercising such sovereignty.

What does the preamble contain?

The preamble contains a list of the purposes for which the Constitution was established.

How many such purposes does the preamble list?

It lists only six, but they are broad.

What purposes of government does the preamble articulate?

The preamble states the following purposes:

1. "To form a more perfect Union,"
2. "To establish justice,"
3. "To insure domestic tranquility,"
4. "To provide for the common defense,"
5. "To promote the general welfare," and
6. "To secure the blessings of liberty to ourselves and our posterity"

Why does the preamble refer to "a more perfect Union"?

At the time the delegates wrote the U.S. Constitution, the 13 former British colonies already had a weak form of government among them known as the Articles of Confederation that the new constitution was designed to replace.

What is the meaning of insuring domestic tranquility?

Obviously, all governments try to provide for peace among their citizens. This is probably a more specific reference to Shays' Rebellion, an uprising among debtors and taxpayers in Massachusetts in the winter of 1786–1787 that persuaded many leading citizens that the Articles of Confederations was inadequate to protect its citizens.

Why did the Framers think it necessary to establish justice?

Attaining justice, or some semblance thereof, is a key goal of any legitimate government. Under the Articles of Confederation, many states, in their quest for democracy, had arguably adopted systems that led to almost complete domination by the legislative branch. Many Framers believed that these state legislatures had enacted laws that unduly favored some social and economic interests (typically debtors over creditors) over others.

How, if at all, did the Framers think that the Articles of Confederation had jeopardized the common defense?

Under the Articles, there was no national army. The national government could request that states supply troops for individual contingencies, but states often proved reluctant to supply troops to defend other states. In addition, the national government was unable to get states to comply with the terms of the Treaty of Paris that had ended the Revolutionary War. In turn, the British refused to remove their troops from the Northwest Territory as stipulated in this treaty. Generally, American diplomats found that their nation was not received abroad with the same kind of respect as were other nations.

What is the general welfare?

Although the Constitution does not define the general welfare, the idea embodies the idea of a commonwealth where individuals and states work on behalf of the common good rather than simply for their own self-interests.

What does the term "the blessings of liberty" mean?

It indicates that liberty is not only an end in and of itself but also a means to other ends. American liberty has arguably led to achievements in art, literature, science, industry, and other fields that would be impossible without such liberty.

How long did the Framers intend for the Constitution to last?

With the short-lived Articles of Confederation in their field of view, the Framers could only hope for greater permanence. The reference to "posterity" in the preamble to the Constitution indicates that the Framers hoped the document would bless succeeding generations. The Framers' inclusion of an amending mechanism further indicates that they recognized that the document would have to change over time if it were to be successful.

BIBLIOGRAPHY

Bernard Bailyn, *The Ideological Origins of the American Revolution* (Cambridge, MA: Harvard University Press, 1967).
Carl L. Becker, *The Declaration of Independence: A Study in the History of Political Ideas* (New York: Vintage Books, 1970).

Richard Beeman, *Our Lives, Our Fortunes & Our Sacred Honor: The Forging of American Independence, 1774–1776* (New York: Basic Books, 2013).

Richard Beeman, *Plain, Honest Men: The Making of the American Constitution* (New York: Random House, 2009).

Carol Berkin, *A Brilliant Solution: Inventing the American Constitution* (New York: Harcourt, 2002).

Sol Bloom, *The Story of the Constitution* (Washington, D.C.: United States Constitution Sesquicentennial Commission, 1937).

Catherine Drinker Bowen, *Miracle at Philadelphia* (Boston: Little, Brown and Company, 1966).

M. E. Bradford, *Founding Fathers: Brief Lives of the Framers of the United States Constitution,* 2nd ed. (Lawrence: University Press of Kansas, 1982).

The Constitution. Special issue of *LIFE,* Vol. 10, Fall 1987.

Max Farrand, *The Records of the Federal Convention of 1787,* 4 vols. (New Haven, CT: Yale University Press, 1966).

Alexander Hamilton, James Madison, and John Jay, *The Federalist Papers,* Clinton Rossiter, ed. (New York: New American Library, 1961).

David D. Hendrickson, *Peace Pact: The Lost World of the American Founding* (Lawrence: University Press of Kansas, 2003).

Merrill Jensen, *The Articles of Confederation* (Madison: University of Wisconsin Press, 1966).

James H. Hutson, ed. *Supplement to Max Farrand's* The Records of the Federal Convention of 1787. New Haven, CT: Yale University Press.

Ralph Ketcham, *Framed for Posterity: The Enduring Philosophy of the Constitution* (Lawrence: University Press of Kansas, 1993).

Donald S. Lutz, *The Origins of American Constitutionalism* (Baton Rouge: Louisiana State University Press, 1968).

Dorothy McGee, *Framers of the Constitution* (New York: Dodd, Mead & Company, 1968).

Pauline Maier, *American Scripture: Making the Declaration of Independence* (New York: Alfred A. Knopf, 1997).

Dumas Malone, *The Story of the Declaration of Independence* (New York: Oxford University Press, 1954).

Forrest McDonald, *Novus Ordo Seclorum: The Intellectual Origins of the Constitution* (Lawrence: The University Press of Kansas, 1985).

William L. Miller, *The Business of May Next: James Madison & the Founding* (Charlottesville: University Press of Virginia, 1992).

Richard B. Morris, *Witnesses at the Creation: Hamilton, Madison, Jay, and the Constitution* (New York: New American Library, 1985).

William Peters, *A More Perfect Union: The Making of the United States Constitution* (New York: Crown Publications, Inc., 1987).

David Brian Robertson, *The Constitution and America's Destiny* (New York: Cambridge University Press, 2005).

Clinton Rossiter, *1787: The Grand Convention* (New York: W. W. Norton and Company, 1966).

Ellis Sandoz, ed. *Political Sermons of the American Founding ERA: 1730–1805* (Indianapolis: Liberty Fund, Inc., 1991).

David O. Stewart, *The Summer of 1787: The Men Who Invented the Constitution* (New York: Simon & Schuster, 2007).

Garry Wills, *Inventing America: Jefferson's Declaration of Independence* (New York: Doubleday & Company, Inc., 1978).

Gordon S. Wood, *The Creation of the American Republic: 1776–1787* (Williamsburg: The University of North Carolina Press, 1969).

John R. Vile, *A Companion to the United States Constitution and Its Amendments,* 5th ed. (Lanham, MD: Rowman & Littlefield, 2011).

John R. Vile, *The Constitutional Convention of 1787: A Comprehensive Encyclopedia of America's Founding,* 2 vols. (Santa Barbara, CA: ABC-CLIO, 2005).

John R. Vile, *The Writing and Ratification of the U.S. Constitution: Practical Virtue in Action* (Lanham, MD: Rowman & Littlefield, 2012).

Chapter 2
Article I: The Legislative Branch

CONSTITUTIONAL DIVISIONS

How did the Framers divide the Constitution?
They divided it into a series of articles, which are much like chapters in a book.

How many articles are there in the U.S. Constitution?
There are seven. These are usually listed as capitalized Roman numerals, much as in an outline. On occasion, scholars sometimes also refer to constitutional amendments as articles, but it is more common to list them by Arabic numbers.

Which of the seven articles in the Constitution is the longest?
Article I is.

Which of the seven articles in the Constitution is the shortest?
Unless one counts the signatures that are attached, Article VII is the shortest. If these signatures are counted, then Article V is the shortest.

The articles are divided into units called sections.
Are all of the articles so subdivided?
No, only the first four are.

What name do scholars often give to the first three articles of the Constitution?
They call these the "distributing articles" because they divide powers among the three branches of government.

BACKGROUND

What is the subject of Article I?
It deals with legislative powers.

The U.S. capitol building in Washington D.C. (Jiawangkun/Dreamstime.com)

Why does the Constitution outline legislative powers in the first article?

In establishing a republican, or representative, form of government, the Founders undoubtedly anticipated that the legislature, as an elected branch of government, would be closest to, and most representative of, the people. This was the only significant branch of government under the previous Articles of Confederation, and it was logical to assume that this branch would be the most powerful under the new constitution as well.

Which organization of the national government exercises legislative powers?

Congress does.

What is a congress?

The term "Congress" is used to refer to an assembly. When the colonists had sent representatives in 1765 to protest the Stamp Act, they called this meeting the Stamp Act Congress. Subsequently, the First and Second Continental Congresses had led the opposition to British assertions of parliamentary sovereignty that eventually led to the Revolutionary War. The legislative branch under the Articles of Confederation was also designated as a congress.

The Framers may have preferred the term "Congress" in order to distinguish their legislature from the British Parliament whose authority to tax and govern they had rejected in the Revolutionary War.

How did the Framers divide Congress?

They divided it into chambers, known as houses.

How many houses does Congress have?

Congress has two houses.

What is the name of a legislature with two houses?

Such a legislature is known as a bicameral body. A unicameral legislature such as that under the Articles of Confederation, by contrast, has only one house.

Where did the principle of bicameralism arise?

The British parliament has two houses—the House of Commons, whose members are elected by the people, and the House of Lords, most of whose members are hereditary and serve for life.

What is the purpose of bicameralism?

In England, bicameralism served to provide representation for different classes. In the United States, by contrast, the people elect members of both houses of Congress (although prior to the adoption of the Seventeenth Amendment, state legislatures selected members of the Senate). The American Framers intended for bicameralism to guard against precipitous and improvident legislation. When Thomas Jefferson asked George Washington about this, Washington reputedly poured some of his coffee into a saucer and blew over it, indicating that the Senate was to serve, like his breath, to cool the passions of the House.

Are there any disadvantages to bicameralism?

The need to get approval of two houses, rather than one, undoubtedly slows the progress, and sometimes results in the death, not only of improvident and unpopular legislation but also of worthy legislation that may have majority support.

THE HOUSE OF REPRESENTATIVES

Which House of Congress does the Constitution mention first?

The Senate (See Article I, Section 1). Generally, however, scholars call the House of Representatives the lower house and the Senate the upper house.

Who selects members of the House of Representatives?

Voters of the states select them.

How long is a term of a member of the House of Representatives?

A term is two years. This is the shortest term that the U.S. Constitution describes.

Why are the terms of members of the House of Representatives so short?

The Framers of the Constitution wanted the House of Representatives to be close to the people, and short terms were thought to be one way of assuring this. Some members of the Constitutional Convention, drawing from state experience, actually wanted members to be elected annually. A popular slogan during the Articles of Confederation asserted that, "Tyranny [or despotic government] begins, when annual elections end." Given the distances that representatives would have to travel to get to the nation's capital and the knowledge and experience that they would need to legislate on matters of national importance, a one-year term was not especially practical.

Are there any adverse consequences of having members of the House of Representatives serve for two-year terms?

Because of their short terms, members of the House of Representatives may sometimes vote on the basis of short-term political considerations of their districts rather than for what they believe to be the long-term good of the nation. They must also devote significant amounts of their time to campaigning and its accompanying fund-raising.

How many terms may a member of the House of Representatives serve?

Currently, the Constitution does not provide any limits. Moreover, like the Senate, the House provides some incentives for members to run for multiple terms by basing many prize committee assignments largely on seniority. In *U.S. Term Limits v. Thornton* (1995), the Supreme Court responded to Arkansas' attempt to impose such limits by ruling that only a constitutional amendment could impose such additional limits.

How many seats are open for election in the House of Representatives in each regular election?

All of them (currently 435) are open every two years. As noted above, members serve for two-year terms, and regular elections for all members are held every two years.

What criteria does the Constitution establish for voting for a member of the U.S. House of Representatives or U.S. Senate?

The criteria for voting for members of Congress are the same as those that a state has specified for voting for the larger house of its state legislature. This provision allowed members of the Constitutional Convention to leave existing state voting qualifications in place rather than having to set a single nationwide standard, which would have been highly contested.

According to the Constitution, how old must an individual be in order to serve as member of the House of Representatives?

Such an individual must be at least 25 years of age.

What, if any, other qualifications does the Constitution require for a person to be a member of the House of Representatives?

An individual must have been a U.S. citizen for at least seven years and must be a resident of the state that elects him.

Does the U.S. Constitution require members of the House to be residents of the districts that select them?

No, it does not. By convention, representatives are expected to be from the districts that select them, but this requirement is not spelled out in the Constitution.

What kind of system of representation does the United States use to select members of the House of Representatives?

The United States currently uses what is known as a single-member district system. To win a House seat, an individual must win a plurality (the highest number) of voters within that district. By contrast, some foreign democratic governments use proportional systems that assign seats to parties based on the percentages of votes that they receive in an election.

What is the central consequence of using a single member system rather than a system of proportional representation?

Most experts believe that a single-member district system is more likely to promote a two-party, rather than to a multiparty, system. Under a single-member district, a party receives no electoral reward for winning a percentage in a district that is less than a plurality, whereas they might get some seats under a proportional system. The winner-take-all presidential system might also reinforce the two-party system since third-and fourth-party candidates rarely, if ever, translate votes into support within the Congress.

How does the Constitution apportion U.S. Representatives?

It apportions them by population. However, the Constitution guarantees each state at least one vote.

How many classes of people does the original formula for representation in the U.S. House of Representatives list?

It lists four. These four classes are as follows:

1. "Free persons." At the time the Constitution was written, white men and women would have been considered to be free, but only men would have had the right to vote. The Constitution does not, however, list this restriction, although Section 2 of the Fourteenth Amendment eventually confirmed the restriction, which was not overturned until states ratified the Nineteenth Amendment in 1920.
2. "Those bound to service for a number of years." This refers to indentured servants who earned their passage to the United States by agreeing to serve as a servant for a specified number of years. Such servants were to count the same as free persons.
3. "Indians not taxed." These individuals, members of sovereign tribes, were not included in the population for determining representation in the House of Representatives.
4. "All other persons." This is an oblique reference to those held as slaves. Undoubtedly cognizant of the manner in which the institution of slavery conflicted with their professed dedication to liberty, the Founders never mentioned the terms "slaves" or "slavery" in the Constitution.

How did the original Constitution count slaves in apportioning the House of Representatives?

It counted such "other persons" as three-fifths of a person for both taxation and representation. This resulted from the Three-Fifths Compromise that was struck at the Constitutional Convention between representatives in the North, who had relatively few slaves, and those in the South, where slavery was still a prominent institution. Fortunately, the Thirteenth and Fourteenth Amendments have superseded the three-fifths clause.

How does the government ascertain the population of states in order to apportion membership in the House of Representatives?

The Constitution directs the government to make an "enumeration," better known as a census, every 10 years to determine such apportionment.

The Constitution specified that the first such enumeration must be made within three years of the meeting of the first Congress.

What is the maximum number of U.S. Representatives that the U.S. Constitution permits?

The Constitution specifies that there shall be no more than 1 representative for every 30,000 persons. Had the nation allocated the maximum number of representatives under this standard, there would be more than 10,000 members of Congress today.

How many representatives did the Constitution initially allocate to the states?

The number varied from 1 to 10, based on estimates of their respective populations. The enumeration of representation for the first Congress gives an idea of the respective population of the states at the time the Constitution was written. The Constitution awarded Rhode Island and Delaware only 1 representative each. Georgia was entitled to 3 representatives and New Jersey to 4. North and South Carolina and Connecticut each had 5 representatives, New York and Maryland had 6, Pennsylvania and Massachusetts had 8, and Virginia had 10. Although New Jersey delegates allied themselves with delegates from the small states at the Constitutional Convention, New Jersey was far from the smallest. By contrast, Virginia, clearly identified at the Convention with the interests of the large states, did have the largest population.

At present, seven states each have only a single representative. California currently has the largest number of representatives—now more than 50.

How did the Constitution provide for filling vacancies in the House of Representatives?

When vacancies occur, state governors call for new elections.

What is the only specific officer of the House of Representatives that the Constitution mentions?

The Speaker of the House is the only officer that the Constitution mentions.

What does the Speaker of the House do?

The Speaker is responsible for helping to set the agenda of the House and for presiding over it (although he often delegates the latter task to others). The Speaker also has a role in the selection of Committee chairs.

How powerful is the Speaker of the House?

Because the Constitution says so little about this office in the Constitution, the power of the Speaker can vary tremendously from one Congress and from one individual to another. Generally speaking, this individual's power as a representative of the most democratic House of the most democratic branch of government is likely to be second only to the president's.

How many Speakers of the House of Representative have become presidents?

To date, the only Speaker to become president was Tennessee's James K. Polk, who served as House Speaker from 1835–1839 and as president from 1845–1849. See appendices marked "U.S. Presidents" and "Speakers of the House of Representatives."

Who chooses the Speaker of the House of Representatives?

The members of that body choose their own speaker. This is typically a partisan vote (with each party member casting a vote for the leaders of his/ her party) that takes place at the beginning of each new Congress or upon the occasion of a vacancy in the speakership.

Is the speaker of the House necessarily from the same political party as the president?

No, the Constitution does not require this. Sometimes there is a president from one party and a majority of one or both houses of Congress from another. This is known as "divided government." Although this has been fairly common in recent American history, such divided governments are almost unknown in parliamentary democracies where the majority party or coalition chooses the prime minister, or chief executive.

Does the Constitution require that the speaker of the House be a member of that body?

No, the Constitution is silent on the subject. To date, however, the House has always chosen its speaker from among its members.

May the speaker of the House vote?

The Constitution does not specify. Traditionally, the speaker votes only in cases of ties.

What is the power of impeachment?

The power of impeachment is the power to bring charges against a government official for wrongdoing.

Which house of Congress has the power of impeachment?

The Constitution vests the power to impeach in the House of Representatives, but trials of impeachment take place in the Senate.

THE SENATE

How many senators does the Constitution designate to each state?

The Constitution grants each state, regardless of its size, two senators. At the Constitutional Convention, the New Jersey Plan had proposed that states have an equal vote in the national legislature, as they had been under the Articles of Confederation. The Virginia Plan had advocated that representation in Congress be based on population. The Connecticut, or Great, Compromise is embodied in the varied scheme of representation used for the House of Representatives and the U.S. Senate.

What provision did the original Constitution make for selecting senators?

It provided that state legislatures would select them.

How do Americans choose such senators today?

The Seventeenth Amendment, adopted in 1913, provided that the people of each state would henceforth directly elect senators.

What is the term of a U.S. senator?

The term is for six years.

Why is the term of senators longer than that of members of the House of Representatives?

The Framers anticipated that the Senate would help to serve as a brake on impetuous actions taken by the House of Representatives. The Framers designed the six-year term to allow senators to keep a longer-term perspective in view when they cast their votes. It also allows individual senators to spend a longer time in that body to develop expertise and thus to provide greater continuity.

Members of the upper house of the English Parliament (the House of Lords) are largely hereditary and serve for life. By comparison, the term of a member of the U.S. Senate is much closer to that of members of the House of Representatives than to the English House of Lords.

What were the terms of senators in the first Congress?

Senators were divided into three groups. Their initial terms were two years, four years, and six years, respectively, to secure the current rotation.

How many senatorial seats are up for election every two years?

Either 33 or 34 seats are up for election every two years.

What age requirement did the Constitution establish for members of the U.S. Senate?

It required that they be 30 years of age or older. This indicates that the Framers were aiming for a somewhat higher level of maturity among senators than among members of the House (who were only required to be 25).

What are the other constitutional requirements for a Senator?

The Constitution requires senators to be citizens of the United States for at least nine years and inhabitants of the states that elect them.

Who does the Constitution designate as president of the U.S. Senate?

It designates the vice president. Other than being prepared to assume the presidency, this is the only formal duty that the Constitution designates for the vice president. This duty means that the vice president plays a role in both the legislative and executive branches, arguably breaching any strict theory of separation of powers.

Does the vice president have authority to vote in the Senate?

Yes, but only in cases of a tie.

Other than the vice president who serves as president of the Senate, what is the only other Senate office that the U.S. Constitution specifically designates?

The Senate pro tempore is.

What does the term "pro tempore" mean?

It means temporarily, or "for the time being."

Who selects the Senate pro tempore?

The Senate selects the Senate pro tempore.

Does the Constitution require that the Senate pro tempore be a member of that body?

No, it does not, but this has been the practice.

What is the function of the Senate pro tempore?

The Constitution designates this individual to preside over the Senate in the absence of the vice president.

Is the Senate pro tempore the most powerful member of the Senate?

Generally speaking, the Senate pro tempore is not the most powerful. Although the Constitution does not mention the office, the most powerful individual in the Senate is typically the Senate majority leader, whose status in the Senate corresponds to that of the House majority leader, who assists the speaker. Other officers include party whips, who are tasked with attempting to line up individuals to vote with their party, especially on key issues.

RULES AND PROCEDURES FOR CONGRESS

Which institution of government has the power to try impeachments?

The U.S. Senate does.

Does any other institution share in this power?

No; the Constitution says the U.S. Senate has the sole power of impeachment. As a result, courts have been extremely hesitant to intervene in such proceedings. In *Nixon v. United States* (1993), the Supreme Court used this language to justify deferring to a Senate procedure whereby 12 senators held impeachment hearings of 2 federal judges, and the full Senate later voted on the basis of a report issued by this committee.

What does the Constitution require senators to do prior to trying a case of impeachment?

It requires them to take an oath or affirmation.

Who presides over Senate trials of the president?

The chief justice of the United States presides in such cases.

Who presides over the Senate when the vice president is on trial?

The Constitution does not specify. Presumably, the vice president would not preside over his own trial. It is unclear whether such a job would ordinarily fall to the president pro tempore of the Senate or the chief justice of the United States.

What vote does the Constitution require in the Senate to convict an individual who has been impeached?

The Constitution requires a two-thirds majority for conviction.

Why does the Constitution require a two-thirds majority in impeachment trials?

The Constitution designed this supermajority vote to assure that individuals were removed for specified crimes rather than because of political unpopularity.

What are the consequences of impeachment and conviction?

The consequences are removal from office and possible disqualification for office.

Can an individual who has been convicted of an impeachable offense and removed from office be subsequently punished in the courts?

Yes.

What is a filibuster?

A filibuster is a procedure by which a determined group of senators can "talk a bill to death," absent a vote of two-thirds of their colleagues to demand a vote on it.

What does the Constitution say about this mechanism?

Nothing; it is an extraconstitutional development. Currently, in due course, rules allow 60 senators to invoke cloture, which brings debate to an end.

Who establishes "the times, places and manner of holding elections for Senators and Representatives"?

The state legislatures have this responsibility.

Does the Constitution subject these state regulations for the times, places, and manner of holding congressional elections to any oversight?

Yes, the Constitution further specifies that Congress may alter such regulations "except as to the places of chusing [sic] Senators." The Seventeenth Amendment—which now specifies that the people, rather than their state legislatures, select senators—further altered this phrase.

How frequently must Congress assemble?

The Constitution specifies that Congress must assemble at least once a year.

What date did the Constitution specify for the meeting of the first Congress?

It specified the first Monday in December.

Under the Constitution of 1787, on what day did Congress hold its first meeting?

It was to begin its first meeting on January 21 of each year. The Twentieth Amendment, which sets the date on January 3, has superseded this provision.

Who does the Constitution designate as the judge of the elections, returns, and qualifications of members of Congress?

It made each house its own judge. However, in *Powell v. McCormack* (1969), the Supreme Court ruled that Congress may not add to the constitutionally prescribed age, citizenship, and residency qualifications of a member of Congress in deciding whether to seat a member. In this case, the Court ruled that if Congress wanted to keep the flamboyant Harlem representative Adam Clayton Powell from serving, the House would have to expel him by the required two-thirds majority.

What is a quorum?

A quorum is the majority required to do business in a governing body.

What constitutes a quorum of each house of Congress?

A majority constitutes such a quorum. In conducting ordinary business, Congress (whose members may also be working on committee assignments) typically designates itself as a committee of the whole, which does not require a majority to be in attendance.

What, if anything, can Congress do to get absent members to attend?

The Constitution enables each house to compel the attendance of members through use of penalties that each house prescribes.

Who determines the rules of each house of Congress?

Each determines its own rules.

On what grounds may Congress punish its members?

The Constitution specifies that members may be punished for "disorderly behavior."

May each house of Congress expel members for such disorderly behavior?

Yes, each house has authority to do so, although censure (reprimand) is more common.

What vote does the Constitution require for a house of Congress to expel one of its members?

The Constitution requires a two-thirds vote in the house expelling such a member.

Does the Constitution require Congress to keep and publish a journal?

Yes, this document is now designated as the *Congressional Record.*

Is the *Congressional Record* required to report all activities of Congress?

No, the Constitution specifically permits some proceedings to be kept secret. Members are also accorded the privilege of editing remarks they have made in chambers. Members also add information about their activities and matters of interest to individuals in their districts.

How many members of Congress must make a request before votes are recorded in the *Record*?

One-fifth of the members must do so.

What is the maximum length of time that one house can adjourn without permission of the other during a regular session?

Three days is the maximum.

Does the Constitution permit one house of Congress to meet at a place other than that designated for such meetings?

No.

Who sets the salaries of members of Congress?

Congress collectively sets these salaries. Voters can retaliate against members of Congress whom they believe have voted for excessive pay increases. Moreover, the Twenty-Seventh Amendment now requires there to be an intervening election before pay raises can go into effect.

Who pays the salaries of members of Congress?

The U.S. Treasury pays them. This undoubtedly gives members, including senators who were—prior to the Seventeenth Amendment—elected by state legislatures, greater freedom from state control than they would otherwise have. Under the Articles of Confederation, which emphasized state sovereignty, states paid for their delegates to Congress.

What privileges do members of Congress have when attending or going to and from sessions?

The Constitution privileges them from arrests except in cases of treason, felony, or breach of the peace. Felonies and breaches of the peace, however, encompass all criminal matters, leaving the protection as a guarantee only against civil arrests, which are no longer made.

Do members of Congress have any privileges other than that against civil arrests when traveling to sessions?

Yes, they may not be questioned (or indicted) for speeches or debates within Congress. This guarantee, which the Framers designed to encourage vigorous legislative debate, preceded the freedom of speech guaranteed in the First Amendment.

Can the president appoint a member of Congress to an office created during the time this member was serving in Congress?

No. The Constitution also prohibits members of Congress from being appointed to any office "the Emoluments whereof shall have been increased during such time." This later restriction has sometimes been evaded by the so-called Saxbe-Fix.

What is an emolument?

An emolument is a payment, salary, or compensation.

What is the "Saxbe-Fix"?

The Saxbe-Fix is a procedure, named after a Nixon cabinet appointee, whereby Congress repeals an increase in salary for an office to which one of its members has been nominated, thus presumably making the individual eligible to this office. Some scholars continue to question the legitimacy of this procedure.

Does the Constitution permit members of Congress to serve simultaneously in any other civil offices?

No. This separates the U.S. system from parliamentary systems. In the latter, members of the legislative body (usually designated at the parliament) may also serve on the cabinet.

Is there any way that a member of Congress may become a cabinet officer?

Yes, a member of Congress may accept a cabinet office by resigning the congressional seat.

PROCEDURES FOR PASSING LEGISLATION

According to the Constitution, where must bills raising revenue originate?

The Constitution specifies that such bills must originate in the House of Representatives.

Where do spending bills originate?

The Constitution does not specify, but, by convention, they also originate in the House of Representatives.

The Constitution specifies that Congress appropriates money. Is the president obligated to spend all that Congress appropriates?

There are numerous occasions where presidents have "rescinded" or delayed funds that Congress has appropriated, but, in the aftermath of perceived abuses of this power in the administration of President Richard Nixon, Congress significantly cut back on the authority.

According to the Constitution, what should the president do if the president approves of a bill submitted to him by the House and Senate?

The president should sign it.

What does the Constitution require of any bill that passes both the House and the Senate?

Each such bill must be presented to the president.

What is a legislative veto?

This was a mechanism developed in the twentieth century whereby Congress would grant power to the president or his or her subordinates subject to the disapproval of one or both houses of Congress. In *Immigration and Naturalization Services v. Chadha* (1983), the Supreme Court ruled that this provision violated both the presentment and bicameralism requirements in the Constitution and struck it down.

According to the Constitution, what should a president do if the president disapproves a bill that the House and Senate present to him?

In such cases, the president should return it, with stated objections, to the House of Congress in which the bill originated.

What is the purpose of the presidential veto power?

This is an element in the delicate system of checks and balances that the Framers established. It is especially useful—albeit not specifically limited to—those cases where the president thinks that Congress is acting unconstitutionally or attempting to tread on the prerogatives of the presidential office.

Is a presidential veto final?

Not necessarily, since Congress has power to override it.

What provision does the Constitution make for overriding a presidential veto?

It requires a two-thirds vote of both houses of Congress for such an override.

Does the Constitution establish any requirements, other than a two-thirds vote, for Congress to override a presidential veto?

Yes, votes must be recorded and entered into the journal.

What happens if a president neither signs nor vetoes a bill adopted by both houses of Congress?

Such a bill becomes law without a presidential signature if the president does not return it within 10 days (excepting Sundays).

Why doesn't the Constitution include Sundays when ascertaining whether a president has returned a bill within 10 days?

The Framers knew that many citizens regarded Sunday as a day of rest and worship on which some presidents might have religious objections to signing legislation.

What is a pocket veto?

The Constitution does not specifically mention this term, but it does provide for this practice. If a congressional adjournment prevents the president from returning a bill to Congress with his veto, it fails to become law. There is some debate over how to define a congressional adjournment.

What is an item veto?

The Constitution does not provide for such a veto, which would allow a president selectively to strike items from an appropriations bill. After years of discussion in which proponents often cited positive state experiences with such a veto, Congress attempted to extend such authority to the president by adopting the Line Item Veto Act, which went into effect in 1997. In *Clinton v. City of New York* (1998), the Supreme Court ruled in a 6–3 decision that the act was unconstitutional because it sought to allow the president to exercise his power, not prior to the adoption of, but after the passage of, an act.

What is the only specified order, resolution, or vote taken by both houses of Congress that the Constitution does not require Congress to present to the president?

The only such specified vote is a question of adjournment. Constitutional amendments are also considered to be exempt.

THE POWERS OF CONGRESS

Which article and section of the Constitution lists the majority of the powers of Congress?

Article I, Section 8 does.

What is the name of the powers of Congress that Article I, Section 8 and other parts of the Constitution specifically list?

Such powers are called enumerated (meaning listed), or granted, powers.

What is the power of the purse?

The Constitution does not specifically mention this term, but in describing the powers of Congress *in The Federalist,* Alexander Hamilton referred to this power to describe the authority of Congress over taxing and spending. In the dispute with England, Americans had asserted the principle of "no taxation without representation." The Framers of the Constitution thus considered it to be especially important that the branch of government that controlled taxes and spending be a branch that was elected by, and accountable to, the people.

What is the first of the powers of Congress that Article I, Section 8 mentions?

The first listed is the power to tax and spend.

What terms does Article I, Section 8 use to describe federal taxes?

Article I, Section 8 mentions taxes, duties, imposts, and excises. The national government did not rely on an income tax until the Civil War, and the Supreme Court later declared it to be unconstitutional, necessitating adoption of the Sixteenth Amendment.

What kind of tax is a duty?

It is a tax on a ship.

What kind of tax is an impost?

This is a tax on imported goods, more frequently referred to as a tariff.

What kind of tax is an excise?

It is a tax on the purchase or consumption of an item.

According to Article I, Section 8, for what purposes may Congress tax and spend?

It has power to tax and spend to pay the debts and to provide for the common defense and general welfare. Despite attempts to widen the meaning of the general welfare clause, U.S. courts have generally tied this clause specifically to taxing and spending power.

Are there occasions where Congress can exercise the power to tax and spend when it cannot justify such power under other clauses?

Yes, in *National Federation of Independent Business v. Sebelius* (2012), Chief Justice John Roberts settled a conflict over the Patient Protection and Affordable Care Act of 2010 (often dubbed Obamacare) on the basis that Congress could tax individuals who refused to purchase health care, even though, like four other members of the Court, he did not think that Congress had the power to control health care under its power through the commerce clause.

Does the congressional power to tax include power to tax the states?

The Constitution does not directly address this subject, but Supreme Court decisions, pointing to the value of federalism, have extended what it designates as the doctrine of intergovernmental tax immunities to most exercises of direct taxes on the states. It does, however, permit Congress to tax the salaries of state officials (and states to tax salaries of federal employees), and it permits taxation of certain state services conducted in competition with private enterprise.

Which branch of government has the power to borrow money on the credit of the United States?

Only the Congress has this power.

Does the Constitution delineate any limits on the congressional power to borrow?

The Constitution does not list any specific limits on borrowing. In the wake of large recent increases in the national debt, numerous members of Congress have proposed a balanced budget amendment to limit or forbid borrowing and/or spending; critics question the enforceability of such a provision.

Which branch of government has the power to regulate interstate and foreign commerce?

Congress has this responsibility. This power has been interpreted quite broadly, and the clause granting such authority has been one of the most expansive sources of federal powers in the twentieth century. This power was one of those that the government under the Articles of Confederation lacked.

What three classes of commerce does the Constitution specifically mention as subjects of congressional regulation?

These three classes are: commerce with foreign nations, among the several states, and with the Indian tribes (whose sovereignty the Constitution still recognizes, much as the sovereignty of foreign nations). Generally, courts allow states to regulate intrastate commerce, absent regulations that might conflict with federal power, but the Constitution does not specifically mention intrastate commerce.

How have the courts interpreted commerce powers?

Ever since the decision in *Gibbons v. Ogden* (1824), courts have interpreted commerce broadly as "intercourse." Courts currently allow Congress to control the following: the channels of commerce; the instrumentalities of commerce; and activities that substantially affect such commerce. Because the latter is a matter of degree, courts continue to hear cases on the boundaries of this power.

Generally speaking, what the national government exercises a power under the commerce clause that interferes with state exercises of power?

As a general rule, federal powers prevail. Thus, in one of the most important cases dealing with this issue, the Supreme Court decided in *Gibbons v. Ogden* (1824) that a grant to navigate interstate waters under a federal pilotage license took priority over a state grant of a steamboat monopoly.

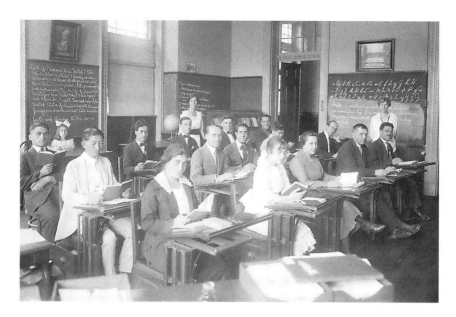

Students prepare for the U.S. citizenship test. Today's American immigrants are even more diverse than when this photo was taken. (Library of Congress)

In a latter case, *Cooley v. Board of Wardens* (1851), the Court ruled that, absent congressional actions, there were some matters that were appropriate for state variation—for example, rules regarding piloting in the Philadelphia harbor that were at issue in this case—and others that required a single uniform national rule.

The only major restraint on current federal powers in the area of commerce is the presence of explicit constitutional prohibitions. When Congress fails to set rules for a given area of commerce, courts often have to examine state laws on a case-by-case basis.

Which branch of government does the Constitution vest with power to establish uniform rules of naturalization?

It gave this power to Congress. Interestingly, the Constitution contained no definition of who qualified for citizenship prior to the adoption of the Fourteenth Amendment (1868).

Does Congress have power over bankruptcy?

Yes, it does; the Constitution grants Congress power to adopt uniform laws on the subject. In the nineteenth century, prior to congressional laws dealing with the subject, courts generally upheld state laws on bankruptcy.

What branch of government has the power to coin money and "regulate the value thereof"?

Congress does. Under the Articles of Confederation, states coined their own money. Under such circumstances, dealing with individuals in other states was akin to dealing with people in foreign nations.

Why did the Constitution also grant Congress the power to regulate the value of foreign coin?

In early American history, when specie was rare, such coins were often used as legal tender.

Which branch of government is responsible for fixing standard weights and measures?

Congress has this responsibility.

Which branch of government does the Constitution vest with the power to punish the counterfeiting of securities and current coin of the United States?

The Constitution vests this power in Congress.

Which branch of government is responsible for establishing post offices and post roads?

The Constitution vests this power in Congress.

What is a post road?

This is a road over which mail is carried. Congressional power over post offices includes power over such roads. During the Eisenhower Administration, Congress used its authority over national defense to build an interstate system of highways, by which it could more easily mobilize troops and evacuate cities in danger of attack.

What are patents and copyrights?

The Constitution does not specifically use these terms, but Article I, Section 8, invests Congress with power to secure to authors and inventors "the exclusive right to their respective writings and discoveries" by giving them such rights for limited time periods. The stated purpose of this provision was "to promote the progress of science and useful arts." Patents give inventors a monopoly over the production of an invention for a given number of years; copyrights give similar powers to authors.

What is the only court that the U.S. Constitution specifically mentions?

Excluding the Senate, which acts as a court when trying cases of impeachment, the Supreme Court is the only court that the Constitution mentions. However, Article I, Section 8 gives Congress power "to constitute Tribunals inferior to the Supreme Court." Currently, the federal courts are arranged in a hierarchy with 94 U.S. district courts at the lowest level, 13 courts of appeal above them, and the U.S. Supreme Court at the apex. The Supreme Court can also accept appeals on federal constitutional issues from state supreme courts.

To which branch of government does the Constitution give the power to "define and punish piracies and felonies committed on the high seas, and offenses against the laws of nations"?

It gives this power to Congress.

Why does the Constitution grant the powers to define and punish piracies and felonies committed on the high seas, and offenses against the laws of nations to Congress rather than to the states, which are responsible for most other matters of criminal law?

Acts on the high seas would not fall within state jurisdiction. Acts involving the laws of nations would affect the foreign policy of the entire country.

Which branch of the government has the power to declare war?

The legislative branch has this power. The Constitution also gives Congress power to grant letters of marque and reprisal, and make rules concerning captures on land and water. Although the Constitution vests Congress with the power to *declare* war, the president typically *wages* war in his capacity as commander in chief of the military.

How effective has the power to declare war been in giving Congress control over foreign policy matters?

In the twentieth century, an increasing number of conflicts have not been declared wars. Most notably, President Truman designated the War in Korea as a "police action," and no declaration of war was made in the case of the war in Vietnam, although Congress did provide some authorization for American participation in what is known as the Gulf of Tonkin Resolution. Both presidents Bush got congressional authorizations, albeit not formal declarations of war, for the attacks against Iraq (the first for its attack on Kuwait and the second to topple a dictator said to have had weapons of mass destruction).

In 1973, Congress adopted the War Powers Resolution, designed to recover some of the authority that it thought it had lost to the president. Under this resolution, presidents are obligated when possible to: consult with Congress before committing American troops abroad, inform Congress of troop deployments and of the reasons for them, and to withdraw troops from conflicts that Congress does not sanction within 60 days (with the possibility of a 30-day extension). Presidents have attempted to skirt this law, and the Supreme Court has yet to decide on its constitutionality.

What are letters of marque and reprisal?

At the time the delegates wrote the U.S. Constitution, it was common to employ privateers for military purposes (as, for example, Francis Drake had raided Spanish shipping on behalf of the English queen). The term "marque" originally designated the frontier of a nation. Letters of marque and reprisal granted authority to such privateers to conduct military operations, on the high seas or in foreign territories, which would, without such authorization, be considered acts of piracy.

Which branches of the military does the Constitution specifically mention?

It specifically mentions the army, the navy, and the state militia.

What does the Constitution say about standing armies?

It does not use this specific term, but many of the Framers of the Constitution were concerned about the perceived evil of such standing, or permanent, armies. The Constitution does not specifically outlaw such armies, but it provided that no appropriations of money for the military shall remain in force for more than two years.

Which branch of the government is responsible for making laws to govern the U.S. military?

The legislative branch is so responsible. Congress has responded by drawing up a special Code of Military Conduct. The military also has a special military court system for its active members.

In what specific cases does the U.S. Constitution authorize "calling forth" the militia?

It authorizes such a call when needed "to execute the laws of the Union, suppress insurrections and repel invasion." This clearly implies that such state militia may not be sent overseas. This constitutional limitation eventually led to the development of the state and national guards, which faced no such constitutional obstacles.

What is a militia?

The militia is an army composed of citizens, designed primarily for defensive purposes. The concept of a militia was particularly important in the republican thought from which the Framers borrowed heavily. Such a militia was often compared favorably to mercenary armies composed of noncitizens such as the British had used during the Revolutionary War.

Where, other than Article I, Section 8, does the Constitution mention militia?

The Second Amendment, which deals with the right to bear arms, also mentions it.

According to the Constitution, who is responsible for "organizing, arming, and disciplining the militia"?

Congress has this responsibility.

What powers over the militia does the Constitution reserve to the states?

The Constitution specifically reserves "the appointment of the Officers, and the authority of training the militia according to the discipline prescribed by Congress."

What is the maximum size of the area that the Constitution designates for the nation's capital?

The maximum area is 10 miles square; the Constitution does not specify a minimum area.

Where was the nation's capital located prior to the federal acquisition of the District of Columbia?

It began in New York City and was later moved to Philadelphia.

How did the Constitution contemplate the creation of the nation's capital?

States were to cede land for a site, subject to congressional approval. States competed vigorously for the prize of having the capital located near them, with New York, Pennsylvania, and Virginia all making strong bids. In the first known example of "logrolling," or trading votes, the Virginians agreed to support some of Alexander Hamilton's financial programs in return for a promise to locate the capital at its present site on the Potomac River. Maryland and Virginia both ceded land for this project, but the land originally ceded by Virginia has since been retroceded, or returned, and it is possible that more such property could eventually be retroceded to Maryland.

How does the Constitution refer to the nation's capital?

The Constitution refers to the capital as the District of Columbia.

According to the Constitution, who is responsible for legislating for the District of Columbia?

Congress is. In 1978 Congress proposed a constitutional amendment that would have enabled members of the District to govern their own affairs, but the necessary number of states did not ratify this amendment.

Who makes rules for federal enclaves where forts, magazines, arsenals, dockyards and other federal facilities are located?

Congress makes such rules.

What is the "sweeping clause"?

This is the last paragraph of Article I, Section 8 of the Constitution—also sometimes called the "elastic clause," or, simply, "the necessary and proper clause." It grants Congress power "to make all laws which shall be necessary and proper for carrying into execution the foregoing Powers, and all other powers vested by this Constitution in the government of the United States, or in any department or officer thereof."

What are implied powers?

These are powers that Congress exercises under the sweeping clause. Chief Justice John Marshall offered a striking analysis of such powers in the case of *McCulloch v. Maryland* (1819). In that case, Marshall approved the constitutionality of the bank of the United States under the sweeping clause, even though the Constitution does not specifically mention the power to establish a bank. Marshall argued that the bank was not an end in and of itself that needed to be listed in the Constitution, but rather a necessary and proper means to powers that were listed in the document.

Where does Congress get its power to conduct investigations?

This is a good example of implied powers. It would be difficult for Congress to legislate on a number of subjects if it had no such investigatory powers. The courts have thus recognized that such investigatory powers are ancillary to the law-making power. The courts have, however, also ruled that Congress does not have power to run roughshod over individual rights when conducting such investigations but is subject, under the Fifth Amendment and elsewhere, to various guarantees of "due process."

In addition to the power to establish a bank and to conduct investigations, are there other recognized powers that the Constitution does not explicitly list?

The Constitution does not directly mention control over agriculture, manufacturing, education, air or water pollution, highway construction and/or maintenance (other than the construction of post roads), internal improvements, or a host of other areas where federal regulations are now fairly commonplace. When challenged, the government generally defends them as exercises of congressional power under the commerce clause and/or under the federal government's power to condition funding of state programs on compliance with specified regulations.

What does the term "resulting powers" mean?

Scholars sometimes employ this term to describe the combination of powers that results from adding enumerated and implied powers.

LIMITS ON THE POWERS OF CONGRESS

What does Article I, Section 9 of the Constitution do?

Article I, Section 9 lists various limits on the power of Congress. Notably, it follows the section (8) that grants powers to Congress.

What does Article I, Section 9 mean when it mentions "the migration or importation of such persons as any of the states now existing shall think proper to admit"?

Like the phrase in Article I, Section 2, which refers to "three-fifths of such others persons," this is a euphemism for those who were held as slaves. It may be significant that this phrase refers to such slaves as "persons" rather than as mere items of "property."

What provision does Article I, Section 9 make respecting slave importation?

It limits congressional control of slave importation until 1808.

Did the Constitution permit any control of slave importation prior to 1808?

Yes, it allowed for a tax of up to $10 per person. Again, the reference to persons might be significant.

What is a writ of habeas corpus?

This is a legal instrument whereby an individual can demand that the government show cause as to why that individual has been arrested or detained. Whereas the writ is today often used by state prisoners who appeal their detentions to federal courts, in the early republic is was more commonly understood as a means by which state courts could question federal detentions.

Under what, if any, circumstances may Congress suspend the writ of habeas corpus?

Ordinarily, the Constitution prohibits Congress from suspending this writ. However, the Constitution permits suspension when "in cases of rebellion or invasion the public safety may require it."

May anyone other than Congress suspend the writ of habeas corpus?

The Constitution is silent on the subject, but President Abraham Lincoln exercised such authority during the Civil War.

Has the Court issued any recent decisions on habeas corpus?

Yes, in *Rasul v. Bush* (2004), the Court decided that it could review habeas corpus petitions from foreign citizens held in a foreign territory where the United States was exercising jurisdiction. In *Hamdan v. Rumsfeld* (2006), it decided that a Yemini national being held by the United States at Guantanamo Bay was entitled to a writ of habeas corpus. *Boudmediene v. Bush* (2008) further invalidated a congressional attempt to deny federal jurisdiction over pending habeas corpus actions.

Article I, Section 9 prohibits Congress from passing a bill of attainder. What is this?

A bill of attainder is a legislative punishment of a specific individual or individuals made without benefit of a trial. The English Parliament had adopted such bills to punish officers of the king with whom it was dissatisfied.

Article I, Section 9 also prohibits ex post facto laws. What are these?

They are retroactive laws. In an early case, *Calder v. Bull* (1798), the Supreme Court decided that the kind of laws that the Constitution was referring to here were criminal, rather than civil, laws. It thus disallowed criminal laws that increased the penalty for crimes already committed or that attempted to punish someone for actions that were not criminal when they were committed.

What is a capitation, or direct tax?

A capitation tax is a tax that applies to individuals as individuals. The Constitution does not define a direct tax, and the debates at the Constitutional Convention are similarly unrevealing. The Supreme Court's decision in *Pollock v. Farmers' Loan & Trust Company* (1895) ruled that the income tax was such a direct tax and thus illegal, but the Sixteenth Amendment permitted such taxes.

What limits did Article I, Section 9 impose on the imposition of capitation, or other direct, taxes?

They were to be apportioned according to the census.

Can Congress adopt legislation that prefers the commerce of some American ports over others?

No, it may not. It is also prohibited from adopting statutes obliging ships leaving one state to go to, or pay duties in, another.

According to the Constitution, what is prerequisite to withdrawing money from the U.S. Treasury?

The Constitution requires an appropriation made by law.

How frequently does the Constitution specify that accounts of governmental receipts and revenues must be made?

It does not set a precise time. Rather the Constitution specifies that this be done "from time to time."

What is a title of nobility?

England and other societies that recognize hereditary families often designate its nobility with such titles such as Lord or Lady, Duke or Duchess. There is little merit in arguments recently advanced linking such titles of nobility to law school degrees, since these are not hereditary titles, are not conferred on Americans by foreign government, and do not entitle those who have them to do anything other than practice the profession for which they were trained.

Does the Constitution permit Congress to confer such titles of nobility?

No, the Framers desired a democratic, rather than an aristocratic, government. They therefore prohibited such titles in Article I, Section 9 of the Constitution. Similarly, Article I, Section 10 prohibits states from granting such titles as well.

Under what, if any, conditions, may an individual receive a present, emolument, office, or title from a foreign king, power or foreign state?

The Constitution only permits individuals to receive such presents with the consent of Congress.

What is an emolument?

An emolument is a payment or other form of remuneration.

LIMITS ON THE STATES

What does Article I, Section 10 do?

Article I, Section 10 specifies limits on the states. Significantly, it follows a section that limits the powers of Congress.

What is the name of powers that only the national government can exercise?

Such powers are called exclusive powers.

Article I, Section 9 prohibits Congress from interfering with the slave trade prior to 1808. Does Article I, Section 10 impose a similar prohibition on the states?

No, states (some of which had already outlawed this trade) were free to regulate such importation prior to 1808.

Are states individually free to enter into treaties, alliances, or confederations or grant letters of marque and reprisal?

No; Article I, Section 10 of the Constitution prohibits this.

Does the Constitution permit states to coin their own money or emit bills of credit?

Not according to Article I, Section 10 of the Constitution. States did exercise this power under the Articles of Confederation.

While prohibiting both state and national governments from passing bills of attainder and ex post facto laws, what additional restriction does Article I, Section 10 place on the states that does not apply to Congress?

It prohibits states from adopting laws "impairing" the obligation of contracts.

Why did the Framers impose this additional restriction on the states?

Under the Articles of Confederation, states had adopted a number of schemes to alleviate the condition of debtors. Many of the Framers thought that these plans had been unfair to creditors and had led to inflation. Most of the Founders probably did not anticipate that the national government, representing a much larger number of economic and other interests, would be as tempted to adopt such legislation.

Has the contract clause been important in American history?

Yes, this clause has been quite important, especially in the nation's early history. In *Dartmouth College v. Woodward* (1819), the Supreme Court ruled that a charter that the English king granted to the college prior to the Revolution was such a contract that the states could not impair. In the case of *Charles River Bridge v. Warren Bridge* (1837) the Court decided to interpret any ambiguities in a contract in favor of the states. In *Home Building and Loan Association v. Blaisdell* (1934), the Court decided that a Minnesota mortgage moratorium law did not involve a breach of the contract clause and, since then, the Court has struck down relatively few laws under this provision.

Under what specified circumstances does the Constitution permit states to lay imposts or duties on imports or exports Congress has not authorized?

According to Article I, section 10 of the Constitution, the states are permitted to levy such imposts or exposts that are "absolutely necessary" for executing its inspection laws.

In *McCulloch v. Maryland* (1819), Chief Justice John Marshall used this qualification to demonstrate that the Constitution recognizes varying degrees of necessity.

Under what circumstances does the Constitution permit states to enter into agreements or compacts with other states or with foreign powers?

Such agreements, known as interstate compacts, require the consent of Congress.

Are there any circumstances in which a state may engage in war without congressional authorization?

Yes, states may engage in unauthorized war in case of actual invasion or cases of "imminent danger" that will not admit of delay.

Are there any unstated limits on the powers of the states?

Yes, courts have recognized a number of such limits. These may occur either because the Constitution entrusts some powers, like the control of interstate commerce, to the national government and they cannot be simultaneously exercised by the states (at least not when the two sets of regulations conflict) or because the exercise of some powers are thought to threaten the independent existence of the national government. Thus, in *McCulloch v. Maryland* (1819), Chief Justice John Marshall ruled that since "the power to tax involves the power to destroy," states did not have the power to tax the bank, which was an instrumentality of the national government.

BIBLIOGRAPHY

Books

Christopher J. Bailey, *The U.S. Congress* (New York: Basil Blackwell Std., 1989).
Barbara J. Craig, *Chadha: The Story of an Epic Constitutional Struggle* (New York: Oxford University Press, 1988).
John H. Ely, *War and Responsibility: Constitutional Lessons of Vietnam and Its Aftermath* (Princeton, N.J.: Princeton University Press, 1993).
Morris Fiorina, *Divided Government,* 2nd ed. (Boston: Allyn and Bacon, 1996).
Louis Fisher, *The Politics of Shared Powers: Congress and the Executive,* 2nd ed. (Washington, D.C.: Congressional Quarterly Press, 1987).
Anthony Gregory, *The Power of Habeas Corpus in America: From the King's Prerogative to the War on Terror.* (New York: Cambridge University Press, 2013).
Thomas E. Mann, *A Question of Balance: The President, the Congress and Foreign Policy* (Washington, D.C.: Brookings, 1989).
Walter J. Oleszek, *Congressional Procedures and the Policy Process,* 4th ed. (Washington, D.C.: Congressional Quarterly, Inc., 1996).
Ronald M. Peters Jr., *The American Speakership: The Office in Historical Perspective* (Baltimore: The Johns Hopkins University Press, 1990).
William H. Rehnquist, *Grand Inquests: The Historic Impeachments of Justice Samuel Chase and President Andrew Johnson* (New York: William Morrow & Company, 1992).
Michael D. Wormser, *Guide to Congress,* 3rd ed. (Washington, D.C.: Congressional Quarterly Inc., 1982).
Justin J. Wert, *Habeas Corpus in America: The Politics of Individual Rights* (Lawrence, KS: University Press of Kansas, 2011).

Cases

Boudmediene v. Bush, 553 U.S. 723 (2008).
Calder v. Bull, 3 U.S. 386 (1798).
Charles River Bridge v. Warren Bridge, 36 U.S. 420 (1837).

Clinton v. City of New York, 524 U.S. 417 (1998).
Cooley v. Board of Wardens of the Port of Philadelphia, 53 U.S. 299 (1852).
Dartmouth College v. Woodward, 17 U.S. 518 (1819).
Gibbons v. Ogden, 22 U.S. 1 (1824).
Hamdan v. Rumsfeld, 548 U.S. 557 (2006).
Home Building and Loan Association v. Blaisdell, 290 U.S. 398 (1934).
Immigration and Naturalization Services v. Chadha, 462 U.S. 919 (1983).
McCulloch v. Maryland, 17 U.S. 316 (1819)
National Federation of Independent Business v. Sebelius (2012).
Pollock v. Farmers' Loan & Trust Company, 158 U.S. 601 (1895).
Powell v. McCormack, 395 U.S. 486 (1969).
Rasul v. Bush, 542 U.S. 466 (2004).
U.S. Term Limits v. Thornton, 115 S. Ct. 1842 (1995).

Chapter 3
Article II: The Executive Branch

SECTION 1: ESTABLISHING THE PRESIDENCY

Article I outlines the powers of the legislative branch; what does Article II do?

It outlines the power of the executive branch. As an elective branch of government, it is logical that the Constitution would treat this branch directly after the other elected branch.

How many sections does Article II of the Constitution have?

It has four.

How does the opening line of Article II, Section 1 differ from that of Article I, Section 1?

Article I, Section 1 refers to all legislative powers "herein granted" whereas Article II, Section 1 refers simply to "the executive power" (omitting the phrase "herein granted").

Front view of the White House in Washington, D.C. (Alice Scully/iStockPhoto.com)

What is the significance of the differing language of the opening lines of Articles I and II?

Some commentators believe this difference in language indicates that the Constitution intended to entrust the president with more discretionary powers than Congress. Prior to the writing of the Constitution, some political theorists, most notably John Locke, associated the executive with the notion of prerogative power, which some believe was implicit in the idea of the presidency.

What two roles does the Constitution consolidate in the American presidency that governments with a monarch often separate?

The president serves both as head of government and head of state.

What does it mean to say that the president serves both as head of the government and as head of state?

As the highest elected official in the United States—indeed, with the vice president, the only official elected by the nation as a whole—the president is the head of the government. In the American system, this status does not necessarily guarantee that the president will have majority support of Congress, but it certainly puts the president in a visible position to influence public policy.

Because the United States does not have a monarch, the president is also head of state. He is responsible for receiving foreign ambassadors, and he frequently serves as a symbol for the nation.

What are the consequences of combining the roles of head of government and head of state in the president?

Undoubtedly, this enhances presidential power. On occasion, it may also enable a president to manipulate the president's role as a symbol of the nation to enhance the president's own political power and gain support for controversial policies.

What principle is the Constitution articulating when it vests the executive power in a president of the United States of America?

The principle is that of a singular executive. Some individuals at the Constitutional Convention had advocated a plural executive, or an executive by committee. A singular executive has undoubtedly increased the visibility and vigor of the presidential office. The *Federalist Papers* frequently refer to the "energy" of the chief executive.

What does the Constitution say about the First Lady (or First Man)?

It makes no mention of the subject. This lack of constitutional foundation may be one factor that makes this position so difficult to fill to everyone's satisfaction.

How long is a single presidential term?

A presidential term is for four years. Significantly, this term does not precisely correspond with the terms either of members of the House of Representatives or the Senate. All members of the House of Representatives who want to continue in office must, of course, run for election in presidential election years, but a popular president who brings other members of his party in on his "coattails" usually finds that his party loses support in the so-called mid-term election held in the middle of his term. Only one-third of the members of the Senate face election in a presidential election year.

By contrast, in parliamentary systems, the prime minister (their nearest equivalent to a president) and the prime minister's party's representatives in Parliament generally rise or fall together.

What other officer of the federal government also serves for a four-year term?

The vice president does.

THE ELECTORAL COLLEGE

What is the name of the mechanism that is used to select the president and vice president?

This indirect mechanism of election is designated as the Electoral College.

What does the word "college" in electoral college mean?

It certainly does not refer to an institution of higher learning from which one can receive a degree. In context, the word "college" simply designates a group of individuals, as in the College of Cardinals.

With the Electoral College in place, is it possible to win a majority of the national popular vote and not win the presidency?

Yes.

Generally speaking, compared to the popular vote, does the Electoral College tend to magnify or minimize the margin of victory of the winner?

Almost invariably, the Electoral College victory tends to be larger than the popular vote victory. In part this results from the winner-take-all system that most states now use in apportioning their electoral votes.

Has an individual ever won the greatest number of popular votes and not been elected president?

Yes, in 1888 Republican Benjamin Harrison won a majority of the Electoral College votes even though he lost the popular vote to Democrat Grover Cleveland. In the election of 1824, no candidate received a majority of the electoral votes, and the election was decided by the House of Representatives; the House awarded the election to John Quincy Adams even though he does not appear to have had as many popular votes as Andrew Jackson. The election of 1876 is also controversial. In that case, electoral fraud made it difficult to know whether Republican Rutherford B. Hayes or Democrat Samuel Tilden had won. An electoral commission appointed by Congress to resolve the controversy ultimately gave disputed electoral votes to Hayes, who won the election. In 2000, Republican George W. Bush won a slight majority of votes in the Electoral College despite the fact that Democrat Al Gore Jr. won a greater number of popular votes. The election was essentially decided when, in its decision in *Bush v. Gore* (2000), the U.S. Supreme Court stopped the recounting of votes in Florida, which it thought was not being done in a manner consistent with equal protection, where Bush remained ahead in the popular vote.

Why did the delegates to the Constitutional Convention settle on an electoral college system rather than on direct popular election of the president?

Some delegates were undoubtedly afraid of direct popular choice, especially at a time when the mass of the population might not be familiar with all the leading candidates for office. In addition, when delegates wrote the Constitution, the direct popular vote throughout all 13 states would have been difficult to tally, and states had significantly different requirements for voting. Also, the Electoral College gave some representation to states as states and thus reflected the constitutional value of federalism.

How many electors does each state have in the electoral college?

Each state has a number of electors equal to its total number of representatives (based on population, with each state guaranteed at least one) and senators (the Constitution grants two to each state).

How does a state choose its electors?

The Constitution does not specify, and, in the early years of the republic, some states allowed their legislators to choose such electors; all states currently select such electors through popular vote.

Who resolves disputes that might occur as to who has been elected to the Electoral College?

Since the adoption of a congressional law in 1887, this matter has now been entrusted to the states. Previously, such matters were resolved by Congress. In the 1876 presidential election, charges that Congress had decided on the legitimacy of Southern electors on the basis of partisanship undercut respect for electoral results that year.

The decision in *Bush v. Gore* (2000) indicates, however, that the Supreme Court also has a role in deciding electoral contests and that it will apply what it considers to be constitutional standards to such elections.

According to the Constitution, is a state required to award all its electoral votes to the individual who receives a plurality of that state's votes?

No, but this general ticket, or unit rule, is now the practice in every state except Maine and Nebraska (both with relatively small numbers of votes), which split their votes among contenders.

What are the most frequently proposed alternatives to the current electoral system of selecting the president?

A district system in which each congressional district would cast a separate vote (typically, with the candidate winning the most votes in the states being awarded the additional two votes of that state) has been a frequently proposed alternative to the present system.

A proportional system, giving each candidate a proportion of the votes the candidate has won in each state, is another frequently proposed alternative. Some variants of both the district system and the proportional systems propose awarding two electoral votes (those based on its senators) to each state's overall winner.

Neither the district nor proportional system plans is probably as popular as simple direct election, but those who like the present federal dimension of the current set-up typically oppose such a change.

Where do presidential electors meet?

Electors meet in their respective states. The Framers of the Constitution thought that this would help eliminate any improper collusion among them.

Under the original Electoral College scheme, how many votes did each elector cast for president?

Each elector voted for two such candidates, one of whom had to be from a state other than the elector's own. This was designed to keep a single state from gaining both the presidency and the vice presidency. The Twelfth Amendment has changed the original system so that each elector now casts one vote for president and another for vice president, but it still requires that at least one of these candidates must be from a state other than the elector's own.

Under the original Electoral College plan, what happened after each elector cast his votes?

Lists were made of all persons voted for and the number of votes they received, and this list was transmitted signed, sealed, and certified to the president of the Senate (the vice president).

Have electors ever unanimously selected a president?

Yes, they unanimously selected George Washington (that is, consistent with the rules of the day, each elector cast at least one of two votes for him). James Monroe, who was later president during the so-called Era of Good Feelings, fell one vote shy of such unanimity, reputedly because one of the electors wanted to reserve the honor of unanimity for Washington.

Under the original Electoral College system, under what circumstances did the person with the highest number of electoral votes become president?

Then as now, such an individual became president only when that individual received a number of votes equal to, or greater than, a majority.

Under the original Electoral College system, what happened in cases of a tie in the Electoral College?

The House of Representatives had to choose between the candidates who tied.

Was there ever a tie under the original Electoral College system?

Yes, in the election of 1800, all the Republican electors who voted for Democrat-Republican Thomas Jefferson also voted for Aaron Burr (an unanticipated result of the development of political parties). It took 35 ballots in the House of Representatives, where there were a good number of lame-duck Federalists (those who had not been reelected to office), to resolve this election in favor of Jefferson (Alexander Hamilton was one Federalist leader who ultimately supported Jefferson over Burr). This impasse also led to the adoption of the Twelfth Amendment, modifying the original Electoral College scheme so as to make ties much less likely.

Under the original Electoral College system, what happened if two candidates did not tie and no individual received a majority of the Electoral College votes?

The House of Representatives chose the president from the five candidates with the greatest number of electoral votes. The Twelfth Amendment subsequently changed this so that, in such circumstances, the House now chooses among the top three candidates.

What special rules apply when the House of Representatives has to choose the president?

Each state delegation has a single vote. Also, members from at least two-thirds of the states must be present, and a candidate must carry a majority of the states (26 at present) to win.

How many times has the House of Representatives decided a presidential election?

This has happened on two occasions. The first such election occurred in 1800 when the House had to resolve the tie between Thomas Jefferson and Aaron Burr. The last such election was in 1824. In this election, the House selected John Quincy Adams over popular vote winner Andrew Jackson as well as over Henry Clay, the speaker of the House, who had thrown his support to Adams (William Crawford had also run but was excluded from consideration by the provision in the Twelfth Amendment, which required that the House choose from among the top three contenders). John Quincy Adams subsequently appointed Clay as his secretary of state, leading Jackson and his supporters to charge that Adams and Clay had engaged in a "corrupt bargain."

How did the original Electoral College system provide for the selection of the vice president in cases where elections went to the House of Representatives?

The vice president was to be the individual with the next highest number of votes to the top presidential candidate.

Did the original Electoral College system require the vice president to have a majority of electoral votes?

No, it did not, but under the Twelfth Amendment, if no candidate now has a majority of the Electoral College, the Senate chooses between the top two contenders.

Under the original Electoral College system, what happened if there was a tie among individuals having the next highest number of votes for president?

The Senate was to make the choice.

In cases where the Senate has to choose the vice president, how do senators vote?

In contrast to cases where the House has to choose among presidential contenders and where each state delegation has a single vote, senators cast their votes individually. Since each state has two senators, using the house system would invalidate a state's vote whenever its two senators disagreed. Today, with 50 states, each of which has two senators, if the choice of the vice president goes to the Senate and all senators attended, a candidate would need to get 51 votes or more to win.

Who determines the time of choosing presidential electors and the day that they give their votes?

Congress makes such determinations.

What date has Congress established for choosing presidential electors?

It has established that such elections should be held on the first Tuesday after the first Monday of November in presidential election years.

Does the Constitution subject Congress to any restrictions in setting the time that presidential electors cast their votes?

Yes, the day that electors cast their vote is to be uniform throughout the United States. Congress has set this date for the first Monday after the second Wednesday in December.

What amendments have modified the original Electoral College system?

The Twelfth and Twenty-Third amendments have both modified the Electoral College. The system has also been modified by customs and usages. Thus, electors rarely exercise independent judgment in choosing a president, as the Framers probably anticipated, but electors typically vote instead for the candidates that they have been prepledged to support.

Is it possible for an elector to vote for a candidate to whom that elector is not pledged?

There is no constitutional prohibition against such "faithless electors," although many states have laws and levy penalties against those maverick delegates who occasionally engage in this practice.

QUALIFICATIONS FOR PRESIDENT

What, if any, qualifications must an individual meet in order to be selected as president?

An individual must be a natural-born citizen or a citizen of the United States at the time of the Constitution's adoption, must be at least 35 years of age, and must have been a resident of the United States for at least 14 years.

What is a natural-born citizen?

A natural-born citizen is a citizen by birth rather than by naturalization. Although the U.S. Supreme Court does not appear to have issued a decision on the subject, presumably, an individual born abroad of American parents would be considered natural born. In 1968, Michigan governor George Romney (the father of the 2012 presidential candidate) vied for the Republican nomination for president even though he had been born abroad of American missionary parents. Similarly, John McCain, the 2008 Republican presidential candidate, had been born in the Panama Canal Zone, but members of Congress adopted a resolution indicating that they thought he was eligible for the presidential office.

Why does the Constitution require that an individual be natural born in order to be president?

The Framers designed this requirement to guard against foreign intrigues. There were some fears that a European monarch might try to lay a claim on the U.S. presidency.

What are the qualifications for a vice president?

The qualifications for vice president are the same as those for a president. The Twelfth Amendment explicitly states that "no person constitutionally ineligible to the office of President shall be eligible to that of Vice-president of the United States."

Can an individual who has served as president run for office as a vice president?

Under term limits now specified in the Twenty-Second Amendment (providing for presidential term limits), this would be possible only in the case of presidents who have not served as president for six years or longer.

MISCELLANEOUS PROVISIONS

Under what circumstances does the vice president assume the duties of the president?

The vice president assumes such duties in cases of removal of the president from office or in cases of his death, resignation, or inability to perform the duties of his office.

Who sets the president's salary?

Congress does.

What limits does the Constitution set on the president's salary?

The Constitution requires that the president shall receive such a salary at stated times. It also specifies that this salary shall not be increased or decreased during his term of office and that he shall not receive any other emolument from the nation or the states during his term.

Does a president have to accept a salary?

The Constitution does not specify, but President George Washington as well as President John F. Kennedy both refused such remuneration.

Why does the Constitution prevent Congress from increasing or decreasing a president's salary during his term of office and prevent the president from accepting any other emoluments from the nation or the states?

Congress sets the salary of the president. If it had the power to raise or lower this salary during a president's term, it might exercise undue control over the president; the same concern would apply to the states.

What is the only oath that the Constitution specifically delineates?

It only specifies the oath of office of the president.

What are the two ways that a president can take his oath?

A president may either swear or affirm this oath.

Why does the Constitution allow a president either to swear or affirm oath?

Some religious groups object to swearing. Individuals from such groups would be permitted to affirm their oaths rather than swearing them.

What is the presidential oath?

The oath provides that, "I do solemnly swear (or affirm) that I will faithfully execute the Office of president of the United States, and will to the best of my Ability, preserve, protect and defend the Constitution of the United States."

Does the Constitution mention the words, "so help me God" in the presidential oath?

No, these words, which most presidents add, are not specifically stated in the Constitution. Similarly, although most presidents swear on a Bible, the Constitution does not require this.

How frequently do presidents take the oath of office?

They do so at the beginning of each term. This reminds the president and the public that the president's term is fixed rather than being for life. When January 20th falls on a Sunday, as in 2013, presidents take an oath in a private ceremony that they repeat publicly the next day.

Barack Obama is sworn in as the 44th president of the United States by Chief Justice John Roberts during a public ceremony in Washington, D.C., January 20, 2009. Obama's wife Michelle holds the Bible on which President Abraham Lincoln took his oath of office. The president takes the Oath of Office at the beginning of his term as president. (U.S. Department of Defense)

SECTION 2: PRESIDENTIAL POWERS

What is the first responsibility that the Constitution lists for a president?

Article II, Section 1 vests all "executive Power" in the president. The first responsibility that Article I, Section 2 lists is actually an office. Thus, it designates the president as commander in chief of the army, navy, and militia when called into service of the United States.

What principle does the president's role as commander in chief incorporate?

As commander in chief, the president, who is not required to have prior military experience, exercises civilian control of the military. Whereas Congress exercises the "power of the purse," the president wields the "power of the sword."

What is the cabinet?

The Constitution does not use the word "cabinet," but it consists of the heads of the chief executive agencies of government, whom the president may consult about pressing issues of public policy.

Does the Constitution make any indirect references to the cabinet?

Yes, Article II, Section 2 of the Constitution enables the president to request written opinions from the heads of his executive departments.

Who has the power to issue reprieves and pardons?

The president has this power.

Which four cabinet-level departments actually preceded the establishment of the Constitution?

The Department of Foreign Affairs, the Treasury, the War Department, and the Post Office all preceded the Constitution and were reestablished by the first Congress, which renamed the Department of Foreign Affairs the Department of State.

What is the purpose of the pardon power?

One purpose might be to provide a remedy in case of manifest injustices. Presidents might also use the power of pardon to extend amnesties to those who have been engaged in, or might otherwise continue to engage in, violence against the United States.

Does the Constitution list any limits on the pardon power?

Yes, a president can only pardon offenses against the United States. A president thus cannot pardon individuals for judgments rendered in state courts or in civil actions. In addition, the president cannot issue a pardon in cases of impeachment. Aside from such restrictions, courts have been fairly generous in delineating presidential pardon powers. Thus, in *Schick v. Reed* (1974), the Court declared that the president has the power to issue conditional pardons.

Can a president issue general pardons?

Yes, these are generally referred to as amnesties. president Jimmy Carter issued such an amnesty for those who had fled the draft during the Vietnam War.

Does a president have to list the specific offenses he is pardoning?

Apparently the president does not have to list such offenses by name. president Gerald Ford pardoned Richard Nixon for "all [unspecified] crimes he may have committed while in office."

Can a president pardon him/herself?

The Constitution does not specifically prohibit this, although the principle that no individual should be judged in his or her own case would seem to call such a pardon into question. The House of Representatives might attempt to impeach a president who pardoned himself, but such an impeachment could be ineffective if a president pardoned himself at the end of his term.

Can a president pardon family members?

Again, such a pardon might appear self-interested and could possibly lead the House of Representatives to impeach the president, but the language of the Constitution does not specifically prohibit it, and president Clinton issued a pardon to his half-brother, who had been convicted of drug charges.

What is executive privilege?

The Constitution does not specifically use the term "executive privilege," but the term embodies the principle that the president has certain prerogatives in connection with his office. In particular, there may be circumstances, especially in areas related to American foreign policy making, where the president may assert a privilege against turning over certain information to other branches of government.

Are there any limits on a president's executive privilege?

There definitely are. In *United States v. Nixon* (1974), the Supreme Court rejected a claim of executive privilege that President Richard M. Nixon raised against requests by a special prosecutor for tapes of conversations in which he had participated in the Oval Office. Although the Court indicated that the president had a presumptive right to the privacy of such conversations, the justices ruled that this privilege could be outweighed by governmental interests. In this case, the government needed such conversations in order to pursue criminal prosecutions.

Can a grand jury indict a sitting president in a court for a crime?

This issue does not appear to have been resolved. Some argue that the president can only be indicted by impeachment. During the Watergate scandal, the special prosecutor chose to name president Nixon as an "unindicted" coconspirator.

Can an individual sue the president for actions the president takes in office?

The Constitution is silent on the subject, but in *Nixon v. Fitzgerald* (1982), the Supreme Court indicated that the president had immunity for actions that he took in office in pursuit of his duties. The Court's rationale was that the president had to exercise a great deal of discretion, and lawsuits could hinder his ability to do his job. Courts have extended similar privileges to members of the judicial branch and to other officers of government.

Can individuals sue a president for actions the president took before assuming the office?

In *Clinton v. Jones* (1997), the Supreme Court unanimously decided that an individual could sue President Clinton for sexual harassment that allegedly occurred when he was governor of Arkansas. Clinton's attorneys had argued that the trial should be postponed until the president's term of office was completed, but the Court noted that this could result in the loss of critical evidence. The Supreme Court did say that lower courts should accommodate the president's busy schedule and indicated that he might be deposed (questioned under oath) at the White House on videotape rather than being required to attend court proceedings.

Who has power to make treaties with foreign nations?

The president has this power.

Are there any limits on a president's treaty-making power?

Yes, such treaties require the concurrence of two-thirds of the Senate.

Does the Senate always approve treaties that the president has negotiated?

No, it does not. Thus, although president Woodrow Wilson had been one of the strongest proponents of the League of Nations, the Senate never approved the treaty that would have made the United States a member. Similarly, president Jimmy Carter was unable to get to Senate to approve the treaty growing out of the second Strategic Arms Limitation Talks.

Are there any ways to bypass the requirement for the Senate to ratify a treaty?

There are occasions, usually authorized by Congress, where the president may enter into agreements with foreign nations, known as executive agreements. By and large, such agreements are limited to fairly routine matters, but the line between treaties and executive agreements can be fuzzy.

Significantly, there are also times, the North American Free Trade Agreement, for example, when, usually in close coordination with the president, both houses vote on an agreement with foreign nations by a majority vote rather than by a two-thirds majority of the Senate alone.

Who is responsible for appointing ambassadors and other public ministers and consuls?

The president has this responsibility. Such appointments are subject to senatorial confirmation.

What differences are there among ambassadors, other public ministers, and consuls?

The head of a U.S. embassy, and the chief U.S. representative abroad, is called the ambassador, but the ambassador typically has other public ministers who work with him or her. The term "consul" is often used to refer to an individual who serves abroad primarily to deal with issues of trade and commerce rather than diplomacy.

Does the president need the Senate's approval to fire members of his cabinet and other officers that he appoints with Senate consent?

No, the president does not need such approval. The Constitution is silent on the matter, but the first Congress—which consisted of many members who had attended the Constitutional Convention—decided that such consent was not necessary. The Supreme Court subsequently affirmed this judgment in *Myers v. United States* (1926) when it declared that the president had the right to fire a first-class postmaster without senatorial consent.

Court decisions, most notably *Humphrey's Executor v. United States* (1935), have subsequently ruled that presidential prerogatives to fire officers are somewhat limited in the cases of officials exercising quasi-judicial or quasi-legislative—as opposed to executive—functions.

What is the rationale behind judicial rulings that the president may fire cabinet and other executive officials without senatorial consent?

As chief executive, the president is responsible for seeing that the laws are faithfully executed, and he has to rely on his subordinates to do this. He is also presumably in the best position to assess the performance of individuals who work for him.

In addition to appointing ambassadors, cabinet members, and other civil officers, what other appointments does the president make?

He appoints members of the Supreme Court and other offices of the United States whose appointments are not otherwise provided for in the Constitution.

Does the Senate always approve presidential nominees to the U.S. Supreme Court?

No, it has rejected almost one-fourth of them.

Are there any limits on the president's power to appoint ambassadors and other public ministers?

Yes, before appointments go into effect, the Senate must first approve of them.

The Constitution refers to "inferior Officers." Who are they?

They are members of the government whose offices are not specifically mentioned in the Constitution and who are under the direct authority of cabinet officers or other individuals appointed by the president rather than being immediately accountable to the president.

Who provides for the appointment of the inferior officers that the Constitution mentions?

Congress makes such provisions.

What three choices does Congress have in deciding who shall appoint inferior officers not otherwise listed in the Constitution?

It may vest such appointments in the president alone, in the courts, or in the heads of departments.

What happens when the president desires to make an appointment during a Senate recess?

The president may make temporary appointments by granting commissions that expire at the end of the congressional session. Congress and the president are engaged in a dispute, which the U.S. Supreme Court will likely ultimately resolve, as to what constitutes an official congressional recess.

Does a president have any powers that are not listed in the Constitution?

The president certainly has some discretionary authority in pursuit of the general powers that the Constitution grants. Some commentators have also argued that, especially in the realm of foreign affairs, the president can exercise certain inherent powers. In *Youngstown Sheet & Tube Co. v. Sawyer,* or the *Steel Seizure Cases* (1951), the Supreme Court ruled that, absent congressional authorization, the president does not have power to seize domestic steel mills to avoid a strike in time of war, but, in other cases, it has recognized that the president has broad discretion in foreign policy matters.

SECTION 3: ADDITIONAL DUTIES

Does the Constitution mention any specific presidential speeches?

The Constitution indirectly refers to the president's annual state of the union address when it specifies that "he shall from time to time give to the Congress information on the state of the Union," but the specific term did not come into common currency until the 1930s and 1940s.

Does the Constitution require the president to give this, or any other speeches before Congress in person?

No. Although George Washington inaugurated this practice, Thomas Jefferson discontinued it, and it was not resumed until Woodrow Wilson (a great admirer of the British system where the prime minister routinely appears before parliament). This has subsequently been standard procedure.

What role, if any, does the president have in the legislative process?

In addition to advocating policies in speeches that they give, the president has the power to "recommend" such measures "as he shall judge necessary and expedient." In addition, the president has the power to veto measures with which he disagrees.

Although Congress has the power to make laws, presidents do in some cases have the authority to issue executive orders. Indeed, they have issued more than 15,000 such orders since they were numbered, beginning in 1907. In most cases, presidents issue such orders under authority granted by Congress.

One of the most controversial orders that a U.S. president has ever promulgated was that which Franklin D. Roosevelt issued at the request of the U.S. military to exclude Americans of Japanese ancestry from areas in California where it was believed that invasion might be threatened during World War II. Although the Supreme Court upheld this order in *Korematsu v. United States* (1944), lower courts declared these actions illegal in the 1980s, and Congress eventually authorized reparation payments for Japanese who had been detained under these orders. The Supreme Court has addressed a number of cases since the terrorist attacks against the United States on September 11, 2001, involving the rights of individuals accused of terrorist actions.

Does the president have the power to convene both houses of Congress?

Yes. This power was more important in the early history of the nation when Congress did not meet throughout the year, as, for all practical purposes, it now does.

If the two houses of Congress disagree on when they should adjourn, who has power to resolve this controversy?

The president is authorized to do so.

Who is responsible for receiving ambassadors and other foreign representatives?

The president is. This highlights the president's role as chief of state.

Who is responsible for seeing that U.S. laws are faithfully executed?

The president is. This is why the presidency is referred to as the head of the executive branch.

What does the executive power involve?

This responsibility gives the president some discretionary power. In the case of *In Re Neagle* (1890), the Court ruled that a president can exercise certain powers that the Constitution does not specifically mention (in this case, appointing a marshal to protect a justice of the U.S. Supreme Court).

Who is responsible for commissioning officers of the United States?

The president is.

Japanese Americans were forced to relocate from the west coast to various internment camps in the United States during World War II. (Library of Congress)

SECTION 4: IMPEACHMENT

Which officers of the government may be removed after being convicted of an impeachable offense?

Article II, Section 4 specifies that "the President, Vice president, and all civil Officers of the United States" are subject to such removal. Civil officers would include cabinet officers and judges but not members of Congress, who are subject to expulsion by a two-thirds vote of other members of their house.

How many grounds for impeachment does the Constitution specify?

It specifies three. They involve conviction of treason, bribery, or other high crimes and misdemeanors.

What is treason?

Article III, Section 3 of the Constitution specifically defines treason as "levying War against them [the United States], or in adhering to their Enemies, giving them Aid and Comfort."

What are "high crimes and misdemeanors"?

The Constitution does not specifically define such offenses, but there is general consensus that such crimes involve either criminal wrongdoing or something closely akin to it. The Constitution did not intend for the House to impeach individuals simply because they have unpopular political beliefs.

How many times has the U.S. House of Representatives impeached a U.S. president?

The House has only impeached two presidents, Andrew Johnson and Bill Clinton. It seems likely that the House would also have impeached Richard M. Nixon had he not resigned from his office.

How many presidents has the U.S. Senate removed from office through an impeachment trial in American history?

None have been so removed. Andrew Johnson avoided conviction in the Senate on impeachment charges by a single vote. Richard Nixon resigned after the House Judiciary Committee voted on articles of impeachment against him but prior to any vote by the entire House or a trial in the Senate. The Senate failed to muster two-thirds majorities to convict Clinton.

BIBLIOGRAPHY

Books

Edward S. Corwin, *The President: Office and Powers, 1787–1984,* ed. Randall W. Bland, Theodore T. Hindson, and Jack W. Peltason, 5th rev. ed. (New York: New York University Press, 1984).

Forrest McDonald, *The American Presidency: An Intellectual History* (Lawrence: University Press of Kansas, 1994).

Robert M. Hardaway, *The Electoral College and the Constitution: The Case for Preserving Federalism* (Westport, CT: Praeger, 1994).

Louis Henkin, *Foreign Affairs and the Constitution* (New York: Norton, 1972).

Charles O. Jones, *The Presidency in a Separated System* (Washington, D.C.: The Brookings Institution, 1994).

Michael Nelson, ed. *Guide to the Presidency and the Executive Branch,* 5th ed., II vols. (Washington, D.C.: Congressional Quarterly, 2013).

Richard E. Neustadt, *Presidential Power* (New York: Wiley, 1980).

Mark J. Rozell, *Executive Privilege: The Dilemma of Secrecy and Democratic Accountability* (Baltimore: The John Hopkins University Press, 1994).

Robert J. Spitzer, *The Presidential Veto: Touchstone of the American Presidency* (Albany: State University of New York Press, 1988).

Jeffrey K. Tulis, *The Rhetorical Presidency* (Princeton, NJ: Princeton University Press, 1987).

Donald Young, *American Roulette: The History and Dilemma of the Vice Presidency* (New York: The Viking Press, 1974).

Cases

Clinton v. Jones, 525 U.S. 820 (1997).

Humphrey's Executor v. United States, 295 U.S. 602 (1935).

In Re Neagle, 135 U.S. 1 (1890).

Korematsu v. United States, 323 U.S. 214 (1944).

Myers v. United States, 472 U.S. 52 (1926).

Nixon v. Fitzgerald, 457 U.S. 731 (1982).

United States v. Nixon, 418 U.S. 174 (1974).

Youngstown Sheet and Tube Co. v. Sawyer, 343 U.S. 579 (1952).

Chapter 4

Article III: The Judicial Branch

SECTION 1: ORGANIZATION, APPOINTMENT, AND TENURE

What does Article III do?

Just as Article I outlines the powers of the legislative branch and Article II outlines the powers of the executive branch, Article III outlines the powers of the judicial branch.

What feature distinguishes the judicial branch from the other two?

It is the only one of the three branches whose members are not elected.

Front view of the U.S. Supreme Court building in Washington, D.C. (VisualField/iStockPhoto.com)

What is the only court that the U.S. Constitution specifically names?

The U.S. Supreme Court is.

According to the Constitution, how many members does the Supreme Court have?

The Constitution does not specify. Throughout American history, the number has varied from 5 to 10. Congress has set the number at 9 (8 associates and a chief justice) since the Civil War, but there is no constitutional obstacle to changing this number. The last serious attempt to change this number, President Franklin Roosevelt's so-called Court-packing plan, was a political disaster.

How do individuals become members of the federal judiciary?

Article II, Section 2 of the Constitution specifies that the president appoints them subject to the advice and consent of the Senate.

On what basis do presidents make their selections to the court?

They select such members much as they might make other appointments to governmental offices, recognizing, of course, that they need to appoint individuals with legal training. Presidents may consider ideology, overall competence, party affiliation, geographical, racial, ethnic, or gender balance, past loyalty and friendship, experience, the likelihood of having nominees confirmed in the Senate, and a variety of other factors.

What qualifications does the Constitution outline for judges and justices?

In contrast to the other branches, and likely because judges are appointed and confirmed rather than elected, the Constitution establishes no such qualifications. Today, a law degree from a recognized institution is almost a sine qua non for a judicial appointment, but this is an extra constitutional requirement.

How long do judges (generally called justices) on the U.S. Supreme Court serve?

They serve "during good Behavior."

How long do other federal judges serve?

They also serve "during good Behavior."

What does the phrase "during good Behavior" mean?

This means that judges serve until they die, resign, or are impeached, convicted, and removed from office.

What process does the Constitution establish for selecting the chief justice?

The president specifically nominates a new chief justice on the death, removal, or resignation of the sitting chief, who must, like other Supreme Court nominees, be confirmed by the Senate. The president may choose someone on the existing court to be the chief, or the president may appoint an outsider to the bench.

What stipulation does the Constitution make in regard to the salaries of judges?

It provides that Congress may increase, but not decrease, such salaries during their terms.

How does the provision for judicial salaries compare with provisions for members of the two elected branches?

The Twenty-Seventh Amendment requires that the salaries of members of Congress cannot be altered until there is an intervening election, and Congress may not raise or lower the salary of a president during the president's term of office.

Why does the Constitution allow Congress to raise, but not lower, the salaries of judges and justices while they remain on the bench?

Because they serve comparatively long terms, many judges would be penalized during times of inflation if their salaries could not be raised during this time. The prohibition against having their salaries lowered is designed to protect them from undue congressional influence.

SECTION 2: JURISDICTION

Do U.S. courts have a general right to examine federal laws?

No, the Constitution only vests courts with jurisdiction over "cases" that arise. Scholars have observed that American courts have no "self-starter." Judges apply and interpret law only in the course of deciding concrete cases and controversies. Courts have developed elaborate rules of "standing" to ascertain whether parties have proper cause to stand before them and "justiciability" to decide whether judicial remedies are appropriate.

What part of the Constitution outlines the jurisdiction of the federal courts?

Article III, Section 2 does.

What did the Constitution mean when it extended judicial power to all cases in law and equity?

Law and equity were the two main divisions of English law. Traditional law proceeded by assessing punishments like fines and imprisonment. Equity law was designed for cases when more flexible remedies—injunctions against certain activities, for example—might be needed.

Does the federal judicial power extend to cases affecting ambassadors, public ministers, and consuls?

Yes.

Article III, Section 2 refers to admiralty jurisdiction. Where else does the Constitution refer to admiralty law?

Article I, Section 8 grants Congress power "to define and punish piracies and felonies committed on the high seas, and offenses against the law of nations."

What two general types of jurisdiction do courts exercise?

The Constitutions grants jurisdiction based on subject matter and on the basis of the parties to suits.

What matters get to federal courts on the basis of their subject matter?

Such cases include those

1. Under (a) the United States Constitution;
           (b) the laws of the United States, and
           (c) treaties made under their authority.
2. Affecting ambassadors and related personnel; and
3. Involving admiralty and maritime law.

Under what circumstances does the Constitution give jurisdiction to federal courts based on the parties to the suits?

Such cases include those involving controversies

1. Where the United States is a party;
2. Between two or more states;

3. Between a state and citizens of another state;

4. Between citizens of different states;

5. Between citizens of the same state claiming lands under grants of different states; and

6. Between a state, or its citizens and foreign states or subjects.

Which, if any, of the provisions in Article III of the Constitution related to judicial jurisdiction did an amendment subsequently modify?

The Eleventh Amendment removed jurisdiction from federal courts in cases where a citizen of one state was sued by a citizen of another state or foreign nation. Courts have subsequently extended this doctrine to encompass other areas of state sovereign immunity.

Article III of the Constitution speaks of original jurisdiction. What is original jurisdiction?

This refers to those cases that a court hears for the first time. Typically, this is a trial court where both law and facts are at issue.

What does Article III of the Constitution mean when it refers to appellate jurisdiction?

This refers to cases that are heard before a higher court "on appeal" from a lower court.

Does the U.S. Supreme Court ever hear cases of original jurisdiction?

Yes, but such cases are rare.

Under what circumstances does the U.S. Supreme Court hear cases for the first time (cases of original jurisdiction)?

The Supreme Court has original jurisdiction (albeit not necessarily "exclusive" original jurisdiction) in cases affecting ambassadors, other public ministers and consuls, and those in which states are parties. In such cases, the Court often appoints a special master, or expert, to make an initial judgment and subsequently reviews the special master's judgment.

Under what circumstances does the Supreme Court hear cases "on appeal"?

It hears cases "on appeal" in all other cases outlined in Article III. The Supreme Court hears most of its cases on appeal.

How do cases get to the Supreme Court on appeal?

The federal system currently consists of three tiers. A set of 94 U.S. District Courts hear most trials. Decisions from these courts may be appealed to 1 of 13 U.S. Courts of Appeal. These decisions may in turn be appealed to the U.S. Supreme Court. Writs of certiorari are the most usual means of registering such appeals. Under current law, the Supreme Court has almost complete discretion over which cases it chooses to hear.

Cases that involve federal constitutional questions may also be appealed to the U.S. Supreme Court from the highest court in each state, usually designated as the state supreme court.

How are Supreme Court decisions publicized?

Such decisions are printed in the official *U.S. Reports* and in a number of unofficial reports. Citations to a Supreme Court decision typically include title of the case, the volume number in which a case may be found, the page on which it starts, and the year in which it was decided. Early cases also include the name of the reporter. A citation to *Marbury v. Madison,* 1 Cranch (5 U.S.) 137 (1803), such as is found in the bibliography at the end of this chapter, thus indicates that this 1803 decision can be found in volume 5 of the *U.S. Reports* (the first volume reported by Cranch) beginning at page 137. Reports of U.S. district and appellate courts use a similar citation system.

Does the U.S. Constitution require that the Supreme Court or other courts rule unanimously?

No. Typically, a justice authors a majority decision for the Court (alternatively, the majority may issue an unsigned per curiam opinion on behalf of the Court), but it is common for judges and justices to file concurring or dissenting opinions.

What is a concurring opinion?

A concurring opinion is one written by a justice who agrees with the Court's decision but not necessarily with all the reasoning advanced to support it.

What is a dissenting opinion?

This is an opinion filed by one of more justices disagreeing with the majority decision. Although such decisions have no legal force, they serve as a kind of appeal to history.

Does the Constitution make any exceptions to the appellate jurisdiction of the U.S. Supreme Court?

It grants such jurisdiction subject to "such exceptions, and under such regulations as the Congress shall make." This is one of the most enigmatic provisions in the Constitution. On occasion, the Supreme Court has acquiesced in laws that have limited its jurisdiction. Could Congress take away all the Court's jurisdiction? Could a law that attempts selectively to remove jurisdiction over certain controversial issues, itself be unconstitutional? Such actions could jeopardize enforcement of amendments that may have subsequently altered the original grant of jurisdiction, but no one can be sure what limits the Court might accept or reject unless and until such an action happens.

Does the Constitution mention the right to a jury trial anywhere other than in the Sixth and Seventh Amendments?

Yes, Article III provides that the trial of all [federal] crimes, other than impeachments, shall be by jury.

What provision does Article III make as to where trials must take place?

If a crime is committed within a state, the trial must be held within that state.

Who decides where trials not committed within the states are held?

Article III grants Congress power to adopt legislation on the subject.

SECTION 3: TREASON

In what two places does the U.S. Constitution mention treason?

In Article II, Section 4, the Constitution lists treason as grounds for impeachment; the Constitution defines treason in Article III, Section 3.

What, if any, conditions does the Constitution establish to convict an individual of treason?

The Constitution requires either the testimony of two or more witnesses to an overt act or a confession in open court.

Why does the U.S. Constitution require that confessions for treason be made in "open" court?

This serves to prevent coerced confessions.

Who establishes the penalties for treason?

Congress does.

What, if any, limits does the Constitution establish on penalties for treason?

It specifies that "no attainder of treason shall work corruption of blood, or forfeiture except during the life of the person attainted."

What is "corruption of blood"?

This is a penalty that extends to the descendants of a lawbreaker.

Why does the Constitution prohibit this?

It did so because the Framers considered guilt to be personal rather than hereditary.

MISCELLANEOUS

What do scholars mean when they refer to the courts' power of statutory construction?

Statutory construction is the process by which courts interpret the meaning of the laws.

What happens if the courts interpret a law in a manner that Congress did not intend?

Congress has the power to adopt a new law, clarifying its earlier language.

What is judicial review?

Judicial review is the power that courts sometimes exercise, in the course of deciding cases, of striking down state laws, acts of Congress, or actions of officials that the courts believe are contrary to the Constitution and thus void.

Where does the Constitution mention judicial review?

The Constitution does not specifically mention either the term or the practice, but judicial review is consistent with checks and balances and with the idea of a written constitution, designed to be superior to ordinary acts of legislation. The Supremacy Clause in Article VI is often cited in justifications of judicial review, especially of state legislation that conflicts with the Constitution.

What are the origins of judicial review?

The power can be traced back to a famous 17th-century precedent known as Dr. Bonhom's Case (1610), in which Sir Edward Coke of England declared that even a law of Parliament was subject to the constraints of right reason. Over time, the English adopted the principle of parliamentary sovereignty whereby the Parliament had complete power. Because Americans had rejected the idea of parliamentary sovereignty in the Revolutionary War period, they chose instead to emphasize the priority of a written constitution, specifically delineating relationships among branches and protecting individual rights.

The first case in which the Supreme Court exercised judicial review to strike down a provision of a law passed by Congress was in the case of *Marbury v. Madison* in 1803. In this case, Chief Justice John Marshall decided that a provision of the Judiciary Act of 1789 under which Marbury had brought his case to the Supreme Court was unconstitutional, and, although he believed Marbury had been wronged, Marshall thus rejected Marbury's plea for an order, or writ of mandamus, to the secretary of state ordering him to deliver a commission for a position of justice of the peace that he had refused to deliver to Marbury.

Who can reverse a court's exercise of judicial review striking down a law or other governmental actions?

Parties who lose cases in lower courts may appeal. If the U.S. Supreme Court issues a decision on a constitutional issue, it remains in place until the Court changes its mind in a similar case and/or until the states ratify a constitutional amendment to reverse the Court's judgment.

Do American courts reverse themselves often?

Although such reversals get considerable attention, courts usually affirm precedents. Courts generally adhere to principle of stare decisis, meaning let the precedent stand.

What are the advantages of judicial adherence to precedents?

Adherence to precedents lends stability to the law and makes it easier for citizens to plan for the future.

Are there examples where the U.S. Supreme Court has changed its mind after exercising judicial review?

Yes, there are. Normally, courts adhere to the principle of stare decisis, or that of adhering to existing precedents. Especially when it comes to constitutional matters, however, the Court is sometimes willing to reconsider its earlier judgments.

Some of the Court's most dramatic decisions have involved reversals of earlier judgments. For example, in *Brown v. Board of Education* (1954) the Court reversed its decision in *Plessy v. Ferguson* (1896) and decided that racial segregation was in violation of the Fourteenth Amendment. In *Baker v. Carr* (1962), the Court reversed earlier precedents and decided that state legislative apportionment was justiciable (or subject to court scrutiny) under the equal protection clause of the Fourteenth Amendment. Many of the Court's judgments in the 1960s regarding the rights of criminal defendants reversed earlier decisions.

Have any constitutional amendments reversed Supreme Court decisions?

Yes.

How many have done so?

There are at least four clear cases. The Eleventh Amendment reversed a Supreme Court decision in *Chisholm v. Georgia* (1793), relative to suits brought against states. The Thirteenth and Fourteenth Amendments reversed the Court's notorious decision in *Scott v. Sanford* (1857), which had said that blacks were not and could not be U.S. citizens. The Sixteenth Amendment reversed the Supreme Court's decision that had invalidated the national income tax in *Pollock v. Farmers' Loan & Trust Company* (1895), and the Twenty-Sixth Amendment reversed the Court's decision in *Oregon v. Mitchell* (1971) and thus lowered the voting age to individuals 18 years or older in both state and federal elections.

Once states ratify an amendment to reverse a Supreme Court decision, does this end the matter?

Not necessarily. The Court still has the power to interpret the new amendment, and new amendments may be adopted. Many commentators believe that in the years immediately following the Civil War American courts gave an overly restrictive reading of the intentions of those who authored the Thirteenth and Fourteenth Amendments. These restrictive readings continued well into the twentieth century.

BIBLIOGRAPHY

Books

Henry J. Abraham, *The Judiciary: The Supreme Court in the Governmental Process,* 10th ed. (New York: New York University Press, 1996).

Henry J. Abraham, *Justices, Presidents, and Senators: A History of U.S. Supreme Court Appointments from Washington to Bush II,* 5th ed. (Lanham MD: Rowman & Littlefield, 2007).

Joan Biskupic and Elder Witt, *Guide to the U.S. Supreme Court,* 3rd ed. (Washington, D.C.: Congressional Quarterly, 1997).

Stephen L. Carter, *The Confirmation Mess: Cleaning Up the Federal Appointment Process* (New York: Basic Books, 1994).

Phillip Cooper and Howard Ball, *The United States Supreme Court: From the Inside Out* (Upper Saddle River, NJ: Prentice Hall, 1996).

John A. Garraty, ed., *Quarrels That Have Shaped the Constitution,* rev. ed. (New York: Harper & Row, Publishers, 1987).

Kermit Hall, ed., *The Oxford Companion to the Supreme Court of the United States,* 2nd ed (New York: Oxford University Press, 2005).

Robert G. McCloskey, *The American Supreme Court,* 2nd ed. (Chicago: University of Chicago Press, 1994).

David M. O'Brien, *Storm Center: The Supreme Court in American Politics,* 7th ed. (New York: W. W. Norton & Company, 2005).

Lisa Paddock, *Facts About the Supreme Court of the United S*tates (New York: H. W. Wilson Company, 1996).

Peter Renstrom, *Constitutional Law and Young Adults,* 2nd ed. (Santa Barbara, California: ABC-CLIO, 1996).

Bernard Schwartz, *A History of the Supreme Court* (New York: Oxford University Press, 1993).

David Schultz, John R. Vile, and Michelle D. Deardorff, *Constitutional Law in Contemporary America,* 2 vols. (New York: Oxford University Press, 2011).

Bernard Schwartz, *Decision: How the Supreme Court Decides Cases* (New York: Oxford University Press, 1996).

Cases

Baker v. Carr, 369 U.S. 186 (1962).

Brown v. Board of Education, 347 U.S. 483 (1954).

Chisholm v. Georgia, 2 U.S. 419 (1793).

Marbury v. Madison, 5 U.S. 137 (1803).

Oregon v. Mitchell, 400 U.S. 112 (1971).

Plessy v. Ferguson, 163 U.S. 537 (1896).

Pollock v. Farmers' Loan & Trust Company, 158 U.S. 601 (1895).

Scott v. Sandford, 60 U.S. 393 (1857).

Chapter 5

Articles IV, V, VI, and VII: Federalism, the Amending Process, Miscellaneous Matters, and Ratification

---

ARTICLE IV: THE FEDERAL SYSTEM

What is the central subject of Article IV of the Constitution?

Article IV deals with relations among states and with relations between the states and the national government.

What name do political scientists give to a government, like that of the United States, which shares powers between a national government and various subgovernments, or states?

They designate such a government as a federal government, and use the term "federalism" to describe state-national relations in such a system. The Constitution does not use either term, but the early defenders of the U.S. Constitution referred to themselves as Federalists.

What are the chief characteristics of a federal government?

In addition to dividing power between state and national authorities, such governments are characterized by written constitutions (needed to delineate powers between the two levels of government). Also, in federal systems, each government has power to operate directly on individual citizens.

What are the alternatives to federalism?

A unitary system, like that in Great Britain, recognizes no permanent state governments. Confederal systems, like those under the Articles of Confederation and the Confederate States of America, divide power between the nation and the states, but give states the upper hand and require the national government to operate through the states in acting on individual citizens.

Why did the Framers of the Constitution choose to establish a federal system?

Most of the Framers recognized that, with existing loyalties, it would be impractical to abolish the states. Not only did the states have the affection and loyalty of many Americans, but they also permitted a degree of variation in a nation that was otherwise quite large and where uniform policies might not always prove to be desirable. Maintaining a system that divides power between a central government and various state governments also seemed to be an appropriate auxiliary mechanism for protecting freedom. The Framers thought that both state and national governments would try to prevent usurpations by the other. Federal governments also give citizens multiple access points to the political process, with positions in state government often proving to be testing grounds for individuals who desire national offices.

Are there any disadvantages to the system of federalism that the U.S. Constitution established?

Although scholars may refer to a "system" of federalism, the Framers left many relationships between state and national governments to be

The Virginia state capitol building in Richmond. States continue to play a role in American government. Virginia's role as the capital of the Confederate States of America shows the dangers of excessive state independence. (Library of Congress)

worked out in the future. Such relationships are thus quite complex and can lead to controversies like those over tariffs and those that precipitated the Civil War. Although the existence of states permits local variation and experimentation, such variations may also mean that some states might not extend the same protections to rights and privileges as do others.

Do states have the right to nullify federal laws?

Politicians in the Southern states (sometimes reflecting arguments that New England Federalists had made during the War of 1812), most notably, Senator (and one-time vice president) John C. Calhoun of South Carolina, argued for such a power in the years prior to the Civil War. This doctrine, however, conflicts with the Supremacy Clause in Article VI of the Constitution—asserting the supremacy of federal laws—and is not generally accepted legal doctrine today.

Does the Constitution allow states to secede from the United States?

The Constitution is silent on the subject. In events leading to the Civil War, a number of Southern states, which sought to preserve the institution of slavery, argued that they had this right, but President Abraham Lincoln (who did not think secession would resolve conflicts between Northern and Southern states, which would necessarily remain in close geographical proximity to one another) asserted that his oath to support the Constitution of the United States mandated that he try to preserve the Union. The force of Northern arms eventually freed the slaves and preserved the Union and is generally believed to have ruled out future attempts at secession. In a case decided shortly after the Civil War, *Texas v. White* (1869), the Supreme Court referred to "an indestructible Union of indestructible states."

What is the first obligation that Article IV describes states as owing one another?

To extend "full faith and credit" to the public acts, records, and judicial proceedings of every other state.

Who is responsible for enacting legislation under which such acts, records, and proceedings shall be proved?

Congress is.

Can Congress adopt laws that allow states some discretion as to which laws they will accept from other states?

In the past, Congress and the courts have granted some leeway in cases involving compelling matters of public policy (states might thus not recognize marriages in other states between underage individuals or next of kin, for example). In 1996, Congress adopted the Defense of Marriage Act (DOMA) limiting the federal definition of marriage to the union of one man and one woman and allowing states to refuse to recognize marriages between homosexual partners that were made in other states. In *United States v. Windsor* (2013), however, the U.S. Supreme Court held that decision by the United States to use DOMA to deny a federal tax exemption for a surviving gay spouse of a gay marriage that was recognized by New York state violated protections of equal liberty guaranteed by the due process clause of the Fifth Amendment.

What parts of the Constitution refer to the "privileges and immunities" of citizens?

This phrase is used in Article IV, Section 2 and in Section 2 of the Fourteenth Amendment.

What privileges and immunities does the U.S. Constitution protect?

The Constitution includes no specific list of such privileges and immunities. The term may be a shorthand expression for fundamental rights, like those included within the federal Bill of Rights, or the Framers may chiefly have designed the term to guarantee that a state treated out of state citizens in the same manner that it treated its own.

What is extradition?

Extradition is the process of moving an individual accused of a crime from one state to another so that the individual can be tried in the state where the crime was committed. The Constitution does not specifically use the term "extradition," but it describes the process in Article IV, Section 2.

According to Article IV, what is the process for extraditing a fugitive from one state to another?

The governor of one state makes a request of the governor of another. Under current law, and contrary to practice in earlier American history, which regarded this as a moral but a legally unenforceable duty, courts may enforce such requests.

What does Article IV, Section 2 mean when it refers to persons "held to Service or Labour in one state" who escape to another?

This is another of the Constitution's euphemistic phrases used to describe individuals who were held in slavery.

What provision did Article IV make for escaped slaves?

It provided that such individuals would not be discharged from their condition by the law of the state into which they fled and that, upon demand, such states should turn them over to the state from which they fled. This led to considerable controversy in the years prior to the U.S. Civil War when Southern states often attempted quite aggressively to capture runaways (and did not always distinguish between runaways and free blacks), and Northern states were often reluctant to return individuals to servitude.

Is it possible for new states to join the Union?

Yes, originally the United States had only 13 states; today there are 50. Congress admits new states by adopting legislation, although members of Congress have introduced amendments to admit the District of Columbia, or parts thereof, as a state. Today, there is some sentiment for admitting Puerto Rico as a state.

Which branch of government is responsible for admitting new states into the Union?

Congress is.

Is it possible to form new states within the jurisdiction of existing states?

Yes.

Is it possible to form a new state by combining parts of existing states?

Yes.

What conditions does the Constitution establish for the formation of such states?

Both Congress and the legislatures of the state involved must give their consent.

What is the status of new states once they are admitted to the Union?

The Constitution does not make any distinction between the original states and new states that have been subsequently admitted. Court decisions have established that old and new states have equal rights.

Which branch of government is responsible for disposing of U.S. property and making rules and regulations for U.S. territories?

Congress is.

What did the Constitution say about prior claims of territory by the United States or by individual states?

It specified that nothing in the document was intended to prejudice any such claims.

What does the Constitution say about the purchase of new territories?

The Constitution is silent on the subject. In 1803, President Thomas Jefferson, who generally favored interpreting the Constitution strictly, decided to purchase the Louisiana Territory from France, even without a constitutional amendment, rather than taking the chance of losing this opportunity. Jefferson's action has served as precedent for subsequent purchases, including that of Alaska from Russia. The United States has acquired other territories (for example, Guam, the Philippines, and Puerto Rico) through war.

Does the Constitution mention national parks?

No, but Congress has interpreted its power to make rules for U.S. territories and property to include federal regulation of such parks.

What is the Guarantee Clause?

This is the name, sometimes spelled as the Guaranty Clause, given to the clause in Article IV, Section 4 of the Constitution.

What does the Guarantee Clause say?

It provides that "the United States shall guarantee to every state in this union a republican form of government."

What does "republican" mean in this context?

It means representative government.

In addition to the Guarantee Clause, what other obligation of the nation to the states does Article IV list?

It also provides that, upon the application of a state, the national government shall protect it against invasion.

According to the Constitution, who has the duty of applying to the national government for help if threatened by such an invasion?

The Constitution designates the state legislature, or, in cases where the legislature cannot be convened, the governor.

What is the "political questions" doctrine?

This doctrine is not specifically mentioned in the Constitution, but Court decisions, most notably *Luther v. Borden* (1849), which involved the legitimacy of state governments in the wake of Dorr's Rebellion, have established that the judgment as to whether or not a state is "republican" is entrusted to the political, or elected, branches of government, rather than to the judiciary.

How do the people of a state know that the Congress accepts its government as "republican"?

Congress recognizes a state government as republican when it seats its representatives. Thus, in the period immediately following the Civil War, Congress refused to seat delegates from certain Southern states that had participated in the rebellion until such states met certain conditions.

What does the Constitution say about local governments?

It is silent on the subject. U.S. law treats local governments as part of state governments.

ARTICLE V: THE AMENDING PROCESS

Where does the Constitution outline an amending process?

It does so in Article V.

Why do scholars sometimes refer to the amending process as an alternative to revolution?

They do so because the process is designed as a substitute for revolutionary change that might otherwise be required. The American Founders recognized that the British inability or failure to respond to colonial grievances short of war had been a major cause of the Revolutionary War.

Who proposes amendments to the Constitution?

Members of Congress may propose amendments or states may call for Congress to call a constitutional convention for this purpose.

Approximately, how many amendments have members introduced in Congress?

As of 2013, members of Congress have introduced more than 11,500 such proposals. Several subjects (like women's rights and prayer in public schools), however, have often generated hundreds of separate proposals.

In addition to proposals members of Congress have introduced, more than 125 groups or individuals have proposed major rewrites of the Constitution; to date, none of these has succeeded in securing sufficient congressional or popular support.

What congressional majorities does the Constitution require to propose an amendment to the Constitution?

It requires two-thirds majorities of both houses of Congress.

Does the Constitution require a president to sign amendments that the necessary majorities of Congress propose?

The Constitution does not directly answer this question, although given that two-thirds majorities of Congress can override such a presidential veto (the same majorities that are required for Congress to propose an amendment), an attempt to veto would appear almost predestined to failure. In an early case, *Hollingsworth v. Virginia* (1798), the Supreme Court ruled that the president's signature was not required for proposed amendments, and it has continued to adhere to that precedent.

Which governments have the responsibility for ratifying constitutional amendments?

The states do.

How may the states ratify an amendment?

They may do so by convening state conventions on the subject or by vote of their legislatures.

Who decides which mechanism shall be used to ratify amendments?

The Constitution specifies that Congress makes such a designation when it submits amendments to the state for ratification.

What majority of states does Article V require to ratify an amendment?

Article V requires three-fourths of the states.

By what votes must states ratify amendments?

The Constitution does not specify a particular majority. Existing case law leaves this matter to the states to decide for themselves.

Does the Constitution require governors to sign state ratifications of amendments?

The Constitution is silent on the subject, but practice suggests that such signatures are unnecessary.

Can a state rescind its ratification of an amendment if three-fourths of the states have not yet ratified it?

The Constitution is silent on the subject, and it continues to be a matter of intense scholarly debate. Some states attempted to rescind their ratification of the proposed Equal Rights Amendment (designed to guarantee equal rights to women), especially after Congress extended the deadline for ratification of this amendment, but, after the new deadline also passed without ratification, the Supreme Court never heard a case on the matter.

Can a state vote to ratify an amendment that it has previously rejected?

Article V is silent on the subject, but current practice accepts such ratifications as valid.

Who certifies that states have ratified a constitutional amendment?

The Constitution is silent on the subject. In early American history, the secretary of state performed this function. Congress subsequently passed this job on to the administrator of the General Services Administration (then responsible for publishing the *Federal Register*). Both functions are now the responsibility of the archivist of the United States. Although such certifications may help inform the public that an amendment has been ratified, it is not altogether clear that such certification is actually necessary for an amendment to go into effect. Supreme Court decisions have indicated that ratification is complete on the day that the last state has ratified an amendment.

What procedure does the Constitution establish in order to call a convention to propose amendments?

Two-thirds of the states must petition Congress for such a convention.

On how many occasions have the necessary majorities under Article V proposed a constitutional convention to propose amendments?

There have been none. States have made more than 300 petitions for conventions in American history, but, to date, two-thirds of the

states do not appear to have called for a convention on a singular subject or subjects in a time that was considered contemporaneous enough to
obligate Congress to call such a convention.

If it receives requests from two-thirds of the states, does Congress have any discretion as to whether to call such a convention?

The language appears obligatory—Congress "shall" call such a convention. There is continuing dispute as to the degree that Congress could adopt
legislation under the necessary and proper clause to govern such a convention and how binding it would be. To date, despite several attempts to do so,
Congress has not adopted legislation on the subject.

Can Congress or the states limit the subject or subjects of a Constitutional Convention called to propose constitutional amendments?

Some states provide for such limits on conventions called to rewrite or
modify their constitutions, but there is disagreement as to whether or not a
national convention could be so limited and whether Congress, the states,
or both could so limit it. Political constraints might be sufficient to limit
the scope of such deliberations.

Once Congress proposes an amendment, how long do states have to ratify it?

The Constitution does not specify. Some amendments have had internal
deadlines—usually seven years. They are presumably self-enforcing. The
proposed Equal Rights Amendment had a seven-year limit in its authorizing resolution, rather than in the amendment's text, and, in a controversial action that the Supreme Court never reviewed, Congress subsequently
extended this deadline.

Congress ratified the Twenty-Seventh Amendment, first proposed as
part of the Bill of Rights with no internal deadline for ratification, in 1992,
over 200 years later.

How many amendments have the necessary majorities of Congress proposed that the required number of states have not ratified?

As of 2013, there have been six. These dealt, respectively, with
representation in Congress (the original proposed First Amendment), titles
of nobility (known as the Reed Amendment), the continuation of slavery

(the Corwin Amendment), child labor, equal rights for women, and representation for the District of Columbia.

Who decides whether states have ratified an amendment?

In *Dillon v. Gloss* (1921), the Supreme Court said that, to be valid, an amendment must express a "contemporary consensus." In *Coleman v. Miller* (1939), however, the Supreme Court said that the matter of time limits and related issues were "political questions" for Congress to decide. In subsequent years, other decisions have modified the political questions doctrine, and in some circumstances courts might be better able to establish consistent rules on the subject.

Does Article V specify any limits on the amending process?

It specifies two limits. Scholars often identify these as "entrenchment clauses."

What are these two entrenchment clauses?

One such limit prohibited any alteration in the prohibition of any congressional regulation of slave importation prior to 1808. The second prohibits states from being deprived of their equal suffrage in the Senate without their consent.

Do either of the two limits on the substance of amendments remain in force?

The provision related to slavery had a built-in time limit that has long since passed. The provision prohibiting states from being deprived of their equal suffrage in the Senate remains in force.

Why did the Framers prohibit states from being deprived of their equality in the Senate?

The Constitutional Convention had been torn over the issue of state representation. The Virginia Plan had proposed that states should be represented in the legislature according to population. The New Jersey Plan had proposed that all states be represented (as under the Articles of Confederation) in the legislature equally. After intense debates, the Great, or Connecticut, Compromise specified that representation in the House of Representatives would be according to population and representation in the Senate would be equal. Small states would have been reluctant to enter a union where their equality could be changed. Interestingly, the Supreme Court has outlawed such equal geographical representation plans at the state level.

Are there any limits on the amending process other than those that Article V specifies?

Some scholars have argued that amendments that radically changed the nature of the Constitution might be improper, and lawyers have presented arguments that a number of amendments were unconstitutional, but, to date, the U.S. Supreme Court has never invalidated an amendment on this ground.

Is the constitutional amending process the exclusive mechanism for changing the Constitution?

Quite clearly, customs and usages have modified many provisions of the Constitution without formal amendments. Scholars have also pointed to some events in constitutional history, including the changes inaugurated in constitutional understandings by the Supreme Court during the New Deal, where political actors have initiated major changes short of constitutional amendment, or where amendments were ratified using somewhat dubious procedures—delegates to the Constitutional Convention did not abide by the guidelines in the Articles of Confederation, and Southern states were required to ratify the Civil War Amendments as a condition to sending representatives back to Congress. Adhering to Article V as the exclusive means of amendment, however, is the best way of assuring that the Constitution retains its place as fundamental law.

Is it possible to amend the Constitution through mechanisms like the initiative or referendum?

Some states allow citizens to propose amendments or laws (an initiative) or to vote on them (a referendum), but the Constitution makes no explicit provision for this.

In recent years, Yale's Professor Akhil Reed Amar has proposed that "We the People" might modify the Constitution by initiatives, referenda, or other mechanisms not specified in Article V, but such theories will be difficult to prove absent such actions by "We the People" and judicial judgments of their constitutionality. Moreover, such attempts could prove to be highly destabilizing.

Does the current amending process mandate periodic review and amendment of the Constitution?

No, there are no such automatic reviews. At the time the Constitution was written, some state constitutional provisions provided mandatory review of their constitutions on a periodic basis by Councils of Revision. Similarly, Thomas Jefferson proposed on several occasions that constitutions should be rewritten every generation, which he calculated at about every 19 or 20. James Madison opposed such periodic revision on the basis that it would lead to instability and would undermine respect for the Constitution and the system of laws that it created.

Is the current amending process too easy?

Given that only 27 amendments have been ratified in a span of time covering more than 200 years, it would certainly be difficult to make this argument. The current process appears to pose major obstacles to speedy or massive constitutional changes that do not have relatively strong and widespread national support.

Is the current amending process too difficult?

This remains a point of controversy. Certainly, the current process is quite difficult, and relatively few amendments have been adopted. Since the founding fathers intended to guard the Constitution against precipitous change, they might be quite happy with the result. Would-be reformers are often more frustrated with such a system, and they have offered numerous proposals to liberalize the process.

Is it possible to repeal a constitutional amendment?

Yes, it is possible but generally difficult.

How can the people repeal an amendment?

Acting through Article V, they can repeal an amendment by adopting another amendment, as they did when the Twenty-First Amendment repealed the Eighteenth and thus eliminated national alcoholic prohibition.

Is it possible to change the amending process?

Yes, with the likely exception of the entrenchment clause related to equal state suffrage in the Senate, Congress and the states can amend Article V in the same manner as any other provision of the Constitution.

ARTICLE VI: MISCELLANEOUS MATTERS

What provision did the Constitution make for debts that the Articles of Confederation had incurred?

The first paragraph of Article VI made provision for the new government to accept this debt.

What is the supremacy clause?

This is the name given to the clause that is found in the second paragraph of Article VI.

What does the supremacy clause say?

It specifies that "[t]his Constitution, and the laws of the United States which shall be made in pursuance thereof, and all treaties made, or which shall be made, under the authority of the United States, shall be the supreme law of the land, and the judges in every state shall be bound thereby; anything in the constitution of laws of any state to the contrary notwithstanding."

Why does the supremacy clause distinguish between laws and treaties?

The Framers appear to have employed the language they used for treaties—treaties made "under the authority of the United States" rather than made "in pursuance thereof"—not to exempt treaties from constitutional restrictions, but to indicate that treaties entered into under the Articles of Confederation, like debts so encumbered, would continue to be in force. Modern Supreme Court decisions, most notably *Reid v. Covert* (1957), have indicated that the Court believes that treaty provisions are subject, like other laws, to constitutional restraints.

What is the importance of the supremacy clause in Article VI of the Constitution?

The clause, which originated in the New Jersey Plan, establishes the supremacy of federal laws over conflicting state laws and obligates state judges to follow the U.S. Constitution in cases of conflict.

The Constitution specifies the oath of the president of the United States. What about other officers?

The Constitution does not spell out a specific oath, but it provides that other officers in both state and federal governments must take an oath or affirmation to support the Constitution.

Does the Constitution place any restrictions on the oaths or affirmations that public office holders take?

Yes, the Constitution prohibits any "religious Tests." Thus, an individual cannot be required to affirm a religious belief, or lack of it, in order to assume a public office. This provision expresses a concern for religious liberty that the First Amendment expanded.

ARTICLE VII: RATIFICATION

How was the Constitution ratified?

It was ratified by conventions held within individual states.

Was the method for ratifying the Constitution consistent with provisions in the Articles of Confederation that were in effect at the time?

No, this method was technically illegal since the Articles required that amendments be proposed by Congress and adopted unanimously by existing state legislatures.

Why did the Framers require state conventions to ratify the new Constitution?

This was consistent with the general theory of constitutions that had developed during the period of state constitution–making that had accompanied the Revolutionary War. Such a method was thought to be more democratic than alternative means. This method also served to bypass existing state legislatures, the members of which would be losing power relative to the new national government.

How many states did the Framers specify must ratify the new Constitution before it went into effect?

They required nine state ratifications, which was equivalent to three-fourths of the states that had sent representatives to the Constitutional Convention.

Where is the only place that the Constitution specifically references the Convention whose authors composed it?

Article VII provides the only such acknowledgment.

Why does Article VII refer to "the states present" when describing who ratified the Constitution?

This phraseology, which Benjamin Franklin suggested, obscured the fact that the state of Rhode Island did not send delegates to the Constitutional Convention.

Did the other states unanimously consent to the Constitution?

One or more delegates from each of the state signed the Constitution. New York had sent three delegates; only one, Alexander Hamilton, signed the Constitution, so he signed on his own behalf rather than for his state. Two Virginia delegates, Edmund Randolph and George Mason, did not sign, although this left a majority of three others, Washington who signed as president of the Convention, and John Blair and James Madison.

Who was most responsible for the final style of the Constitution?

Gouverneur Morris of Pennsylvania served on the final Committee of Style at the Constitutional Convention and is thought to have had the greatest influence on its final style.

Who wrote out the Constitution by hand prior to its signing?

Jacob Shallus (whose name does not appear on the document) so copied, or "engrossed" the document. He was the assistant clerk of the Pennsylvania State Assembly.

How long is the Constitution?

The original is 4,543 words, including the names of the signers.

How many pages did it take to record the original Constitution?

It took four pages. Each was just over 28 inches in length and about 23.5 inches in width.

On what date did delegates present at the Convention agree to adopt the Constitution?

They did so on September 15, 1787.

By what vote did the states represented at the Convention adopt the Constitution?

The states who were present adopted it unanimously. This excluded Rhode Island, which sent no delegates, and New York, which had only one delegate (Alexander Hamilton) still present. The vote was thus 11–0.

On what date did the delegates sign the Constitution?

They signed on September 17, 1787. September 17 is appropriately designated as "Constitution Day."

How many delegates signed the Constitution?

A total of 39 of the 42 remaining delegates signed.

What physical instrument did the signing of the Declaration of Independence and the U.S. Constitution have in common?

For both, the delegates used a silver inkstand that had been hidden when the British had occupied Philadelphia.

According to the Constitution, when did American independence begin?

It began in 1776. The last clause in Article VII identifies 1787 as the 12th year of American independence.

How did George Washington identify himself when he signed the Constitution?

He identified himself as president [of the Convention] and as a "deputy" from Virginia.

Who among the remaining delegates, other than the two Virginia delegates specified above (Edmund Randolph and George Mason), decided not to sign the Constitution?

Elbridge Gerry of Massachusetts also decided not to sign.

Which delegate to the Convention had another delegate sign the Constitution for him?

Delaware's John Dickinson, a Quaker who had refused to sign the Declaration of Independence and who was absent when fellow delegates signed the Constitution, had his colleague George Read, also from Delaware, sign for him.

Which state had the largest number of individuals who signed the Constitution?

Pennsylvania, with seven delegates, had the largest number.

In what order were the states whose delegates signed the Constitution listed?

They are listed from north to south beginning on the right side of the document (where delegates ran out of space) and continuing on the left. The first two states listed are thus New Hampshire and Massachusetts (Vermont and Maine had not yet been formed) and the last two are South Carolina and Georgia (the United States had not yet acquired Florida).

Was ratification of the Constitution a foregone conclusion?

No, it was not. There were many who feared the new Constitution.

What was the name of those who supported the new constitution?

They called themselves Federalists.

What was the name of those who opposed the new constitution?

They were called Anti-Federalists.

Which state ratified the Constitution first?

Delaware was the first to ratify, voting unanimously to do so on December 6, 1787. Pennsylvania followed two days later by a much closer vote of 46–23.

What was the critical ninth state to ratify the Constitution?

New Hampshire, which ratified in June 21, 1788. Virginia, then the most populous state, followed five days later, and New York ratified one month after Virginia.

Which state was the last of the original 13 to ratify the Constitution?

Rhode Island was; it ratified on May 29, 1790, after the new Constitution had gone into effect among other ratifying states.

What would have happened if Rhode Island had never ratified the Constitution?

Presumably, the other states would have treated it as a foreign nation.

How intense was the debate over ratification of the Constitution?

It was very intense.

What records do we have of these debates?

There are ample records from this time period. The best-known apology for the new Constitution was a series of 85 newspaper articles titled *The Federalist Papers* that Alexander Hamilton, James Madison, and John Jay authored under the pen name of Publius. Scholars still consult this book to gain insight into the meaning of the Constitution.

In addition, there are several collections of Anti-Federalist writings, the most complete by Herbert Storing titled *The Complete Anti-Federalist*. Records of debates are also available from many of the state conventions that debated the Constitution (See Elliott).

Where is the original Constitution stored today?

It is now stored in the National Archives in Washington, D.C. The Declaration of Independence and the Bill of Rights are also there on display for public view. There is an elaborate security system at the Archives designed to preserve these documents in perpetuity.

BIBLIOGRAPHY

Books

Bruce Ackerman, *We the People: Foundations* (Cambridge, MA: The Belknap Press of Harvard University Press, 1991).

Richard B. Bernstein, with Jerome Agel, *Amending America: If We Love the Constitution So Much, Why Do We Keep Trying to Change It?* (New York: Times Books, 1993).

Steven R. Boyd, *Alternative Constitutions for the United States: A Documentary History* (Westport, CT: Greenwood Press, 1992).

Russell L. Caplan, *Constitutional Brinkmanship: Amending the Constitution by National Convention* (New York: Oxford University Press, 1988).

Jonathan Elliott, ed. *The Debates in the Several State Conventions on the Adoption of the Federal Constitution,* 5 vols., 2nd ed. (Philadelphia: J. B. Lippincott, 1861–1863).

Michael A. Gillespie and Michael Lienesch, eds., *Ratifying the Constitution* (Lawrence: University Press of Kansas, 1989).

Robert A. Goldwin, ed., *A Nation of States,* 2nd ed. (Chicago: Rand McNally & Company, 1974).

Alan P. Grimes, *Democracy and the Amendments to the Constitution* (Lexington, MA: Lexington Books, 1978).

Morton Grodzins, *The American System: A New View of Government in the United States* (Chicago: Rand McNally & Company, 1966).

Darren Patrick Guerra, *Perfecting the Constitution: The Case for the Article V Amendment Process* (Lanham, MD: Lexington Books, 1913).

Alexander Hamilton, James Madison, and John Jay, *The Federalist Papers,* ed. Clinton Rossiter (New York: New American Library, 1961).

Scott J. Hill and Adam Wright, eds. *Amending the Constitution by an Article V Convention* (New York: Nova Science Publishers, 2013).

David Kyvig, *Explicit and Authentic Acts: Amending the U.S. Constitution, 1776–1995* (Lawrence: University of Kansas Press, 1986).

Sanford Levinson, ed., *Responding to Imperfection: The Theory and Practice of Constitution Amendment* (Princeton, NJ: Princeton University Press, 1995).

David C. Nice, *Federalism: The Politics of Intergovernmental Relations* (New York: St. Martin's Press, 1987).

Herbert Storing, ed., *The Complete Anti-Federalist,* 7 vols. (Chicago: The University of Chicago Press, 1981).

John R. Vile, *Constitutional Change in the United States: A Comparative Study of the Role of Constitutional Amendments, Judicial Interpretations, and Legislative and Executive Actions* (Westport, CT: Praeger, 1994).

John R. Vile, *Contemporary Questions Surrounding the Constitutional Amending Process* (Westport, CT: Praeger, 1993).

John R. Vile, *Encyclopedia of Constitutional Amendments, Proposed Amendments, and Amending Issues, 1789–2010,* 3rd ed. (Santa Barbara, CA: ABC-CLIO, 2010).

John R. Vile, *Rewriting the United States Constitution: An Examination of Proposals From Reconstruction to the Present* (New York: Praeger, 1991).

Cases

Coleman v. Miller, 307 U.S. 433 (1939).
Dillon v. Gloss, 256 U.S. 368 (1921).
Hollingsworth v. Virginia, 3 U.S. 379 (1798).
Luther v. Borden, 48 U.S. 1 (1849).
Reid v. Covert, 354 U.S. 1 (1957).
Texas v. White, 74 U.S. 700 (1969).
United States v. Windsor, 570 U.S. (2013).

Chapter 6

The Adoption of the Bill of Rights and the Meaning of the First Amendment

---

THE BILL OF RIGHTS: BACKGROUND

What is the name of the first 10 amendments to the Constitution?

Today, scholars designated them collectively as the Bill of Rights; however, the amendments are not phrased so much as rights as they are as prohibitions on governmental control.

When did Congress first propose these amendments?

The first Congress proposed them in September of 1789.

How many signatures are on the congressional copy of this document?

There are two. They were those of Frederick Augustus Muhlenberg, the speaker of the House, and John Adams, the vice president.

How did Congress identify these amendments?

It referred to them as "Articles in addition to, and amendments of, the Constitution of the United States of America proposed by Congress and ratified by the Legislatures of the several states, pursuant to the Fifth Article of the original Constitution." It did not specifically mention a bill of rights.

When did the states ratify the Bill of Rights?

They ratified them on December 15, 1791, when Virginia became the 11th of 14 states to approve. In a symbolic gesture, Connecticut and Georgia added their ratifications on the sesquicentennial celebration of the adoption of the Bill of Rights in 1939.

Who was president when the Bill of Rights was ratified?

George Washington was president; he had indicated his support for such a bill in his first inaugural address.

What was the origin of the term "bill of rights"?

Most American states already had such a "bill" or "declaration" of rights prior to the addition of such a bill of rights to the national Constitution. In 1689, the English Parliament had adopted a declaration of rights of British subjects based on "A Declaration of Rights" that William of Orange had made the previous year upon his acceptance of the English crown in the "Glorious Revolution" of 1688.

What are rights?

Rights are generally defined as legitimate claims, or entitlements. The Declaration of Independence had proclaimed that all men were entitled to certain natural, or human, rights. Rights listed in a Constitution are generally referred to as constitutional, or civil, rights. Americans generally believe that just governments must protect basic individual rights.

What is the link between rights and responsibilities?

The Constitution is silent on the subject, but it is logical to assume that the two are related in at least a negative sense. If an individual is to

A guard stand on duty at the National Archives in Washington, D.C., as visitors observe the Bill of Rights, Constitution, and Declaration of Independence. (Alex Wong/Getty Images)

exercise rights, that individual is presumably obligated to refrain from interfering with similar rights exercised by other individuals.

In addition, the references in the Constitution to state militia, to voting rights, and to grand and petit juries all imply that citizens may be called upon to serve, thus again balancing rights with responsibilities.

What kind of rights does the Constitution enumerate?

By and large, the Constitution lists political rights. Unlike a number of 20th-century constitutions, the U.S. Constitution generally does not list social and economic rights. Thus, it contains no guarantees of welfare, unemployment compensation, paid vacations, minimum wages, prohibitions against child labor, and the like. Congress and the states, have, of course, adopted laws on many of these subjects.

In enforcing the Constitution, have courts treated all rights in that document equally?

No, they have not. In the years prior to 1937, the courts often gave greater attention to the protection of economic rights than to others. Since 1937, the courts have abandoned this approach but have sometimes indicated that certain other rights should be given a "preferred position."

In a famous footnote to the Carolene Products Case (*United States v. Carolene Products,* 1938), Justice Harlan Fiske Stone offered justification for extending heightened judicial scrutiny to at least three areas. These involved: (1) specific provisions within the Bill of Rights and the Fourteenth Amendment; (2) situations in which normal democratic processes appeared to be blocked; and (3) the rights of religious and ethnic minorities. To a large extent, these areas have served as the focal point of much judicial decision making since 1937.

How many amendments did Congress propose to the states as the Bill of Rights?

It proposed 12.

If the states had ratified all 12 amendments, what would have been the first 2 amendments?

The original first amendment, which fell a single state short of ratification, dealt with the formula for representation in Congress, a matter subsequently dealt with by legislation. States ratified the original second amendment in 1992 as the Twenty-Seventh Amendment. It deals with congressional pay raises.

James Madison was the fourth president of the United States from 1809–1817. He is considered to be the father of the Bill of Rights. (Library of Congress)

Who do scholars consider to be the "father" of the Bill of Rights?

James Madison. As a representative from Virginia to the first Congress, Madison compiled the proposals that became, and led the fight for, the Bill of Rights. Initially, Madison was at best a tepid supporter of such provisions. He advocated a bill of rights as a way to head off a second constitutional convention that might undo or jeopardize the work of the first, and to fulfill a campaign promise to his constituents who wanted such a bill of rights. Madison's friend Thomas Jefferson had also written letters to him touting the advantages of a bill of rights and arguing that even if such a bill did not help, it would surely do no harm.

Why did the original constitution omit a bill of rights?

Many Federalist supporters of the Constitution argued that, by creating a government with limited, separated, and balanced powers, the entire Constitution was designed to serve as a bill of rights. In addition, a number of provisions, most notably in Article I, Sections 9 and 10, serve, like the Bill of Rights, to limit governmental power.

For whatever reason, delegates to the Constitutional Convention of 1787 devoted little thought to such a bill of rights, and some critics subsequently objected to its omission, Federalist supporters of the Constitution tended to argue either that, as a government of limited powers, the national government would have no power to violate the rights for which protections were being sought or that an enumeration of such protected rights could prove dangerous if the list proved to be incomplete and the conclusion was drawn that certain cherished rights could therefore be invaded.

Where are the provisions of the Bill of Rights and other amendments located?

They are located at the end of the document in the order of their ratification.

Why did Congress add amendments the provisions of the Bill of Rights and subsequent amendment to the end of the Constitution rather than integrating them into its text?

James Madison (VA) actually argued for this latter procedure in the first congress, but Roger Sherman (CT) objected that this would make it appear as though George Washington and other Framers had approved amendments that were not then in existence. Having the amendments at the end of the Constitution certainly makes it much easier to trace constitutional history than it would otherwise be.

What sources did James Madison utilize in formulating the Bill of Rights?

He drew primarily from provisions within existing state constitutions and from proposals that the states recommended when they ratified the Constitution.

Did Madison succeed in incorporating all the provisions that he thought were important within the Bill of Rights?

No, Madison actually thought the most important change that the nation could make would be to limit the right of *states* to abridge rights of conscience. The Congress decided to include only provisions that limited the national government.

How important was the Bill of Rights in early American history?

Judging by the small number of cases that were argued before courts on the subject, it appears to have had little impact, but the values that it embodied continued to inform constitutional discourse.

What limited the impact of the Bill of Rights in early American history?

As Federalists had originally predicted, the national government made relatively few attempts to interfere with basic rights, and not all of them were adjudicated in the Supreme Court. Moreover, in *Barron v. Baltimore* (1833) the Supreme Court decided that the provisions in the Bill of Rights applied only to the national government, and thus not also to the states.

What role does the Bill of Rights play in modern American history?

Most scholars consider the Bill of Rights to be essential. In part because courts otherwise interpreted federal powers quite expansively, and in part because they have paid less attention to traditional separation of powers and federalism concerns, the constraints in the Bill of Rights have become increasingly important as restraints on governmental powers. Also, the modern understanding of the scope of the Bill of Rights has been significantly expanded.

In what way has the scope of the Bill of Rights expanded in modern times?

Today courts have applied most provisions within the Bill of Rights to limit not only the national government but also the states (through the due process clause of the Fourteenth Amendment).

What led to this expansion of the Bill of Rights as a limitation on the states as well as the national government?

The Fourteenth Amendment, ratified in 1868, protected individuals against state actions that would interfere with the due process of law or abridge their privileges and immunities as U.S. citizens. Over time, some justices and scholars came to argue that the authors of one or both of these clauses intended to "incorporate" or "absorb" various provisions within the Bill of Rights and apply them to the states.

According to current case law, do all provisions of the Bill of Rights apply to the states?

No, not quite all do. Courts have "incorporated" or applied all but about half a dozen such provisions to the states.

What theory explains why courts have applied some, but not all, provisions in the Bill of Rights to the states?

Justices have advanced several theories about the relation between the Bill of Rights and the Fourteenth Amendment. The dominant view that the

Court has taken is called "selective incorporation." Under this view, which Justice Benjamin Cardozo advanced and defended in *Palko v. Connecticut* (1937), the Fourteenth Amendment does not incorporate the entire Bill of Rights but only those provisions that deal with "fundamental rights." Over time, the Court has identified an increasing number of such rights that it considers to be fundamental, but it has generally done so on a case-by-case basis.

What other theories have justices advanced about the relationship between the Bill of Rights and the Fourteenth Amendment?

Justice Hugo Black articulated the view of "total incorporation," which would apply all the provisions within the Bill of Rights to the states.

Another view, prominently associated with former Supreme Court justice Felix Frankfurter, is that the Fourteenth Amendment provides for "fundamental fairness," rather than specifically incorporating one or another amendment.

Other views are designated as "selective incorporation plus," or "total incorporation plus." Advocates of these views argue that, in addition to provisions within the Bill of Rights, the Fourteenth Amendment incorporates more general principles of justice.

Justices articulated most of these views in opinions in the case of *Adamson v. California* (1947), which involved application of the Fifth Amendment right against self-incrimination.

When did the idea of incorporation develop?

Some argue that the proponents of the Fourteenth Amendment, most notably Representative John Bingham of Ohio, specifically intended for the Amendment to overturn *Barron v. Baltimore* (1833) and incorporate the Bill of Rights. In 1897, the Supreme Court decided that the Fifth Amendment provision prohibiting the taking of property without just compensation was incorporated into the Fourteenth Amendment. In *Gitlow v. New York* (1925), the Supreme Court ruled that the Fourteenth Amendment protected freedom of speech that was outlined in the First Amendment. The Court has incorporated other provisions on a piecemeal basis, with the most additions being made to the list during the tenure of the Warren Court in the 1950s and 1960s.

Have subsequent amendments limited any of the freedoms listed in the Bill of Rights?

To date, none have been so limited. One of the arguments that opponents advanced against the amendment designed to protect the flag from desecration was that it would be the first to weaken one of these freedoms (freedom of speech as guaranteed in the First Amendment).

THE FIRST AMENDMENT

What is the first word of the First Amendment?

"Congress" is.

How, if at all, is it significant that the first word of the First Amendment refers to Congress?

It is a strong indication that Chief Justice John Marshall was correct when he ruled in *Barron v. Baltimore* (1833) that those who framed and ratified the Bill of Rights did not originally intend for it to apply to the states but only to the national government; alternatively, one could argue that the Framers intended for other amendments without such a limitation to cover all governments.

The First Amendment begins with the word "Congress" and appears on its face only to limit that body. How restrictively does the Court read the term "Congress" today?

It does not read it very restrictively. Not only have the courts "incorporated" most provisions of the Bill of Rights into the Fourteenth Amendment where they now limit the states, but it is also doubtful that courts would allow actions by other branches of the federal government restricting First Amendment freedoms. Thus, in the Pentagon Papers Case, *New York Times Co. v. U.S.* (1971), the Court struck down an injunction against publication of governmental documents that the president and the attorney general, rather than Congress, had requested.

What is the subject of the first two guarantees of the First Amendment?

They deal with religion.

Are the references to religion in the First Amendment the first constitutional references to the subject?

No, they are not. The last clause of Article VI prohibits "religious tests" as a condition for assuming office.

Does the Constitution ever refer directly to God?

No, not unless one counts the phrase "in the year of our Lord one thousand seven hundred and Eighty seven" that is included in what is known as the attestation clause in the last paragraph of Article VII just before the delegates' signatures on the original manuscript. The Constitution of the Confederate States of America did make a direct reference to God in its preamble.

Does the U.S. Constitution define religion?
No, the Framers left this to subsequent legislation and judicial decisions.

THE ESTABLISHMENT CLAUSE

What is the name of the first clause of the First Amendment?
This provision is usually called the establishment clause.

Why is this title, the establishment clause, something of a misnomer?
This clause might be better designated as the "disestablishment," "anti-establishment," or "nonestablishment" clause, since it attempts not to establish, but to prevent the establishment, of religion.

What does the establishment clause say?
It prohibits Congress from making any "law respecting an establishment of religion."

What is the most obvious meaning of the establishment clause?
The clause is clearly intended to prevent the government from establishing an official church or mandating adherence to its beliefs or contributions to its coffers. When states originally ratified the amendment; however, some of them did give such recognition to favored churches, and the Amendment did not immediately eliminate these.

According to contemporary court decisions, does the establishment clause do anything other than prevent the government from establishing an official church or mandating adherence to its beliefs or contributions to its coffers?
In the 20th and 21st centuries, courts have used the establishment clause to strike down a variety of governmental activities that appear to endorse or support not only particular religions but religion in general.

What does the Constitution say about the separation of church and state?
The Constitution does not use this specific phrase, but the Supreme Court has often cited this principle in its interpretation of the establishment clause of the First Amendment.

Where did the expression "separation of church and state" originate?

Roger Williams, the founder of Rhode Island and an early American advocate of religious freedom, appears to have been the first to use this expression. Thomas Jefferson, proud enough of his authorship of the Virginia Statute for Religious Freedom that it was recorded on his tombstone, subsequently referred to a wall of separation of church and state when, as president, he rejected a petition asking that he call for a national day of prayer.

What are some contemporary applications of the establishment clause?

Courts have applied the provision to prayer and Bible reading in public schools, to governmental aid to parochial schools, and to governmentally sponsored religious displays.

How has the Court applied the establishment clause to the issue of prayer in public schools?

In *Engel v. Vitale* (1962), the Court ruled that a nondenominational prayer, which the state board of regents composed for schoolchildren to say before lunch, was unconstitutional. The Court has subsequently struck down laws that appear to endorse prayer in public schools over corresponding secular activities, and it has ruled it unconstitutional for public schools to post copies of the Ten Commandments (*Stone v. Graham,* 1980) or bring in a rabbi to deliver prayers at high school graduations.

The status of student-initiated and student-led prayers has not been fully established as yet. It would appear that schools may designate a time of silence that students can use for prayer as long as the schools do not appear to be endorsing prayer over corresponding secular activities, as the Court felt it had done in striking down such a law in *Wallace v. Jaffree* (1985).

How has the Court applied the establishment clause to the issue of Bible reading in public schools?

In *Abington School District v. Schempp* (1963) the Court ruled that devotional readings from the Bible and recitations of the Lord's Prayer do not have a place in public schools. It was concerned in part about who would choose the passages and translations of the Bible, as well as the effect that nonparticipation might have on nonbelievers.

Courts have not, of course, outlawed the academic study or discussion of religion in public schools. Moreover, citing what is known as the "open forum" doctrine, courts have allowed student religious groups to meet on school grounds as long as nonreligious groups are also allowed to meet.

How has the Court applied the establishment clause to the issue of state aid to parochial schools?

Generally, the Court has ruled that such aid is unconstitutional. The Court has permitted states to provide secular textbooks to students in parochial schools (partly on the basis that such books benefit the child rather than the school itself), and it has approved a limited number of other such aids—for example, services for deaf students, tax deductions for school expenses (including tuition to parochial schools), and state provision of remedial classes to needy students in public schools. Also, the Court has permitted some aid for construction of religious colleges and universities on the basis that such institutions are less pervasively sectarian than corresponding elementary or high schools.

How has the Court applied the establishment clause to governmentally sponsored religious displays?

This has been a very confusing area of the law in which clear guidelines have yet to emerge. The Court has generally allowed for religious displays, at Christmas holidays, for example, that are integrated into displays with secular symbols while rejecting displays that are solely religious or where the religious elements so dominate that the display appears to send a message that the government favors one religion over another, or religion over nonreligion.

Does the Court simply judge each establishment clause case according to its unique facts?

Certainly facts play an important role in such decisions. The Court has also formulated a standard known as the Lemon test that it uses fairly consistently, albeit not always, in establishment clause cases.

What is the Lemon test?

The Lemon test is a three-part test that the Supreme Court first formulated in a case dealing with aid to parochial schools known as *Lemon v. Kurtzman* (1971) and that courts often use in addressing establishment clause issues.

What are the three prongs of the Lemon test?

The first prong provides that, for a law to be constitutional, it must have a clear secular legislative purpose. In context, secular means non-religious.

The second prong provides that, for a law to be constitutional, its primary effect must neither advance nor inhibit religion.

The third prong provides that, for a law to be constitutional, it must not lead to excessive entanglement between church and state. This part of the test probably comes closest to incorporating the idea that there should be a wall of separation between church and state.

On what basis does the Court sometimes ignore this Lemon test?

The Court is most likely to ignore the Lemon test in cases where there is a clear historical practice that sanctions an activity that might not otherwise be permitted. Thus, tracing the practice back to the first Congress, the Supreme Court ruled in *Marsh v. Chambers* (1983) that it is not unconstitutional for a state legislature to hire a chaplain to begin each day's session with prayer.

The Court also appears to be unlikely to strike down the words "in God we trust" on coins or the practice of using governmental funds to hire chaplains in the military. The first practice is arguably fairly innocuous and dates back to the Civil War, while the second practice furthers the free exercise rights of military personnel.

THE FREE EXERCISE CLAUSE

In addition to the establishment clause, what other provision of the First Amendment relates to religion?

The free exercise clause does.

What does the free exercise clause of the First Amendment say?

It prohibits Congress from interfering "with the free exercise" of religion.

What is the relationship between the establishment clause and the free exercise clause?

There is obviously some potential for conflict between these two provisions. Scholars continue to dispute which clause courts should favor in cases of apparent conflict.

Is freedom of religion absolute?

No, it is not. Few, if any, rights listed in the Constitution are absolute. When the exercise of one person's rights come into conflict with another person's, courts must often adjudicate. It seems clear that individuals could

Amish schoolchildren run to school. In 1972, the Supreme Court upheld the right of the Amish to take their children out of school after the eighth grade. (Amy Sancetta/AP/Corbis)

not legally offer up child sacrifices in pursuit of their religion, but matters that affect other individuals less seriously may have to be judged on a case-by-case basis. Some commentators distinguish between religious belief, religious advocacy (or speech), and religious practice and argue that, while the Constitution protects all three, belief has the strongest claim to protection, and practice the least.

What are some examples of rights that courts have upheld under the free exercise clause?

The Court has ruled that individuals have the right to go door to door on behalf of their religious beliefs. The Court has ruled that individuals who are fired from their jobs because they refuse to work on Sunday can still qualify for unemployment benefits (*Sherbert v. Verner,* 1963). Courts have ruled that the Amish may take their children out of school after the eighth grade because of their belief that such education will undermine their children's faith (*Wisconsin v. Yoder,* 1972). Linking freedom of speech and freedom of religion, the Supreme Court overruled an earlier decision and decided that schoolchildren who have religious objections to the practice cannot be forced to salute the American flag in public schools (*West Virginia State Board of Education v. Barnette,* 1943).

What are some asserted rights that courts have rejected under the free exercise clause?

The Court has not upheld cases of drug use or tax evasion that have been justified on religious grounds. Clearly, acts of violence or destruction of property are not so justified except under the most unusual circumstances.

What, if anything, has Congress done in the area of religious freedom?

In 1984, Congress adopted an Equal Access Act designed to extend a Supreme Court decision relative to colleges and universities to high schools by providing that public schools that allow noncurricular organizations to operate must allow religious groups to participate equally. The Court upheld this law in *Westside Community Board of Education v. Mergens* (1990).

However, in *City of Boerne, Texas v. Floeres* (1997), the Court struck down the Religious Freedom Restoration Act (RFRA) of 1994, in which Congress had specified that the courts should only uphold general laws that indirectly affect religious practices when states could offer a "compelling interest" for so doing. Congress designed the law to overturn the Court's decision in *Employment Division v. Smith* (1990) where, in upholding a state's denial of unemployment benefits to two Native Americans who had lost their jobs as drug rehabilitation counselors because they had used peyote during religious rituals, the Court had denied that a state was required to show a "compelling interest" in such circumstances.

What subjects, other than religion, does the First Amendment cover?

It also deals with freedom of speech, freedom of the press, the right to assemble peaceably, and the right to petition government for redress of grievances. At their inception, as today, many of these rights were tied to religious, as well as political, liberties.

FREEDOM OF SPEECH

Does the First Amendment define freedom of speech?

No.

Is freedom of speech absolute?

This depends in part on how speech is defined. Most individuals who have studied the matter have concluded that, however liberal constitutional protections for freedom of speech are, they are not absolute.

Justice Oliver Wendell Holmes Jr. made one of the most convincing arguments against absolute freedom of speech in the case of *Schenck v. United States* (1919). He argued that even the most stringent protection of freedom of speech would not protect an individual who falsely shouted fire in a crowded theater and caused a panic. Holmes subsequently formulated what has been called the clear and present danger test. This test was most commonly used in cases where speech was thought to be subversive of the existing government.

What is the clear and present danger test?

According to this test, which is a judicial gloss on the Constitution, government has a right to suppress speech, especially of a subversive nature, that poses "a clear and present danger" that the government has a right to prevent. Speech thus has to be judged in context. A speech that an individual makes to a small group of supporters might pose less of a clear and present danger than a speech that the same individual delivered to a large hostile crowd that is about to erupt into rioting.

Is the clear and present danger test the only one that courts have used in the area of subversive speech?

No, it is not. A more restrictive test, which the Supreme Court majority applied in the case of *Gitlow v. New York* (1925), provided that the government could suppress speech that had a "dangerous tendency." Similarly, in *Dennis v. United States* (1951), the Court applied the "gravity of the evil test" to convict leading members of the U.S. Communist Party. According to this test, the Court must weigh the gravity, or seriousness, of an evil threatened by subversive speech against its probability or improbability.

Does the Supreme Court currently use the clear and present danger test?

No, it does not. In *Brandenburg v. Ohio* (1969), a case involving prosecution against a member of the Ku Klux Klan who uttered veiled threats at a rally, the Court largely abandoned the clear and present danger test for a tougher standard. The Court was particularly concerned that any danger posed by speech be considered to be immediate, or imminent, before government has the right to suppress such speech.

Does the government have to permit the exercise of free speech at any place, at any time, and under any circumstances?

Governments are expected to give wide leeway to speech and are usually prohibited from suppressing speech on the basis of its content, but they are generally permitted to adopt reasonable "time, place, and manner" restrictions on freedom of speech, as long as restrictions are uniformly and fairly enforced. It is thus perfectly acceptable for governments to ban sound trucks from residential neighborhoods during certain hours, to prohibit street demonstrations without permits, or to prevent individuals from using speech to disrupt public meetings.

In examining such regulations, the courts usually require the government to use the "least restrictive means" possible to meet objectives of public safety and welfare. They also see that governmental officials are not granted arbitrary discretion over which speech to accept and which to reject.

Do students enjoy the same rights of freedom of speech and press as adults?

The Supreme Court recognized in *Tinker v. Des Moines* (1969) that students enjoyed some First Amendment rights (in this case, the right to wear black armbands in protest of the Vietnam War), but courts have limited student speech in ways that courts would not do for adults.

What are some examples where courts have upheld greater restrictions of student speech than that of adults?

In *Bethel School District No. 403 v. Frazer* (1986), the Supreme Court ruled that a school could discipline a student for a lewd (but not obscene) speech that he gave before a student assembly. Similarly, in *Hazelwood School District v. Kuhlmeier* (1988), the Court gave a high school principal the right to delete an article in a student newspaper that he thought was inappropriate for a school setting. In *Morse v. Frederick* (2007), the Supreme Court allowed a school to discipline a student who held up a sign on an Olympic run past the school saying "Bong Hits 4 Jesus" on the basis that school officials had the right to suppress speech that might appear to be advocating drug use. Such censorship would be highly inappropriate outside the school context.

Do individuals have a right not to speak?

As the discussion of the Fifth Amendment later in this book will show, a criminal defendant has a right not to speak in a criminal trial. In addition, the Supreme Court's decision in *West Virginia State Board of Education v. Barnette* (1943) supporting students' rights not to salute the American flag indicates that the government does not have the right to compel individuals to make affirmations contrary to their beliefs.

Does the First Amendment protect commercial speech?

Yes, it does. Earlier in this century, the Supreme Court sometimes spoke as though commercial speech had substantially less protection than more overtly political types of speech. Freedom of speech does not, of course, enable companies to engage in false advertising, but the Court has extended fairly wide protection to truthful information, even when companies disseminate it with the intention of making money rather than convincing others of a political or religious opinion.

What, if any, impact does the First Amendment have on contributions to candidates who are running for office?

In *Buckley v. Valeo* (1976), the Supreme Court effectively decided that, in some cases, money was equivalent to speech, or effective advocacy, but that in others the government could regulate contributions in order to avoid political corruption. It thus decided that laws could limit the amount of contributions that a candidate receives from other individuals, but it ruled that there was no limit on the amount of money that individuals could spend on their own campaigns. The Court also invalidated overall spending limits on campaigns, except in cases where individuals voluntarily agreed to accept such limits in exchange for some governmental financing of their campaigns (at present, this is largely limited to U.S. presidential campaigns).

What is symbolic speech?

This is "speech" that consists of gestures and/or symbols rather than, or in conjuction with, spoken words.

Does the First Amendment protect symbolic speech?

The First Amendment does not specifically mention such symbolic speech, but the Supreme Court has ruled that many forms of symbolic speech are closely akin to "pure" speech and are thus protected by that amendment.

What are some examples of exercises of symbolic speech that courts have protected?

In *Tinker v. Des Moines School District* (1969), the Supreme Court ruled that students in a high school could wear black armbands in protest of the Vietnam War. In much more controversial decisions in *Texas v. Johnson* (1989) and *United States v. Eichman* (1990) the Court ruled that individuals could burn an American flag as a form of symbolic protest.

Mary Beth and John Tinker display the black armbands embellished with a peace sign that they wore to school to protest the Vietnam War in Des Moines, Iowa, on March 4, 1968. Both students, along with their friend Christopher Eckhardt, were suspended from school for wearing them. (Bettmann/Corbis)

Are there examples of symbolic speech that the Court has ruled that the First Amendment does not protect?

Yes. Symbolic speech often blends into actions, some of which may be illegal. In *United States v. O'Brien* (1968), for example, the Supreme Court decided that the First Amendment did not allow individuals to burn their draft registration cards. The Court considered such draft cards to be governmental property, and it also thought that the system of identification established by such cards was essential to the national defense, especially in times of emergency. When symbolic speech is involved, the Court usually looks to see whether it is possible to regulate the activity apart from the speech with which it is connected.

Are there any other kinds of speech that have been especially prominent in First Amendment law?

Yes, the areas of fighting words, libel, and obscenity (libel and obscenity are treated below under freedom of the press) have all posed special problems. In effect, the Court has ruled that the First Amendment does not protect these kinds of utterances, but the Court has had a difficult time attempting to define any of these areas with great precision.

What are fighting words?

Fighting words are words spoken face to face to another individual and intended to arouse intense hostile emotions rather than to stimulate reasoned thought.

Does the Constitution protect fighting words?

The Supreme Court has ruled that such words are not necessarily protected, but there is only one major case in which this exception has been specifically applied.

Does the Supreme Court consider vulgar words printed on clothing that individuals wear in public to be fighting words?

No. In *Cohen v. California* (1971), the Supreme Court upheld an individual's right to wear a jacket with a four-letter sexual expletive directed against the draft. The Court reasoned that, in context, the word was not erotic (and thus not obscene) and that it was not directed toward any particular individual (and thus not an example of fighting words). The Court further noted that individuals who were offended could avert their eyes.

FREEDOM OF THE PRESS

Why does the First Amendment list freedom of the press immediately after freedom of speech?

The two rights are intimately connected. The first consists primarily of spoken words while the second consists of written and published ones.

Historically, what principle has been most important to the American understanding of freedom of the press?

The presumption against prior restraint of publications has been.

What is the presumption against prior restraint?

Generally speaking, courts are quite reluctant to suppress publications prior to their publication and distribution where they can be assessed by the public. Thus, in *Near v. Minnesota* (1931), the Supreme Court lifted an injunction (or order) against publication of a scandal-mongering newspaper. The Court made it clear that publications of this type might be subject to prosecution for libel or obscenity after they were published, but it refused to prohibit such publication beforehand.

Has the Supreme Court based any contemporary cases on the presumption against prior restraint of publication?

Yes, the most important of these cases is the Pentagon Papers Case, *New York Times v. United States* (1971).

What happened in the Pentagon Papers Case?

The U.S. attorney general and the president attempted to enjoin publication of a top-secret and critical study of the history of American participation in the Vietnam War. The Supreme Court voided this injunction, citing the strong presumption against prior restraint of publication.

According to the decision in the Pentagon Papers Case, are there any circumstances under which courts might permit prior restraint of publication?

Yes, the Court indicated that publications that might put lives in immediate jeopardy—stories, for example, attempting to publish troop positions or the sailing dates of warships—might be subject to such restraint.

Does freedom of the press involve any protections other than the presumption against prior restraint of publication?

Yes. Freedom to publish would be of little value if all who did so could be immediately prosecuted thereafter. In the United States, there are a quite limited number of offenses for which a publisher can be punished.

What would be some examples of publications for which an individual or industry could be punished?

A publication whose story revealed that its author had broken laws to get information could subject its author to penalties. A publication might also be punished if courts judge it to be libelous or obscene.

What is libel?

Libel is the legal term for publications that attempt to slander others.

If a medium publishes derogatory information about an individual that is truthful, will courts consider it to be legally libelous?

No, in American law, truth has long been accepted as a defense in cases where libel is alleged. In English colonial law, by contrast, truth was not considered to be a defense. Indeed, it used to be said that, "[t]he greater the truth, the greater the libel."

Do courts consider the publication of all untruthful derogatory information to be legally libelous?

No, American courts have recognized that a free press needs considerable "breathing space" or "play in the joints" if it is to flourish. Moreover, courts have ruled that publications should have extra leeway when commenting on public policies or dealing with public figures, especially those who have run for public offices.

What is the Court's rationale for giving publications greater leeway when dealing with public, rather than private, individuals?

Courts reason both that public officials have bargained for publicity when they sought their jobs and that such officials generally have access to the media to respond to charges that are raised against them.

Can individuals who are considered to be public figures ever collect libel judgments?

Yes, but the standard of proof they have to offer is difficult to prove.

What standard must public figures meet when attempting to show that others have libeled them?

In *New York Times v. Sullivan* (1964), the Court established what is known as the "actual malice" test to govern such situations. Under this test, public officials can prove libel only in cases where they can show that damaging information about them was published either with knowledge that it was false or with reckless disregard for its truth or falsity.

Can public figures collect judgments for "emotional duress" that they suffer as a result of mean-spirited parodies against them?

Apparently not. In *Hustler Magazine v. Falwell* (1988), the Supreme Court unanimously decided that a parody of a liquor advertisement claiming that a well-known minister first had sex with his mother in an outhouse was part of the wide-open freedom to criticize that was permitted by the First Amendment.

Do First Amendment freedoms of speech and press protect obscenity?

The courts have said that the provisions do not protect obscenity, but they have had great difficulty in defining obscenity. In one of the most candid statements that has arguably ever been made on the subject, one-time Supreme Court Justice Potter Stewart, professing that he could not come up with a definition, indicated that "I know it when I see it."

How did governments handle the issue of obscenity throughout most of American history?

Prior to the incorporation of the guarantees of the First Amendment into the due process clause of the Fourteenth Amendment, states had considerable leeway in suppressing obscenity. For many years, courts relied on what was known as the Hicklin Test.

What was the Hicklin Test?

Under this relatively restrictive test, courts asked "whether the tendency of the matter charged as obscenity is to deprave and corrupt those whose minds are open to such immoral influences, and into whose hands a publication of this sort may fall."

Do courts still use the Hicklin Test for obscenity?

No; over time, courts concluded that this test was too restrictive and that it suppressed meritorious speech as well as obscenity.

What test do courts currently use in ascertaining whether works are obscene?

Basically, the courts rely on a test that Chief Justice Warren Burger developed and articulated in the case of *Miller v. California* (1973). This test, called the Miller Test, has three prongs.

What are the three prongs of the Miller Test for obscenity?

The first asks whether an average person, applying contemporary community standards of a local community would find that a work as a whole appeals to a prurient (lustful) interest in sex. Under this standard, a work that is judged to be obscene in small-town America might not be considered obscene in a major city. Also, obscenity is confined to matters related to sex. Moreover, works must be judged as a whole and not by isolated passages.

The second prong asks whether a work depicts or describes in a patently offensive way, sexual conduct specifically defined by law.

The third prong, sometimes known as the LAPS Test, asks whether a work has any serious literary, artistic, political, or scientific value. Such value might redeem a work that would otherwise be considered obscene.

What, if any, other principles other than those which the Miller Test articulates, apply to obscenity regulations?

Courts are less protective of speech that is thrust upon unwilling viewers than it is to obscenity that is not this obtrusive. Similarly, courts have shown special solicitude for laws designed to protect juveniles for participation in, or exposure to, pornography. The courts have also upheld zoning laws that are designed to control the types of neighborhoods in which the sale and distribution of obscenity is allowed, and it has enforced laws against public nudity, even in establishments that advertise nude dancing.

Does the Constitution grant rights of access to members of the press that it does not grant to others?

Generally speaking, courts have ruled that it does not.

If a grand jury summons a member of the press to testify about information secured from individuals by promising to keep their names confidential, does the Constitution exempt such members of the press from testifying?

In *Branzburg v. Hayes* (1972) and companion cases, the Supreme Court ruled that it did not. However, many states have subsequently adopted laws, known as shield laws, to protect reporters in such cases where they are not themselves implicated in any criminal wrongdoing.

Do courts treat different kinds of media identically when it comes to issues of speech and press?

No. Both because the number of available radio and television stations has been technologically limited and because these media reach more pervasively into homes (and can be directed to individuals not yet old enough to read), Courts have sometimes upheld restrictions on programming and scheduling by electronic media that they have not applied to the print media. In addition, courts have sometimes upheld requirements for electronic media to provide opponents of editorials to respond to editorials, but they have not required printed media to do so. There is currently considerable controversy about what, if any, regulations should apply to communications via the Internet and other computer hookups, but a 1997 Supreme Court decision in *Reno v. American Civil Liberties Union,* striking down the Communications Decency Act of 1997, indicated that the First Amendment did protect freedom of expression on the Internet.

FREEDOM OF PETITION AND ASSEMBLY

What, if any, limitation does the Constitution mention with regard to the right of assembly?

It only extends protections to assemblies that are peaceable.

What corollary right have the courts generally tied to the right of peaceable assembly in the First Amendment?

The Court has interpreted this provision to extend to a wider free-dom of association. Thus, in the case of *NAACP v. Alabama* (1958), the Court ruled that the National Association for the Advancement of Colored People did not have to release a list of its members when it was judged that disclosure of such a list could lead to recriminations against members and discourage others from joining. Similarly, in *Hurley v. Irish-American Gay, Lesbian and Bisexual Group of Boston* (1995), the Court permitted a private group to deny a group advocating gay rights the right to carry a banner in a parade that it was sponsoring.

What is the last provision in the First Amendment?

It deals with the right to petition the government for redress of griev-ances.

Why did the Framers consider the right of petition to be especially important?

The English king's failure to heed colonial petitions had been a major impetus for the Revolutionary war. Representative government would be ineffective if individuals did not have the right to petition such representatives.

BIBLIOGRAPHY

Books

Henry J. Abraham and Barbara A. Perry, *Freedom & the Court: Civil Rights and Liberties in the United States,* 8th ed. (Lawrence: University Press of Kansas, 2003).

Allen Alderman and Caroline Kennedy, *In Our Defense: The Bill of Rights in Action* (New York: William Morrow Co., 1991).

Irving Bryant, *The Bill of Rights: Its Origin and Meaning* (Indianapolis, IN: Bobbs-Merrill, 1965).

Robert S. Peck, *The Bill of Rights and the Politics of Interpretation* (St. Paul, MN: West Publishing Company, 1992).

Robert A. Rutland, *The Birth of the Bill of Rights, 1776–1791* (Chapel Hill: University of North Carolina Press, 1955).

Bernard Schwartz, *A History of the American Bill of Rights* (New York: Oxford
      University Press, 1977).
Herbert J. Storing, *What the Anti-Federalists Were For: The Political Thought of
      the Opponents of the Constitution* (Chicago: The University of Chicago
      Press, 1981).
Helen E. Veit, Kenneth R. Bosling, and Challene B. Bickford, eds., *Creating the
      Bill of Rights: The Documentary Record from the First Federal
      Congress* (Baltimore: The Johns Hopkins University Press, 1991).
John R. Vile, David L. Hudson Jr., and David Schultz, eds. *Encyclopedia of the
      First Amendment* (Washington, D.C.: Congressional Quarterly
      Press, 2009).

Cases

Abington School District v. Schempp, 374 U.S. 203 (1963).
Adamson v. California, 332 U.S. 46 (1947).
Barron v. Baltimore, 32 U.S. 243 (1833).
Bethel School District No. 403 v. Frazer, 478 U.S. 675 (1986).
Board v. Education v. Earls, 536 U.S. 822 (2002).
Brandenburg v. Ohio, 395 U.S. 494 (1969).
Branzburg v. Hayes, 408 U.S. 665 (1972).
Buckley v. Valeo, 424 U.S. 1 (1976).
City of Boerne, Texas v. Flores, 65 U.S.L.W. 4612 (1997).
Cohen v. California, 403 U.S. 15 (1971).
Dennis v. United States, 341 U.S. 494 (1951).
Employment Division v. Smith, 494 U.S. 872 (1990).
Florence v. Board of Chosen Freeholders of County of Burlington, 566
      U.S. ___ (2012).
Gitlow v. New York, 268 U.S. 652 (1925).
Hazelwood School District v. Kuhlmeier, 484 U.S. 260 (1988).
Hurley v. Irish-American Gay, Lesbian and Bisexual Group of Boston, 515 U.S.
      557 (1995).
Hustler Magazine Inc. v. Falwell, 485 U.S. 46 (1988).
Lemon v. Kurtzman, 403 U.S. 602 (1971).
McCulloch v. Maryland, 17 U.S. 316 (1819).
Marsh v. Chambers, 463 U.S. 783 (1983).
Miller v. California, 413 U.S. 15 (1973).
Morse v. Frederick, 551 U.S. 000 (2007).
NAACP v. Alabama, 357 U.S. 449 (1958).
Near v. Minnesota, 283 U.S. 697 (1931).
New Jersey v. T.L.O. 469 U.S. 325 (1985).
New York Times Co. v. Sullivan, 376 U.S. 254 (1964).
New York Times Co. v. United States, 403 U.S. 713 (1971).
Palko v. Connecticut, 302 U.S. 319 (1937).
Reno v. American Civil Liberties Union, 65 U.S.L.W. 4715 (1997).
Safford Unified School District v. Redding, 557 U.S. 364 (2009).

Schenck v. United States, 244 U.S. 47 (1919).

Sherbert v. Verner, 374 U.S. 398 (1963).

Stone v. Graham, 449 U.S. 39 (1980).

Texas v. Johnson, 491 U.S. 397 (1989).

Tinker v. Des Moines Independent County School District, 393 U.S. 503 (1969).

United States v. Eichman, 496 U.S. 310 (1991).

United States v. O'Brien, 391 U.S. 367 (1968).

Veronia School District v. Acton, 515 U.S. 646 (1995).

Wallace v. Jaffree, 472 U.S. 38 (1985).

Westside Community Board of Education v. Mergens, 496 U.S. 226 (1990).

West Virginia State Board of Education v. Barnette, 319 U.S. 624 (1943).

Wisconsin v. Yoder, 406 U.S. 205 (1972).

Chapter 7

The Rest of the Bill of Rights and the Eleventh and Twelfth Amendments

THE SECOND AMENDMENT

What is the only amendment in the Bill of Rights with its own preface?

The Second Amendment is.

What is the subject of the Second Amendment?

It focuses on the right to bear arms.

How did the right to bear arms originate?

Citizens of republics have often been expected to defend their community and their nation. This obligation became a right that was recognized in the English Bill of Rights of 1689.

What necessity does the Second Amendment mention?

It mentions the need to provide for "the security of a free state."

Does the Second Amendment make any direct reference to hunting?

No, but at the time it was written, many families would have supplemented their diets with wild game.

What does the Second Amendment say is necessary for preserving the security of a free state?

It specifies the presence of a "well regulated" militia.

Outside the Second Amendment, does the Constitution mention the militia anywhere else?

Yes, Article I, Section 8 allows Congress to "provide for organizing, arming, and disciplining the Militia" and to call out the militia to execute national laws and suppress rebellions.

According to the U.S. Supreme Court, does an individual have to be a member of the militia in order to claim the right to own a gun?

No; in *District of Columbia v. Heller* (2008), the Court overturned a law in the District of Columbia banning the possession of handguns in the home and decided that the right to bear arms, while subject to reasonable governmental limitations, was an individual right that was not limited by the Amendment's prefatory clause. In *McDonald v. Chicago* (2010), the Court further decided that the Fourteenth Amendment extended the right to bear arms as a limitation on states and localities as well as the national government.

As the courts currently interpret the U.S. Constitution, do state and national governments have the right to regulate the sale of firearms?

Yes. Most existing laws are designed to limit the kinds of weapons that can be bought or sold, to provide some kind of waiting period before such weapons can be purchased, or attempt to limit purchases by individuals who have had mental illnesses or been convicted of criminal acts (governments often limit gun ownership by felons and ex-felons). There is continuing dispute as to whether or not decisions recognizing such laws give proper force to the Second Amendment's right to bear arms.

Does the Second Amendment protect the right *not* to keep guns in one's house?

A number of municipalities have adopted laws requiring homeowners (at least those who did not have religious objections) to have guns to protect themselves, but, as yet, the U.S. Supreme Court has not decided whether the laws are constitutional. There are certainly other rights, like the right of association, the right to jury trials, and protections against self-incrimination that the Constitution does not require individuals to exercise.

THE THIRD AMENDMENT

What is the subject of the Third Amendment?

It deals with the quartering of soldiers in private houses.

What is the origin of the Third Amendment?

Prior to and during the American Revolution, the British sometimes commandeered the homes of private individuals for quartering troops, particularly in Boston and other American cities.

According to the Third Amendment, are there peacetime circumstances during which the government may quarter soldiers in private homes?

Yes, the Third Amendment permits this when the owner gives consent to this lodging.

Does the Constitution place any limits on quartering troops in private homes during times of war?

Yes, according to the Third Amendment, governments must do so "in a manner to be prescribed by law."

Has the Third Amendment been the subject of frequent litigation?

No, it has not. Once the British left American soil, there have been few occasions where the military has attempted to commandeer private homes for its troops.

THE FOURTH AMENDMENT

What is the chief subject of the Fourth Amendment?

It deals chiefly with searches and seizures.

What kinds of searches and seizures does the Fourth Amendment prohibit?

It prohibits those that are "unreasonable." Because the Fourth Amendment goes on to specify the requirement for search warrants, readers often associate warrantless searches with unreasonable searches, but courts have not found all such warrantless searches to be unreasonable. In making judgments about the reasonableness of searches, courts will often ask whether an individual had an expectation of privacy in certain circumstances and, if so, whether such an expectation was reasonable.

What are some examples of searches that police conduct without a warrant that courts are likely to uphold as reasonable?

The Court has recognized exceptions in certain cases of stop and frisk (especially in cases where concealed weapons may pose a danger to an officer or to the public; see, for example, *Terry v. Ohio*, 1968), in cases involving the pursuit of fleeing felons, in cases where contraband is within arm's reach of a suspect, in cases where contraband is in "open fields" or "plain view," in cases where a suspect has given consent to such a search, and in cases where individuals have abandoned property. The Court has also been more lenient in approving searches of movable vehicles than it has of private homes, and, in some cases, the court has allowed the introduction of evidence secured without a warrant when it was thought that police would have invariably discovered such evidence as part of an ongoing systematic search or when a search was conducted in "good faith" that courts later found to be in technical violation of the law.

Why do courts typically give greater leeway to police searches of automobiles than to other searches?

Courts typically give greater leeway because individuals can move vehicles prior to issuance of a warrant. Moreover, individuals expose themselves to public view when driving in a way that they typically do not do at home or other more private places.

What happens in cases where officers engage in "unreasonable" searches and seizures?

Courts typically apply what is known as the exclusionary rule.

What is the exclusionary rule?

This is the judge-made practice whereby courts exclude from consideration evidence that police have obtained illegally.

Does the Fourth Amendment specifically mention the exclusionary rule?

No.

Do courts apply the exclusionary rule only to the national government, or do they also apply it to the states?

Initially, in *Weeks v. United States* (1914), the Supreme Court applied this rule only to the national government. In *Mapp v. Ohio* (1961), however, the Supreme Court extended this rule to the states as well.

What are the purposes of the exclusionary rule?

Courts chiefly designed the rule to prevent illegal police conduct, but it arguably also sets a good example for the citizenry and helps keep judicial hands clean from wrongdoing.

What is the primary drawback of the exclusionary rule?

Application of the rule sometimes means that criminals go free because law enforcement officials have blundered.

Have courts recognized any exceptions to the exclusionary rule?

Yes, they have. Courts have ruled that there is a "good faith" exception to the exclusionary rule when officers thought their search warrants were proper but were later found to be otherwise. Similarly, in some cases the courts will accept illegally obtained evidence if police can establish that they inevitably would have discovered such evidence (as, for example, in an ongoing search) using legal means.

What four categories did the Fourth Amendment seek to secure for individuals against unreasonable searches and seizures?

The amendment specifically refers to persons, houses, papers, and effects.

What is the significance of this list?

It is designed to be fairly inclusive. The order in which the items are listed suggests that the Constitution sought to be particularly solicitous of personal privacy and of the privacy of homes. In applying the Fourth Amendment, judges often repeat the principle, which has deep roots in English common law, that a person's home is that individual's castle and that governments should accord special deference to privacy at this location.

What does the Fourth Amendment mean when it refers to effects?

These are items of personal property that individuals can move or carry with them.

Do contemporary interpretations of the Fourth Amendment extend protection against wiretaps and other forms of electronic surveillance?

Yes. In *Olmstead v. United States* (1928), the Court decided that a conversation was not included among an individual's "persons, houses, papers, and effects," that police could not describe such a conversation in advance, and that police could therefore seize it without a warrant as long as they did not commit physical trespass or commit violence to obtain it. In *Katz v. United States* (1967), the Court overruled this and declared that such surveillance, like most other searches, must be authorized by prior search warrants. It recently extended the warrant requirement to Global Positioning System (GPS) devices. In *City of Ontario v. Quon* (2010), the Court did find that governmental employees had the right to conduct audits of pagers that they provided for use by their employees.

Are there any cases in which the government may legally engage in warrantless electronic eavesdropping?

Court prevents such surveillance of American citizens in the United States. It is not clear whether it can do so in cases of alien spies or in jurisdictions outside of the United States.

What standard does the Constitution establish for such a warrant?

It established the standard of "probable cause."

What is probable cause?

As the name implies, probable cause suggests that police have a reasonable belief to think that what they are searching for is to be found where they are searching. The standard does not rise to the level of preponderance of the evidence (the typical standard in a civil case) or beyond a reasonable doubt (the typical standard in a criminal case). Generally, such probable cause has to be beyond a mere hunch but requires less than absolute certainty.

How does the government establish probable cause under the Fourth Amendment?

It does so through oath or affirmation.

Who decides whether there is probable cause to conduct a search?

The Constitution does not specifically say so, but established practice calls for an impartial judge or magistrate to make this decision.

According to the Fourth Amendment, what kinds of description must a search warrant include?

The description must include the place to be searched and the persons or things to be seized.

What is the purpose of this provision?

The Framers intended to prevent the use of general warrants, or so-called writs of assistance, whose previous abuse by the British authorities had been one of the causes of the Revolutionary War. Such warrants did not require individualized suspicion but permitted officials to conduct broad searches of areas on the basis of a general order issued by the king.

When executing search warrants, may police use evidence that they find if the warrant did not list it?

This will depend on the facts. Courts generally permit police to use evidence that they discover in the course of executing a warrant if such evidence is in plain view or if it does not exceed the scope of the search. By contrast, police looking for machine guns would have no cause to empty a sugar bowl, so, if they discovered contraband in the process of doing so, they probably would not be able to use it.

According to existing practice, must police officers announce their presence and request that occupants voluntarily open their premises prior to executing a search warrant?

Yes; generally courts expect police to follow a "knock and announce" rule. Such a rule is designed to protect individuals against unexpected and frightening invasions of their privacy, to prevent occupants from reacting violently, to preserve property, and to guard against the possibility that officers may be at the wrong place.

In recent years, however, the Supreme Court has recognized certain exigent circumstances—when residents are believed to be armed or likely to destroy evidence or escape, for example—under which police may enter without a prior announcement. Rather than creating blanket exceptions (all felony drug busts, for example) to the knock and announce rule, the Supreme Court prefers to let lower courts decide on the appropriateness of such exceptions on a case-by-case basis.

To what degree does the Fourth Amendment protect students in school settings?

Students retain some privacy rights but do not generally have the same expectations of privacy in school settings than they would elsewhere. Thus in *New Jersey v. T.L.O* (1985), the Supreme Court ruled that school officials could search the purse of a student suspected of smoking. In *Veronia School District v. Acton* (1995) and *Board of Education v. Earls* (2002), it subsequently upheld random drug tests for students participating in extracurricular activities. The Court did rule in *Safford Unified School District v. Redding* (2009) that school officials had gone too far in conducting a strip search of a student suspected of possessing illicit pills, but in *Florence v. Board of Chosen Freeholders of County of Burlington* (2012), it permitted such searches of adults, even those arrested for minor offenses, who were kept in the general prison population.

May police detain individuals who are on the premises during a legally executed search?

Yes, they may do so to protect the search site and to secure their own safety, but in *Bailey v. United States* (2013), the Court ruled that they do not have similar authority to arrest individuals who had left the house and were not stopped by police until they were a mile away. *Chimel v. California* (1969) had further limited searches incident to arrests within the home to the area in direct control of the individual arrested.

THE FIFTH AMENDMENT

What is the primary subject of the Fifth Amendment?

This amendment deals primarily with the rights of individuals who have been accused of crimes. The last provision deals with governmental takings of property.

What is the implicit assumption behind the guarantees of rights found in the Fifth through Eighth Amendments?

These amendments require that governments assume that individuals that they have charged with crimes are presumed innocent until proven guilty. Although the Constitution never directly mentions this presumption, it serves as a linchpin of the American criminal justice system. This is the assumption behind the practice requiring that defendants in criminal cases be proved guilty "beyond a reasonable doubt," rather than as, in civil cases, by a simple "preponderance of the evidence."

Do juvenile defendants have the same constitutional protections as adults?

Since the case of *In re Gault* (1967), courts have applied most, but not all, of the procedural protections in the Bill of Rights to juveniles. In some cases, however, juveniles may be tried before a separate system of juvenile courts. Although such courts are typically more lenient, they are not bound by all the procedural protections of adult courts.

GRAND JURY INDICTMENTS

What does the Fifth Amendment mean when it refers to capital crimes?

Capital crimes are those that are punishable by death. The term "capital punishment" remains a synonym for the death penalty.

What does the Fifth Amendment mean when it refers to a presentment or indictment?

These are terms for formal legal charges against a criminal. A grand jury makes a "presentment" on the basis of its own knowledge or observation and an "indictment" on the basis of information presented to be by a prosecutor.

What does the Fifth Amendment mean when it refers to a grand jury?

A grand jury is a body of citizens charged with deciding whether prosecutors have brought enough evidence to bring an individual to trial. Such a jury does not decide on ultimate guilt or innocence.

In what cases does the Fifth Amendment guarantee indictment or presentment by a grand jury?

It requires grand jury presentments or indictments in the case of "capital, or otherwise infamous, crimes."

In what circumstances does the Fifth Amendment exempt the government from obtaining an indictment by a grand jury?

It exempts cases "arising in the land or naval forces, or in the Militia, when in actual service in time of War of public danger."

What method of indictment does the Constitution omit?

Many states, which are still not subject to this provision of the Fifth Amendment, indict individuals through a process of "information" where a state prosecutor, rather than a grand jury, presents evidence to a judge that there is sufficient evidence to pursue a prosecution.

What is the purpose of a grand jury?

Such juries are designed to shield innocent individuals against vindictive or overly aggressive prosecutors.

PROTECTION AGAINST DOUBLE JEOPARDY

Does the Constitution specifically use the term "double jeopardy"?

No, but it comes close. The Fifth Amendment provides "nor shall any person be subject for the same offense to be twice put in jeopardy of life or limb."

What is the purpose of the Fifth Amendment provision against double jeopardy?

Like the provision for grand jury indictments, it keeps prosecutors from wearing individuals out or bankrupting them by continual prosecutions for crimes for which they have already been exonerated.

Are there any limits on the Fifth Amendment provision relative to double jeopardy?

Yes. Although state and federal authorities generally cooperate on such matters, this provision does not necessarily protect individuals against separate prosecutions by state and national authorities. Similarly, an individual who is exonerated on a criminal charge brought by the state may subsequently be brought to court on a civil charge brought by a private individual. Thus, although a jury declared that former football legend O. J. Simpson was not guilty of murder in his criminal trial, a civil court subsequently found him liable for wrongful death and battery in a subsequent civil suit that families of the victims brought to court.

If a jury deadlocks (a so-called hung jury), does the Fifth Amendment prohibit the government from bringing this individual to trial again?

No, it does not. The double jeopardy provision applies only in cases where a jury has issued a "not guilty" verdict.

If a judge invalidates a verdict because prosecutors have used evidence that was illegally obtained, can prosecutors retry the individual?

Yes, a retrial in such cases (absent the illegally obtained evidence) is not considered to be a violation of the double jeopardy provision.

PROTECTION AGAINST SELF-INCRIMINATION

What amendment protects individuals from being witnesses against themselves in criminal trials?

The Fifth Amendment does.

How do scholars generally identify this provision?

They generally call it the provision against self-incrimination.

What is the origin of the Fifth Amendment privilege against self-incrimination?

There are several theories behind this privilege. Some believe it is unfair to force individuals to testify against themselves; others think it leads to shoddy police work; others think it demeans human dignity; and still others argue that it does not give defendants a sporting chance. By whatever rationale, this privilege has deep roots in English common law.

Does the Fifth Amendment privilege against self-incrimination extend to congressional hearings?

Yes, courts have ruled that it does.

Is there a mechanism by which governments can induce an individual to testify to self-incriminating information?

Yes, governments can grant such individuals immunity against prosecution for their testimony, and punish those who still refuse to testify for contempt.

Does the Fifth Amendment privilege against self-incrimination apply to civil cases?

No, it does not; the Fifth Amendment specifically mentions "any criminal case." Thus, to cite an earlier example, a civil court required O. J. Simpson to take the witness stand, but the criminal case that preceded it did not.

Does the privilege against self-incrimination prohibit the government from taking blood or other bodily fluids or from requiring individuals to give fingerprints or stand in lineups that might help identify (and thus incriminate) such individuals?

No, court decisions have generally permitted the introduction of such real, or physical, evidence, by distinguishing it from compelled verbal ("testimonial") evidence that the Fifth Amendment protects. There is currently debate about the degree to which police may collect and keep DNA samples from suspects who are not convicted of crimes.

THE DUE PROCESS CLAUSE

Which provision of the Constitution is the first to mention "due process of law"?

The Fifth Amendment is.

What three values does the due process clause specifically protect?

It protects "life, liberty, and property."

Why might the words "life, liberty, and property" sound familiar to someone reading the Constitution for the first time?

The words come close to the words "life, liberty, and the pursuit of happiness," which are contained in the Declaration of Independence.

What insight does the Fifth Amendment give into the Framers' view of the death penalty?

The fact that they expected that the government could take life away with "due process" indicates that they did not think the penalty was per se unconstitutional.

Where, other than the Fifth Amendment, does the Constitution mention "due process" of law?

Section 1 of the Fourteenth Amendment also mentions this.

What does the Fifth Amendment mean when it refers to "due process"?

The term appears to be much broader than many other phrases that the Constitution employs. Some scholars believe it was intended to mirror provisions in the English Magna Carta (1215) providing that individuals should be treated "according to the law of the land." Clearly, the term is designed to assure fundamental fairness. It many cases, it may be impossible to specify precisely what process is "due" until presented with facts in individual cases. Ultimately, courts serve as judges of whether governmental efforts have followed due process.

Is the idea of due process confined to criminal trials?

No, courts have ruled that certain administrative hearings and other noncriminal proceedings also have to adhere to due process requirements.

THE TAKINGS CLAUSE

What is the last provision of the Fifth Amendment?

The last provision of the Fifth Amendment prohibits governmental takings of private property for public use without just compensation. This provision reinforces the free enterprise system by preventing the government from nationalizing industries without providing compensation to the owners.

What name do scholars generally give to the last provision of the Fifth Amendment?

They generally call this the takings clause.

What name do scholars give to compensated governmental takings of property, which the Fifth Amendment permits?

They generally call this the right of eminent domain.

Does the government actually have to take physical possession of a person's property before such an action falls under the takings clause?

No, courts have ruled that the imposition of certain governmental regulations can be so stringent (for example, a complete ban on building in an area where it was previously permitted), and can so negatively affect the value of property, as to constitute a governmental taking that requires governmental compensation.

Why do most governments exercise the right of eminent domain?

Certain projects in the public interest—the acquisition of land for parks and highways, public schools, and other public buildings, for example— would be quite difficult, if not impossible, without such a power.

How have governments interpreted the "public use" requirement of the takings clause?

They have generally interpreted this provision liberally, leaving the governments themselves to determine what uses they consider to be on behalf of the public good. In *Kelo v. City of New London* (2005), the Supreme Court allowed a city to allow a private entity to use eminent domain to condemn a well-kept private home in order to further economic development. Some states have reacted by providing stronger state constitutional protections that the U.S. Supreme Court recognizes at the federal level.

THE SIXTH AMENDMENT

What is the central purpose of the Sixth Amendment?

Its central purpose is to outline the rights of defendants in criminal trials.

What is the first guarantee that the Sixth Amendment articulates?

The first is the right of criminal defendants to speedy criminal trials.

What are the purposes of the Sixth Amendment's right to a speedy trial?

Courts have identified at least three such purposes. These include avoiding extensive pretrial detention for individuals accused of crime, minimizing the damage to reputation that occurs when an accusation is made public, and assuring that the fairness of a trial will not be compromised by undue delay during which memories fade and witnesses may die.

In addition to requiring that they be speedy, what other requirement does the Sixth Amendment require for criminal trials?

It specifies that they be public.

Why does the Sixth Amendment provide
for public criminal trials?

This requirement subjects such trials to public scrutiny and enables the public to become better familiar with the criminal justice system.

Does the Sixth Amendment refer to a jury of one's peers
(equals)?

It does not do so directly, but it does specifically refer to an "impartial jury."

What does the Sixth Amendment mean when it refers
to an impartial jury?

The term "impartial" implies that the jury has not already made up its mind as to a defendant's guilt or innocence. Jury selection procedures are designed to assure that a jury is fair.

Does the Sixth Amendment refer to a petit jury
or a grand jury?

It refers to a petit jury.

What is a petit jury and what does it do?

A petit jury decides on a defendant's guilt or innocence; it may also select, or recommend, an appropriate penalty.

Does the Sixth Amendment specify how many individuals must
sit on a petit jury?

No, it does not. In federal criminal cases, 12 jurors are the rule, but the Supreme Court has ruled that states can have smaller juries in such cases, since the amendment does not list the number 12.

Does the Constitution require that juries
in criminal cases be unanimous?

No, it does not. Although this is the practice in federal cases, the Supreme Court has allowed states to make decisions by less than unanimous verdicts.

Does the Sixth Amendment specify where criminal cases must
be tried?

Yes, it specifies that such cases are to be tried in the state and district, previously specified by law, where a crime was committed. In cases where local prejudice may predominate, defendants may ask for a change of venue, or location. Thus, the trial of Timothy McVeigh for bombing the federal building in Oklahoma City was held in Denver.

Why does the Sixth Amendment require the government to inform individuals of the nature and cause of the accusations against them?

Without such notice, defendants would find it quite difficult to prepare adequate defenses.

What is the purpose of the provision in the Sixth Amendment that provides that defendants have the right to confront the witnesses against them?

It allows an individual accused of crime to refute false accusations.

What precisely does the Sixth Amendment right to confrontation involve?

There is some dispute on this subject. Some commentators believe this provision requires that defendants be able to observe witnesses against them in a face-to-face setting (an interpretation that can present problems in cases where children are called upon to testify in traumatic situations, such as sex offenses against them). Others think the confrontation clause primarily means that a defendant's lawyers should be able to cross-examine witnesses against their clients. Such interpreters are likely to connect this provision to rules against the use of hearsay evidence, that is, of the use of statements offered for their truth and made by individuals who are not in the court to testify. To date, Supreme Court decisions have not been completely consistent as to which interpretation should prevail.

What does the Sixth Amendment mean by "compulsory process"?

This refers to the power individual defendants have to subpoena, or get court orders, requiring individuals to appear at trial to answer questions on their behalf. If only the state had this power, trials would be tilted unfairly toward the prosecution.

Where does the Bill of Rights list the right to counsel?

It does so in the Sixth Amendment.

What did the right to counsel mean in early American history?

It meant that a defendant, who could afford to do so, could hire an attorney. Later the Court extended this right to poor defendants in cases that involved major crimes and in cases where courts thought that defendants were unable, because of special circumstances (for example, youth, ignorance, a hostile environment, racial prejudice, etc.), to defend themselves.

What does the right to counsel mean in modern circumstances?

According to the Supreme Court's decision in *Gideon v. Wainwright* (1963), the right to counsel now requires that the state provide an attorney to an individual unable to afford one. The right begins from the point that an individual becomes a suspect and not simply at a trial itself.

Are there any criminal cases in which an indigent defendant is not entitled to appointed counsel?

Courts do not typically require counsel in misdemeanor cases involving small fines rather than imprisonment.

How do defendants learn about their right to counsel and other such rights?

Ever since the Supreme Court's decision in *Miranda v. Arizona* (1966), courts have required arresting and interrogating officers to inform suspects that they have a right to remain silent, that what they say can and will be used against them in a court of law, and that, if they cannot afford counsel, the government will provide such representation for them.

Does the right to counsel include the right to effective counsel?

Not necessarily. Although it is possible to challenge the effectiveness of counsel, the Supreme Court ruled in *Strickland v. Washington* (1984), that to win on such a claim a defendant has the onus of showing both that representation "fell below an objective standard of reasonableness," and that there is a "reasonable probability that, but for the counsel's unprofessional errors, the result of the proceeding would have been different."

THE SEVENTH AMENDMENT

What is the subject of the Seventh Amendment?

The Seventh Amendment deals with the right to a petit jury in civil cases.

What does the Seventh Amendment mean by a civil case?

A civil case is a dispute in court between private individuals rather than a prosecution that the state brings.

Do courts require defendants to exercise their Sixth and Seventh Amendment rights to jury trials?

No. Defendants are entitled to such jury trials, but, under current law, they are not required to choose them. Indeed, not only do many defendants choose to be tried by a judge rather than by a jury, but, in criminal cases, many defendants enter into plea bargains with the district attorney.

What is a plea bargain?

In a plea bargain, a defendant agrees to plead guilty, typically to a lesser charge, without going through a trial, or before a trial has ended. Typically, a plea bargain results in a lesser penalty than that which a defendant would receive if the defendant had been convicted of the most serious offense or offenses charged against him or her.

Are plea bargains legal?

Yes; the Supreme Court has approved such plea bargains that parties knowingly and fairly agree to and where the prosecutor does not exert undue coercion.

According to the Seventh Amendment, what amount of money has to be involved in a civil (noncriminal) case before an individual is entitled to a jury?

It specifies an amount of $20 or more. This specification indicates that the Framers intended for the right of a jury to be a broad one.

What does the Seventh Amendment mean when it refers to "suits at common law"?

Common law is the system of judge-made law used both in England and the states (with some modifications for unique American circumstances) at the time the Constitution was written. Common law differs from civil, or code, law that is typical in European nations like France and Spain and that (a variant of which) persists in Louisiana.

What does the Seventh Amendment mean when it says that "no fact tried by a jury, shall be otherwise re-examined in any Court of the United States, than according to the rules of the common law"?

Under common law, the function of juries was to ascertain matters of fact. Higher courts were charged with reviewing matters of law rather than matters of fact. Presumably, the Seventh Amendment intended to sanction this procedure and to keep appellate courts from redeciding matters of fact.

Does the Seventh Amendment requirement for a jury require 12 persons?

No, the Supreme Court has upheld six-person juries in civil cases.

THE EIGHTH AMENDMENT

What is the shortest Amendment in the Constitution?

The shortest amendment is the Eighth Amendment. It only has 16 words.

What amendment mentions bail?

The Eighth Amendment does.

What is bail?

Bail consists of money that a defendant advances as a condition for the defendant's freedom prior to a trial.

What is the purpose of bail?

Judges often require defendants to post bail to guarantee that the defendants, who might otherwise attempt to flee and escape justice, will show up for such a trial.

How, if at all, does the Eighth Amendment limit such bail?

It prohibits "excessive" bail.

Does the Eighth Amendment prohibition against "excessive bail" mean that every defendant is entitled to such bail?

No, it does not. The risks that individuals who are insane, violent, or likely to escape, could pose could be too great. Congress has adopted laws that specify the conditions under which individuals can qualify for bail.

What is a fine?

A fine is a payment of money that governments sometimes use to penalize individuals for wrongdoing.

What, if any, kind of fines does the Eighth Amendment prohibit?

It prohibits "excessive" fines. Legislatures and courts ultimately have to decide what kinds of fines are excessive.

What, if any, kinds of punishments does the Eighth Amendment prohibit?

It prohibits "cruel and unusual" punishments. The Supreme Court has held that modern punishments need to be considered not at one fixed point, but in light of evolving standards of decency. Thus, in *Trop v. Dulles* (1954), it decided that it was cruel and unusual to strip an individual of citizenship for military desertion.

Did the Framers of the Constitution consider capital punishment to be cruel and unusual punishment?

Not in and of itself. The Fifth Amendment (like the later Fourteenth Amendment) allowed for deprivation of life (along with liberty and property), albeit only through "due process of law." Still, many Framers of the Constitution had been influenced by Cesare Beccaria's essay, *On Crimes and Punishments*, which had sought to limit the crimes for which the death penalty would be applied.

Does the contemporary Supreme Court consider the death penalty per se to be unconstitutional "cruel and unusual punishment"?

No, it does not. In *Furman v. Georgia* (1973), the Court struck down the death penalty as it was then administered on the basis that the penalty was being inflicted arbitrarily, but it has subsequently accepted more carefully drawn death-penalty statutes.

How does the imposition of the death penalty differ from that of other punishments?

Because the penalty is irrevocable, there is no room for error; states can compensate an individual who has been wrongly incarcerated, but they cannot restore a life wrongfully taken. Moreover, the penalty is retributive rather than restorative; unlike some other penalties, it is not aimed at rehabilitation of the offender.

What rules has the Supreme Court adopted to prevent the death penalty from being "cruel and unusual" punishment in violation of the Eighth Amendment?

The Court has not allowed states to inflict an automatic penalty for the conviction of a certain crime. Instead, the Court has specified that trials must be divided into bifurcated proceedings, separate phases—one that determines guilt or innocence and another that decides on the penalty. Courts have also required juries to weigh a variety of aggravating, extenuating, and mitigating circumstances when deciding whether the death penalty is an appropriate punishment for a given crime.

Courts have recently decided that it is also cruel and unusual to execute defendants who were under 18 at the age they committed their crimes (*Roper v. Simmons,* 2005); indeed, it further decided that juveniles cannot be sentenced to life in prison without the possibility of parole for noncapital offenses (*Graham v. Florida,* 2010). The Court has also prohibited capital punishment of individuals whose diminished intelligence levels kept them from a full realization of what they were doing (*Atkins v. Virginia,* 2002).

Do Supreme Court interpretations of the Eighth Amendment permit imposition of the death penalty for heinous but nonlethal crimes like rape?

No, not unless the crimes are also accompanied by murder.

Does the Court currently allow jurors to consider the impact on victims when deciding whether to inflict the death penalty?

Yes; in *Payne v. Tennessee* (1991), the Court overturned earlier decisions and decided that the Constitution did not bar consideration of the impact that such crimes had on friends and family members when making such decisions.

How has the Supreme Court reacted to recidivism ("three strikes and you're out") laws that provide enhanced penalties for repeat offenders?

It has generally upheld such laws, deciding that it would apply only what in *Harmelin v. Michigan* (1991) it called a "narrow proportionality principle" to noncapital cases.

THE NINTH AMENDMENT

What constitutional amendment deals with unenumerated rights?

The Ninth Amendment does.

What are unenumerated rights?

Unenumerated rights are rights that the Constitution does not specifically list.

How did the Ninth Amendment respond to objections that Anti-federalists had raised against adoption of the Bill of Rights?

Anti-Federalists initially argued that, if the Framers of such a bill omitted any rights, the government might thus think that it had the right to deny that they existed. The Ninth Amendment made it clear that those who wrote the amendment did not intend for the government to interpret the Constitution in that fashion.

Have U.S. courts recognized any unenumerated rights?

Yes; these have included the right to travel, the right to educate one's children in private schools, and the right of privacy.

What is the classic case in which the Supreme Court outlined its justification for a right to privacy?

In *Griswold v. Connecticut* (1965), the Supreme Court struck down Connecticut's prohibition against birth control by articulating a right of privacy based on emanations (extensions) and penumbras (shadows) of the First, Third, Fourth, Fifth, Ninth, and Fourteenth Amendments.

How has the Supreme Court expanded the right of privacy since *Griswold v. Connecticut*?

The most significant expansion of this right occurred in *Roe v. Wade* (1973) where the Court ruled that the right to privacy encompassed a woman's right, in consultation with her doctor, to choose an abortion throughout the first two trimesters (six months) of her pregnancy. In recent years, the Court has accepted some laws providing for short waiting periods, for the consent of a parent (with a provision for a judicial bypass), and for similar restrictions. Also, the Court has ruled that, although individuals have a right to abortion, the government is not necessarily required to pay for it.

Does the right to privacy extend to homosexual conduct?

In *Bowers v. Hardwick* (1986) the Court upheld a state law against sodomy, even when applied to private homosexual conduct, but in *Lawrence v. Texas* (2003), it decided that such laws unduly interfered with the liberty guaranteed by the due process clause of the Fourteenth Amendment. State governments have come to different conclusions as to whether their constitutions protect homosexual marriage.

THE TENTH AMENDMENT

What amendment of the Constitution refers to rights reserved to the states, or to the people?

The Tenth Amendment deals with such reserved rights.

According to the Tenth Amendment, what are the two characteristics of the rights reserved to the states?

Such rights must neither be delegated to the United States nor prohibited by the Constitution to the states. Most rights delegated to the United States are found in Article I, Section 8 of the Constitution; most prohibitions on the states are found in Article I, Section 10, in the Fourteenth Amendment, and in other amendments.

What kinds of rights does the Tenth Amendment reserve to the states?

Scholars generally call these either reserved rights or state police powers. Traditionally, states maintain primary control over such areas as police protection, health, welfare, education, and property regulations.

What role has the Tenth Amendment played in American history?

The amendment was fairly important from the time that Roger Taney became chief justice of the Supreme Court in 1836 through 1936. The use of the amendment declined with a change in judicial philosophy in 1937. In recent years, however, the Tenth Amendment has received renewed attention. In the 1995 case of *United States v. Lopez,* the Supreme Court ruled that the Gun-Free School Zones Act of 1990, making it illegal to possess a gun within 1,000 feet of a public school, violated the Tenth Amendment by exceeding congressional powers under the commerce clause. Similarly in 1997 in *Printz v. United States* and *Mack v. United States* the Court cited the Tenth Amendment in voiding the requirement of the Brady Handgun Violence Prevention Act requiring local law enforcement officials to do background checks of would-be gun purchasers.

Does the Tenth Amendment eliminate the possibility that the national government might exercise implied powers?

No, it does not. The Tenth Amendment is phrased differently from a similar provision in the Articles of Confederation. In *McCulloch v. Maryland* (1819), Chief Justice John Marshall noted that the amendment did not reserve to the states all powers not *expressly* delegated to the United States but only those that were not delegated. This leaves open the possibility that the Constitution delegates some powers to the national government implicitly rather than explicitly.

THE ELEVENTH AMENDMENT

What Supreme Court decision prompted the Eleventh Amendment?

In *Chisholm v. Georgia* (1793), the Court ruled that a state could be sued by citizens of another state without the consent of the state being sued. In so ruling, the Court had at least temporarily overturned the widespread view known as sovereign immunity whereby a state was thought to be immune to suits to which it did not consent.

When did the states ratify the Eleventh Amendment?

1795.

How did the Eleventh Amendment respond to the Supreme Court's decision in *Chisholm v. Georgia*?

The amendment withdrew judicial jurisdiction from cases "commenced or prosecuted against one of the United States by Citizens of another State, or by Citizens or Subjects of any Foreign State."

Are there any circumstances in which federal courts can hear cases between a citizen of another state or nation against a state?

Yes, states may consent to such suits. Similarly, the prohibition in the Eleventh Amendment applies only in cases where citizens initiate such suits.

THE TWELFTH AMENDMENT

What is the subject of the Twelfth Amendment?

It deals with the electoral college system for selecting presidents.

When did the states ratify the Twelfth Amendment?

1804.

What presidential election led to adoption of the Twelfth Amendment?

The election of 1800 immediately preceded the introduction of this amendment.

What problem, arising in the election of 1800, led to the Twelfth Amendment?

In the election of 1800, all of the Republican electors who cast ballots for their presidential candidate, Thomas Jefferson, also cast ballots for Aaron Burr, whom the electors had intended to serve as vice president.

The result was a tie in the Electoral College. This tie sent the election to the House of Representatives where many Federalists, defeated for re-election (so-called lame ducks), were still sitting. Although the House eventually cast a majority of votes for Jefferson, this vote pointed to a problem in the existing system, which the Twelfth Amendment sought to rectify.

Had there been problems in the Electoral College prior to the election of 1800?

Yes, the election of 1796 had resulted in the election of a president (John Adams, a Federalist) from one party and a vice president (Thomas Jefferson, a Democratic-Republican) from another, and not only did they rarely cooperate, but Jefferson subsequently ran against Adams in the next election.

Did the Framers of the U.S. Constitution anticipate political parties?

They probably did not anticipate parties as they developed after the Constitution was written. James Madison's cogent analysis in *Federalist* No. 10 indicates that he anticipated that groups would divide into factions centering on their personal interests, but Madison and other Framers probably did not anticipate nationwide parties such as we have come to expect since the early administration of George Washington, one of the Founders who expressed his dislike for such parties.

What is the most important change that the Twelfth Amendment initiated?

The Amendment provided that electors would now cast separate ballots for president and vice president.

What changes did the Twelfth Amendment make in House procedures for selecting a president?

Prior to the Twelfth Amendment, when each elector cast two votes, the Constitution required the House to choose between them in the case of a tie. Since it is no longer possible for more than one presidential candidate to get more than a majority when each elector casts a single presidential vote, the Twelfth Amendment eliminates this contingency. The Twelfth Amendment does provides that, when no candidate receives a majority, the House of Representatives will now choose "from the persons having the highest numbers not exceeding three of the list of those voted for as President," rather than from among the top five.

Is it possible for a president and a vice president to be from different political parties?

The Constitution nowhere mentions parties, but, by now specifying that electors will cast separate votes for president and vice president, the Twelfth Amendment makes it likely that electors will vote for presidential and vice presidential candidates of the same party.

Is it possible for the president and vice president to be residents of the same state?

It is possible but unlikely. The Twelfth Amendment specifies that electors must vote for at least one presidential or vice presidential candidate from another state, but, if a vice president could win without the votes from the state that the president is from, the Twelfth Amendment would appear to pose no obstacle.

According to the Twelfth and Twentieth Amendments, what happens if no presidential candidate receives a majority of the Electoral College, and the House of Representatives is unable to make such a choice prior to the presidential inauguration?

The vice president acts as president until such a choice is made.

If no individual receives a majority of the electoral votes cast for vice president, how many names of the top contenders are sent on to the Senate for review?

The Twelfth Amendment specifies that the top two names will be sent to the Senate. By contrast, the top three presidential contenders are sent to the House of Representatives. This creates a remote possibility that a president and vice president could be selected from different parties, a situation that occurred prior to the adoption of the Twelfth Amendment.

BIBLIOGRAPHY

Books

Henry J. Abraham and Barbara A. Perry, *Freedom and the Court: Civil Rights and Liberties in the United States,* 8th ed. (Lawrence: University Press of Kansas, 2003).

Allen Alderman and Caroline Kennedy, *In Our Defense: The Bill of Rights in Action* (New York: William Morrow Co., 1991).

Akhil Reed Amar, *The Constitution and Criminal Procedure: First Principles* (New Haven, NJ: Yale University Press, 1997).

Walter Berns, ed., *After the People Vote: A Guide to the Electoral College,* rev. ed. (Washington, D.C.: American Enterprise Institute, 1992).

John D. Bessler, *Cruel and Unusual: The American Death Penalty and the Founders' Eighth Amendment* (Boston, MA: Northeastern University Press, 2012).

Judith A. Best, *The Choice of the People: Debating the Electoral College* (Lanham, MD: Rowman & Littlefield, 1996).

David J. Bodenhamer, *Fair Trial: Rights of the Accused in American History* (New York: Oxford University Press, 1991).

Martin Clancy and Tim O'Brien, *Murder at the Supreme Court: Lethal Crimes and Landmark Cases* (Amherst, NY: Prometheus Books, 2013).

James W. Ely Jr., *The Guardian of Every Other Right: A Constitutional History of Property Rights* (New York: Oxford University Press, 1992).

David Fellman, *The Defendant's Rights Today* (Madison: University of Wisconsin Press, 1976).

David J. Garrow, *Liberty & Sexuality: The Right to Privacy and the Making of Roe v. Wade* (New York: Macmillian, 1994).

Radahisa Kuroda, *The Origins of the Twelfth Amendment: The Electoral College in the Early Republic, 1787–1804* (Westport, CT: Greenwood Press, 1994).

Melvin I. Urofsky, *The Continuity of Change: The Supreme Court and Individual Liberties, 1953–1986* (Belmont, CA: Wadsworth Publishing Company, 1991).

John R. Vile, and David L. Hudson Jr., eds. *Encyclopedia of the Fourth Amendment,* 2 vols. (Washington, D.C.: Sage, 2013).

Cases

Atkins v. Virginia, 536 U.S. 304 (2002).
Bailey v. United States, No 11–770 (2013).
Board v. Education v. Earls, 536 U.S. 822 (2002).
Chimel v. California, 395 U.S. 752 (1969).
Chisholm v. Georgia, 2 U.S. 419 (1798).
District of Columbia v. Heller, 128 S. Ct. 2783 (2008).
Florence v. Board of Chosen Freeholders of County of Burlington, 566 U.S._(2012).
Furman v. Georgia, 408 U.S. 238 (1973).
Gideon v. Wainwright, 372 U.S. 335 (1963).
Graham v. Florida, 560 U.S._(2010).
Griswold v. Connecticut, 381 U.S. 479 (1965).
Harmelin v. Michigan, 501 U.AS. 957 (1991).
In Re Gault, 387 U.S. 1 (1967).
Katz v. United States, 389 U.S. 347 (1967).
Kelo v. City of New London, 545 U.S. 469 (2005).
Lawrence v. Texas, 539 U.S. 558 (2003).

McCulloch v. Maryland, 17 U.S. 316 (1819).
McDonald v. Chicago, 561 U.S. 3025 (2010).
Mapp v. Ohio, 367 U.S. 643 (1961).
Miranda v. Arizona, 384 U.S. 436 (1966).
New Jersey v. T.L.O. 469 U.S. 325 (1985).
Olmstead v. United States, 277 U.S. 438 (1928).
Payne v. Tennessee, 501 U.S. 808 (1991).
Printz v. United States, Mack v. United States, 65 U.S.L.W. 4731 (1997).
Roe v. Wade, 410 U.S. 113 (1973).
Romer v. Evans, 116 S. Ct. 1620 (1996).
Roper v. Simmons, 543 U.S. 551 (2005).
Safford Unified School District v. Redding, 557 U.S. 364 (2009).
Strickland v. Washington, 466 U.S. 668 (1984).
Trop v. Dulles, 356 U.S. 86 (1954).
United States v. Lopez, 63 LW 4343 (1995).
Veronia School District v. Acton, 515 U.S. 646 (1995).

Chapter 8

Amendments Thirteen through Fifteen: The Post-Civil War Amendments

THE THIRTEENTH AMENDMENT

What three amendments did the states ratify in the years immediately following the U.S. Civil War?

States ratified the Thirteenth, Fourteenth, and Fifteenth Amendments all within five years of the end of the war.

What role did the Civil War have in the adoption of these amendments?

It is unlikely that states would have adopted any of these amendments had the Civil War not demonstrated the consequences of slavery and the need to alleviate the problems that it had caused.

What is the subject of the Thirteenth Amendment?

The amendment outlaws "slavery" and "involuntary servitude." Notably, this is the first place where the Constitution directly mentions slavery.

Hadn't Lincoln's Emancipation Proclamation already abolished slavery?

Lincoln's proclamation, which went into effect on January 1, 1863, was indeed an important step on the road to freedom, but it only applied to slaves held behind enemy lines. Moreover, a presidential proclamation would not have the same permanency as a constitutional amendment.

When did the states ratify the Thirteenth Amendment?

They ratified in 1865, the same year that the Civil War ended.

How many years transpired between the ratification of the Twelfth and Thirteenth Amendments?

Sixty-one years passed between ratification of these two amendments, the longest such time period between amendments in American history.

Had Congress proposed any amendments by the necessary majorities between adoption of the Twelfth and Thirteenth Amendments?

Yes, Congress had actually proposed two amendments during this time period.

What amendment did Congress first propose as the Thirteenth Amendment?

In 1810 Congress proposed what is often called the Reed Amendment. This amendment, which fell shy of ratification by the required number of states, would have stripped citizenship from any individuals who accepted titles of nobility without the consent of Congress. It would also have prohibited such individuals from holding office.

In addition to the Reed Amendment, what other amendment did Congress propose by the necessary majorities between 1804 and 1865?

In 1861, in an attempt to head off the Civil War, Congress proposed the Corwin Amendment. This proposal would have prohibited Congress from eliminating slavery in a state without its consent. Three states ratified the amendment, but the Civil War quickly changed attitudes on the subject.

Does the Constitution permit involuntary servitude in any situations?

Yes, the Thirteenth Amendment specifies that such slavery can be used "as a punishment for crime whereof the party shall have been duly convicted."

Did the Thirteenth Amendment permit slavery within American territories?

No, the prohibition of slavery in the Thirteenth Amendment extended to any place subject to United States jurisdiction.

How many sections are there in the Thirteenth Amendment?

There are two. The first abolishes slavery and the second grants Congress the power to enforce that prohibition through appropriate legislation.

Would Congress have had power to enforce the Thirteenth Amendment through legislation if its authors had failed to include the second section?

Presumably this power would still have been implied. Congress appears to have added the second section of the Thirteenth Amendment to avoid misunderstanding on the subject. In *Plessy v. Ferguson* (1896), the decision in which the Court majority later legitimized the doctrine of "separate but equal," Justice John Marshall Harlan (I) unsuccessfully argued in dissent that the Thirteenth Amendment was designed not only to eliminate slavery itself but also its "badges and incidents," among which Harlan included racial segregation.

What was the last state to ratify the Thirteenth Amendment?

Mississippi, which did so in 2013, was the last. It had instituted this process decades earlier but had not sent relevant paperwork to the director of Archives until then.

THE FOURTEENTH AMENDMENT

Section 1
What is the longest amendment to the Constitution?

The Fourteenth Amendment, which resembles the Bill of Rights both because it is concerned with the protection of individual rights and because it addresses multiple subjects.

When did the states ratify the Fourteenth Amendment?

They ratified it in 1868.

What, if anything, was unusual about the ratification of the Fourteenth Amendment?

Congress required Southern states to ratify the amendment before it recognized their governments as "republican" and seated their delegates.

What was the primary purpose of the Fourteenth Amendment?

Its primary purpose was to guarantee rights to those who had previously been held in slavery.

What is the first subject that the Fourteenth Amendment addresses?

It is citizenship.

How did the original Constitution define citizenship?

It did not directly address the subject other than to give Congress the responsibility for naturalization.

What is the importance of citizenship?

Citizenship ties together a unique blend of rights and responsibilities that are especially important in representative governments.

Portrait of Dred Scott. The decision of the 1857 case *Scott v. Sandford* was famously overturned by the Fourteenth Amendment. (Library of Congress)

What two ways does the Fourteenth Amendment provide for individuals to become citizens?

Individuals can become a citizen either by birth or by naturalization.

What historic Supreme Court decision did the Fourteenth Amendment modify?

The Fourteenth Amendment overturned *Scott v. Sandford* (1857).

What had the Supreme Court decided in the *Dred Scott Decision* of 1857?

The Court had ruled that Dred Scott, his wife Harriet, and other blacks who were suing for their freedom because they had lived in free territories, were not and could not be citizens of the United States. The decision also declared that the Missouri Compromise of 1820, which had prohibited slavery in certain American territories, was unconstitutional.

Which individuals does Section 1 of the Fourteenth Amendment identify as citizens?

It referred to "[a]ll persons born or naturalized in the United States, and subject to the jurisdiction thereof."

Is it possible for a person to be born in the United States but not subject to its jurisdiction?

Apparently it is possible. Scholars generally believe that this phrase refers to individuals who are serving in the United States as diplomats. If the United States were ever invaded, it is also possible that the phrase would include individuals who might be born in the United States to enemies who were occupying the country at the time.

According to the Fourteenth Amendment, what leads to state citizenship?

The amendment links state citizenship to residence therein. This indicates that individuals do not have to be born within a state in order to be citizens thereof.

What governments does the Fourteenth Amendment limit?

The Fourteenth Amendment is directed to state governments. By and large, the provisions within the Bill of rights had protected individuals against national deprivations of civil rights and liberties.

What three prohibitions does Section 1 of the Fourteenth Amendment contain?

It prohibits states from making or enforcing any laws that "abridge the privileges or immunities of citizens of the United States," that "deprive any person of life, liberty, or property, without due process of law," or that "deny to any person within its jurisdiction the equal protection of the laws."

Which of the three guarantees of liberty that Section 1 of the Fourteenth Amendment outlines has been the least effective in protecting individual rights?

The privileges and immunities clause has proved to be the least effective.

Why has the privileges and immunities clause of the Fourteenth Amendment proven to be largely ineffective?

In an early interpretation of this clause in the *Slaughterhouse Cases* (1873) involving the employment of butchers in the city of New Orleans, the Supreme Court ruled that citizens enjoyed most privileges and immunities by reason of their state constitutions rather than by reason of national citizenship. The Court has never overturned this decision, leaving relatively few privileges and immunities for this clause to protect.

How have courts interpreted the due process clause of the Fourteenth Amendment?

The courts sometimes distinguish between procedural due process and substantive due process. The first, emphasizing the term "process," focuses on whether governments have acted with procedural fairness. The second, with a greater focus on what process is *due,* recognizes that some laws may be procedurally fair but substantively flawed.

Is the Fourteenth Amendment the first constitutional provision that mentions the right to due process?

No, the Fifth Amendment, which initially limited only the national government, also mentions the right of due process.

Historically, why has the due process clause of the Fourteenth Amendment been especially important?

In addition to the limitations that the clause carries on its own, this clause has been the primary mechanism through which courts have applied most of the guarantees in the Bill of Rights to the states, and not simply to the national government, as appears to have been originally intended.

Does the Fourteenth Amendment eliminate all discriminatory actions?

No, it does not.

Does the Fourteenth Amendment prohibit all discriminatory actions?

No; in the *Civil Rights Cases of 1883* and other cases, the Supreme Court has ruled that the prohibitions against discriminatory actions listed in the amendment apply to "state" rather than "private" actions. It is thus sometimes possible for individuals to act in discriminatory ways that would violate the law if states engaged in them. Courts must often decide whether an action is primarily public, and thus subject to legal control, or private, and thus up to individual discretion.

What previous document most clearly embodies the idea of "equal protection" of the laws as found in the Fourteenth Amendment?

The Declaration of Independence, adopted in 1776 by the Second Continental Congress, had declared that "all men are created equal."

Does the guarantee of equal protection allow for racial segregation?

There is still disagreement about the intentions of those who authored the Fourteenth Amendment. For a long time, the Supreme Court approved of racial segregation under the doctrine of "separate but equal" that it had articulated in the case of *Plessy v. Ferguson* (1896). In *Brown v. Board of Education* (1954), one of the landmark cases of 20th-century law involving segregation in education, the Court overturned this decision and decided that separate facilities were inherently unequal.

"Jim Crow Laws" are often mentioned in reference to the Fourteenth Amendment. What are Jim Crow Laws?

Jim Crow laws were laws (named after a minstrel star) that the Supreme Court upheld from 1896 to 1954 and which were especially prominent in southern states that required racial segregation in places of public accommodation such as motels, restaurants, theaters, hospitals, etc.

Now that such Jim Crow laws are unconstitutional, does the prohibition against racial segregation apply only to segregation by law (de jure segregation), or does it also apply to de facto segregation?

Supreme Court decisions since *Brown* have made it clear that the Fourteenth Amendment prohibits de jure segregation and that the Court will allow a wide use of remedies, including school busing, to eliminate such segregation (See *Swann v. Charlotte-Mecklenburg Board of Education,* 1970).

Subsequent cases, most notably *Milliken v. Bradley* (1974), have indicated that the Court is less likely to attempt to remedy segregation that it considers to be the result of voluntary choice, so-called de facto segregation, rather than direct state action. It is not always easy to draw the line between de jure and de facto segregation.

Does the Fourteenth Amendment make any explicit reference to race or color?

No, although the authors of the amendment were chiefly concerned with race and color, the amendment does not specifically mention either term.

How does the modern Supreme Court typically deal with laws that rely upon racial classifications?

Because the Framers of the Fourteenth Amendment were especially concerned with racial discrimination, the Court typically requires governments to justify racial classifications (or those related to alienage or national origin) by a "compelling state interest." By contrast, in examining most other types of legislation, the courts typically require the government only to offer a "rational basis" for its actions.

Does the Fourteenth Amendment's omission of the words "race" or "color" mean that Congress can use it to limit other types of discrimination?

Because those who wrote and ratified the amendment did so primarily to address issues involving race, some commentators favor largely confining its interpretation to this and similar classifications. Pointing to the generality of language in the amendment, others believe that Congress should also use it to address other forms of discrimination.

Do Congress and the courts currently utilize the equal protection clause of the Fourteenth Amendment to limit gender discrimination?

Yes, Congress has mandated equal protection of the laws for men and women, and in a number of cases, courts have used the equal protection clause to strike down discrimination based on gender. Typically, however, the Court uses a standard of review in gender cases that requires more than a rational basis but that is not as strict as the compelling state interest standard that it uses in cases of racial discrimination; thus, in gender cases, the modern Court will typically require that the government advance an "important governmental interest." Had the states ratified the proposed Equal Rights Amendment, the Court might have used a somewhat stricter standard.

What are some examples of gender discrimination that courts have struck down under authority of the equal protection clause of the Fourteenth Amendment?

The Supreme Court ruled in *Reed v. Reed* (1971) that the state cannot automatically prefer a man over a woman when deciding who should administer an estate. In *Frontiero v. Richardson* (1973) the Court also ruled that the military should not use different standards for determining whether spouses of women were dependent upon them. More recently, in a case involving the Virginia Military Academy, the Court decided that, in order to continue as a state institution, Virginia's historical all-male academy had to admit women.

Do courts allow governments to make any distinctions on the basis of gender?

Yes; it permits some such distinctions, especially in regard to military matters. In *Rostker v. Goldberg* (1981), for example, the Court upheld a congressional law that provided for mandatory selective service registration for men but not for women.

Have courts applied the equal protection clause to any areas other than race or gender?

Yes; courts sometimes apply the clause to distinctions based on such factors as age, wealth, legitimacy, etc. The court has generally proven more willing to allow states to classify individuals on the basis of such characteristics than on the basis of race or gender, but its decisions on this point have not always been consistent.

In two companion cases that the Supreme Court decided in 1997 (*Vacco v. Quill* and *Washington v. Gluksberg*), advocates of a constitutional "right to die" argued that the equal protection clause did not permit states to distinguish between the termination of life support from a doctor's active assistance in helping terminally ill patients commit suicide. The Court unanimously rejected this argument and refused to create a constitutional right to die.

Some proponents of gay marriage argue that the equal protection clause should put such commitments on an equal ground with others.

Does the equal protection program permit affirmative action programs designed to provide privileges for, rather than to discriminate against, minority groups?

This is currently a matter of great controversy. To date, the Court has tended to judge such programs on a case-by-case basis. It has accepted some such programs designed to make up for past discrimination or to provide greater racial diversity, but it had ruled more negatively in cases involving programs that establish strict goals or quotas. Thus in *Regents of the University of California v. Bakke* (1978), the Supreme Court ruled that the medical school at the University of California at Davis could give some weight to racial considerations in admission while rejecting a strict quota system. The Court took a similar stance in *Gratz v. Bollinger* (2003) and *Grutter v. Bollinger* (2003), which, respectively, addressed undergraduate admissions at the University of Michigan and admissions to its law school. In the latter case, Justice Sandra Day O'Connor did suggest that affirmative action program might no longer be needed in another 25 years. More recently, in *Fisher v. University of Texas,* the Court ruled that it would apply "strict scrutiny," its highest standard of review, to any use of racial classification in college admissions.

How, if at all, has the Supreme Court applied the equal protection clause to legislative apportionment?

Beginning with the case of *Baker v. Carr* (1962), the Court subjected the apportionment of legislative districts to scrutiny under the equal protection clause. In *Colegrove v. Green* (1946), the Court had previously ruled that such legislative apportionment was not justiciable (it had considered the issue to be a "political question") under the Guarantee Clause of Article IV, Section 4 of the Constitution.

What areas of apportionment do courts currently subject to equal protection scrutiny?

They extend such scrutiny both to apportionment of congressional districts and to state legislative apportionment.

What central principle does the Supreme Court apply in apportionment cases?

The basic standard, which the Supreme Court first articulated in a case involving Georgia primary elections (*Gray v. Sanders,* 1963) and subsequently extended in *Reynolds v. Sims* (1964) to both houses of a state legislature, is the "one-person/one-vote" standard. In effect, this means that legislative districts must have—so far as this is possible—equal populations.

Have court decisions under the equal protection clause led to substantial legislative reapportionment?

Yes, prior to the decision in *Baker v. Carr* (1962), many states had not reapportioned for decades, and rural districts often received representation that was disproportionate to their populations. States have subsequently reapportioned all such legislatures.

Has the U.S. Supreme Court applied its guidelines for state legislative apportionment to the U.S. Senate?

No, each state continues to have two senators regardless of its population.

How can the Court justify requiring both houses of a state legislature to be apportioned according to population when the U.S. Senate is not so apportioned?

The Court ruled that the compromise establishing equal representation in the Senate was a unique agreement essential to the establishment of the Constitution but not a valid precedent for the state level.

Does the equal protection clause of the Fourteenth Amendment limit the national government?

It does not explicitly do so. In *Bolling v. Sharpe* (1954), a companion case to *Brown v. Board of Education,* however, the Court ruled that a denial of equal protection could be so blatant as also to constitute a denial of Fifth Amendment due process rights. In *Bolling,* the Court therefore outlawed racially segregated schools in Washington, D.C. (governed by the federal government) just as *Brown* outlawed such segregation in the states.

Section 2
What is the subject of Section 2 of the Fourteenth Amendment?

Section 2 of the Fourteenth Amendment deals with state representation in the U.S. House of Representatives.

What previous provision of the Constitution does Section 2 of the Fourteenth Amendment modify?

Section 2 of the Fourteenth Amendment modifies the three-fifths clause.

What modification did Section 2 of the Fourteenth Amendment make in the three-fifths clause?

It provided that representation in the U.S. House of Representatives would now be based on "the whole number of persons in each State, excluding Indians not taxed"; previously the three-fifths clause had counted slaves as three-fifths of a person for purposes of representation.

Where is the first place that the Constitution mentions a voting age?

Section 2 of the Fourteenth Amendment provides that states may lose representation in the House of Representatives in cases where they deny voting rights to non-Indian males over the age of 21.

How supportive of the Fourteenth Amendment were advocates of women's suffrage?

Many were only tepid supporters. Contrary to their hopes, the postwar amendments not only failed to extend the right to vote to women, but Section 2 of the amendment makes the first mention of males in connection with voting. The Supreme Court cited this language in *Minor v. Happersett* (1875) to deny that the amendment intended to extend voting rights to women.

Does the Fourteenth Amendment mention any acceptable cases in which states may abridge voting rights?

Yes; it permitted such abridgment in the case of those who had participated in rebellion or another crime. Many states continue to deny voting rights to felons, especially those who are incarcerated, or ex-felons, although a strong argument can be made that such rights should be restored once individuals have paid their due by serving their sentences.

Why did the Fourteenth Amendment use the term "rebellion"?

Lincoln had used this term. By designating the Civil War as a rebellion, an internal condition, he had a better chance of keeping other nations from joining in the conflict on the side of the South. Southern states preferred to refer to the Civil War as a War Between the States, by which they meant to say that the North and South were separate nations, each of whom were entitled to solicit foreign recognition and support.

What provision did Section 2 of the Fourteenth Amendment make for states that denied voting rights to citizens who were not criminals or participants in the rebellion?

It provided for a reduction of their representation in the House of Representatives.

Why did Section 2 of the Fourteenth Amendment provide for reduced state representation for states that limited such rights?

Its authors were influenced by a mixture of motives based on justice and partisanship. Not only did it seem unfair to give states representation for individuals whom they had disenfranchised, but this also seemed likely to increase the power of Democrats in Congress at a time when most white Southerners were Democrats and most southern African Americans identified themselves as Republicans--Lincoln, a Republican president, fought to preserve the Union, issued the Emancipation Proclamation, and pushed for adoption of the amendment.

Did Congress enforce the provision in Section 2 of the Fourteenth Amendment providing for reduced representation for states that deprived individuals of their right to vote?

No, this proved to be both politically and practically difficult.

Section 3
What is the subject of Section 3 of the Fourteenth Amendment?

It limits the offices that former officers or supporters of the Confederate States of America could fill.

What limits did Section 3 of the Fourteenth Amendment place on former supporters of the Confederacy?

It specifically excluded them from serving as president and vice president or any civil office under the United States or under any state.

Did the Fourteenth Amendment provide any way to remove the limitations on former supporters of the Confederacy?

Yes, it granted Congress the power to remove such disabilities by a two-thirds vote.

Did Congress ever exercise its power to remove the limitation in Section 3 of the Fourteenth Amendment on offices that former supporters of the Confederate States of America could hold?

Yes, it removed most such restrictions by legislation.

Section 4
What is the subject of Section 4 of the Fourteenth Amendment?

Section 4 deals with the assumption of debts.

What did Section 4 say with respect to debts that Congress incurred while fighting the Civil War?

It specified that such debts "shall not be questioned."

What, if any, debts did Section 4 of the Fourteenth Amendment invalidate?

It invalidated any debts incurred by the state or national governments in aid of the "insurrection" against the United States. Section 4 also specified that the United States would not be responsible for "any claim for the loss or emancipation of any slave."

According to Section 4 of the Fourteenth Amendment, what was the status of any claims that individuals made for the loss or emancipation of slaves?

It held that all such claims were to "be held illegal and void."

Why did Section 4 of the Fourteenth Amendment prohibit compensation for slave loss or emancipation?

Individuals had discussed this option prior to the Civil War, but the conflict made it virtually unthinkable to compensate the slaveholders who were blamed for precipitating and perpetuating the conflict.

Section 5
What is the subject of Section 5 of the Fourteenth Amendment?

This section entrusts Congress with power to enforce the amendment by appropriate legislation.

Does Section 5 of the Fourteenth Amendment vest Congress with any power to expand civil rights protections that it would not otherwise have?

On at least some occasions, the Courts have been willing to defer to congressional judgments widening civil rights protections on the basis that Congress had enhanced discretion on this subject because of this enforcement provision in Section 5. For example, the Court allowed Congress to prohibit certain voter literacy requirements under Section 5 of the Fourteenth Amendment in *Katzenbach v. Morgan* (1966) without declaring that such tests would otherwise be in violation of Section 1 of that amendment. In 1997, however, in a case striking down the Religious Freedom Restoration Act, the Supreme Court indicated that, although Congress had the power to protect existing rights guaranteed by the Fourteenth Amendment, it did not have the right to create new rights.

Does Section 5 of the Fourteenth Amendment vest Congress with any power to restrict civil rights protections that it would not otherwise have?

It probably does not. Some commentators and Supreme Court justices have argued that this section serves as a kind of "one-way ratchet" that enables Congress to expand, but not to restrict, such powers. Still, there may be legitimate dispute as to whether any given congressional action—a racial set-aside, for example—actually expands or restricts civil rights.

THE FIFTEENTH AMENDMENT

When did the states ratify the Fifteenth Amendment?

They did so in 1870.

What was the last state to ratify the Fifteenth Amendment?

In a symbolic act, Tennessee (the only state that had yet to ratify the amendment) did so on April 2, 1997. Kentucky had taken a similar symbolic vote on the amendment in 1976.

What is the subject of the Fifteenth Amendment?

The Fifteenth Amendment deals with voting rights.

How many sections are there in the Fifteenth Amendment?

The Amendment has two sections.

What three factors does Section 1 of the Fifteenth Amendment prohibit the United States or individual states from using to abridge voting rights?

The factors are "race, color, or previous condition of servitude." Contrary to the hopes of many advocates of women's rights, the amendment did not ban discrimination on the basis of sex. The Constitution did not end such discrimination until states adopted the Nineteenth Amendment in 1920.

How effective has the Fifteenth Amendment been in protecting voting rights against racial discrimination?

Especially during its early years, the amendment was quite ineffective. States devised, or consented to, a number of mechanisms including literacy tests (which states typically administered to favor whites over blacks), poll taxes, all-white primary elections, grandfather clauses (one had to take a literacy test unless one's grandfather had voted; since most grandfathers of African Americans had been slaves, this clause again fell disproportionately

---

EXCERPTS FROM THE CONSTITUTION

Part 1. In case of the removal of the president from office, or of his death, resignation, or inability to discharge the powers and duties of the said office, the same shall devolve on the vice-president, and the congress may by law provide for the case of removal, death, resignation or inability, both of the president and vice-president, declaring what officer shall then act as president, and such officer shall act accordingly, until the disability be removed, or a president shall be elected.

Part 2. In all cases affecting ambassadors, other public ministers and consuls, and those in which a state shall be a party, the supreme court shall have original jurisdiction.

Part 3. In all the other cases before mentioned, the supreme court shall have appellate jurisdiction, both as to law and fact, with such exceptions, and under such regulations as the congress shall make.

Part 4. Neither slavery nor involuntary servitude, except as a punishment for crime whereof the party shall have been duly convicted, shall exist within the United States, or any place subject to their jurisdiction.

INSTRUCTION "C"

(After applicant has read, not aloud, the foregoing excerpts from the Constitution, he will answer the following questions in writing and without assistance:)

1. In case the president is unable to perform the duties of his office, who assumes them? _____

2. "Involuntary servitude" is permitted in the United States upon conviction of a crime. (True or False)_____

3. If a state is a party to a case, the constitution provides that original jurisdiction shall be in_____

4. Congress passes laws regulating cases which are included in those over which the United States Supreme Court has_____

_____ jurisdiction.

I hereby certify that I have received no assistance in the completion of this citizenship and literacy test, that I was allowed the time I desired to complete it, and that I waive any right existing to demand a copy of same. (If for any reason the applicant does not wish to sign this, he must discuss the matter with the board of registrars.)

Signed: _____
                                          (Applicant)

Page of Alabama Voters Literacy Test, 1960s. (National Archives)

on them), and even physical intimidation by the Ku Klux Klan and other vigilante groups to keep African Americans from voting.

What does Section 2 of the Fifteenth Amendment do?

It grants Congress power to enforce the amendment by appropriate legislation.

Does Section 2 of the Fifteenth Amendment grant Congress any power that it would not otherwise have?

Certain 20th-century Supreme Court decisions have cited this provision as authority for giving greater deference to congressional judgments in this area than it might otherwise do. This section proved to be important in the Court's decision to uphold the Voting Rights Act of 1965, which has been extended on a number of occasions, and the continued coverage formula (that focused on a limited number of states and localities) which the Supreme Court recently invalidated in *Shelby County v. Holder* (2013). Under Section 2, the Court recognized the authority of Congress to suspend literacy tests in certain states even though the Court had previously ruled that such tests were not per se in violation of Section 1 of the Fourteenth Amendment.

BIBLIOGRAPHY

Books

Richard C. Cortner, *The Supreme Court and the Second Bill of Rights: The Four-teenth Amendment and the Nationalization of Civil Liberties* (Madison: University of Wisconsin Press, 1981).

Don E. Fehrenbacher, *The Dred Scott Case: Its Significance in American Law and Politics* (New York: Oxford University Press, 1978).

Harold M. Hyman, *A More Perfect Union: The Impact of the Civil War and Reconstruction on the Constitution* (Boston: Houghton Mifflin Company, 1975).

Donald W. Jackson, *Even the Children of Strangers: Equality Under the U.S. Constitution* (Lawrence: University Press of Kansas, 1992).

Richard Kluger, *Simple Justice,* 2 vols. (New York: Alfred A. Knopf, 1975).

Earl M. Maltz, *Civil Rights, the Constitution, and Congress, 1863–1869* (Lawrence: University Press of Kansas, 1990).

Howard N. Meyer, *The Amendment that Refused to Die* (Radnor, PA: The Chilton Book Company, 1973).

William E. Nelson, *The Fourteenth Amendment: From Political Principle to Judicial Doctrine* (Cambridge, MA: Harvard University Press, 1988).

C. Vance Woodward, *The Strange Career of Jim Crow,* 3rd rev. ed. (New York: Oxford University Press, 1974).

Cases

Baker v. Carr, 369 U.S. 186 (1962).
Bolling v. Sharpe, 347 U.S. 497 (1954).
Brown v. Board of Education, 347 U.S. 483 (1954).
Civil Rights Cases, 109 U.S. 3 (1883).
Fisher v. University of Texas, 570 U.S. _ (2013).
Frontiero v. Richardson, 411 U.S. 677 (1973).
Gratz v. Bollinger, 539 U.S. 244 (2003).
Gray v. Sanders, 372 U.S. 368 (1963).
Grutter v. Bollinger, 539 U.S. 306 (2003).
Katzenbach v. Morgan, 384 U.S. 641 (1966).
Milliken v. Bradley, 418 U.S. 717 (1974).
Minor v. Happersett, 88 U.S. 162 (1871).
Plessy v. Ferguson, 163 U.S. 537 (1896).
Reed v. Reed, 404 U.S. 71 (1971).
Regents of the University of California v. Bakke, 438 U.S. 265 (1978).
Reynolds v. Sims, 377 U.S. 533 (1964).
Rostker v. Goldberg, 453 U.S. 57 (1981).
Scott v. Sandford, 60 U.S. 393 (1857).
Shelby County v. Holder, 570 U.S. (2013).
Slaughterhouse Cases, 83 U.S. 36 (1973).
Swann v. Charlotte Mecklenburg Board of Education, 401 U.S. 1 (1970).
Vacco v. Quill, 65 U.S.L.W. 4695 (1997).
Washington v. Glucksberg, 521 U.S. 702 (1997).

Chapter 9

Amendments Sixteen through Nineteen: The Progressive Era Amendments

---

THE SIXTEENTH AMENDMENT

How many amendments did the states ratify from 1913 to 1920?

The states ratified four amendments, namely amendments Sixteen through Nineteen, during this time, which roughly corresponds to a time period in American history referred to as the Progressive Era. Progressive leaders were especially concerned with democratizing American government and with eliminating governmental corruption; many were also concerned about the perceived negative impact that immigrants, many from Southern and Eastern Europe, were having on the nation.

What is the subject of the Sixteenth Amendment?

It deals with the power to levy taxes.

When did the states ratify the Sixteenth Amendment?

They ratified it in 1913.

How many years transpired between the adoption of the Fifteenth and Sixteenth Amendments?

Forty-three years transpired between the adoption of the Fifteenth and Sixteenth Amendments. This is thus the second longest period under the Constitution (the first transpired between 1804 and 1865) during which the states did not adopt any amendments.

How many sections does the Sixteenth Amendment contain?

Perhaps because it consists of a single paragraph, this amendment is not divided into sections.

What prompted the Sixteenth Amendment?

In *Pollock v. Farmers Loan Association* (1895), the Supreme Court ruled that the income tax was a form of direct tax that could only be apportioned among the states according to population rather than income. This decision had effectively invalidated the national income tax.

How did the Sixteenth Amendment overturn the decision in *Pollock v. Farmers' Loan & Trust Co.*?

The amendment provided that Congress could levy taxes on income without apportioning such taxes among the states or without respect to any census or enumeration.

Are there any purposes for an income tax other than raising revenue?

Such taxes, if levied in a progressive fashion—taking a higher percentage of income from those who earn more money—also have to potential to redistribute income. Proponents of the amendment thought that this could reduce distances between income groups whereas opponents considered this to be an undesirable "socialistic" feature.

What is the only year in American history, other than 1791 (the ratification of the Bill of Rights) when the states ratified more than one amendment?

The year 1913 was the only such year.

THE SEVENTEENTH AMENDMENT

What other amendment did the states ratify in 1913?

They also ratified the Seventeenth Amendment, which provided for the popular election of senators.

How many sections are there in the Seventeenth Amendment?

The amendment has three paragraphs, but it is not divided into sections.

What is the subject of the Seventeenth Amendment?

The Seventeenth Amendment provides for the popular election of U.S. senators.

What amending mechanism helped to secure the Seventeenth Amendment?

Because proponents feared that many appointed senators would reject such popular election, states sent numerous petitions to Congress requesting that it call a constitutional convention to propose amendments on this subject. Such petitions helped persuade Congress to propose this amendment on its own.

Prior to the Seventeenth Amendment, did voters select any U.S. senators by popular election?

Yes. Although the U.S. Constitution had entrusted this responsibility to the state legislatures, many had already agreed to appoint the popular choice to this office.

According to the Seventeenth Amendment, which individuals have the right to vote for U.S. senators?

All individuals who are eligible to vote for representatives to the most numerous branch of the state legislature are eligible.

How does the Seventeenth Amendment provide for the filling of vacancies in the U.S. Senate?

The amendment entrusts state governors, which it calls "state executives," with calling elections to fill such vacancies.

Does the Seventeenth Amendment make provision for state representation in the Senate between a vacancy and an election to fill such a vacancy?

Yes, it provides that state governors may make temporary appointments so the state will continue to be represented fully during this time.

How, if at all, did the adoption of the Seventeenth Amendment affect the terms of senators who were in office when states ratified it?

The last paragraph of the amendment provides that the amendment "shall not be so construed as to affect the election or term of any Senator chosen before it becomes valid as part of the Constitution."

THE EIGHTEENTH AMENDMENT

What is the subject of the Eighteenth Amendment?

It provided for national alcoholic prohibition.

In what year did the states ratify the Eighteenth Amendment?

They ratified it in 1919, shortly after the end of World War I.

How many sections does the Eighteenth Amendment have?

The amendment has three sections, each of which corresponds to a separate paragraph.

What is the first amendment that did not go into effect immediately upon ratification?

The Eighteenth Amendment is the first.

What time did Section 1 of the Eighteenth Amendment allow to transpire between its ratification and its implementation?

It provided for a one-year transition period.

What aspects of national alcoholic prohibition did the Eighteenth Amendment specifically mention?

It mentioned the "manufacture, sale, or transportation" of such beverages, including their importation or exportation.

What definition did the Eighteenth Amendment provide for determining whether beverages were intoxicating?

The amendment provided no such definition. Congress subsequently adopted a very restrictive definition in the Volstead Act, and the courts subsequently upheld it.

Where is the only place that the Constitution uses the term "concurrent powers"?

Section 2 of the Eighteenth Amendment is the only one.

What are concurrent powers?

These are powers that the state and national governments jointly exercise. By contrast, there are some exclusive powers that only one or the other government (or set of governments) can exercise.

What is the first amendment to the Constitution that included a ratification deadline?

The Eighteenth Amendment was the first to include such a deadline.

What time did the Eighteenth Amendment set for states to ratify?

The amendment provided for a ratification time of seven years, a formula that all subsequent amendments that have included such a limit have used.

Women march in support of the Nineteenth Amendment in New York City on May 6, 1912. The movement for women's suffrage is often traced back to the Seneca Falls Convention of 1848. (Library of Congress)

Why did the Eighteenth Amendment include a ratification deadline?

Some of its opponents incorrectly thought that the amendment would not be ratified with this period.

Is the Eighteenth Amendment still in effect?

No, the Twenty-First Amendment repealed it in 1933.

THE NINETEENTH AMENDMENT

What amendment prohibits state and national governments from denying or abridging the right to vote to women?

The Nineteenth Amendment does.

When had the drive for women's suffrage begun?

It is common for historians to trace this movement to the Seneca Falls Convention of 1848. Many proponents of the Fifteenth Amendment, which prohibited discrimination in voting on the basis of race, hoped that it would also secure women's suffrage, but it did not do so. The proposal for secure women's suffrage was first formally introduced in Congress in 1878.

When did the states ratify the Nineteenth Amendment?

1920.

Susan B. Anthony is often referred to as the mother
of the Nineteenth Amendment, which granted
women the right to vote. (Library of Congress)

What is another name for the Nineteenth Amendment?

It is often called the Susan B. Anthony Amendment in honor of the
woman (1820–1906) who served as one of the greatest leaders of the
American women's suffrage movement, but many women (and men) contributed to its proposal and ratification.

How many sections does the Nineteenth Amendment contain?

The amendment is not divided into sections, but it has two paragraphs.

What does the first paragraph of the Nineteenth Amendment say?

It prohibits the government from denying the right to vote to women.

What does the second paragraph of the Nineteenth Amendment say?

It grants power to enforce the amendment through appropriate legislation.

Did any women have the right to vote prior to ratification of the Nineteenth Amendment?

Yes, prior to this time, states individually decided whether or not to allow women to exercise the franchise.

Who was the first president elected after the right to vote was extended to women?

Warren G. Harding was the first elected president after ratification of the amendment.

BIBLIOGRAPHY

Books

Richard F. Hamm, *Shaping the 18th Amendment: Temperance Reform, Legal Culture, and the Polity, 1880–1929* (Chapel Hill: The University of North Carolina Press, 1995).

C. H. Hoebeke, *The Road to Mass Democracy: Original Intent and the Seventeenth Amendment* (New Brunswick: Transaction, 1995).

Richard Hofstader, *The Age of Reform: From Bryan to F.D.R.* (New York: Vintage Books, 1955).

Aileen S. Kraditor, *The Ideas of the Women's Suffrage Movement, 1890–1920* (New York: Columbia University Press, 1965).

David E. Kyvig, *Alcohol and Order: Perspectives on National Prohibition* (Westport, CT: Greenwood Press, 1985).

Arthur S. Link and Richard L. McCormick, *Progressivism* (Arlington Heights, IL: Harlan Davidson, Inc., 1983).

David Okrent, *Last Call: The Rise and Fall of Prohibition* (New York: Scribners, 2011).

Majorie S. Wheeler, ed. *One Woman, One Vote: Rediscovering the Woman Suffrage Movement* (Troutdale, OR: New Sage Press, 1995).

Case

Pollock v. Farmers' Loan & Trust Company, 158 U.S. 601 (1895).

Chapter 10

Amendments Twenty through Twenty-Seven: The Modern Amendments

THE TWENTIETH AMENDMENT
What is a "lame duck"?

The Constitution does not specifically use this term, but a lame duck is an individual who remains in elective office after being defeated, but prior to the time that the new elected official assumes office.

What, if any, problems do lame ducks pose?

As individuals who are leaving office, they may not be as responsive and accountable to the will of their constituents as if they were returning.

What constitutional amendment sought to reduce the problem of "lame duck" representatives?

The Twentieth Amendment addressed this problem.

When did the states ratify the Twentieth Amendment?

1933.

George Washington presides over the Constitutional Convention of 1787. (National Archives)

How many sections are there in the Twentieth Amendment?

The Twentieth Amendment has six sections, more than in any other amendment that has been adopted.

According to the Twentieth Amendment, do the terms of new members of Congress or that of a new president begin first?

According to the amendment, the terms of new members of Congress begin before the term of a new president.

According to the Twentieth Amendment, when do the terms of the president and vice president begin?

The terms begin on noon on the 20th day of January.

Why did proponents of shortening lame duck terms think that it was necessary to adopt an amendment to change the dates that elected officials took office, rather than doing this by legislation?

By moving forward the dates for congressional and presidential terms, the change inaugurated by the amendment altered the terms of sitting members of Congress, which the Constitution had specified.

According to the Twentieth Amendment, when do the terms of senators and representatives begin?

Their terms begin at noon on the third day of January.

Section 2 of the Twentieth Amendment sets a day for the first meeting of Congress, unless Congress provides otherwise by law. What day is this?

January 3 is the day that it designates.

What happens if a president-elect dies before the president-elect can assume office?

According to the Twentieth Amendment, the vice president elect shall become president.

According to the Twentieth Amendment, who serves as president if a president shall not have been chosen by January 20?

The vice president elect serves in such circumstances.

According to the Twentieth Amendment, who is supposed to provide for cases where neither a president nor a vice president have been selected prior to January 20?

Congress is vested with this responsibility. To date, Congress has not adopted legislation on this subject.

According to the Twentieth Amendment, who becomes president in case both the president and vice president die?

The amendment does not specify. A Succession Act of 1947 has established that the president and vice president are succeeded by the speaker of the House of Representatives and the president pro tempore of the Senate (both elected officials). These officers are succeeded by the following members of the cabinet: secretary of state, secretary of the treasury, secretary of defense, attorney general, secretary of the interior, secretary of agriculture, secretary of commerce, secretary of labor, secretary of health and human service, secretary of housing and urban development, secretary of transportation, secretary of energy, secretary of education, and secretary of veterans affairs.

To date, no one other than a president or vice president has ever had to succeed to office.

According to the Twentieth Amendment, who is responsible for providing for cases in which a candidate for president or vice president dies when such candidates have not received a majority and the House and Senate are still resolve the issue?

The amendment vests this responsibility in Congress.

On what day of the year did Sections 1 and 2 of the Twentieth Amendment take effect?

Section 5 of the amendment specified October 15.

How many years did Congress give the states to ratify the Twentieth Amendment?

It gave them seven years to ratify.

THE TWENTY-FIRST AMENDMENT

What is the only constitutional amendment that another amendment has explicitly repealed?

The Eighteenth Amendment is.

What amendment repealed the Eighteenth Amendment?
The Twenty-First Amendment did.

What is the subject of the Twenty-First Amendment?
The Amendment provided for the repeal of national alcoholic prohibition.

When did the states ratify the Twenty-First Amendment?
1933.

Who was president when the Twenty-First Amendment was ratified?
Franklin D. Roosevelt was president.

How many sections does the Twenty-First Amendment contain?
It has three.

What does each section of the Twenty-First Amendment say?
The first provides for the repeal of the Eighteenth Amendment. The second allows states to continue to regulate the subject. The third specifies the time period during which the amendment must be ratified.

Did the repeal of national alcoholic prohibition allow any remaining restrictions on the transportation of importation of alcohol?
Yes, Section 2 of the Twenty-First Amendment specifically recognizes state powers to prohibit such "transportation of importation into" any such states "in violation of the laws thereof."

What is the only amendment that state conventions, rather than state legislatures, have ratified?
The Twenty-First Amendment is the only amendment to be so ratified.

Why did Congress specify that state conventions rather than state legislatures would ratify the Twenty-First Amendment?
Congress believed that such conventions would be more likely to endorse the amendment than legislatures, many of whom were dominated at the time by rural interests that were generally more favorable to "drys" (proponents of prohibition) than to "wets" (opponents of prohibition).

What deadline did the Twenty-First Amendment provide for its own ratification?
Section 3 provided that such ratification must take place within seven years from the time that Congress submitted it to the states.

THE TWENTY-SECOND AMENDMENT

What is the subject of the Twenty-Second Amendment?

The amendment limits the number of terms that a president can serve.

What limit on presidential terms does the Twenty-Second Amendment establish?

It specifies that a president cannot be elected to that office more than twice and that a vice president who serves for more than 2 years of a president's term cannot be elected more than once. The amendment thus establishes 10 years as the maximum length of time that a modern president can serve.

When did the states ratify the Twenty-Second Amendment?

They ratified it in 1951.

How many presidents in American history have served more than two terms?

Only one president, Franklin D. Roosevelt, has served for more than two terms. Roosevelt was elected to four terms but served just over three before dying. Roosevelt's long service appears to have been a primary impetus for adoption of the Twenty-Second Amendment, an amendment that was especially popular among Republicans (Roosevelt had been a Democrat).

Who had established the two-term precedent that lasted until the time of Franklin D. Roosevelt?

George Washington had retired after two terms. John Adams did not win reelection to a second term. Thomas Jefferson reaffirmed Washington's precedent after he decided not to run for a third term.

Who was president when the Twenty-Second Amendment was ratified?

Harry S. Truman was president at that time.

Did the Twenty-Second Amendment limit the number of terms that President Truman could serve?

No, it did not. Section 1 of the amendment specifically exempted "any person holding the office of President when this Article was proposed by Congress." It further specified that it "shall not prevent any person who may be holding the office of President, or acting as President, during the term within which this Article becomes operative from holding the office of President or acting as President during the remainder of such term."

Does the Twenty-Second Amendment limit the number of terms that a vice president can serve?
No, it does not.

What time limit for ratification did Section 2 of the Twenty-First Amendment establish?
It established a seven-year ratification limit.

THE TWENTY-THIRD AMENDMENT
What is the subject of the Twenty-Third Amendment?
It deals with Electoral College representation for the District of Columbia.

When did the states ratify the Twenty-Third Amendment?
1961.

How many amendments did the states ratify during the 1960s?
States ratified three amendments, the Twenty-Third, the Twenty-Fourth, and the Twenty-Fifth, in the 1960s.

How many sections are there in the Twenty-Third Amendment?
It has two sections.

How does the Twenty-Third Amendment apportion presidential electors for the District of Columbia?
It is to have the same number of electors to which it would be entitled if it were a state, but no more than the least populous state.

What is the number of presidential electors to which the least populous states (and thus the District of Columbia) are entitled?
The District is entitled to three electors. Each state has a minimum of one representative and two senators. Each state's electoral votes are equal to its total number of representatives and senators. States with the minimum three votes currently include Alaska, Delaware, Montana, North Dakota, South Dakota, Vermont, and Wyoming.

How many total votes are there in the Electoral College?
There are currently 538 total votes in the Electoral College. This number consists of the total number of U.S. senators (currently 100) to the total number of voting members of the U.S. House of Representatives

(currently set by law at 435) and to the 3 electoral votes to which the District of Columbia is entitled under the Twenty-Third Amendment. An individual must secure 270 electoral votes, a majority of 538, to become president or vice president.

According to the Twenty-Third Amendment, where do electors from the District of Columbia meet?

Such electors meet in the District.

What is the subject of Section 2 of the Twenty-Third Amendment?

It deals with congressional enforcement powers.

THE TWENTY-FOURTH AMENDMENT

When did the states ratify the Twenty-Fourth Amendment?

They ratified in 1964, the same year that Congress adopted the historic Civil Rights Act of 1964, outlawing racial discrimination in most places of public accommodation. Lyndon B. Johnson was president at this time.

How many sections are there in the Twenty-Fourth Amendment?

It has two sections.

What is the subject of the Twenty-Fourth Amendment?

The amendment prevents individuals from being deprived of their right to vote on the basis of their failure to pay poll taxes.

What are poll taxes?

Poll taxes are taxes required as a condition for voting; such taxes are head taxes in that each person typically pays the same amount.

Why did governments initially institute poll taxes?

Originally, many of the Framers thought that by tying voting to some property qualification they would limit votes to individuals with a greater stake in society. Although they did not mandate such qualifications, they allowed states to enact them.

After the Civil War, many states began to enact poll taxes as a way of making it more difficult for lower-income groups, among which African Americans predominated, to vote. Other mechanisms that states adopted or that individuals employed to constrict the suffrage included so-called grandfather clauses (exempting individuals, mostly white, from literacy tests if their grandfathers had voted), all-white primaries, literacy tests, and physical intimidation. This use of poll taxes in a racially discriminatory manner ultimately led to adoption of the Twenty-Fourth Amendment.

What are primary elections?

Primary elections are elections in which political parties nominate candidates for office.

Where is the only place that the Constitution mentions primary elections?

The Twenty-Fourth Amendment is the only one to mention such elections. This amendment eliminates the poll tax in primary elections as well as other general elections.

What is the subject of Section 2 of the Twenty-Fourth Amendment?

It gives enforcement power to Congress over the poll tax.

THE TWENTY-FIFTH AMENDMENT

What is the primary subject of the Twenty-Fifth Amendment?

Its primary subject is presidential disability.

What, if any, other subjects does the Twenty-Fifth Amendment address?

The amendment also deals with vacancies in the vice presidency.

When did the states ratify the Twenty-Fifth Amendment?

They ratified in 1967.

What were some of the events that precipitated the adoption of the Twenty-Fifth Amendment?

The most immediate catalyst was the assassination of President John F. Kennedy in 1963, but several previous events had brought to public attention the possibility of presidential disability. In addition to the deaths and assassinations of a number of 19th-century presidents, William G. Harding and Franklin D. Roosevelt had died in office in the 20th century. Woodrow Wilson had suffered a debilitating stroke during his second term of office; there had been an assassination attempt against Harry

Truman; Dwight D. Eisenhower had suffered a heart attack and a stroke while in office; and Lyndon Johnson had heart trouble.

What three ways does the Twenty-Fifth Amendment mention that a sitting president can leave office?

According to the amendment, a president can leave office by removal, by death, or by resignation.

Prior to the Twenty-Fifth Amendment, what happened in cases of the death, removal, or resignation of a vice president?

The office remained vacant. Congressional law specified the individual who would assume the presidency in the case of the president's death.

According to the Twenty-Fifth Amendment, who is responsible for nominating a vice president in the case of a vacancy in this office?

The president is.

According to the Twenty-Fifth Amendment, who confirms a presidential nomination for a vacancy in the vice presidency?

A majority vote of both houses of Congress is required for such confirmation.

How does the method for confirming nominees for vacancies in the vice president differ from that of confirming judges and ambassadors?

Both houses of Congress confirm presidential nominations for vice presidential vacancies by majority vote, whereas a simple majority of the Senate confirms judges and ambassadors.

Which, if any, individuals have presidents appointed to vacancies in the vice presidency subsequent to adoption of the Twenty-Fifth Amendment?

Congress approved President Nixon's appointment of Gerald Ford as vice president when Spiro Agnew (who pleaded nolo contendere, or no contest, to bribery charges) resigned as vice president in the Nixon administration. When Ford became president at Richard Nixon's resignation, he appointed Nelson Rockefeller, a former New York governor and one-time candidate for the Republican nomination for president, to succeed him. However, when Ford ran for reelection in 1976, he ran with Kansas senator Robert Dole (who was the Republican nominee for president in 1996) rather than with Rockefeller.

Who is the only president who was never selected through the electoral college system?

President Gerald Ford is the only president to have been selected apart from the Electoral College. He became president after having been previously appointed vice president upon Spiro Agnew's resignation from this job and was defeated when he ran to continue in office in 1976.

According to the Twenty-Fifth Amendment, what happens when a president transmits a message to Congress saying that he is "unable to discharge the powers and duties of his office"?

The vice president is to serve as "Acting President" until the president sends Congress another declaration to the contrary.

If a president is unable to carry on presidential duties, who should he inform of this disability?

The Twenty-Fifth Amendment requires the president to send such notice to the president pro tempore of the Senate and the speaker of the House of Representatives. Apart from the vice president, who serves as president of the Senate, these are the only two congressional offices that the Constitution designates.

According to the Twenty-Fifth Amendment, which individuals, other than the president himself, are responsible for transmitting to Congress information that the president is unable to carry out his constitutional duties?

The Constitution designates the vice president and a majority of either the principal officers of the executive departments or of such other body as Congress may by law provide.

According to the Twenty-Fifth Amendment, what happens in cases where the vice president and a majority of either the principal officers of the executive departments or of such other body as Congress has designated informs Congress that the president is unable to carry out his duties?

The vice president immediately assumes the powers and duties of the presidential office.

If the vice president has assumed duties in light of his and designated officers' findings that the president is incapacitated, what must the president do in order to recover his or her powers?

In such a case, the president must send a written message to the president pro tempore of the Senate and the speaker of the House of Representatives indicating that no disability exists.

According to the Twenty-Fifth Amendment, who is responsible for resolving the issue if there is a dispute between the president and the body that Congress designates as to whether a president is disabled?

Congress is.

If Congress is not in session and a dispute develops between the president and the group designated by Congress to ascertain whether or not he is disabled, how long does Congress have to assemble?

The Twenty-Fifth Amendment specifies that it must assemble within 48 hours.

If Congress is unable to vote within 21 days after being informed that there is a disagreement between the president and designated officers as to whether the president can carry out his duties, what happens?

The Twenty-Fifth Amendment specifies that the president resumes his duties.

In cases of dispute between a president and other delegated officials, by what vote must Congress decide that a president is disabled?

The Twenty-Fifth Amendment specifies a two-thirds vote, presumably as a way of guaranteeing that Congress does not seek to use this power simply to remove a president with whom it disagrees politically.

THE TWENTY-SIXTH AMENDMENT

What is the subject of the Twenty-Sixth Amendment?

It deals with voting rights for U.S. citizens 18 years of age or older.

In what year did the states ratify the Twenty-Sixth Amendment adopted?

They ratified in 1971.

What Supreme Court decision did the Twenty-Sixth Amendment modify?

It modified *Oregon v. Mitchell* (1971). In this decision, the Court had decided that the national government could lower the voting age in national elections but not in state elections.

What factors, other than *Oregon v. Mitchell,* led to the Twenty-Sixth Amendment?

The war in Vietnam played some part. Many individuals argued that it was unfair to ask young people to fight and die for a country in which they could not vote. Supporters of the amendment also noted the rising educational attainments of those who were 18 years and older.

Prior to adoption of the Twenty-Sixth Amendment, what was the most common voting age?

Most states did not allow individuals to vote until the age of 21.

How many sections are there in the Twenty-Sixth Amendment?

The amendment has two sections.

What does Section 2 of the Twenty-Sixth Amendment contain?

Section 2 of the Twenty-Sixth Amendment contains the provision for congressional enforcement of the 18-year-old voting age.

THE TWENTY-SEVENTH AMENDMENT

What amendment did Congress originally propose as the Twenty-Seventh Amendment?

In 1972, Congress proposed the Equal Rights Amendment, which it designed to give equal rights to women, as the Twenty-Seventh Amendment. In 1978, it subsequently proposed an amendment to give statehood to the District of Columbia. The requisite number of states did not ratify either amendment.

In what year did Congress first propose the Twenty-Seventh Amendment?

Congress proposed the amendment in 1791. It was originally the second of 12 proposals that Congress proposed to the states as the Bill of Rights.

In what year did state ratify the Twenty-Seventh Amendment?

States ratified in 1992. Some scholars have argued that the length of the time between this amendment's proposal and its ratification was too long to express a "contemporary consensus" of the states.

What individual was most responsible for getting the Twenty-Seventh Amendment ratified?

Gregory Watson, an aide to a Texas state legislator, became interested in the amendment when writing a term paper for a government class (for which he received a C) and subsequently spent nearly $5,000 of his own money to get the amendment ratified.

What is the subject of the Twenty-Seventh Amendment?

It deals with congressional pay.

What limit does the Twenty-Seventh Amendment place on congressional pay?

It says that pay "varying such compensation" shall not take effect, "until an election of Representatives shall have intervened." Such elections are held every two years.

Does the Twenty-Seventh Amendment limit congressional pay cuts as well as pay increases?

This was probably not its intention, but its language does not distinguish between these two actions, so it would presumably limit both.

How many sections does the Twenty-Seventh Amendment contain?

Like other amendments originally proposed as part of the Bill of Rights, the amendment has only a single paragraph. In contrast to many of the other first 10 amendments, it deals only with a single subject.

BIBLIOGRAPHY

Books

Richard B. Bernstein with Jerome Agel, *Amending America: If We Love the Constitution So Much, Why Do We Keep Trying to Change It?* (New York: Random House, 1993).

John D. Feerick, *The Twenty-Fifth Amendment: Its Complete History and Earliest Applications* (New York: Fordham University Press, 1976).

David E. Kyvig, *Explicit and Authentic Acts: Amending the U.S. Constitution, 1776–1995* (Lawrence: University Press of Kansas, 1996).

David E. Kyvig, *Repealing National Prohibition* (Chicago: University of Chicago Press, 1979).

John R. Vile, *Encyclopedia of Constitutional Amendments, Proposed Amendments, and Amending Issues, 1789–2010, 3rd ed.* (Santa Barbara, CA: ABC-CLIO, 2010).

Case

Oregon v. Mitchell, 400 U.S. 112 (1971).

Chapter 11

1215 through 2013: A Walk through American Constitutional History

---

FAMOUS QUOTATIONS ABOUT THE U.S. CONSTITUTION

What contemporary of the Constitutional Convention called it "an assembly of demigods"?

Thomas Jefferson made this comment in a letter to John Adams.

Who once referred to the Constitutional Convention as "the greatest single effort of national deliberation that the world has ever seen"?

John Adams did.

Who once said that the Constitution appeared to him as "little short of a miracle"?

George Washington made this observation in a letter to the Marquis de Lafayette. Catherine Drinker Bowen has subsequently written a popular book on the Constitutional Convention entitled *Miracle at Philadelphia.*

Who once called the Constitution "a covenant with death"?

William Lloyd Garrison, a prominent abolitionist, made this statement because he felt that the Constitution had sanctioned slavery.

Who once said that the Constitution was "the most wonderful work ever struck off at a given time by the brain and purpose of man"?

William Gladstone (See Kammen, p. 162) made this statement. Gladstone also said that "the British Constitution is the most subtle organism which had proceeded from the womb and the long gestation of progressive history. . . ."

Who once said that "Some men look at constitutions with sanctimonious reverence, and deem them like the arc [*sic*] of the covenant, too sacred to be touched. They ascribe to the men of the preceding age a wisdom more than human, and suppose what they did to be beyond amendment. I knew that age well; I belonged to it, and labored with it. It deserved well of its country. It was very like the present, but without the experience of the present; and forty years of experience in government is worthy a century of book-reading; and this they would say for themselves were they to rise from the dead"?

Thomas Jefferson did. He was specifically referring to the Virginia state constitution, but successors have sometimes applied his words to the U.S. Constitution as well.

Who referred to the United States government as a "government of the people, by the people, and for the people"?

Abraham Lincoln uttered these words in his famous Gettysburg Address.

Who proclaimed, "Our Union, it must be preserved"?

This was the position that President Andrew Jackson took when he was presented with the doctrine of state nullification of federal laws. By contrast, Senator John C. Calhoun is reputed to have said, "The Union, next to our liberties [by which he probably meant to highlight states' rights], most dear."

KEY DATES AND CASES IN AMERICAN CONSTITUTIONAL HISTORY

THE YEARS PRIOR TO THE U.S. CONSTITUTION

The Magna Carta is often considered as a fountain of English and American rights. When did King John sign it?

1215.

Slavery was one of the most difficult issues that the United States has ever confronted. When was slavery first introduced in North America?

It was introduced with the landing of slaves at Jamestown in 1619.

When did the Pilgrims sign the Mayflower Compact, which is often cited as a constitutional prototype?

1620.

In what year did the English Parliament adopt a Declaration of Rights?

It did so in 1689, a year after King William and Queen Mary assumed the throne.

Scholars often cite the French and Indian War as a turning point, after which the British ended their policy of "salutary neglect" and began taking a more direct hand in the governance of the colonies. What were the dates of the French and Indian War?

It lasted from 1754 to 1763.

The colonists resisted efforts by the British Parliament to tax them. When did the Stamp Act Congress meet?

It met in 1765.

The colonists later sent representatives to two continental congresses. When did these meet?

The first Continental Congress met in 1774. The second began in 1775.

In what year did the Revolutionary War begin?

It began in 1775.

In what year did Thomas Paine publish his influential *Common Sense*?

It was published in January of 1776.

When did Thomas Jefferson write and the Second Continental Congress adopt the Declaration of Independence?

1776.

The first form of government established for the former 13 colonies was the Articles of Confederation. When did Congress write the Articles?

Delegates wrote the Articles in 1776 and 1777.

When did the last state ratify the Articles of Confederation?

1781.

One of the preludes to the Constitutional Convention was the Annapolis Convention. When did it meet?

In September of 1786.

When did Shays' Rebellion begin?

It began in the winter of 1786.

THE FIRST 100 YEARS OF THE CONSTITUTION

When did the Constitutional Convention meet?

It met from May 25 through September 17, 1787.

In what year did George Washington become the first president?

He became president in 1789, the same year that the first Congress under the new Constitution met.

In what year did Congress adopt the first Judiciary Act?

1789.

When did the states ratify the Bill of Rights?

The states ratified in 1791, two years after being proposed in Congress.

The Whiskey Rebellion provided a good opportunity for the assertion of national power. When was this rebellion?

It occurred in 1794–1795.

In what year did states ratify the Eleventh Amendment?

1795.

When did Congress adopt the Alien and Sedition Acts, which made it more difficult for immigrants to become citizens and which limited and punished speech that criticized the government?

Congress adopted them during the administration of John Adams in 1798.

When did Jefferson and Madison author the Virginia and Kentucky Resolutions?

They anonymously wrote these documents, arguing that states had the right to "interpose" against laws with which they disagree, in 1798, largely in response to the Alien and Sedition Acts.

John Marshall was the fourth chief justice of the
Supreme Court. His efforts helped to make the
Supreme Court an equal branch of government
next to the executive and legislative branches.
(Library of Congress)

**Thomas Jefferson often claimed that his election brought about
a "revolution" in American government. When was he elected?**

His first election was held in 1800. The election had to be resolved
in the House of Representatives in 1801 because of a tie in the Electoral
College between Aaron Burr and him.

**When did John Marshall become chief justice of the United
States?**

He took his seat in 1801; he was an outgoing appointment of President
John Adams.

**The Louisiana Purchase called into question Jefferson's view
that the Constitution should be strictly construed. In what year
did the United States make this purchase from France?**

1803.

In what year did the Supreme Court justify judicial review of federal legislation in the famous decision of *Marbury v. Madison*?
1803.

When did the states ratify the Twelfth Amendment?
1804.

During the War of 1812, northern state delegations met at the Hartford Convention to decide whether to remain in the Union. When did this convention meet?
It met in 1815.

The Supreme Court affirmed the constitutionality of the national bank in *McCulloch v. Maryland*. When did the Court decide this landmark case?
1819.

The Missouri Compromise brought to the surface serious sectional divisions in the United States over the issue of slavery. What was the date of this compromise?
Congress adopted it in 1820.

In what year did Marshall rule in *Gibbons v. Ogden* that commerce should be defined broadly as "intercourse"?
He made this decision in 1824.

In what year did the House of Representatives have to resolve a presidential election contest among Andrew Jackson, John Quincy Adams, and Henry Clay?
1824. The House awarded the presidency to Adams even though Jackson had garnered more votes.

On what date did John Adams and Thomas Jefferson both die?
They both died on July 4, 1826, 50 years to the day that the Declaration of Independence was adopted. James Monroe, the last of the Founding Fathers to serve as president, died on this same day 5 years later.

The controversy over the admission of Missouri and Maine was followed by southern opposition to tariffs. What years marked this "nullification crisis"?
This crisis occurred from 1828 to 1832.

In *Barron v. Baltimore,* Chief Justice John Marshall decided
that the Bill of Rights applied only to the national government.
When did he write this decision?
  1833.

In what year did Roger Taney become chief justice of the
United States?
  1836.

When did James Madison, the "father" of both the
Constitution and the Bill of Rights, die?
  1836.

Who was president when the Constitution was 50 years old?
  In 1837, Martin Van Buren was president.

The movement for women's suffrage is often traced to the
Seneca Falls Convention, which met in Seneca Falls, New York.
When was this convention held?
  It was held in 1848.

In the *Dred Scott Decision,* Chief Justice Roger Taney ruled
that blacks were not and could not become citizens of the
United States. When did he write this decision?
  1857.

Abraham Lincoln's election helped precipitate the Civil War.
When was he first elected president?
  He was first elected in 1860; Lincoln was the first Republican elected
to this office.

The greatest test of the Constitution occurred with the Civil
War. What were its dates?
  It lasted from 1861–1865.

When did the Emancipation Proclamation go into effect?
  It went into effect on January 1, 1863.

In what year did Salmon Chase become chief justice of the
United States?
  He became chief justice in 1864.

When did the states ratify the Thirteenth Amendment?
    1865.

What dates mark the period of Reconstruction during which northern troops occupied the southern states?
    Reconstruction dates from 1865 to 1877.

When did the states ratify the Fourteenth Amendment?
    1868.

In what year did the House of Representatives vote impeachment charges against President Andrew Johnson?
    It took this vote in 1868. The Senate would fall a single vote shy of the necessary two-thirds vote needed to convict him.

In what year did Congress establish the number of Supreme Court Justices at nine?
    Congress set the number at 9 in 1869; prior to this time, the number had ranged from 6 to 10. The Constitution still does not specify the number of Supreme Court justices.

In what year did the Supreme Court drastically limit the privileges and immunities clause of the Fourteenth Amendment?
    The *Slaughterhouse Cases* of 1877 severely limited the scope of this clause.

In what year did Morrison Waite become chief justice of the United States?
    He became chief justice in 1877.

In what year did the Supreme Court decide that the Fourteenth Amendment applied only to "state action"?
    It made this decision in the Civil Rights Cases of 1883.

Who was president when the Constitution was 100 years old?
    Grover Cleveland was president in 1887. Cleveland has been the only U.S. president to serve two nonsuccessive terms, the first from 1885 to 1889 and the second from 1893 to 1897.

THE SECOND 100 YEARS OF THE CONSTITUTION

In what year did Melville Fuller become chief justice of the United States?

1888.

In what year did the U.S. Supreme Court invalidate the national income tax?

It invalidated this tax in 1895 in the case of *Pollock v. Farmers' Loan & Trust Co.*

In what year did the Supreme Court endorse the policy of "separate but equal"?

It did so in the case of *Plessy v. Ferguson* in 1896.

In *Lochner v. New York*, which scholars often identify as the embodiment of the idea of substantive due process, the Supreme Court overturned a New York law regulating the hours of bakers. In what year was this case decided?

1905.

In what year did Edward White become chief jusice of the United States?

He became chief in 1910.

In what year did the states ratify the Sixteenth and Seventeenth Amendments?

1913. The first sanctioned the income tax; the second provided for direct election of the Senate.

When did the Supreme Court first apply the exclusionary rule to the national government?

It did so in 1914 in the case of *Weeks v. United States.*

In *Schenck v. United States*, Justice Oliver Wendell Holmes Jr. articulated the "clear and present danger test." In what year did the Supreme Court decide this case?

1919.

In what year did the states ratify the Eighteenth Amendment, establishing national alcoholic prohibition?

1919.

In what year did the states ratify the Nineteenth Amendment, extending suffrage to women?

1920.

Only one individual, William Howard Taft, has ever served as president and as chief justice of the United States. When did Taft assume the latter position?

He did so in 1921 and served until 1929. Taft had previously served as president from 1909–1913.

In what year did Congress propose a child labor amendment?

It proposed this amendment in 1924, but the necessary majority of the states never ratified it.

In *Gitlow v. New York* the Supreme Court ruled that the protection for freedom of speech applied to states as well as to the national government. In what year did the Court decide *Gitlow*?

1925.

In what year did Charles Evans Hughes become chief justice of the United States.

1930.

In what year did the states ratify the Twentieth and Twenty-First Amendments?

1933.

In what year did the Supreme Court make its decision in *Schechter Poultry Corp v. United States*, invalidating Roosevelt's National Industrial Recovery Act?

It made this decision in 1935. This is one of the few cases in which the Supreme Court has voided a law because it was thought to be an improper delegation of legislative power.

In what year did President Franklin D. Roosevelt introduce his famous "court-packing" plan?

He introduced it in 1937, shortly after his second election.

In what year did the Supreme Court make its historic "switch in time that saved nine"?

In 1937, it took an ideological turn that many have attributed to Roosevelt's "court-packing" plan. From 1937 forward, the Court has given fairly minimal scrutiny to legislation dealing with economic matters and has focused primarily on issues thought to be related more directly to the protection of other civil rights and liberties.

Who was president when the sesquicentennial of the U.S. Constitution was celebrated?

Franklin D. Roosevelt was president in 1937. This was the same year that he offered his famous court-packing plan to add members to the U.S. Supreme Court.

In what year did Harlan Fiske Stone become chief justice of the United States?

1941. He has previously served as an associate justice.

In what year did the Supreme Court outlaw the all-white primary?

It did so in 1944 in the case of *Smith v. Allwright.*

In what year did Fred Vinson become chief justice of the United States?

1946.

In what year did the states ratify the Twenty-Second Amendment?

1951.

In what year did the Supreme Court overturn President Truman's seizure of U.S. steel mills in order to avoid a strike?

It did so in 1951 in the case of *Youngstown Sheet & Tube Co. v. Sawyer.*

In what year did President Dwight D. Eisenhower appoint Earl Warren as chief justice of the United States?

President Eisenhower appointed Warren, a former California governor, to this post in 1953.

In what year did the Court render its decision in *Brown v. Board of Education*, declaring an end to the doctrine of "separate but equal"?

1954.

In what year did President Eisenhower send troops to Little Rock, Arkansas, to restore order in the wake of negative reaction to the Court's desegregation decision?

Eisenhower sent in troops in 1958 after Governor Orval Faubus stirred up opposition to integration and defied federal law.

In what year did the Supreme Court declare that the exclusionary rule applied to the states?
It decided this in the case of *Mapp v. Ohio* in 1961.

In what year did the states ratify the Twenty-Third Amendment?
1961.

In what year did the Supreme Court decide that the issue of legislative apportionment was appropriate for judicial resolution?
It made this decision in the 1962 case of *Baker v. Carr.*

In what year did the Supreme Court make its historic decision in *Engel v. Vitale* dealing with public prayer in public schools?
1962.

In what year did the Supreme Court extend its decision on prayer in public schools to include public Bible reading?
It did so in the case of *Abington v. Schempp* in 1963.

In what year did the Supreme Court decide that the right to counsel applied to defendants unable to afford their own attorneys?
It made this ruling in *Gideon v. Wainwright* in 1963.

In what year did Dr. King make his famous "I have a dream" speech at the March on Washington?
1963.

In what year did the Supreme Court apply the principle of "one person, one vote" to both houses of the state legislatures?
It did so in the 1964 case of *Reynolds v. Sims.*

In what year did Congress adopt the Gulf of Tonkin Resolution which supplied some authority for the continuing war in Vietnam?
1964.

In what year did the states ratify the Twenty-Fourth Amendment?
1964.

In what year did Congress outlaw racial discrimination in most places of public accommodation?

It adopted the Civil Rights Act, doing this in 1964. The Supreme Court had invalidated a similar law, the Civil Rights Act of 1875, in 1883 as an improper attempt by the government to regulate private conduct under the Fourteenth Amendment, but the Supreme Court upheld the 1964 law as a legitimate exercise of congressional authority under the commerce clause.

In what year did the Court recognize a right to privacy?

Although there are prior precedents, this right is often traced to the Supreme Court's historic decision in *Griswold v. Connecticut* in 1965 when it struck down a Connecticut birth-control statute.

In what year did the Supreme Court formulate the Miranda Rules governing warnings that police were obligated to give before interrogating suspects?

These rules were established in the case of *Miranda v. Arizona* in 1966; they required police officers to tell individuals of their right to remain silent, of their right to an attorney, and of their right to have an appointed attorney if they could not afford one on their own.

In what year did Congress adopt its most far-reaching voting rights legislation?

It did so in 1965 with the adoption of the Voting Rights Act of 1965.

In what year did a president appoint the first African American to the U.S. Supreme Court?

In 1967 President Lyndon B. Johnson appointed Thurgood Marshall to the Court. Marshall had previously served as counsel to the National Association for the Advancement of Colored People and as the solicitor general of the United States.

In what year did the states ratify the Twenty-Fifth Amendment?

1967.

In what year did the Supreme Court outlaw warrantless electronic surveillance?

It did so in 1967 in the case of *Katz v. United States*.

In what year Warren Burger become chief justice of the United States?

President Nixon appointed Burger to this post in 1969.

In what year did the states ratify the Twenty-Sixth Amendment?
1971.

The Pentagon Papers Case was quite important in reaffirming the presumption against prior restraint of publication. In what year was this case decided?
1971.

In what year was the Equal Rights Amendment proposed?
Congress proposed the amendment in 1972, but the necessary number of states never ratified it.

In what year did the Supreme Court include the right to an abortion under the right of privacy?
It did so in *Roe v. Wade* in 1973.

In what year did the Supreme Court say that the military had to treat men and women equally when it came to ascertaining whether their spouses were financially dependent on them?
It did so in 1973 in the case of *Frontiero v. Richardson.*

In what year did Congress adopt the War Powers Resolution, by which it sought to restrain presidential war-making powers?
1973.

In what year did the Supreme Court adopt the three-part Miller Test defining obscenity?
It did so in *Miller v. California* in 1973.

In what year did the Supreme Court reject President Nixon's claim of executive privilege?
It did so in *United States v. Nixon* in 1974.

In what year did President Nixon resign from office?
1974.

In what year did Congress propose an amendment that would have treated the District of Columbia as a state for purposes of representation?
It proposed this amendment in 1978, but it was never ratified by the necessary number of states.

In what year did a president appoint the first woman to the U.S. Supreme Court?

In 1981, President Ronald Reagan appointed Sandra Day O'Connor as the first woman on the Court.

In what year did the Supreme Court outlaw the legislative veto?

It did so in *Immigration and Naturalization Service v. Chadha,* which it decided in 1983.

In what year did William Rehnquist become chief justice of the United States?

President Ronald Reagan elevated him to this post (Rehnquist was previously an associate justice) in 1986.

EVENTS FROM THE BICENTENNIAL OF THE CONSTITUTION TO THE PRESENT

Who was president when the bicentennial of the U.S. Constitution was celebrated?

Ronald Reagan was president in 1987. Former chief justice Warren Burger headed the committee charged with commemorating the bicentennial of the Constitution. This celebration continued into 1991 with the commemoration of the bicentennial of the ratification of the Bill of Rights.

In what year did the Supreme Court rule that flag burning was a right protected by the First Amendment?

It first made this decision protecting flag burning as a type of symbolic expression in the 1989 case of *Texas v. Johnson.* The Court reaffirmed this decision the following year in *United States v. Eichman.*

In what year did the Supreme Court decide that states did not have the right to limit terms of their members of Congress?

It made this decision in 1995 in *U.S. Term Limits, Inc. v. Thornton.* This decision effectively means that term limits would have to be effected by a constitutional amendment.

In what case did the Supreme Court hear arguments in the case of *Clinton v. Jones*?

1997.

In what year did the Supreme Court hear its first case dealing with regulation of the Internet?

1997.

In what year did the Supreme Court issue a decision that resolved the presidential election?

2000.

In what year did terrorist attacks against the United States prompt a new "war on terrorism" that raised significant issues for civil liberties?

2001.

In what year did the Supreme Court invalidate state laws prohibiting private consensual acts of sodomy?

It did so in the case of *Lawrence v. Texas* in 2003.

In what year did the first state issue licenses for gay marriages?

Massachusetts was the first to do so in 2004.

In what year did George W. Bush appoint Chief Justice John Roberts to the U.S. Supreme Court?

2005.

When did Americans elect the first African American to the presidency?

Barack Obama was so elected in 2008 and reelected in 2012.

In what year did President Obama appoint the first Hispanic American to the Supreme Court?

He so appointed Sonia Sotomayor in 2009. Justice Benjamin Cardozo, a Sephardic Jew (from Spain), has also served on the Court.

In what year did the U.S. Supreme Court uphold the constitutionality of the Patient Protection and Affordable Care Act of 2010?

2012.

What year marked the 225th Anniversary of the Ratification of the U.S. Constitution?

2013.

BIBLIOGRAPHY
Books

Charles A. Beard, *An Economic Interpertation of the Constitution of the United States.* (New York: Macmillan, 1949).

David P. Currie, *The Constitution of the United States: A Primer for the People* (Chicago: University of Chicago Press, 1988).

John A. Garraty, ed., *Quarrels That Have Shaped the Constitution,* rev. ed. (New York: Harper & Row, Publishers, 1987).

Michael Kammen, *A Machine That Would Go of Itself: The Constitution in American Culture* (New York: Alfred A. Knopf, 1987).

Alfred H. Kelly, Winfred A. Harbison, and Herman Belz, *The American Constitution: Its Origin and Development,* 7th ed. 2 vols. (New York: W. W. Norton & Company, 1991).

Jethro L. Lieberman, *The Evolving Constitution: How the Supreme Court Has Ruled on Issues from Abortion to Zoning* (New York: Random House, 1992).

Forrest McDonald, *A Constitutional History of the United States* (New York: Franklin Watts, 1982).

Peter G. Renstrom, *Constitutional Law and Young Adults,* 2nd ed. (Santa Barbara, CA: ABC-CLIO, 1996).

Melvin I., Urofsky, *A March of Liberty: A Constitutional History of the United States* (New York: Alfred A. Knopf, 1988).

John R. Vile, *A Companion to the United States Constitution and Its Amendments,* 5th ed. (Lanham, MD: Rowman & Littlefield, 2011).

Cases

Abington School District v. Schempp, 374 U.S. 203 (1963).

Baker v. Carr, 369 U.S. 186 (1962).

Brown v. Board of Education, 347 U.S. 483 (1954).

Bush v. Gore, 531 U.S. 98 (2000).

Clinton v. Jones, 536 U.S. 820 (1997).

Engel v. Vitale, 370 U.S. 421 (1962).

Gideon v. Wainwright, 372 U.S. 335 (1963).

Gitlow v. New York, 268 U.S. 652 (1925).

Immigration and Naturalization Services v. Chadha, 462 U.S. 919 (1983).

Katz v. United States, 389 U.S. 347 (1967).

Lawrence v. Texas, 539 U.S. 558 (2003).

Lochner v. New York, 198 U.S. 45 (1905).

Mapp v. Ohio, 367 U.S. 643 (1961).

Marbury v. Madison, 5 U.S. 137 (1803).

Miller v. California, 413 U.S. 15 (1973).

Miranda v. Arizona, 384 U.S. 436 (1966).

New York Times v. United States, 403 U.S. 713 (1971).

Pollock v. Farmers' Loan & Trust Co., 158 U.S. 601 (1895).

Reynolds v. Sims, 377 U.S. 533 (1964).

Roe v. Wade, 410 U.S. 113 (1973).

Schechter Poultry Corp. v. United States, 295 U.S. 495 (1935).

Schenck v. United States, 249 U.S. 47 (1919).

Scott v. Sandford, 60 U.S. 393 (1857).

Smith v. Allwright, 321 U.S. 649 (1944).

Texas v. Johnson, 491 U.S. 397 (1989).

United States v. Eichman, 496 U.S. 310 (1990).

United States v. Nixon, 418 U.S. 683 (1974).

U.S. Term Limits Inc., v. Thornton, 115 S. Ct. 1842 (1995).

Weeks v. United States, 232 U.S. 383 (1914).

Youngstown Sheet & Tube Co. v. Sawyer, 343 U.S. 579 (1952).

APPENDIX A

The Constitution
of the United States

Note: The following text is a transcription of the Constitution in its original form.
Items that are italicized have since been amended or superseded.

We the People of the United States, in Order to form a more perfect Union, establish Justice, insure domestic Tranquility, provide for the common defence, promote the general Welfare, and secure the Blessings of Liberty to ourselves and our Posterity, do ordain and establish this Constitution for the United States of America.

ARTICLE. I.

Section. 1.

All legislative Powers herein granted shall be vested in a Congress of the United States, which shall consist of a Senate and House of Representatives.

Section. 2.

The House of Representatives shall be composed of Members chosen every second Year by the People of the several States, and the Electors in each State shall have the Qualifications requisite for Electors of the most numerous Branch of the State Legislature.

No Person shall be a Representative who shall not have attained to the Age of twenty five Years, and been seven Years a Citizen of the United States, and who shall not, when elected, be an Inhabitant of that State in which he shall be chosen.

Representatives and direct Taxes shall be apportioned among the several States which may be included within this Union, according to their respective Numbers, which shall be determined by adding to the whole Number of free Persons, including those bound to Service for a Term of Years, and excluding Indians not taxed, three fifths of all other Persons.

The actual Enumeration shall be made within three Years after the first Meeting of the Congress of the United States, and within every subsequent Term of ten Years, in such Manner as they shall by Law direct. The Number of Representatives shall not exceed one for every thirty Thousand, but each State shall have at Least one Representative; and until such enumeration shall be made, the State of New Hampshire shall be entitled to chuse three, Massachusetts eight, Rhode-Island and Providence Plantations one, Connecticut five, New-York six, New Jersey four, Pennsylvania eight, Delaware one, Maryland six, Virginia ten, North Carolina five, South Carolina five, and Georgia three.

When vacancies happen in the Representation from any State, the Executive Authority thereof shall issue Writs of Election to fill such Vacancies.

The House of Representatives shall chuse their Speaker and other Officers; and shall have the sole Power of Impeachment.

Section. 3.

The Senate of the United States shall be composed of two Senators from each State, *chosen by the Legislature thereof* for six Years; and each Senator shall have one Vote.

Immediately after they shall be assembled in Consequence of the first Election, they shall be divided as equally as may be into three Classes. The Seats of the Senators of the first Class shall be vacated at the Expiration of the second Year, of the second Class at the Expiration of the fourth Year, and of the third Class at the Expiration of the sixth Year, so that one third may be chosen every second Year; *and if Vacancies happen by Resignation, or otherwise, during the Recess of the Legislature of any State, the Executive thereof may make temporary Appointments until the next Meeting of the Legislature, which shall then fill such Vacancies.*

No Person shall be a Senator who shall not have attained to the Age of thirty Years, and been nine Years a Citizen of the United States, and who shall not, when elected, be an Inhabitant of that State for which he shall be chosen.

The Vice President of the United States shall be President of the Senate, but shall have no Vote, unless they be equally divided.

The Senate shall chuse their other Officers, and also a President pro tempore, in the Absence of the Vice President, or when he shall exercise the Office of President of the United States.

The Senate shall have the sole Power to try all Impeachments. When sitting for that Purpose, they shall be on Oath or Affirmation. When the President of the United States is tried, the Chief Justice shall preside: And no Person shall be convicted without the Concurrence of two thirds of the Members present.

Judgment in Cases of Impeachment shall not extend further than to removal from Office, and disqualification to hold and enjoy any Office of honor, Trust or Profit under the United States: but the Party convicted shall nevertheless be liable and subject to Indictment, Trial, Judgment and Punishment, according to Law.

Section. 4.

The Times, Places and Manner of holding Elections for Senators and Representatives, shall be prescribed in each State by the Legislature thereof; but the Congress may at any time by Law make or alter such Regulations, except as to the Places of chusing Senators.

The Congress shall assemble at least once in every Year, and such Meeting shall be on *the first Monday in December,* unless they shall by Law appoint a different Day.

Section. 5.

Each House shall be the Judge of the Elections, Returns and Qualifications of its own Members, and a Majority of each shall constitute a Quorum to do Business; but a smaller Number may adjourn from day to day, and may be authorized to compel the Attendance of absent Members, in such Manner, and under such Penalties as each House may provide.

Each House may determine the Rules of its Proceedings, punish its Members for disorderly Behaviour, and, with the Concurrence of two thirds, expel a Member.

Each House shall keep a Journal of its Proceedings, and from time to time publish the same, excepting such Parts as may in their Judgment require Secrecy; and the Yeas and Nays of the Members of either House on any question shall, at the Desire of one fifth of those Present, be entered on the Journal.

Neither House, during the Session of Congress, shall, without the Consent of the other, adjourn for more than three days, nor to any other Place than that in which the two Houses shall be sitting.

Section. 6.

The Senators and Representatives shall receive a Compensation for their Services, to be ascertained by Law, and paid out of the Treasury of the United States. They shall in all Cases, except Treason, Felony and Breach of the Peace, be privileged from Arrest during their Attendance at the Session of their respective Houses, and in going to and returning from the same; and for any Speech or Debate in either House, they shall not be questioned in any other Place.

No Senator or Representative shall, during the Time for which he was elected, be appointed to any civil Office under the Authority of the United States, which shall have been created, or the Emoluments whereof shall have been encreased during such time; and no Person holding any Office under the United States, shall be a Member of either House during his Continuance in Office.

Section. 7.

All Bills for raising Revenue shall originate in the House of Representatives; but the Senate may propose or concur with Amendments as on other Bills.

Every Bill which shall have passed the House of Representatives and the Senate, shall, before it become a Law, be presented to the President of the United States: If he approve he shall sign it, but if not he shall return it, with his Objections to that House in which it shall have originated, who shall enter the Objections at large on their Journal, and proceed to reconsider it. If after such Reconsideration two thirds of that House shall agree to pass the Bill, it shall be sent, together with the Objections, to the other House, by which it shall likewise be reconsidered, and if approved by two thirds of that House, it shall become a Law. But in all such Cases the Votes of both Houses shall be determined by yeas and Nays, and the Names of the Persons voting for and against the Bill shall be entered on the Journal of each House respectively. If any Bill shall not be returned by the President within ten Days (Sundays excepted) after it shall have been presented to him, the Same shall be a Law, in like Manner as if he had signed it, unless the Congress by their Adjournment prevent its Return, in which Case it shall not be a Law.

Every Order, Resolution, or Vote to which the Concurrence of the Senate and House of Representatives may be necessary (except on a question of Adjournment) shall be presented to the President of the United States; and before the Same shall take Effect, shall be approved by him, or being disapproved by him, shall be repassed by two thirds of the Senate and House of Representatives, according to the Rules and Limitations prescribed in the Case of a Bill.

Section. 8.

The Congress shall have Power To lay and collect Taxes, Duties, Imposts and Excises, to pay the Debts and provide for the common Defence and general Welfare of the United States; but all Duties, Imposts and Excises shall be uniform throughout the United States;

To borrow Money on the credit of the United States;

To regulate Commerce with foreign Nations, and among the several States, and with the Indian Tribes;

To establish an uniform Rule of Naturalization, and uniform Laws on the subject of Bankruptcies throughout the United States;

To coin Money, regulate the Value thereof, and of foreign Coin, and fix the Standard of Weights and Measures;

To provide for the Punishment of counterfeiting the Securities and current Coin of the United States;

To establish Post Offices and post Roads;

To promote the Progress of Science and useful Arts, by securing for limited Times to Authors and Inventors the exclusive Right to their respective Writings and Discoveries;

To constitute Tribunals inferior to the supreme Court;

To define and punish Piracies and Felonies committed on the high Seas, and Offences against the Law of Nations;

To declare War, grant Letters of Marque and Reprisal, and make Rules concerning Captures on Land and Water;

To raise and support Armies, but no Appropriation of Money to that Use shall be for a longer Term than two Years;

To provide and maintain a Navy;

To make Rules for the Government and Regulation of the land and naval Forces;

To provide for calling forth the Militia to execute the Laws of the Union, suppress Insurrections and repel Invasions;

To provide for organizing, arming, and disciplining, the Militia, and for governing such Part of them as may be employed in the Service of the United States, reserving to the States respectively, the Appointment of the Officers, and the Authority of training the Militia according to the discipline prescribed by Congress;

To exercise exclusive Legislation in all Cases whatsoever, over such District (not exceeding ten Miles square) as may, by Cession of particular States, and the Acceptance of Congress, become the Seat of the Government of the United States, and to exercise like Authority over all Places purchased by the Consent of the Legislature of the State in which the Same shall be, for the Erection of Forts, Magazines, Arsenals, dock-Yards, and other needful Buildings;—And

To make all Laws which shall be necessary and proper for carrying into Execution the foregoing Powers, and all other Powers vested by this Constitution in the Government of the United States, or in any Department or Officer thereof.

Section. 9.

The Migration or Importation of such Persons as any of the States now existing shall think proper to admit, shall not be prohibited by the Congress prior to the Year one thousand eight hundred and eight, but a Tax or duty may be imposed on such Importation, not exceeding ten dollars for each Person.

The Privilege of the Writ of Habeas Corpus shall not be suspended, unless when in Cases of Rebellion or Invasion the public Safety may require it.

No Bill of Attainder or ex post facto Law shall be passed.

No Capitation, or other direct, Tax shall be laid, unless in Proportion to the Census or enumeration herein before directed to be taken.

No Tax or Duty shall be laid on Articles exported from any State.

No Preference shall be given by any Regulation of Commerce or Revenue to the Ports of one State over those of another; nor shall Vessels bound to, or from, one State, be obliged to enter, clear, or pay Duties in another.

No Money shall be drawn from the Treasury, but in Consequence of Appropriations made by Law; and a regular Statement and Account of the Receipts and Expenditures of all public Money shall be published from time to time.

No Title of Nobility shall be granted by the United States: And no Person holding any Office of Profit or Trust under them, shall, without the Consent of the Congress, accept of any present, Emolument, Office, or Title, of any kind whatever, from any King, Prince, or foreign State.

Section. 10.

No State shall enter into any Treaty, Alliance, or Confederation; grant Letters of Marque and Reprisal; coin Money; emit Bills of Credit; make any Thing but gold and silver Coin a Tender in Payment of Debts; pass any Bill of Attainder, ex post facto Law, or Law impairing the Obligation of Contracts, or grant any Title of Nobility.

No State shall, without the Consent of the Congress, lay any Imposts or Duties on Imports or Exports, except what may be absolutely necessary for executing it's inspection Laws: and the net Produce of all Duties and Imposts, laid by any State on Imports or Exports, shall be for the Use of the Treasury of the United States; and all such Laws shall be subject to the Revision and Controul of the Congress.

No State shall, without the Consent of Congress, lay any Duty of Tonnage, keep Troops, or Ships of War in time of Peace, enter into any Agreement or Compact with another State, or with a foreign Power, or engage in War, unless actually invaded, or in such imminent Danger as will not admit of delay.

ARTICLE. II.

Section. 1.

The executive Power shall be vested in a President of the United States of America. He shall hold his Office during the Term of four Years, and, together with the Vice President, chosen for the same Term, be elected, as follows:

Each State shall appoint, in such Manner as the Legislature thereof may direct, a Number of Electors, equal to the whole Number of Senators and Representatives to which the State may be entitled in the Congress: but no Senator or Representative, or Person holding an Office of Trust or Profit under the United States, shall be appointed an Elector.

The Electors shall meet in their respective States, and vote by Ballot for two Persons, of whom one at least shall not be an Inhabitant of the same State with themselves. And they shall make a List of all the Persons voted for, and of the Number of Votes for each; which List they shall sign and certify, and transmit sealed to the Seat of the Government of the United States, directed to the President of the Senate. The President of the Senate shall, in the Presence of the Senate and House of Representatives, open all the Certificates, and the Votes shall then be counted. The Person having the greatest Number of Votes shall be the President, if such Number be a Majority of the whole Number of Electors appointed; and if there be more than one who have such Majority, and have an equal Number of Votes, then the House of Representatives shall immediately chuse by Ballot one of them for President; and if no Person have a Majority, then from the five highest on the List the said House shall in like Manner chuse the President. But in chusing the President, the Votes shall be taken by States, the Representation from each State having one Vote; A quorum for this purpose shall consist of a Member or Members from two thirds of the States, and a Majority of all the States shall be necessary to a Choice. In every Case, after the Choice of the President, the Person having the greatest Number of Votes of the Electors shall be the Vice President. But if there should remain two or more who have equal Votes, the Senate shall chuse from them by Ballot the Vice President.

The Congress may determine the Time of chusing the Electors, and the Day on which they shall give their Votes; which Day shall be the same throughout the United States.

No Person except a natural born Citizen, or a Citizen of the United States, at the time of the Adoption of this Constitution, shall be eligible to the Office of President; neither shall any Person be eligible to that Office who shall not have attained to the Age of thirty five Years, and been fourteen Years a Resident within the United States.

In Case of the Removal of the President from Office, or of his Death, Resignation, or Inability to discharge the Powers and Duties of the said Office, the Same shall devolve on the Vice President, and the Congress may by Law provide for the Case of Removal, Death, Resignation or Inability, both of the President and Vice President, declaring what Officer shall then act as President, and such Officer shall act accordingly, until the Disability be removed, or a President shall be elected.

The President shall, at stated Times, receive for his Services, a Compensation, which shall neither be increased nor diminished during the Period for which he shall have been elected, and he shall not receive within that Period any other Emolument from the United States, or any of them.

Before he enter on the Execution of his Office, he shall take the following Oath or Affirmation:—"I do solemnly swear (or affirm) that I will faithfully execute the Office of President of the United States, and will to the best of my Ability, preserve, protect and defend the Constitution of the United States."

Section. 2.

The President shall be Commander in Chief of the Army and Navy of the United States, and of the Militia of the several States, when called into the actual Service of the United States; he may require the Opinion, in writing, of the principal Officer in each of the executive Departments, upon any Subject relating to the Duties of their respective Offices, and he shall have Power to grant Reprieves and Pardons for Offences against the United States, except in Cases of Impeachment.

He shall have Power, by and with the Advice and Consent of the Senate, to make Treaties, provided two thirds of the Senators present concur; and he shall nominate, and by and with the Advice and Consent of the Senate, shall appoint Ambassadors, other public Ministers and Consuls, Judges of the supreme Court, and all other Officers of the United States, whose Appointments are not herein otherwise provided for, and which shall be established by Law: but the Congress may by Law vest the Appointment of such inferior Officers, as they think proper, in the President alone, in the Courts of Law, or in the Heads of Departments.

The President shall have Power to fill up all Vacancies that may happen during the Recess of the Senate, by granting Commissions which shall expire at the End of their next Session.

Section. 3.

He shall from time to time give to the Congress Information of the State of the Union, and recommend to their Consideration such Measures as he shall judge necessary and expedient; he may, on extraordinary Occasions, convene both Houses, or either of them, and in Case of Disagreement between them, with Respect to the Time of Adjournment, he may adjourn them to such Time as he shall think proper; he shall receive Ambassadors and other public Ministers; he shall take Care that the Laws be faithfully executed, and shall Commission all the Officers of the United States.

Section. 4.

The President, Vice President and all civil Officers of the United States, shall be removed from Office on Impeachment for, and Conviction of, Treason, Bribery, or other high Crimes and Misdemeanors.

ARTICLE III.

Section. 1.

The judicial Power of the United States shall be vested in one supreme Court, and in such inferior Courts as the Congress may from time to time ordain and establish. The Judges, both of the supreme and inferior Courts, shall hold their Offices during good Behaviour, and shall, at stated Times, receive for their Services a Compensation, which shall not be diminished during their Continuance in Office.

Section. 2.

The judicial Power shall extend to all Cases, in Law and Equity, arising under this Constitution, the Laws of the United States, and Treaties made, or which shall be made, under their Authority;—to all Cases affecting Ambassadors, other public Ministers and Consuls;—to all Cases of admiralty and maritime Jurisdiction;—to Controversies to which the United States shall be a Party;—to Controversies between two or more States;—*between a State and Citizens of another State,—between Citizens of different States,*—between Citizens of the same State claiming Lands under Grants of different States, *and between a State, or the Citizens thereof, and foreign States, Citizens or Subjects.*

In all Cases affecting Ambassadors, other public Ministers and Consuls, and those in which a State shall be Party, the supreme Court shall have original Jurisdiction. In all the other Cases before mentioned, the supreme Court shall have appellate Jurisdiction, both as to Law and Fact, with such Exceptions, and under such Regulations as the Congress shall make.

The Trial of all Crimes, except in Cases of Impeachment, shall be by Jury; and such Trial shall be held in the State where the said Crimes shall have been committed; but when not committed within any State, the Trial shall be at such Place or Places as the Congress may by Law have directed.

Section. 3.

Treason against the United States, shall consist only in levying War against them, or in adhering to their Enemies, giving them Aid and Comfort. No Person shall be convicted of Treason unless on the Testimony of two Witnesses to the same overt Act, or on Confession in open Court.

The Congress shall have Power to declare the Punishment of Treason, but no Attainder of Treason shall work Corruption of Blood, or Forfeiture except during the Life of the Person attainted.

ARTICLE. IV.

Section. 1.

Full Faith and Credit shall be given in each State to the public Acts, Records, and judicial Proceedings of every other State. And the Congress may by general Laws prescribe the Manner in which such Acts, Records and Proceedings shall be proved, and the Effect thereof.

Section. 2.

The Citizens of each State shall be entitled to all Privileges and Immunities of Citizens in the several States.

A Person charged in any State with Treason, Felony, or other Crime, who shall flee from Justice, and be found in another State, shall on Demand of the executive Authority of the State from which he fled, be delivered up, to be removed to the State having Jurisdiction of the Crime.

No Person held to Service or Labour in one State, under the Laws thereof, escaping into another, shall, in Consequence of any Law or Regulation therein, be discharged from such Service or Labour, but shall be delivered up on Claim of the Party to whom such Service or Labour may be due.

Section. 3.

New States may be admitted by the Congress into this Union; but no new State shall be formed or erected within the Jurisdiction of any other State; nor any State be formed by the Junction of two or more States, or Parts of States, without the Consent of the Legislatures of the States concerned as well as of the Congress.

The Congress shall have Power to dispose of and make all needful Rules and Regulations respecting the Territory or other Property belonging to the United States; and nothing in this Constitution shall be so construed as to Prejudice any Claims of the United States, or of any particular State.

Section. 4.

The United States shall guarantee to every State in this Union a Republican Form of Government, and shall protect each of them against Invasion; and on Application of the Legislature, or of the Executive (when the Legislature cannot be convened), against domestic Violence.

ARTICLE. V.

The Congress, whenever two thirds of both Houses shall deem it necessary, shall propose Amendments to this Constitution, or, on the Application of the Legislatures of two thirds of the several States, shall call a Convention for proposing Amendments, which, in either Case, shall be valid to all Intents and Purposes, as Part of this Constitution, when ratified by the Legislatures of three fourths of the several States, or by Conventions in three fourths thereof, as the one or the other Mode of Ratification may be proposed by the Congress; Provided that no Amendment which may be made prior to the Year One thousand eight hundred and eight shall in any Manner affect the first and fourth Clauses in the Ninth Section of the first Article; and that no State, without its Consent, shall be deprived of its equal Suffrage in the Senate.

ARTICLE. VI.

All Debts contracted and Engagements entered into, before the Adoption of this Constitution, shall be as valid against the United States under this Constitution, as under the Confederation.

This Constitution, and the Laws of the United States which shall be made in Pursuance thereof; and all Treaties made, or which shall be made, under the Authority of the United States, shall be the supreme Law of the Land; and the Judges in every State shall be bound thereby, any Thing in the Constitution or Laws of any State to the Contrary notwithstanding.

The Senators and Representatives before mentioned, and the Members of the several State Legislatures, and all executive and judicial Officers, both of the United States and of the several States, shall be bound by Oath or Affirmation, to support this Constitution; but no religious Test shall ever be required as a Qualification to any Office or public Trust under the United States.

ARTICLE. VII.

The Ratification of the Conventions of nine States, shall be sufficient for the Establishment of this Constitution between the States so ratifying the Same.

The Word, "the," being interlined between the seventh and eighth Lines of the first Page, the Word "Thirty" being partly written on an Erazure in the fifteenth Line of the first Page, The Words "is tried" being interlined between the thirty second and thirty third Lines of the first Page and the Word "the" being interlined between the forty third and forty fourth Lines of the second Page.

Attest William Jackson Secretary done in Convention by the Unanimous Consent of the States present the Seventeenth Day of September in the Year of our Lord one thousand seven hundred and Eighty seven and of the Independance of the United States of America the Twelfth In witness whereof We have hereunto subscribed our Names,

G°. Washington   Abr Baldwin
Presidt and deputy from Virginia   New Hampshire
Delaware   John Langdon
Geo: Read   Nicholas Gilman
Gunning Bedford jun   Massachusetts
John Dickinson   Nathaniel Gorham
Richard Bassett   Rufus King
Jaco: Broom   Connecticut
Maryland   Wm. Saml. Johnson
James McHenry   Roger Sherman
Dan of St Thos. Jenifer   New York
Danl. Carroll   Alexander Hamilton
Virginia   New Jersey
John Blair   Wil: Livingston
James Madison Jr.   David Brearley
North Carolina   Wm. Paterson
Wm. Blount   Jona: Dayton
Richd. Dobbs Spaight   Pennsylvania
Hu Williamson   B Franklin
South Carolina   Thomas Mifflin
J. Rutledge   Robt. Morris
Charles Cotesworth Pinckney   Geo. Clymer
Charles Pinckney   Thos. FitzSimons
Pierce Butler   Jared Ingersoll
Georgia   James Wilson
William Few   Gouv Morris

AMENDMENTS TO THE CONSTITUTION

The Bill of Rights: A Transcription

The Preamble to The Bill of Rights

Congress of the United States

begun and held at the City of New-York, on

Wednesday the fourth of March, one thousand seven hundred and eighty nine.

THE Conventions of a number of the States, having at the time of their adopting the Constitution, expressed a desire, in order to prevent misconstruction or abuse of its powers, that further declaratory and restrictive clauses should be added: And as extending the ground of public confidence in the Government, will best ensure the beneficent ends of its institution.

RESOLVED by the Senate and House of Representatives of the United States of America, in Congress assembled, two thirds of both Houses concurring, that the following Articles be proposed to the Legislatures of the several States, as amendments to the Constitution of the United States, all, or any of which Articles, when ratified by three fourths of the said Legislatures, to be valid to all intents and purposes, as part of the said Constitution; viz.

ARTICLES in addition to, and Amendment of the Constitution of the United States of America, proposed by Congress, and ratified by the Legislatures of the several States, pursuant to the fifth Article of the original Constitution.

Note: The following text is a transcription of the first ten amendments to the Constitution in their original form. These amendments were ratified December 15, 1791, and form what is known as the "Bill of Rights."

AMENDMENT I

Congress shall make no law respecting an establishment of religion, or prohibiting the free exercise thereof; or abridging the freedom of speech, or of the press; or the right of the people peaceably to assemble, and to petition the Government for a redress of grievances.

AMENDMENT II

A well regulated Militia, being necessary to the security of a free State, the right of the people to keep and bear Arms, shall not be infringed.

AMENDMENT III

No Soldier shall, in time of peace be quartered in any house, without the consent of the Owner, nor in time of war, but in a manner to be prescribed by law.

AMENDMENT IV

The right of the people to be secure in their persons, houses, papers, and effects, against unreasonable searches and seizures, shall not be violated, and no Warrants shall issue, but upon probable cause, supported by Oath or affirmation, and particularly describing the place to be searched, and the persons or things to be seized.

AMENDMENT V

No person shall be held to answer for a capital, or otherwise infamous crime, unless on a presentment or indictment of a Grand Jury, except in cases arising in the land or naval forces, or in the Militia, when in actual service in time of War or public danger; nor shall any person be subject for the same offence to be twice put in jeopardy of life or limb; nor shall be compelled in any criminal case to be a witness against himself, nor be deprived of life, liberty, or property, without due process of law; nor shall private property be taken for public use, without just compensation.

AMENDMENT VI
In all criminal prosecutions, the accused shall enjoy the right to a speedy and public trial, by an impartial jury of the State and district wherein the crime shall have been committed, which district shall have been previously ascertained by law, and to be informed of the nature and cause of the accusation; to be confronted with the witnesses against him; to have compulsory process for obtaining witnesses in his favor, and to have the Assistance of Counsel for his defence.

AMENDMENT VII
In Suits at common law, where the value in controversy shall exceed twenty dollars, the right of trial by jury shall be preserved, and no fact tried by a jury, shall be otherwise re-examined in any Court of the United States, than according to the rules of the common law.

AMENDMENT VIII
Excessive bail shall not be required, nor excessive fines imposed, nor cruel and unusual punishments inflicted.

AMENDMENT IX
The enumeration in the Constitution, of certain rights, shall not be construed to deny or disparage others retained by the people.

AMENDMENT X
The powers not delegated to the United States by the Constitution, nor prohibited by it to the States, are reserved to the States respectively, or to the people.

AMENDMENT XI
Passed by Congress March 4, 1794. Ratified February 7, 1795.

Note: Article III, section 2, of the Constitution was modified by amendment 11.

The Judicial power of the United States shall not be construed to extend to any suit in law or equity, commenced or prosecuted against one of the United States by Citizens of another State, or by Citizens or Subjects of any Foreign State.

AMENDMENT XII

Passed by Congress December 9, 1803. Ratified June 15, 1804.

Note: *A portion of Article II, section 1 of the Constitution was superseded by the 12th amendment.*

The Electors shall meet in their respective states and vote by ballot for President and Vice-President, one of whom, at least, shall not be an inhabitant of the same state with themselves; they shall name in their ballots the person voted for as President, and in distinct ballots the person voted for as Vice-President, and they shall make distinct lists of all persons voted for as President, and of all persons voted for as Vice-President, and of the number of votes for each, which lists they shall sign and certify, and transmit sealed to the seat of the government of the United States, directed to the President of the Senate; — the President of the Senate shall, in the presence of the Senate and House of Representatives, open all the certificates and the votes shall then be counted; — The person having the greatest number of votes for President, shall be the President, if such number be a majority of the whole number of Electors appointed; and if no person have such majority, then from the persons having the highest numbers not exceeding three on the list of those voted for as President, the House of Representatives shall choose immediately, by ballot, the President. But in choosing the President, the votes shall be taken by states, the representation from each state having one vote; a quorum for this purpose shall consist of a member or members from two-thirds of the states, and a majority of all the states shall be necessary to a choice. [And if the House of Representatives shall not choose a President whenever the right of choice shall devolve upon them, before the fourth day of March next following, then the Vice-President shall act as President, as in case of the death or other constitutional disability of the President. —]* The person having the greatest number of votes as Vice-President, shall be the Vice-President, if such number be a majority of the whole number of Electors appointed, and if no person have a majority, then from the two highest numbers on the list, the Senate shall choose the Vice-President; a quorum for the purpose shall consist of two-thirds of the whole number of Senators, and a majority of the whole number shall be necessary to a choice. But no person constitutionally ineligible to the office of President shall be eligible to that of Vice-President of the United States.

* *Superseded by section 3 of the 20th amendment.*

AMENDMENT XIII
Passed by Congress January 31, 1865. Ratified December 6, 1865.

Note: A portion of Article IV, section 2, of the Constitution was superseded by the 13th amendment.

Section 1.
Neither slavery nor involuntary servitude, except as a punishment for crime whereof the party shall have been duly convicted, shall exist within the United States, or any place subject to their jurisdiction.

Section 2.
Congress shall have power to enforce this article by appropriate legislation.

AMENDMENT XIV
Passed by Congress June 13, 1866. Ratified July 9, 1868.

Note: Article I, section 2, of the Constitution was modified by section 2 of the 14th amendment.

Section 1.
All persons born or naturalized in the United States, and subject to the jurisdiction thereof, are citizens of the United States and of the State wherein they reside. No State shall make or enforce any law which shall abridge the privileges or immunities of citizens of the United States; nor shall any State deprive any person of life, liberty, or property, without due process of law; nor deny to any person within its jurisdiction the equal protection of the laws.

Section 2.
Representatives shall be apportioned among the several States according to their respective numbers, counting the whole number of persons in each State, excluding Indians not taxed. But when the right to vote at any election for the choice of electors for President and Vice-President of the United States, Representatives in Congress, the Executive and Judicial officers of a State, or the members of the Legislature thereof, is denied to any of the male inhabitants of such State, being twenty-one years of age,* and citizens of the United States, or in any way abridged, except for participation in rebellion, or other crime, the basis of representation therein shall be reduced in the proportion which the number of such male citizens

* *Changed by section 1 of the 26th amendment.*

shall bear to the whole number of male citizens twenty-one years of age in such State.

Section 3.

No person shall be a Senator or Representative in Congress, or elector of President and Vice-President, or hold any office, civil or military, under the United States, or under any State, who, having previously taken an oath, as a member of Congress, or as an officer of the United States, or as a member of any State legislature, or as an executive or judicial officer of any State, to support the Constitution of the United States, shall have engaged in insurrection or rebellion against the same, or given aid or comfort to the enemies thereof. But Congress may by a vote of two-thirds of each House, remove such disability.

Section 4.

The validity of the public debt of the United States, authorized by law, including debts incurred for payment of pensions and bounties for services in suppressing insurrection or rebellion, shall not be questioned. But neither the United States nor any State shall assume or pay any debt or obligation incurred in aid of insurrection or rebellion against the United States, or any claim for the loss or emancipation of any slave; but all such debts, obligations and claims shall be held illegal and void.

Section 5.

The Congress shall have the power to enforce, by appropriate legislation, the provisions of this article.

AMENDMENT XV

Passed by Congress February 26, 1869. Ratified February 3, 1870.

Section 1.

The right of citizens of the United States to vote shall not be denied or abridged by the United States or by any State on account of race, color, or previous condition of servitude—

Section 2.

The Congress shall have the power to enforce this article by appropriate legislation.

AMENDMENT XVI

Passed by Congress July 2, 1909. Ratified February 3, 1913.

Note: Article I, section 9, of the Constitution was modified by amendment 16.

The Congress shall have power to lay and collect taxes on incomes, from whatever source derived, without apportionment among the several States, and without regard to any census or enumeration.

AMENDMENT XVII
Passed by Congress May 13, 1912. Ratified April 8, 1913.

Note: *Article I, section 3, of the Constitution was modified by the 17th amendment.*

The Senate of the United States shall be composed of two Senators from each State, elected by the people thereof, for six years; and each Senator shall have one vote. The electors in each State shall have the qualifications requisite for electors of the most numerous branch of the State legislatures.

When vacancies happen in the representation of any State in the Senate, the executive authority of such State shall issue writs of election to fill such vacancies: *Provided,* That the legislature of any State may empower the executive thereof to make temporary appointments until the people fill the vacancies by election as the legislature may direct.

This amendment shall not be so construed as to affect the election or term of any Senator chosen before it becomes valid as part of the Constitution.

AMENDMENT XVIII
Passed by Congress December 18, 1917. Ratified January 16, 1919. Repealed by amendment 21.

Section 1.
After one year from the ratification of this article the manufacture, sale, or transportation of intoxicating liquors within, the importation thereof into, or the exportation thereof from the United States and all territory subject to the jurisdiction thereof for beverage purposes is hereby prohibited.

Section 2.
The Congress and the several States shall have concurrent power to enforce this article by appropriate legislation.

Section 3.
This article shall be inoperative unless it shall have been ratified as an amendment to the Constitution by the legislatures of the several States, as provided in the Constitution, within seven years from the date of the submission hereof to the States by the Congress.

AMENDMENT XIX

Passed by Congress June 4, 1919. Ratified August 18, 1920.

The right of citizens of the United States to vote shall not be denied or abridged by the United States or by any State on account of sex.

Congress shall have power to enforce this article by appropriate legislation.

AMENDMENT XX

Passed by Congress March 2, 1932. Ratified January 23, 1933.

Note: Article I, section 4, of the Constitution was modified by section 2 of this amendment. In addition, a portion of the 12th amendment was superseded by section 3.

Section 1.

The terms of the President and the Vice President shall end at noon on the 20th day of January, and the terms of Senators and Representatives at noon on the 3rd day of January, of the years in which such terms would have ended if this article had not been ratified; and the terms of their successors shall then begin.

Section 2.

The Congress shall assemble at least once in every year, and such meeting shall begin at noon on the 3d day of January, unless they shall by law appoint a different day.

Section 3.

If, at the time fixed for the beginning of the term of the President, the President elect shall have died, the Vice President elect shall become President. If a President shall not have been chosen before the time fixed for the beginning of his term, or if the President elect shall have failed to qualify, then the Vice President elect shall act as President until a President shall have qualified; and the Congress may by law provide for the case wherein neither a President elect nor a Vice President shall have qualified, declaring who shall then act as President, or the manner in which one who is to act shall be selected, and such person shall act accordingly until a President or Vice President shall have qualified.

Section 4.

The Congress may by law provide for the case of the death of any of the persons from whom the House of Representatives may choose a President whenever the right of choice shall have devolved upon them, and for the case of the death of any of the persons from whom the Senate may choose a Vice President whenever the right of choice shall have devolved upon them.

Section 5.
Sections 1 and 2 shall take effect on the 15th day of October following the ratification of this article.

Section 6.
This article shall be inoperative unless it shall have been ratified as an amendment to the Constitution by the legislatures of three-fourths of the several States within seven years from the date of its submission.

AMENDMENT XXI
Passed by Congress February 20, 1933. Ratified December 5, 1933.

Section 1.
The eighteenth article of amendment to the Constitution of the United States is hereby repealed.

Section 2.
The transportation or importation into any State, Territory, or Possession of the United States for delivery or use therein of intoxicating liquors, in violation of the laws thereof, is hereby prohibited.

Section 3.
This article shall be inoperative unless it shall have been ratified as an amendment to the Constitution by conventions in the several States, as provided in the Constitution, within seven years from the date of the submission hereof to the States by the Congress.

AMENDMENT XXII
Passed by Congress March 21, 1947. Ratified February 27, 1951.

Section 1.
No person shall be elected to the office of the President more than twice, and no person who has held the office of President, or acted as President, for more than two years of a term to which some other person was elected President shall be elected to the office of President more than once. But this Article shall not apply to any person holding the office of President when this Article was proposed by Congress, and shall not prevent any person who may be holding the office of President, or acting as President, during the term within which this Article becomes operative from holding the office of President or acting as President during the remainder of such term.

Section 2.

This article shall be inoperative unless it shall have been ratified as an amendment to the Constitution by the legislatures of three-fourths of the several States within seven years from the date of its submission to the States by the Congress.

AMENDMENT XXIII

Passed by Congress June 16, 1960. Ratified March 29, 1961.

Section 1.

The District constituting the seat of Government of the United States shall appoint in such manner as Congress may direct:

A number of electors of President and Vice President equal to the whole number of Senators and Representatives in Congress to which the District would be entitled if it were a State, but in no event more than the least populous State; they shall be in addition to those appointed by the States, but they shall be considered, for the purposes of the election of President and Vice President, to be electors appointed by a State; and they shall meet in the District and perform such duties as provided by the twelfth article of amendment.

Section 2.

The Congress shall have power to enforce this article by appropriate legislation.

AMENDMENT XXIV

Passed by Congress August 27, 1962. Ratified January 23, 1964.

Section 1.

The right of citizens of the United States to vote in any primary or other election for President or Vice President, for electors for President or Vice President, or for Senator or Representative in Congress, shall not be denied or abridged by the United States or any State by reason of failure to pay poll tax or other tax.

Section 2.

The Congress shall have power to enforce this article by appropriate legislation.

AMENDMENT XXV

Passed by Congress July 6, 1965. Ratified February 10, 1967.

Note: Article II, section 1, of the Constitution was affected by the 25th amendment.

Section 1.

In case of the removal of the President from office or of his death or resignation, the Vice President shall become President.

Section 2.

Whenever there is a vacancy in the office of the Vice President, the President shall nominate a Vice President who shall take office upon confirmation by a majority vote of both Houses of Congress.

Section 3.

Whenever the President transmits to the President pro tempore of the Senate and the Speaker of the House of Representatives his written declaration that he is unable to discharge the powers and duties of his office, and until he transmits to them a written declaration to the contrary, such powers and duties shall be discharged by the Vice President as Acting President.

Section 4.

Whenever the Vice President and a majority of either the principal officers of the executive departments or of such other body as Congress may by law provide, transmit to the President pro tempore of the Senate and the Speaker of the House of Representatives their written declaration that the President is unable to discharge the powers and duties of his office, the Vice President shall immediately assume the powers and duties of the office as Acting President.

Thereafter, when the President transmits to the President pro tempore of the Senate and the Speaker of the House of Representatives his written declaration that no inability exists, he shall resume the powers and duties of his office unless the Vice President and a majority of either the principal officers of the executive department or of such other body as Congress may by law provide, transmit within four days to the President pro tempore of the Senate and the Speaker of the House of Representatives their written declaration that the President is unable to discharge the powers and duties of his office. Thereupon Congress shall decide the issue, assembling within forty-eight hours for that purpose if not in session. If the Congress, within twenty-one days after receipt of the latter written declaration, or, if Congress is not in session, within twenty-one days after Congress is required to assemble, determines by two-thirds vote of both Houses that the President is unable to discharge the powers and duties of his office, the Vice President shall continue to discharge the same as Acting President; otherwise, the President shall resume the powers and duties of his office.

AMENDMENT XXVI

Passed by Congress March 23, 1971. Ratified July 1, 1971.

Note: *Amendment 14, section 2, of the Constitution was modified by section 1 of the 26th amendment.*

Section 1.

The right of citizens of the United States, who are eighteen years of age or older, to vote shall not be denied or abridged by the United States or by any State on account of age.

Section 2.

The Congress shall have power to enforce this article by appropriate legislation.

AMENDMENT XXVII

Originally proposed Sept. 25, 1789. Ratified May 7, 1992.

No law, varying the compensation for the services of the Senators and Representatives, shall take effect, until an election of representatives shall have intervened.

Source: National Archives
http://www.archives.gov/exhibits/charters/bill_of_rights_transcript.html and http://
www.archives.gov/exhibits/charters/constitution_amendments_11-27.html

Source: National Archives.
http://www.archives.gov/exhibits/charters/constitution_transcript.html

APPENDIX B

The Declaration of Independence

IN CONGRESS, JULY 4, 1776.

**The unanimous Declaration of the
thirteen united States of America,**

When in the Course of human events, it becomes necessary for one people to dissolve the political bands which have connected them with another, and to assume among the powers of the earth, the separate and equal station to which the Laws of Nature and of Nature's God entitle them, a decent respect to the opinions of mankind requires that they should declare the causes which impel them to the separation.

We hold these truths to be self-evident, that all men are created equal, that they are endowed by their Creator with certain unalienable Rights, that among these are Life, Liberty and the pursuit of Happiness.—That to secure these rights, Governments are instituted among Men, deriving their just powers from the consent of the governed, —That whenever any Form of Government becomes destructive of these ends, it is the Right of the People to alter or to abolish it, and to institute new Government, laying its foundation on such principles and organizing its powers in such form, as to them shall seem most likely to effect their Safety and Happiness. Prudence, indeed, will dictate that Governments long established should not be changed for light and transient causes; and accordingly all experience hath shewn, that mankind are more disposed to suffer, while evils are sufferable, than to right themselves by abolishing the forms to which they are accustomed. But when a long train of abuses and usurpations, pursuing invariably the same Object evinces a design to reduce them under absolute Despotism, it is their right, it is their duty, to throw off such Government, and to provide new Guards for their future security.—Such has been the patient sufferance of these Colonies; and such is now the necessity which constrains them to alter their former Systems of Government. The history of the present King of Great Britain is a history of repeated injuries and usurpations, all having in direct object the establishment of an absolute

Tyranny over these States. To prove this, let Facts be submitted to a candid world.

He has refused his Assent to Laws, the most wholesome and necessary for the public good.

He has forbidden his Governors to pass Laws of immediate and pressing importance, unless suspended in their operation till his Assent should be obtained; and when so suspended, he has utterly neglected to attend to them.

He has refused to pass other Laws for the accommodation of large districts of people, unless those people would relinquish the right of Representation in the Legislature, a right inestimable to them and formidable to tyrants only.

He has called together legislative bodies at places unusual, uncomfortable, and distant from the depository of their public Records, for the sole purpose of fatiguing them into compliance with his measures.

He has dissolved Representative Houses repeatedly, for opposing with manly firmness his invasions on the rights of the people.

He has refused for a long time, after such dissolutions, to cause others to be elected; whereby the Legislative powers, incapable of Annihilation, have returned to the People at large for their exercise; the State remaining in the mean time exposed to all the dangers of invasion from without, and convulsions within.

He has endeavoured to prevent the population of these States; for that purpose obstructing the Laws for Naturalization of Foreigners; refusing to pass others to encourage their migrations hither, and raising the conditions of new Appropriations of Lands.

He has obstructed the Administration of Justice, by refusing his Assent to Laws for establishing Judiciary powers.

He has made Judges dependent on his Will alone, for the tenure of their offices, and the amount and payment of their salaries.

He has erected a multitude of New Offices, and sent hither swarms of Officers to harrass our people, and eat out their substance.

He has kept among us, in times of peace, Standing Armies without the Consent of our legislatures.

He has affected to render the Military independent of and superior to the Civil power.

He has combined with others to subject us to a jurisdiction foreign to our constitution, and unacknowledged by our laws; giving his Assent to their Acts of pretended Legislation:

For Quartering large bodies of armed troops among us:

For protecting them, by a mock Trial, from punishment for any Murders which they should commit on the Inhabitants of these States:

For cutting off our Trade with all parts of the world:

For imposing Taxes on us without our Consent:

For depriving us in many cases, of the benefits of Trial by Jury:

For transporting us beyond Seas to be tried for pretended offences

For abolishing the free System of English Laws in a neighbouring Province, establishing therein an Arbitrary government, and enlarging its Boundaries so as to render it at once an example and fit instrument for introducing the same absolute rule into these Colonies:

For taking away our Charters, abolishing our most valuable Laws, and altering fundamentally the Forms of our Governments:

For suspending our own Legislatures, and declaring themselves invested with power to legislate for us in all cases whatsoever.

He has abdicated Government here, by declaring us out of his Protection and waging War against us.

He has plundered our seas, ravaged our Coasts, burnt our towns, and destroyed the lives of our people.

He is at this time transporting large Armies of foreign Mercenaries to compleat the works of death, desolation and tyranny, already begun with circumstances of Cruelty & perfidy scarcely paralleled in the most barbarous ages, and totally unworthy the Head of a civilized nation.

He has constrained our fellow Citizens taken Captive on the high Seas to bear Arms against their Country, to become the executioners of their friends and Brethren, or to fall themselves by their Hands.

He has excited domestic insurrections amongst us, and has endeavoured to bring on the inhabitants of our frontiers, the merciless Indian Savages, whose known rule of warfare, is an undistinguished destruction of all ages, sexes and conditions.

In every stage of these Oppressions We have Petitioned for Redress in the most humble terms: Our repeated Petitions have been answered only by repeated injury. A Prince whose character is thus marked by every act which may define a Tyrant, is unfit to be the ruler of a free people.

Nor have We been wanting in attentions to our Brittish brethren. We have warned them from time to time of attempts by their legislature to extend an unwarrantable jurisdiction over us. We have reminded them of the circumstances of our emigration and settlement here. We have appealed to their native justice and magnanimity, and we have conjured them by the ties of our common kindred to disavow these usurpations, which, would inevitably interrupt our connections and correspondence. They too have been deaf to the voice of justice and of consanguinity. We must, therefore, acquiesce in the necessity, which denounces our Separation, and hold them, as we hold the rest of mankind, Enemies in War, in Peace Friends.

We, therefore, the Representatives of the united States of America, in General Congress, Assembled, appealing to the Supreme Judge of the world for the rectitude of our intentions, do, in the Name, and by Authority of the good People of these Colonies, solemnly publish and declare, That these United Colonies are, and of Right ought to be Free and Independent States; that they are Absolved from all Allegiance to the British Crown, and that all political connection between them and the State of Great Britain, is and ought to be totally dissolved; and that as Free and Independent States, they have full Power to levy War, conclude Peace, contract Alliances, establish Commerce, and to do all other Acts and Things which Independent States may of right do. And for the support of this Declaration, with a firm reliance on the protection of divine Providence, we mutually pledge to each other our Lives, our Fortunes and our sacred Honor.

The 56 signatures on the Declaration appear in the positions indicated:

COLUMN 1
Georgia
Button Gwinnett
Lyman Hall
George Walton

COLUMN 2
North Carolina
William Hooper
Joseph Hewes
John Penn

South Carolina
Edward Rutledge
Thomas Heyward, Jr.
Thomas Lynch, Jr.
Arthur Middleton

COLUMN 3
Massachusetts
John Hancock

Maryland
Samuel Chase
William Paca

Thomas Stone
Charles Carroll of Carrollton

Virginia
George Wythe
Richard Henry Lee
Thomas Jefferson
Benjamin Harrison
Thomas Nelson, Jr.
Francis Lightfoot Lee
Carter Braxton

COLUMN 4
Pennsylvania
Robert Morris
Benjamin Rush
Benjamin Franklin
John Morton
George Clymer
James Smith
George Taylor
James Wilson
George Ross

Delaware
Caesar Rodney
George Read
Thomas McKean

COLUMN 5

New York
William Floyd
Philip Livingston
Francis Lewis
Lewis Morris

New Jersey
Richard Stockton
John Witherspoon
Francis Hopkinson
John Hart
Abraham Clark

COLUMN 6

New Hampshire
Josiah Bartlett
William Whipple

Massachusetts
Samuel Adams
John Adams
Robert Treat Paine
Elbridge Gerry

Rhode Island
Stephen Hopkins
William Ellery

Connecticut
Roger Sherman
Samuel Huntington
William Williams
Oliver Wolcott

New Hampshire
Matthew Thornton

Source: National Archives. http://www.archives.gov/exhibits/charters/declaration_transcript.html

APPENDIX C
Articles of Confederation

To all to whom these Presents shall come, we the undersigned Delegates of the States affixed to our names send greeting.

Whereas the Delegates of the United States of America in Congress assembled did on the fifteenth day of November in the Year of our Lord One Thousand Seven Hundred and Seventy seven, and in the Second Year of the Independence of America agree to certain articles of Confederation and perpetual Union between the States of Newhampshire, Massachusetts-bay, Rhodeisland and Providence Plantations, Connecticut, New York, New Jersey, Pennsylvania, Delaware, Maryland, Virginia, North-Carolina, South Carolina and Georgia in the Words following, viz.

"Articles of Confederation and perpetual Union between the states of Newhampshire, Massachusetts-bay, Rhodeisland and Providence Plantations, Connecticut, New-York, New-Jersey, Pennsylvania, Delaware, Maryland, Virginia, North-Carolina, South-Carolina and Georgia.

ARTICLE I.

The Stile of this confederacy shall be "The United States of America."

ARTICLE II.

Each state retains its sovereignty, freedom and independence, and every Power, Jurisdiction and right, which is not by this confederation expressly delegated to the United States, in Congress assembled.

ARTICLE III.

The said states hereby severally enter into a firm league of friendship with each other, for their common defence, the security of their Liberties, and their mutual and general welfare, binding themselves to assist each other, against all force offered to, or attacks made upon them, or any of them, on account of religion, sovereignty, trade, or any other pretence whatever.

ARTICLE IV.

The better to secure and perpetuate mutual friendship and intercourse among the people of the different states in this union, the free inhabitants of each of these states, paupers, vagabonds and fugitives from Justice excepted, shall be entitled to all privileges and immunities of free citizens in the several states; and the people of each state shall have free ingress and regress to and from any other state, and shall enjoy therein all the privileges of trade and commerce, subject to the same duties, impositions and restructions as the inhabitants thereof respectively, provided that such restruction shall not extend so far as to prevent the removal of property imported into any state, to any other state of which the Owner is an inhabitant; provided also that no imposition, duties or restriction shall be laid by any state, on the property of the united states, or either of them.

If any Person guilty of, or charged with treason, felony, or other high misdemeanor in any state, shall flee from Justice, and be found in any of the united states, he shall upon demand of the Governor or executive power, of the state from which he fled, be delivered up and removed to the state having jurisdiction of his offence.

Full faith and credit shall be given in each of these states to the records, acts and judicial proceedings of the courts and magistrates of every other state.

ARTICLE V.

For the more convenient management of the general interests of the united states, delegates shall be annually appointed in such manner as the legislature of each state shall direct, to meet in Congress on the first Monday in November, in every year, with a power reserved to each state, to recall its delegates, or any of them, at any time within the year, and to send others in their stead, for the remainder of the Year.

No state shall be represented in Congress by less than two, nor by more than seven Members; and no person shall be capable of being a delegate for more than three years in any term of six years; nor shall any person, being a delegate, be capable of holding any office under the united states, for which he, or another for his benefit receives any salary, fees or emolument of any kind.

Each state shall maintain its own delegates in a meeting of the states, and while they act as members of the committee of the states.

In determining questions in the united states, in Congress assembled, each state shall have one vote.

Freedom of speech and debate in Congress shall not be impeached or questioned in any Court, or place out of Congress, and the members of

congress shall be protected in their persons from arrests and imprison-
ments, during the time of their going to and from, and attendance on congress, except for treason, felony, or breach of the peace.

ARTICLE VI.

No state without the Consent of the united states in congress assembled,
shall send any embassy to, or receive any embassy from, or enter into
any conference, agreement, or alliance or treaty with any King, prince or
state; nor shall any person holding any office of profit or trust under the
united states, or any of them, accept of any present, emolument, office or
title of any kind whatever from any king, prince or foreign state; nor shall
the united states in congress assembled, or any of them, grant any title of
nobility.

No two or more states shall enter into any treaty, confederation or
alliance whatever between them, without the consent of the united states
in congress assembled, specifying accurately the purposes for which the
same is to be entered into, and how long it shall continue.

No state shall lay any imposts or duties, which may interfere with any
stipulations in treaties, entered into by the united states in congress assembled, with any king, prince or state, in pursuance of any treaties already
proposed by congress, to the courts of France and Spain.

No vessels of war shall be kept up in time of peace by any state, except
such number only, as shall be deemed necessary by the united states in
congress assembled, for the defence of such state, or its trade; nor shall
any body of forces be kept up by any state, in time of peace, except such
number only, as in the judgment of the united states, in congress assembled, shall be deemed requisite to garrison the forts necessary for the
defence of such state; but every state shall always keep up a well regulated and disciplined militia, sufficiently armed and accoutred, and shall
provide and constantly have ready for use, in public stores, a due number
of field pieces and tents, and a proper quantity of arms, ammunition and
camp equipage.

No state shall engage in any war without the consent of the united states
in congress assembled, unless such state be actually invaded by enemies,
or shall have received certain advice of a resolution being formed by some
nation of Indians to invade such state, and the danger is so imminent as
not to admit of a delay, till the united states in congress assembled can be
consulted: nor shall any state grant commissions to any ships or vessels
of war, nor letters of marque or reprisal, except it be after a declaration of
war by the united states in congress assembled, and then only against the
kingdom or state and the subjects thereof, against which war has been so

declared, and under such regulations as shall be established by the united states in congress assembled, unless such state be infested by pirates, in which case vessels of war may be fitted out for that occasion, and kept so long as the danger shall continue, or until the united states in congress assembled shall determine otherwise.

ARTICLE VII.

When land-forces are raised by any state for the common defence, all officers of or under the rank of colonel, shall be appointed by the legislature of each state respectively by whom such forces shall be raised, or in such manner as such state shall direct, and all vacancies shall be filled up by the state which first made the appointment.

ARTICLE VIII.

All charges of war, and all other expences that shall be incurred for the common defence or general welfare, and allowed by the united states in congress assembled, shall be defrayed out of a common treasury, which shall be supplied by the several states, in proportion to the value of all land within each state, granted to or surveyed for any Person, as such land and the buildings and improvements thereon shall be estimated according to such mode as the united states in congress assembled, shall from time to time direct and appoint. The taxes for paying that proportion shall be laid and levied by the authority and direction of the legislatures of the several states within the time agreed upon by the united states in congress assembled.

ARTICLE IX.

The united states in congress assembled, shall have the sole and exclusive right and power of determining on peace and war, except in the cases mentioned in the sixth article-of sending and receiving ambassadors--entering into treaties and alliances, provided that no treaty of commerce shall be made whereby the legislative power of the respective states shall be restrained from imposing such imposts and duties on foreigners, as their own people are subjected to, or from prohibiting the exportation or importation of any species of goods or commodities whatsoever-of establishing rules for deciding in all cases, what captures on land or water shall be legal, and in what manner prizes taken by land or naval forces in the service of the united states shall be divided or appropriated,-of granting letters of marque and reprisal in times of peace-appointing courts for the trail of piracies and felonies committed on the high seas and establishing courts for receiving and determining finally appeals in all cases of captures, provided that no member of congress shall be appointed a judge of any of the said courts.

The united states in congress assembled shall also be the last resort on appeal in all disputes and differences now subsisting or that hereafter may arise between two or more states concerning boundary, jurisdiction or any other cause whatever; which authority shall always be exercised in the manner following. Whenever the legislative or executive authority or lawful agent of any state in controversy with another shall present a petition to congress, stating the matter in question and praying for a hearing, notice thereof shall be given by order of congress to the legislative or executive authority of the other state in controversy, and a day assigned for the appearance of the parties by their lawful agents, who shall then be directed to appoint by joint consent, commissioners or judges to constitute a court for hearing and determining the matter in question: but if they cannot agree, congress shall name three persons out of each of the united states, and from the list of such persons each party shall alternately strike out one, the petitioners beginning, until the number shall be reduced to thirteen; and from that number not less than seven, nor more than nine names as congress shall direct, shall in the presence of congress be drawn out by lot, and the persons whose names shall be so drawn or any five of them, shall be commissioners or judges, to hear and finally determine the controversy, so always as a major part of the judges who shall hear the cause shall agree in the determination: and if either party shall neglect to attend at the day appointed, without showing reasons, which congress shall judge sufficient, or being present shall refuse to strike, the congress shall proceed to nominate three persons out of each state, and the secretary of congress shall strike in behalf of such party absent or refusing; and the judgment and sentence of the court to be appointed in the manner before prescribed, shall be final and conclusive; and if any of the parties shall refuse to submit to the authority of such court, or to appear or defend their claim or cause, the court shall nevertheless proceed to pronounce sentence, or judgment, which shall in like manner be final and decisive, the judgment or sentence and other proceedings being in either case transmitted to congress, and lodged among the acts of congress for the security of the parties concerned: provided that every commissioner, before he sits in judgment, shall take an oath to be administered by one of the judges of the supreme or superior court of the state, where the cause shall be tried, "well and truly to hear and determine the matter in question, according to the best of his judgment, without favour, affection or hope of reward:" provided also that no state shall be deprived of territory for the benefit of the united states.

All controversies concerning the private right of soil claimed under different grants of two or more states, whose jurisdictions as they may respect such lands, and the states which passed such grants are adjusted, the said grants or either of them being at the same time claimed to have originated antecedent to such settlement of jurisdiction, shall on the petition of either party to the congress of the united states, be finally determined as near as may be in the same manner as is before prescribed for deciding disputes respecting territorial jurisdiction between different states.

The united states in congress assembled shall also have the sole and exclusive right and power of regulating the alloy and value of coin struck by their own authority, or by that of the respective states-fixing the standard of weights and measures throughout the United States.-regulating the trade and managing all affairs with the Indians, not members of any of the states, provided that the legislative right of any state within its own limits be not infringed or violated-establishing and regulating post-offices from one state to another, throughout all the united states, and exacting such postage on the papers passing thro' the same as may be requisite to defray the expences of the said office-appointing all officers of the land forces, in the service of the united states, excepting regimental officers - appointing all the officers of the naval forces, and commissioning all officers whatever in the service of the United States-making rules for the government and regulation of the said land and naval forces, and directing their operations.

The united states in congress assembled shall have authority to appoint a committee, to sit in the recess of congress, to be denominated "a Committee of the States," and to consist of one delegate from each state; and to appoint such other committees and civil officers as may be necessary for managing the general affairs of the united states under their "direction-to" appoint one of their number to preside, provided that no person be allowed to serve in the office of president more than one year in any term of three years; to ascertain the necessary sums of Money to be raised for the service of the united states, and to appropriate and apply the same for defraying the public "expences; to" borrow money, or emit bills on the credit of the united states, transmitting every half year to the respective states an account of the sums of money so borrowed or "emitted,-to" and equip a "navy-to" agree upon the number of land forces, and to make requisitions from each State for its quota, in proportion to the number of white inhabitants in such state; which requisition shall be binding, and thereupon the legislature of each state shall appoint the regimental officers, raise the men and cloath, arm and equip them in a soldier like manner, at the expence of the united states, and the officers and men so cloathed, armed and equipped shall march to the place appointed, and within the time agreed on by the united states in congress assembled: But if the united states in congress assembled shall, on consideration of circumstances judge proper that any state should not raise men, or should raise a smaller number than its quota, and that any other state should raise a greater number of men than the quota thereof, such extra number shall be raised, officered, cloathed, armed and equipped in the same manner as the quota of such state, unless the legislature of such state shall judge that such extra number cannot be safely spared out of the same, in which case they shall raise officer, cloath, arm and equip as many of such extra number as they judge can be safely spared. And the officers and men so cloathed, armed and equipped, shall march to the place appointed, and within the time agreed on by the united states in congress assembled.

The united states in congress assembled shall never engage in a war, nor grant letters of marque and reprisal in time of peace, nor enter into any treaties or alliances, nor coin money, nor regulate the value thereof, nor ascertain the sums and expenses necessary for the defence and welfare of the united states, or any of them, nor emit bills, nor borrow money on the credit of the united states, nor appropriate money, nor agree upon the number of vessels of war, to be built or purchased, or the number of land or sea forces to be raised, nor appoint a commander in chief of the army or navy, unless nine states assent to the same: nor shall a question on any other point, except for adjourning from day to day be determined, unless by the votes of a majority of the united states in congress assembled.

The congress of the united states shall have power to adjourn to any time within the year, and to any place within the united states, so that no period of adjournment be for a longer duration than the space of six Months, and shall publish the Journal of their proceedings monthly, except such parts thereof relating to treaties, alliances or military operations as in their judgment require secresy; and the yeas and nays of the delegates of each state on any question shall be entered on the Journal, when it is desired by any delegate; and the delegates of a state, or any of them, at his or their request shall be furnished with a transcript of the said Journal, except such parts as are above excepted, to lay before the legislatures of the several states.

Article X. The committee of the states, or any nine of them, shall be authorised to execute, in the recess of congress, such of the powers of congress as the united states in congress assembled, by the consent of nine states, shall from time to time think expedient to vest them with; provided that no power be delegated to the said committee, for the exercise of which, by the articles of confederation, the voice of nine states in the congress of the united states assembled is requisite.

ARTICLE XI.

Canada acceding to this confederation, and joining in the measures of the united states, shall be admitted into, and entitled to all the advantages of this union: but no other colony shall be admitted into the same, unless such admission be agreed to by nine states.

ARTICLE XII.

All bills of credit emitted, monies borrowed and debts contracted by, or under the authority of congress, before the assembling of the united states, in pursuance of the present confederation, shall be deemed and considered as a charge against the united states, for payment and satisfaction whereof the said united states, and the public faith are hereby solemnly pledged.

ARTICLE XIII.

Every state shall abide by the determinations of the united states in congress assembled, on all questions which by this confederation are submitted to them. And the Articles of this confederation shall be inviolably observed by every state, and the union shall be perpetual; nor shall any alteration at any time hereafter be made in any of them; unless such alteration be agreed to in a congress of the united states, and be afterwards confirmed by the legislatures of every state.

And Whereas it hath pleased the Great Governor of the World to incline the hearts of the legislatures we respectively represent in congress, to approve of, and to authorize us to ratify the said articles of confederation and perpetual union. Know Ye that we the undersigned delegates, by virtue of the power and authority to us given for that purpose, do by these presents, in the name and in behalf of our respective constituents, full and entirely ratify and confirm each and every of the said articles of confederation and perpetual union, and all and singular the matters and things therein contained: And we do further solemnly plight and engage the faith of our respective constituents, that they shall abide by the determinations of the united states in congress assembled, on all questions, which by the said confederation are submitted to them. And that the articles thereof shall be inviolably observed by the states we respectively represent, and that the union shall be perpetual. In Witness whereof we have hereunto set our hands in Congress. Done at Philadelphia in the state of Pennsylvania the ninth Day of July in the Year of our Lord one Thousand seven Hundred and Seventy-eight, and in the third year of the independence of America.

On the part & behalf of the State of New Hampshire
JOSIAH BARTLETT
JOHN WENTWORTH JUNR
August 8th 1778

On the part and behalf of The State of Massachusetts Bay
JOHN HANCOCK
SAMUEL ADAMS
ELBRIDGE GERRY
FRANCIS DANA
JAMES LOVELL
SAMUEL HOLTEN

On the part and behalf of the State of Rhode-Island and
Providence Plantations
WILLIAM ELLERY
HENRY MARCHANT
JOHN COLLINS

On the part and behalf of the State of Connecticut
ROGER SHERMAN
SAMUEL HUNTINGTON
OLIVER WOLCOTT
TITUS HOSMER
ANDREW ADAMS

On the Part and Behalf of the State of New York
JAS DUANE
FRAS LEWIS
WM DUER
GOUVMORRIS

On the Part and in Behalf of the State of
New Jersey Novr 26, 1778.
JNO WITHERSPOON
NATHL SCUDDER

On the part and behalf of the State of Pennsylvania
ROSTMORRIS DANIEL
ROBERDEAU JONA
BAYARD SMITH
WILLIAM CLINGAN
JOSEPH REED 22d July 1778

On the part & behalf of the State of Delaware
THOM:KEANFEBY 121779
JOHN DICKINSON
May 5th 1779
NICHOLAS VAN DYKE

On the part and behalf of the State of Maryland
JOHN HANSON
March 1 1781
DANIEL CARROLL DO

On the Part and Behalf of the State of Virginia
RICHARD HENRY LEE
JOHN BANISTER
THOMAS ADAMS
JN° HARVIE
FRANCIS LIGHTFOOT LEE

On the part and Behalf of the State of N°
Carolina
JOHN PENN JULY 21ST 1778
CORNS HARNETT
JN° WILLIAMS

On the part & behalf of the State of South-Carolina
HENRY LAURENS
WILLIAM HENRY DRAYTON
JN° MATHEWS
RICHD HUTSON
THOS HEYWARD JUNR

On the part & behalf of the State of Georgia
JN° WALTON 24TH JULY 1778
EDWD TELFAIR
EDWD LANGWORTHY

APPENDIX D
Speakers of the House of Representatives*

Name & State Represented	Political Party	Years as Speaker
Frederick A. C. Muhlenberg (PA)**	Federalist	1789–1791
Jonathan Trumbull (CT)	Federalist	1791–1793
Frederick A. C. Muhlenberg (PA)**	Democratic-Republican	1793–1795
Jonathan Dayton (CT)	Federalist	1795–1799
Theodore Sedgwick (MA)	Federalist	1799–1801
Nathaniel Macon (NC)	Democratic-Republican	1801–1807
Joseph B. Varnum (MA)	Democratic-Republican	1807–1811
Henry Clay (KY)**	Democratic-Republican	1811–1814
Langdon Cheves (SC)	Democratic-Republican	1814–1815
Henry Clay (KY)**	Democratic-Republican	1815–1820
John W. Taylor (NY)**	Democratic-Republican	1820–1821
Philip B. Barbour (VA)	Democratic-Republican	1821–1823
Henry Clay (KY)**	Democratic-Republican	1823–1825
John W. Taylor (NY)**	National Republican	1825–1827
Andrew Stevenson (VA)	Democrat	1827–1834
John Bell (TN)	Whig	1834–1835
James K. Polk (TN)	Democrat	1835–1839
Robert M. T. Hunter (VA)	Democrat	1839–1841
John White (KY)	Whig	1841–1843
John W. Jones (VA)	Democrat	1843–1845

---

*Adapted from Ronald M. Peters, Jr., *The American Speakership: The Office in Historical Perspective* (Baltimore: The Johns Hopkins University Press, 1990), pp. 299–306.
**Served for nonsuccessive terms.

Name & State Represented	Political Party	Years as Speaker
John W. Davis (IN)	Democrat	1845–1847
Robert C. Winthrop (MA)	Whig	1847–1849
Howell Cobb (GA)	Democrat	1849–1851
Linn Boyd (KY)	Democrat	1851–1855
Nathaniel P. Banks (MA)	American Party	1856–1857
	Coalition with Democrats	
James Orr (SC)	Democrat	1857–1859
William Pennington (NJ)	Whig	1860–1861
Galusha A. Grow (PA)	Republican	1861–1863
Schuyler Colfax (IN)	Republican	1863–1869
James G. Blaine (ME)	Republican	1869–1875
Michael C. Kerr (IN)	Democrat	1875–1876
Samuel J. Randall (PA)	Democrat	1876–1881
J. Warren Keifer (OH)	Republican	1881–1883
John G. Carlisle (KY)	Democrat	1883–1889
Thomas B. Reed (ME)**	Republican	1889–1891
Charles T. Crisp (GA)	Democrat	1891–1895
Thomas B. Reed (ME)**	Republican	1895–1899
David Henderson (IA)	Republican	1899–1903
Joseph G. Cannon (IL)	Republican	1903–1911
James B. (Champ) Clark (MO)	Democrat	1911–1919
Frederick H. Gillett (MA)	Republican	1919–1925
Nicholas Longworth (OH)	Republican	1925–1931
John N. Garner (TX)	Democrat	1931–1933
Henry R. Rainey (IL)	Democrat	1933–1934
Joseph W. Byrns (TN)	Democrat	1935–1936
William B. Bankhead (AL)	Democrat	1936–1940
Sam Rayburn (TX)**	Democrat	1940–1947
Joseph W. Martin Jr. (MA)**	Republican	1947–1949
Sam Rayburn (TX)**	Democrat	1949–1953
Joseph W. Martin Jr. (MA)**	Republican	1953–1955
Sam Rayburn (TX)**	Democrat	1955–1961

Name & State Represented	*Political Party*	*Years as Speaker*
John W. McCormack (MA)	Democrat	1962–1971
Carl B. Albert (OK)	Democrat	1971–1977
Thomas P. O'Neill Jr. (MA)	Democrat	1977–1987
James C. Wright Jr. (TX)	Democrat	1987–1989
Thomas S. Foley (WA)	Democrat	1989–1994
Newt Gingrigh (GA)	Republican	1989–1999
Dennis Hastert (IL)	Republican	1999–2007
Nancy Pelosi (CA)	Democrat	2007–2011
John Boehner (OH)	Republican	2011–

APPENDIX E
United States Presidents*

Name	Political Party	Years Served
George Washington	(Federalist.)	1789–1797
John Adams	(Federalist)	1797–1801
Thomas Jefferson	(Democratic-Republican)	1801–1809
James Madison	(Democratic-Republican)	1809–1817
James Monroe	(Democratic-Republican)	1817–1825
John Q. Adams	(Democratic-Republican)	1825–1829
Andrew Jackson	(Democrat)	1829–1837
Martin Van Buren	(Democrat)	1837–1841
William Henry Harrison	(Whig)	1841
John Tyler	(Whig)	1841–1845
James K. Polk	(Democrat)	1845–1849
Zachary Taylor	(Whig)	1849–1850
Millard Fillmore	(Whig)	1850–1853
Franklin Pierce	(Democrat)	1853–1857
James Buchanan	(Democrat)	1857–1861
Abraham Lincoln	(Republican)	1861–1865
Andrew Johnson	(Republican)	1865–1869
Ulysses S. Grant	(Republican)	1869–1877
Rutherford B. Hayes	(Republican)	1877–1881
James A. Garfield	(Republican)	1881
Chester A. Arthur	(Republican)	1881–1885
Grover Cleveland	(Democrat)	1885–1889

*Material has been adapted from *Guide to the Presidency,* ed. Michael Nelson, 2nd ed. (Washington, D.C.: Congressional Quarterly Inc., 1996). II, 1633.

Name	*Political Party*	*Years Served*
Benjamin Harrison	(Republican)	1889–1893
Grover Cleveland	(Democrat)	1893–1897
William McKinley	(Republican)	1897–1901
Theodore Roosevelt	(Republican)	1901–1909
William Howard Taft	(Republican)	1909–1913
Woodrow Wilson	(Democrat)	1913–1921
Warren G. Harding	(Republican)	1921–1923
Calvin Coolidge	(Republican)	1923–1929
Herbert Hoover	(Republican)	1929–1933
Franklin D. Roosevelt	(Democrat)	1933–1945
Harry S. Truman	(Democrat)	1945–1953
Dwight D. Eisenhower	(Republican)	1953–1961
John F. Kennedy	(Democrat)	1961–1963
Lyndon B. Johnson	(Democrat)	1963–1969
Richard M. Nixon	(Republican)	1969–1974
Gerald R. Ford	(Republican)	1974–1977
Jimmy Carter	(Democrat)	1977–1981
Ronald Reagan	(Republican)	1981–1989
George Bush	(Republican)	1989–1993
Bill Clinton	(Democrat)	1993–2001
George W. Bush	(Republican)	2001–2009
Barack Obama	(Democrat)	2009–

APPENDIX F
United States Supreme Court Justices[1]

Name (Chief Justices in Bold)	Appointing President	Years of Service
John Jay	Washington	1789–1795
John Rutledge	Washington	1790–1791
William Cushing	Washington	1790–1810
James Wilson	Washington	1789–1798
John Blair Jr.	Washington	1790–1795
James Iredell	Washington	1790–1799
Thomas Johnson	Washington	1791–1793
William Paterson	Washington	1793–1806
John Rutledge	Washington	1795
Samuel Chase	Washington	1796–1811
Oliver Ellsworth	Washington	1796–1800
Bushrod Washington	Adams	1798–1829
Alfred Moore	Adams	1800–1804
John Marshall	Adams	1801–1835
William Johnson	Jefferson	1804–1834
Henry B. Livingston	Jefferson	1807–1823
Thomas Todd	Jefferson	1807–1826
Joseph Story	Madison	1812–1845
Gabriel Duvall	Madison	1811–1835
Smith Thompson	Monroe	1824–1843
Robert Trimble	J. Q. Adams	1826–1828
John McLean	Jackson	1830–1861

[1] Adapted from John J. Patrick, *The Young Oxford Companion to the Supreme Court of the United States* (New York: Oxford University Press, 1994), pp. 352–355.

Name (Chief Justices in Bold)	Appointing President	Years of Service
Henry Baldwin	Jackson	1830–1844
James M. Wayne	Jackson	1835–1867
Roger B. Taney	Jackson	1836–1864
Philip P. Barbour	Jackson	1836–1841
John Catron	Jackson	1837–1865
John McKinley	Van Buren	1838–1852
Peter V. Daniel	Van Buren	1842–1860
Samuel Nelson	Tyler	1845–1872
Levi Woodbury	Polk	1845–1851
Robert C. Grier	Polk	1846–1870
Benjamin R. Curtin	Fillmore	1851–1857
John A. Campbell	Pierce	1853–1861
Nathan Clifford	Buchanan	1858–1881
Noah H. Swayne	Lincoln	1862–1881
Samuel F. Miller	Lincoln	1862–1890
David Davis	Lincoln	1862–1877
Stephen J. Field	Lincoln	1863–1897
Salmon P. Chase	Lincoln	1864–1873
William Strong	Grant	1870–1880
Joseph P. Bradley	Grant	1870–1892
Ward Hunt	Grant	1873–1882
Morrison R. Waite	Grant	1874–1888
John Marshall Harlan	Hayes	1877–1911
William B. Woods	Hayes	1881–1887
Stanley Matthews	Garfield	1881–1889
Horace Gray	Arthur	1882–1902
Samuel Blatchford	Arthur	1882–1893
Lucius Q.C. Lamar	Cleveland	1888–1893
Melville W. Fuller	Cleveland	1888–1910
David Brewer	Harrsion	1890–1910
Henry B. Brown	Harrison	1891–1906
George Shiras Jr.	Harrison	1892–1903
Howell E. Jackson	Harrison	1893–1895

Name (Chief Justices in Bold)	*Appointing President*	*Years of Service*
Edward D. White	Cleveland	1894–1910
Rufus W. Peckham	Cleveland	1896–1909
Joseph McKenna	McKinley	1898–1925
Oliver Wendell Holmes Jr	T. Roosevelt	1902–1932
William R. Day	T. Roosevelt	1902–1922
William H. Moody	T. Roosevelt	1906–1910
Horace H. Lurton	Taft	1910–1914
Charles Evans Hughes	Taft	1910–1916
Edward D. White	Taft	1910–1921
Willis Van Devanter	Taft	1911–1937
Joseph R. Lamar	Taft	1911–1916
Mahlon Pitney	Taft	1912–1922
James C. McReynolds	Wilson	1914–1941
Louis D. Brandeis	Wilson	1916–1939
John H. Clarke	Wilson	1916–1922
William Howard Taft	Harding	1921–1930
George Sutherland	Harding	1922–1938
Pierce Butler	Harding	1923–1939
Edward T. Sanford	Harding	1923–1930
Harlan Fiske Stone	Coolidge	1925–1941
Charles Evans Hughes	Hoover	1930–1941
Owen J. Roberts	Hoover	1930–1945
Benjamin N. Cardozo	Hoover	1932–1938
Hugo L. Black	F. Roosevelt	1937–1931
Stanley F. Reed	F. Roosevelt	1938–1957
Felix Frankfurter	F. Roosevelt	1939–1962
William O. Douglas	F. Roosevelt	1939–1975
Frank Murphy	F. Roosevelt	1940–1949
Harlan Fiske Stone	F. Roosevelt	1941–1946
James F. Byrnes	F. Roosevelt	1941–1942
Robert H. Jackson	F. Roosevelt	1941–1954
Wiley B. Rutledge	F. Roosevelt	1943–1949
Harold H. Burton	Truman	1945–1958

Name (Chief Justices in Bold)	Appointing President	Years of Service
Fred M. Vinson	Truman	1946–1953
Tom Clark	Truman	1949–1967
Sherman Minton	Truman	1949–1956
Earl Warren	Eisenhower	1953–1969
John M. Harlan II	Eisenhower	1955–1971
William J. Brennan Jr.	Eisenhower	1956–1990
Charles E. Whittaker	Eisenhower	1957–1962
Potter Stewart	Eisenhower	1958–1981
Byron R. White	Kennedy	1962–1993
Arthur J. Goldberg	Kennedy	1962–1965
Abe Fortas	L. Johnson	1965–1969
Thurgood Marshall	L. Johnson	1967–1991
Warren E. Burger	Nixon	1969–1986
Harry A. Blackmun	Nixon	1970–1994
Lewis F. Powell Jr.	Nixon	1972–1987
William H. Rehnquist	Nixon	1972–1986
John Paul Stevens	Ford	1975–
Sandra Day O'Connor	Reagan	1981–
William H. Rehnquist	Reagan	1986–2005
Antonin Scalia	Reagan	1986–
Anthony M. Kennedy	Reagan	1988–
David H. Souter	Bush	1990–
Clarence Thomas	Bush	1991–
Ruth Bader Ginsberg	Clinton	1993–
David Breyer	Clinton	1994–
John R. Roberts Jr.	G. W. Bush	2005–
Samuel A. Alito Jr.	G. W. Bush	2006–
Sonia Sotomayor	Obama	2009–
Elena Kagan	Obama	2010–

APPENDIX G
The Fifty States[*]

Name	Date of Admission	Members in House of Representatives (1990 Census)
Alabama	1819	7
Alaska	1959	1
Arizona	1912	8
Arkansas	1836	4
California	1850	53
Colorado	1876	7
Connecticut	1788	5
Delaware	1787	1
Florida	1845	25
Georgia	1788	13
Hawaii	1959	2
Idaho	1890	2
Illinois	1818	19
Indiana	1816	9
Iowa	1838	5
Kansas	1861	4
Kentucky	1792	6
Louisiana	1812	7
Maine	1820	2
Maryland	1788	8
Massachusetts	1788	10

---

[*]Adopted from information in *The Book of the States, 1994–95,* Vol. 30 (Lexington, Kentucky: The Council of State Governments, 1994), pp. 633, 635–636.

Name	Date of Admission	Members in House of Representatives (1990 Census)
Michigan	1837	15
Minnesota	1858	8
Mississippi	1817	4
Missouri	1821	4
Montana	1889	1
Nebraska	1867	3
Nevada	1864	3
New Hampshire	1788	2
New Jersey	1787	13
New Mexico	1912	3
New York	1788	29
North Carolina	1789	12
North Dakota	1889	1
Ohio	1803	19
Oklahoma	1907	6
Oregon	1859	5
Pennsylvania	1787	21
Rhode Island	1790	2
South Carolina	1788	6
South Dakota	1889	1
Tennessee	1796	9
Texas	1845	32
Utah	1896	3
Vermont	1791	1
Virginia	1788	11
Washington	1889	9
West Virginia	1863	3
Wisconsin	1848	8
Wyoming	1890	1

About the Author

DR. JOHN R. VILE is a professor and dean of the University Honors College at Middle Tennessee State University in Murfreesboro. Vile has written numerous articles, reviews, chapters, and encyclopedia entries. He is the author, editor, and coeditor of such books as *A Companion to the United States Constitution and Its Amendments*; the *Encyclopedia of Constitutional Amendments, Proposed Amendments, and Amending Issues, 1789–2010*; *Essential Supreme Court Decisions: Summaries of Leading Cases in U.S. Constitutional Law*; *The Encyclopedia of the First Amendment*; *The Encyclopedia of the Fourth Amendment*; *The Constitutional Convention of 1787: A Comprehensive Encyclopedia of America's Founding*; and *The Writing and Ratification of the U.S. Constitution: Practical Virtue in Action*.

The American Mock Trial Association awarded Vile the Congressman Neal Smith Award in 2000 recognition of outstanding and exemplary contributions to law-related education and its mission to promote public understanding of law and the legal process, and designated him in 2008 as a member of the AMTA Coaches Hall of Fame. MTSU awarded Vile its Outstanding Career Achievement Award in 2011. Vile's wife, Linda, is an elementary schoolteacher, and they have two grown children and one grandchild.

Index